AFTER THE FIRE

KATHRYN SHAY

BERKLEY SENSATION, NEW YORK

This is a work of fiction. Names, characters, places, and incidents either are the product of the author's imagination or are used fictitiously, and any resemblance to actual persons, living or dead, business establishments, events, or locales is entirely coincidental.

AFTER THE FIRE

A Berkley Sensation Book / published by arrangement with the author

PRINTING HISTORY
Berkley Sensation edition / November 2003

A BERKLEY SENSATION™ BOOK
Berkley Sensation Books are published by The Berkley Publishing Group, a division of Penguin Group (USA) Inc.,
375 Hudson Street, New York, New York 10014.
BERKLEY SENSATION and the "B" design
are trademarks belonging to Penguin Group (USA) Inc.

PRINTED IN THE UNITED STATES OF AMERICA

10 9 8 7 6 5

To my son Ben, as you begin your college journey. Like the characters in this book, may you love, laugh, and accomplish great things in your life.

↦ PROLOGUE

"OH, MY GOD, the ceiling's coming down!" It was all Mitch Malvaso got out. In seconds, a crushing weight slammed him into the floor, face first. As he hit the concrete, he thought of his sister Jenny, who was also in the warehouse, slapping water on the fire that caused the collapse. "Please, God, don't let her die," he murmured. Then the world went black.

When he awoke outside in the bright sunshine, he started. Pain lacerated the backs of his legs. Burns. Through his bunker pants.

Sucking in a breath, he slitted his eyes and forced them to focus. The first thing he saw was that the fire, which had blazed like an angry monster, consuming Sinco Automotive's five-hundred-square-foot warehouse, was out. Black smoke still curled from the building, where several companies of the Hidden Cove Fire Department had been called to the four-alarm blaze.

Were some of his men still inside?

He took inventory. He was lying on a stretcher, his airpack gone and his turnout coat off. Then things crystallized.

And reality hit him—where was Jenny?

When he tried to move, the burns scraped raw. He let out a long, low moan and consciousness momentarily dimmed. Then, he heard sirens and shouting, and people barking out orders. He shifted, and his breathing escalated with what now felt like hundreds of tiny pinpricks on the backs of his legs. He caught sight of his sister, lying on a blanket off to the left. He managed to yell, "Jenny, you okay?" but it came out like a rusty saw on wood.

After worrisome seconds, she inched up onto her elbows, groaning with the effort. "Yeah. I'm okay." As if she'd been awakened from a deep sleep, she looked around. "Oh, no." She scrambled to a sitting position. "Ahh . . . shit, that hurts," she spat out but came up on all fours and crawled over. Kneeling above him, she said, "Mitch, oh, God, Mitch, are you all right?"

He drew in a breath. "I'm burned. But all right." He reached out and gripped her hand, which was streaked with grime like her face. Her dark hair was damp and matted. "You sure you are?"

"I guess."

Someone approached them. A medic, Jimmy, from Engine 12. "Hey, you two hanging in here?"

"Yeah." Mitch surveyed the scene. Several smoke eaters lay on stretchers, the ground, or blankets. Some coughing, some too still. Medical personnel were tending to a few, left others alone.

Jimmy frowned. "Don't worry, Cap, we're working on getting your brother outta there."

Both Jenny and he gasped. "Our brother?" Mitch said. "Zach's not here, he's on the night shift this week."

All three Malvaso firefighters worked at the same station, he on the elite Rescue Squad, Jenny on Group One, Zach on Group Two of Quint/Midi 7, housed at fire department headquarters.

The young medic's face blanked. Then he said, "Mitch, Zach showed up here when he heard about the fire on his scanner. He barreled inside when he realized the damn thing was out of control and you two were in there."

"Son of a bitch." Mitch gripped the medic's arm. "You know anything else?"

"The men that've been rescued said he pushed them out of the way when the wall started to cave on them after the ceiling fell on you guys."

Mitch struggled to get up. He couldn't. "Fuck, I can't move."

"You're burned bad. We did some work on you already, but others were hurt worse so . . . we're gonna take you to the hospital right now."

"No, I'm not leaving here until I know Zach's okay."

"Mitch—"

"No!" He reached out again for his sister; she flinched when he made contact with her arm. Burns reddened her skin. "Get Jenny some help. Do what you can for me, but I'm staying."

His heart in his throat, Mitch shifted his gaze to the building, watched the smoke circle like a lazy cat along the flat roof, and wondered if his baby brother was alive.

FIFTEEN MINUTES LATER, they still didn't know what was happening with Zach. Jenn sat beside Mitch, ignoring the pain that danced along her upper body like electrical sparks. She stared at the warehouse where her brother was still inside. The medics had done some preliminary burn treatment on both her and Mitch, but since Mitch had dug in his heels and there were so many casualties and life-threatening injuries, they were allowed to stay here and wait.

It had been the worst fifteen minutes of her life.

"You okay, kiddo?" Mitch asked in the tone that always made her soft. The oldest of all five of them, he played the father role much of the time.

"Uh-huh." She stifled a sob. As one of twenty-five female firefighters in the Hidden Cove Fire Department, about a hundred miles north of New York City and west of the Hudson, Jenn was tough. But this . . .

The fire had been routine; five trucks had arrived within minutes of each other. Three of the crews had mounted an interior attack when the ceiling fell, complete with beams and searing plaster; several firefighters had been trapped. Apparently they'd rescued her and Mitch's crews. Now, special teams were digging the rest out.

She rubbed her eyes with her thumb and forefinger.

"Does it hurt bad, honey?" Mitch asked.

"No. Yeah. I guess." She looked down at him and smoothed back his hair. "You?"

"Like a bitch." Mitch coughed and sputtered. He'd removed his SCBA gear—his air had run out because he'd been in the warehouse longer than her—while waiting to be rescued. Consequently, he'd inhaled a lot of smoke.

Again she nodded toward the warehouse. "Mitch, Zach's still in there . . . do you think he's . . ." Jenn's eyes focused on the structure. There were dead smoke eaters inside and out here. She just prayed Zach wasn't one of them.

Though her brother rode through life on a short fuse and chased after too many skirts for her taste, she didn't know what she'd do if something happened to Zach. All three Malvaso firefighters were close—since childhood they'd stuck together against their other brother and sister, and the world in general. What if . . .

Her hand crept out to the side. "Mitello?"

They only used their given Italian names when things were really bad.

Mitch found her hand, clasped it. "Yeah, Genevieve?"

"If he gets out of there . . ."

"*When* he gets out of there."

"When. We're going to do things different. All of us."

"What do you mean?"

"I wanna have a baby."

Her brother chuckled, then choked like a rookie eating his first smoke. His voice came out in a wheezy rumble. "Better find yourself a fella first."

"What would you do different, if you had the chance?" Pain turned her voice raw. "I know you haven't been happy with Cindy."

"No, I haven't been happy. And my kids need help."

"Promise me, when this is over—" She gripped his hand tighter. "—you'll do something about all that. You'll make your life better."

"Okay, I promise."

She glanced back at the warehouse. "Zaccaria, too. He's gotta get his act together. We'll help him."

Momentarily, Mitch closed his eyes. He looked like he was struggling to stay conscious. "All right. The three of us, we'll do better. We'll live better lives."

Just then a shadow came over them. Both she and Mitch looked up, and when she saw who it was, Jenny's eyes started to tear. "Oh, God, Grady."

Her best friend in the world, and coworker on her crew, crouched down. Despite the cast on his arm, which had kept him off the line and out of harm's way for this fire, he clasped her to him. She buried her face in his big, safe chest. "I just heard and came over." He knelt to hold her more securely. She felt a hand in her hair. Soothing her, he said to Mitch, "What's going on?"

"Zach . . ." Mitch cleared his throat. "He's in there."

"What?"

Jenny heard Mitch mumble an explanation.

Grady said, "Son of a—" but stopped. Stilled. His body went taut. Jenny drew back; Grady was staring at the building. She turned to see two firefighters stumble out. Both were covered with layers of grime and white dust.

One held on to the shoulders, the other on to the feet of an HCFD smoke eater.

She tensed. Though she couldn't make out who they carried, Jenny knew in her heart it was her brother.

He looked dead.

≈ ONE

Clouds of gray smoke billowed from the old two-story house as the Rescue Squad vehicle swerved onto North Park Avenue. The blare of sirens and the screech of the tires made adrenaline pump double-time through Mitch's veins. Hopping off the truck, he hurried to Incident Command, the makeshift site where the battalion chief had spread out a sketch of the house on the hood of his truck and diagrammed how they would fight the blaze. The nearest firehouse rig, Engine 12, was first-in and had already set up hose in the front.

"Malvaso," the battalion chief called out. "Get your crew around back." He pointed to a drawing. "Engine Four's laying a hose here, in the rear. We laid a line in the front but the entry's blocked now." He nodded to the aerial ladder rising from the truck, already dumping a master stream on the outside. "The bucket's up and they're about to ventilate."

"Who's in there?" Mitch asked. His men came up behind him. They'd be conducting search and rescue.

"Kids. Teenagers. We have reason to believe they were doing drugs upstairs."

Mitch cringed, thinking of his daughter, Trish. The school's "intervention" meeting last week, called with him and Cynthia, flashed through his mind. He suppressed it ruthlessly to concentrate on the present.

Without further discussion, Mitch hustled around the back of the house with his squad. It was dark in the rear. Somebody from the second-in group, Engine 4, was hooking up a generator for light, but it wasn't on yet. The huge wooden door to the house was locked or stuck; firefighters were taking it with the rabbit ram. Mitch and his crew stood back as they popped the door. Then the spotlight came on, blindingly bright after the darkness.

The lieutenant on 4 nodded to Mitch. "We'll go in first with the hose."

"I'm right behind you." Mitch yanked off his helmet, donned his airpack over his Nomex hood, hooked up the hose, and situated his helmet again. Then he followed the two inside, his men trailing him. Engines 12 and 4 would knock down the fire and his guys would find survivors. Or victims.

A semiopaque curtain of charcoal-gray smoke assaulted them as soon as they stepped through the doorway. Something must be burning that they didn't expect; the color of the smoke darkened—and was more dangerous—depending on how noxious the substance was that caught fire. Was it lead? Asbestos? Two feet in, he heard the chief's instructions over his radio. "Stairway's through the kitchen to the right. A neighbor says the kids' bedrooms are at the top of the stairs."

"Confirmed. I—"

Mitch heard somebody yell in the background and the battalion chief barked something out to them. They'd just reached the doorway leading to the living area when a sudden blast slammed them back. Flames roared in a fireball in front of them. The linemen with the hose landed on their asses, as did Mitch and his four men.

What the hell? He thought the first-in group had already ventilated. They all scrambled up; the guy on the nozzle slapped water on the fire, trying to knock it down. Everybody was grumbling and swearing.

Mitch plodded on; later, he'd haul somebody's ass about the delay in ventilating. When he entered the living room, he was hit by an inferno so potent, he dropped to his knees, signaling his men to go down. The Red Devil burned hot, taunting them with its fiery breath.

It was slow going up the stairs. Rivulets of sweat ran down Mitch's back and dripped into his eyes. Even with the airpack, he was sucking in breaths. He unbuttoned the top of his navy-blue turnout coat. Finally, he reached the second floor. Still crouched down where it was cooler, his hand sliding along the wall, he made his way to what he hoped was the first bedroom, per the chief's instructions.

Pitch black in here and furnace hot, the place reminded him of Sinco. For a minute, his heart constricted. Every time they went into a fire now, all HCFD firefighters experienced momentary unease. Mitch did, too, even though his sister and brother had survived. Mitch shook off his fear and stopped to listen; a smoke eater's sense of hearing could save his life, or the lives of others. He heard faint moaning.

"Somebody's in the first bedroom," he yelled into his radio to his men. "Snyder, search the left side with Thomas. McKenna, you're with me. LoTurco, stay back in case we need you."

He found a bed by sheer blind luck and pressed on the mattress. It bounced, indicating somebody was on it. He gripped a solid form: a leg. It kicked in response.

"I got one." He dragged the victim toward him. He groped around. "Shit, more than one." His hands slid up and down a body, which again moved. From across the room, Snyder called out, "There's a couple here. Both movin'."

It was a minute before Mitch said, "Jesus H. Christ, mine's fuckin' naked."

He heard laughs. "Mine, too."

"Birthday suit on mine."

Hoisting his victim up in a traditional fireman's carry, Mitch fitted the boy over his shoulders. Slowly, he found the wall again and, squatting as much as he could, given the weight of the kid, he made his way to the door of the bedroom.

Out of it.

The victim was heavy; Mitch's shoulder muscles burned with the load. Navigating the stairs was a bitch. He shifted gingerly with each step. Once, he'd seen a firefighter and victim tumble down stairs, causing major injuries to both of them. "Careful," he said into the radio. "Railing'll be loose." He took another step, stumbled, gained his balance, and inched down.

By rights, the fire should have been out by now. That he could see flames to the left, along with the thick black smoke encompassing the first floor, told him something had gone wrong.

And the hose to follow out was no longer there.

Capitalizing on a well-honed sense of direction, Mitch felt his way. He made it through the living room, to the kitchen, where he heard noise. The battalion chief was at the back door yelling, "Right here, Mitch baby. We're right here. Follow my voice."

For some reason, he thought of the men and one woman who didn't make it out of the Sinco fire. They'd been trapped, but died before an encouraging voice could lead them out or rescue crews could find them.

Shit, he couldn't afford this now.

Following the BC's voice, Mitch found his way to the exit. When he reached the clean air, the absence of heat hit him first. Someone slid the kid off his back and Mitch fell to his knees. His head down, he tried to regain his equilibrium. Finally he was able to stand.

Whipping off his helmet and hood, yanking open his coat, he pulled off his gloves and surveyed the scene. Son of a bitch. Four teenagers, three boys and a girl, naked as the day they were born and covered with smoky grime, lay sprawled out on the grass. "Somebody get blankets," Mitch yelled.

"Why?" Snyder asked, still on his knees. "They aren't modest. They were probably having some kind of orgy."

Still, it didn't sit well with Mitch to gawk at them. He reissued the order.

Amidst the wail of sirens and flashing red lights, another person appeared on the scene. Mitch didn't recognize her. Tall, solid but slender, with wispy blond hair, she wore a navy pantsuit with a white blouse underneath. She crossed to the officer in charge, who was within hearing distance of Mitch. "Battalion Chief Jackson?" she asked.

"Yes, ma'am."

She flashed a badge. "Detective Hale."

Ah, the new addition to Hidden Cove's Finest. Mitch had heard a woman from New York City had come on board their police force a few weeks ago.

"The radio report said suspicion of drug use," Jackson commented.

"Yeah, there is."

A kid writhed on the ground. The sound of his moans caught Hale's attention and she crossed to him. Mitch shifted and saw the boy was about Bobby's age, only sixteen. Detective Hale picked up a blanket someone had brought, draped it over the kid, then squatted down. "You okay?"

"Man, I'm gonna puke."

Gently, Hale eased the boy on his side, straightened, and stepped back. She turned to a uniformed cop while the kid barfed violently on the ground. "They going in the ambulance?"

"Yeah."

"Go with them. Get down what they say."

Her gaze locked on Mitch. As she crossed to him, he unhooked his turnout coat and shrugged it off, noticing his white captain's shirt was streaked with grime. The October night had turned warm and he was sweating like a pig.

Up close, Hale was attractive enough, though not what Zach would call a fox. But those eyes—they were huge, light brown, and almost almond shaped. He wondered briefly if she was a real blond.

Only one way to tell, his brother often crudely commented.

". . . Detective Hale," the woman was saying.

"Mitch Malvaso." He wiped his hand on his shirt and held it out.

"Hell, you're burned."

He glanced down. His wrist had gotten singed where the turnout coat met his gloves—a common side effect of fire fighting.

"Get a medic over here," Hale yelled.

The ambulance had pulled in and an EMT Mitch knew approached him. "Let me see, Mitch."

"It's nothing, Louise." Louise Schroeder—a big German woman with nerves of steel—had grown up three streets over from him. Hale watched for a minute as she got out a cloth to clean away the dirt.

"You see anything suspicious up there?" Hale asked when the doctoring was under way.

"No, ma'am. Not a thing. It was pitch black."

"You sure?"

"Hard not to be sure when it's totally dark."

"Damn. We've had this house under watch for days." At his questioning look, she said, "Got a tip about drugs."

"Kids must be stoned on something. They were all—" He started. "Christ, Louise, that hurts like hell."

"I'll kiss and make it better when I'm done."

Hale glanced at the EMT. From a big city, she probably wasn't used to knowing all the rescue personnel on a call.

"I'd like to talk to you, Firefighter Malvaso," she said.

"It's Captain Malvaso," Louise said with pride in her voice.

"Yeah, sure. You going back to the firehouse, Captain?"

"Uh-huh."

She checked her watch with brisk efficiency. "I'm coming over as soon as I get a statement from these kids."

"I told you I didn't see anything."

"I still want a formal report."

"It's your time," he said easily.

"That it is." Turning, she walked away.

"I'm on the Rescue Squad. We're housed at Quint 7,

connected to headquarters," he called out after her.

She waved her hand above her head without looking back. He noticed she had a nice ass.

When Louise was done with the bandages—geez, he was glad the burns were only first degree—Mitch followed his crewmen to the truck. The first-in group would stick around for salvage and overhaul. Cleanup was one thing he didn't miss being on the Rescue Squad. He slid into the shotgun seat.

As they pulled away from the curb, Snyder angled his head to the left. "She's a looker, isn't she?"

"Who?" Mitch asked. He was thinking about how young those kids were.

"The detective."

"Is she?"

"Hey, just 'cause you ordered don't mean you can't read the menu, Cap."

He thought about his wife, Cynthia. Yeah, he'd *ordered* all right. But had he made the right choice? It was such a cliché. She came from a wealthy family in New York. He'd met her when he was twenty and in the city for a convention. There had been such sizzle between them that neither had thought of what their life would be like if they hooked up. He'd gone through a fancy wedding and taken money from her parents to buy her the house she wanted. She'd moved to Hidden Cove, had his babies, but had never truly accepted his lifestyle as a firefighter. He was away too much. He should move up the ladder faster. He should quit altogether and go back to school, make something of himself like his brother Paulie. For the last five years, up until the Sinco fire, their relationship had been a constant battle. The worst part had been her temper tantrums. They were worthy of a five-year-old.

But, he held his ground about the fire department he loved. And he rarely considered leaving her because of the kids. She could never be trusted alone with them. For Cindy's part, overly concerned with appearances, she'd kept up the front. As far as everybody outside the family knew, they had a good relationship. Amazing how you could hide the truth from so many people for so long.

Only now, since Sinco, Mitch didn't want to keep everything to himself anymore. He wanted to be fully involved in life, like he'd promised Jenny that day. Truth be told, he wanted out of the dead-end relationship that his marriage had become.

Too bad Cynthia didn't feel the same.

Christ, she'd turned from Shrew of the Month to June Cleaver since the fire. Mitch wasn't buying it, though. Mostly, he was just waiting for the old Cynthia to show her colors. Meanwhile, he didn't know how to handle her "rekindled feelings" for him and her desire to "keep the marriage together for the kids."

As if he hadn't been doing that for a decade.

Exhausted, his wrist throbbing, he lay his head back on the seat as the men joked around him and the rig bumped its way back to the station house. Nothing made sense to Mitch anymore, so why should Cynthia's behavior? Since the fire, all of life had turned murky.

Wearily, he wondered if anything would ever be right again.

MEGAN HALE JUST wanted to make it through the day. Or rather, she thought, glancing at her watch, the night. But she had one more stop to make before she headed home.

Some home. A little rented studio on Fourth Street. Well, hell, she'd only been in Hidden Cove a few weeks. Who would expect her to morph into Martha Stewart so fast?

She could almost hear her police chief father laugh. *Martha Stewart, my ass. That'll be the ever lovin' day.*

Thinking of her dad made her heart clutch. Just three months ago, the big, strapping Englishman had raced into a drug bust and been ruthlessly gunned down by cops turned bad.

Damn! She wasn't going to go there. Especially since she'd felt the stirrings of a migraine coming on. She'd taken the medicine she was never without, but still, she didn't want to tempt fate. Banishing the images with a cop's cool efficiency, she concentrated on the task at hand.

Quint 7 station house was connected to the fire department headquarters and City Hall and housed the Rescue Squad; it was quiet at ten at night. As she entered the bay area, she stared at the rigs; she only recently learned the difference between them. There was the Rescue Squad vehicle, a five-person truck with equipment for accidents, water rescue, rappelling, etc., but which carried no water or ladders. The two-person Midi was smaller, and went on EMS calls as well as to fires. And the premier truck was the Quint, which could perform five different functions—seating for five, dumping water, carrying ladders, and housing EMS and car accident equipment. Hard to believe it cost more than half a million dollars.

The faint smell of smoke and gasoline surrounded her as she crossed through the bay; she called out but no one answered. Usually firehouses would be all locked up, but the trucks had just returned and the big, garage-like doors were open wide. Hidden Cove was a small town, anyway, unlike New York City. Apparently they didn't worry all the time about crime.

Which is one of the reasons you left the city.

"Can I help you?" A firefighter had come out from the glassed-in watch station beside the last bay. He looked ridiculously young, with a buzz haircut and a freshly shaven jaw.

She flipped her star. "I'd like to see Mitch Malvaso."

The man studied her. "You must be the new detective."

"Guilty as charged." She introduced herself.

He stuck out his hand. "Tim Townsend. Come on in and sit. I'll get Mitello."

Mitello? Would she ever understand men's penchant for nicknaming each other?

That's your problem, Meggie, her dad once said. *Always tryin' to figure out men. We like to eat, drink, and watch TV.* Then he'd winked. *Throw in some hot sex, some close football games, and we're happy as pigs in shit.*

Townsend showed her to the kitchen. "Want some coffee?"

"Sure. Black."

"Have a seat." He motioned to a man-size table, poured coffee, brought it to her, and left to get Malvaso.

Wearily she sank down into a chair and sipped from the mug that said, "Firefighters do it on their knees." The coffee was hot and strong—typical firefighter's brew. And hers. While she waited, she scanned the kitchen. One big rectangle, it had been recently painted a light yellow— she could smell a faint whiff of the paint—which made the space bright. There were huge appliances, a double sink, a big row of windows, and a black-and-white lino- leum floor, which was spotless. Though they might be slobs at home, firefighters were renowned for keeping the station house clean.

She picked up a flyer lying on the table and shook her head. Man, here it was again; this thing was haunting her. It was the same newsletter she'd gotten in the mail the other day. The same one she couldn't stop thinking about. Taking a breath, she reread the article on page one. It was about an upstate New York camp established a few years ago for kids of rescue personnel who'd been killed in the line of duty. Part of the nationally known Bright Horizon Camps, which started off as a recreational summer facility for children with cancer, it had expanded to encompass kids with HIV, sickle-cell anemia, kids who were victims of violence, and most recently, the law enforcement/fire- fighter camp for the children of slain firefighters and po- lice officers. She and her dad had worked at it for three summers.

"Detective Hale?"

Looking up from the newsletter, she saw Mitch Malvaso standing at the end of the table. Without his gear and the grime that covered his face, he seemed different—bigger and more muscular in a navy T-shirt that outlined his broad chest. With it he wore sweatpants and no shoes or socks. His still-wet dark hair glinted almost black in the overhead lights. A faint growth of beard shadowed his jaw.

"I didn't mean to rush your shower."

"You didn't." He raised his arm; a gauze bandage

bound his wrist. "McKenna wouldn't let me go until I got this doctored again."

"Hurt?"

"Like a bitch."

Crossing to the pot, he poured coffee, asked if she wanted a refill, then sat adjacent to her. She got a whiff of subtle aftershave that made her think of one of those underwear models on TV. Up close, his eyes were bloodshot, but they were a soft, velvety brown. His lashes were girl thick. "So, you enjoying your new job at Hidden Cove?" he asked.

"Uh-huh."

"Settling in okay?"

"Yep." She drew out a small notepad and peeled back the cover. "I need to ask you some questions."

His brows rose in annoyance. Well, shit, it was late, she didn't know the guy, and she wasn't exactly interested in making friends with a group of firefighters. What she needed was information. "Are you sure you didn't see anything when you walked into that upstairs bedroom?"

"I'm sure, Detective. Like I said before, it was totally black."

"Totally?"

"Yeah." His tone was exasperated. "I take it you never been inside a burning building."

"Can't say I have."

"It can be like wearing a blindfold. At the risk of spouting clichés, I couldn't see the hand in front of my face."

"Then how did you find your way in and get to those kids?"

"Instinct. Feeling the walls. Knowing what to look for."

"Like?"

"Beds are usually against the wall. If they bounce, people are on them. That kind of thing."

"Did you kick anything on the floor?"

"Nope."

"Smell anything?"

He snorted. "Black smoke stinks worse than cow shit, Detective Hale."

She closed her book. "I'd like to talk to your men."

"Fine, but they're bunked in now. I'd rather not wake them. Mostly because they won't have seen anything, either."

"Statistics show people remember more in the immediate aftermath of an incident. At the risk of ruining their sleep, I'd like to question them now."

Friendly dark eyes turned hard as steel. "Is this necessary?"

Sighing, she rubbed the back of her neck wearily. She felt like she'd gone a couple of rounds with a violent suspect. "Look, Captain, those kids were sixteen and seventeen. I need some answers here."

His jaw tightened. Used to studying people, she took note of the reaction. He was pissed at her. Finally he said, "I'll go get—"

Static blasted out of the loudspeaker. "Structure fire at the corner of Wilson and Main. Rescue Squad, go into service."

"Sorry, Detective, you're going to have to wait after all."

She rose, too, as he headed for the bay. On impulse she followed him. He ducked into the watch station, ripped a paper from the printer, and strode toward the rig. Several men raced into the area. "Another fire," Malvaso shouted. "It's a bad one."

The firefighters hurried to the truck.

Boots stood by the Rescue Squad rig, all cleaned up and ready to go with their droopy pants folded over them. She'd read somewhere this was called turnout gear because it was what firefighters *turned out* in for an alarm. Malvaso quickly donned socks, stuck his feet in the boots, and pulled up the bunker pants—she guessed they were called that because fighting a fire was a lot like fighting a war. Suspenders crisscrossed his back. He grabbed a coat from a hook, along with his helmet, and jumped into the front seat. The truck pulled out just as the last guy tagged on.

Megan stared after them, wondering how these exhausted men were going to deal with a yet another fire.

TWO

"GRADY, GET THE lead out." In the bunk room of the Quint/Midi 7 firehouse, Jenn tapped her foot impatiently as she waited for her best friend to finish tying his sneakers.

"Hold your horses." Grady's blue eyes twinkled. "Not in a hurry to get beaten at racquetball, are you?"

She flopped down and stretched out on one of the cots. They were big, easily accommodating her five-eight muscular build. Scanning the sleeping quarters—stark, nondescript beige walls, no pictures, and ten cots lined up with military precision—she snorted. "Beaten? In your dreams, pal. I'm ready to trounce you."

Grady finished with his sneakers, then poked arms and head through a navy HCFD sweatshirt. He crossed to the cot and sank down on the edge. Before she could get up, he braced his arms on either side of her. "You gotta stop moving sometime, babe."

She tried to keep the emotion from showing on her face. Since the Sinco warehouse fire six months ago that had claimed the lives of ten Hidden Cove firefighters, and injured several more who'd been trapped or who were part of the rescue effort, nothing had been right. "Can it, Gray. I'm not up for this."

"You haven't been up for anything lately." Mile-wide shoulders shrugged. "You won't even talk to me. The cap's thinking about recommending you see Harrison."

"Fuck that. I don't need a psychologist. I only had second-degree burns on my arms. Mitch and Zach were hurt a lot worse." She started to rise.

Strong hands held her in place. "Uh-uh. You're not escaping. Not till you talk to me."

"I talk to you every freakin' day."

She and Grady worked on the same shift, Group One, at the firehouse, which also was the home of the Rescue Squad that Mitch headed; Zach worked at Quint 7, too, but on a different shift.

"And most every night."

A few years ago, right after Jenn's divorce, she and Grady had bought, renovated, and lived side-by-side in a duplex in a quiet residential neighborhood in town. Though the house was built for two separate families, they'd installed connecting French doors in the foyer, which most of the time were left open. Together, they ate meals, watched TV, and often socialized with their dates at home. They also shared most of the same interests—camping, sports, and fast and sleek cars.

"You might talk, but I don't think I've heard an honest word out of that pretty little mouth of yours since the Sinco fire."

She swallowed hard.

Gently, Grady tucked a strand of hair behind her ear. "Jenny, you gotta get it out."

"I can't, Grady."

He sighed. "I wish I'd been with you." He'd broken his arm and had been on sick leave when the warehouse fire in this sleepy little town had rocked their worlds. Jenn knew that not being able to help put out the fire, and then to stand by while Zach, whom he loved like a brother, was trapped, had been horrible for him.

She gripped his biceps. "No, no, you don't. *I* don't. You could have been hurt, like us. Then, lying there outside with all those dead . . ." She couldn't finish.

"Jenn, please. Talk to me."

"No!" She pushed at his chest and met with pure steel. "Let me up."

"All right. But we're not done with this. And I'm gonna beat your ass on the court."

He did. She scored only two points in game one. In game two, she had him twelve to eleven, but he won. Halfway through game three, she flung her racket onto the floor. It clattered, wood against wood, in the cavernous room. "This sucks. I'm done." She headed for the gear she'd stowed on the side of the court. He caught up with her before she reached it and grasped on to her arm.

"Hold on."

"Nope. I'm done. I lost, you won."

"Jenny, stop."

Shaking her head, she pivoted. Their earlier conversation had distracted her so she couldn't even play a decent game of racquetball. Talking about the fire conjured images she tried to squelch every waking second. "I can't stop."

"I know, honey."

Something warm flickered inside her. He always did this to her—made her go soft and mushy with just a sweet word. Unbidden, tears welled in her eyes. "Oh, God." She sank onto the cold wood floor. Her sweaty body tensed at the contrast to her heated skin. "Every time I stop, I see it. All those guys dying. I can still hear Mitch moaning in pain." Not to mention the agony she herself felt from being covered by plaster that burned her skin raw. "Then, Zach was trapped . . ."

Grady plunked down next to her and slid an arm around her. The white T-shirt she wore felt sticky. "I'm sorry. Maybe it would help to talk about it."

"How, Gray? How would that help?"

"I don't know. I'm not a psychologist. But you could use one."

"No, it's not what I need."

"What *do* you need?" he said, exasperated. "I'm worried sick about you."

She didn't answer.

"Jenny, I'm not watching you suffer like this any-more." He sounded like an officer scolding a probie.

She knew he meant it. He could get her to tell him anything, like he had their whole lives . . . the time she'd slept with Johnny Stone after the senior ball . . . the morning her dad died in a fire and she thought her world had ended . . . the night she admitted to Grady that her first husband had hit her when she asked him for a divorce.

With a heavy sigh, she stared hard at him. "All right. I made a decision. When I was waiting outside to see if Zach was okay."

"A decision?" That classic forehead furrowed. He had tawny golden looks and blue eyes the color of a lagoon, in direct contrast to her dark hair and eyes that were Mal-vaso family traits. "What kind of decision?"

"While I was in there, I got to thinking about how I've lived my life."

"Yeah. A lot of us did, after all that loss."

"I'm happy now with most aspects except one."

Wheat-colored brows rose in surprise. "You want to get married again?"

"God, no." Jenn had had two disastrous marriages and divorces, which had soured her completely on the insti-tution. But poor Grady—he'd had it a lot worse. He'd been engaged and that had ended nastily when he realized he and his fianceé wanted different things out of life. But his marriage had wreaked catastrophic consequences that he still struggled with. "Do you want to get married again?" she asked carefully.

"Never." His eyes shadowed every time he talked about Sheila or Linda. "So, tell me what you want. Maybe I can help you get it."

"I'm afraid to tell you."

"*What?* Jenny, you can tell me anything."

Sucking in a breath, she just blurted it out. "I want to have a baby."

His face blanked. "Oh."

"See, I knew it would hurt you."

"No, it's okay. Just because that didn't work out for me doesn't mean you shouldn't have it."

"I'm sorry, Gray." His wife, Linda, ended her seven-month pregnancy when she killed herself; her suicide had stunned all of them. Grady had never been the same since then. Jenn knew he still carried a truckload of guilt about them.

He swallowed hard. "That was four years ago. I'm better about it. Anyway, I'd hate for that to stop you." He grinned. "You always wanted a kid. Ever since we were little." Living next door to each other, they'd been best friends all their lives. Grady had spent most of his time at their house to escape his alcoholic father and enabling mother and Sabina Malvaso, their mother, had practically raised him. "Jesus Christ, remember how you made me play house all the time?"

She smiled at the memory, then said, "I'm thirty-six, Gray. My time's running out. And even if it wasn't, I could walk into a burning building like all those guys at Sinco—or at the World Trade Center—and never come out."

He grasped her hand. "I understand." Squeezed it. "How would you go about this?"

"Artificial insemination, of course. But there's a problem."

"What?"

"I, um, don't want an anonymous donor. Somebody who's selling his sperm for money."

He shuddered. "Guys do it, I guess, but it still gives me the creeps."

"I want somebody I *know* to give me their little soldiers. Somebody whose medical history I have ahead of time. Somebody smart. Somebody handsome. Somebody brave and strong and—"

"Whoa, Genevieve. Where you going with this?"

"It's what I was afraid to tell you."

"Honey, just say it outright."

"I want you to be the donor, Grady."

*   *   *

LIKE THE PRODIGAL son, who returned home after years of debauchery, Zach Malvaso rang the doorbell to his own house. He still had a key tucked in his wallet, had used it numerous times. Not since Sinco, though. He waited, then rang again. Jamming his hands in his jeans pockets, he shifted from one foot to the other and waited some more. Finally the door swung open.

"Dad!" Nicky, his pajama-clad six-year-old, launched himself into Zach's arms. On the porch he'd built with his brother and his best friend, Grady, Zach held on to his child, breathing in the scent of his shampoo and soap after a bath.

"Hey, buddy, how ya doing?"

Nicky pulled back. His dark hair was still damp and his blue eyes gleamed with mischief as he toyed with the buttons on Zach's cotton shirt. "JayJay hit me." Sure enough, Nicky's lip was swollen.

"Jason hit you? I don't believe it."

"We were just playing." Eleven-year-old Jason stood back, his hands jammed into the pockets of jeans that bagged and belled at the bottom. With them he wore a Nike sweatshirt. He was almost a replica of Zach with his dark hair and eyes—that now were as hesitant and wary as a beaten puppy.

Just another little result of your stupidity, Malvaso. His "former life," as he'd come to call it, hung over him like a cloud of noxious black smoke.

Zach stepped into his house and shut the door.

"How come you ring the doorbell, Dad?" Nicky asked, hugging Zach's neck, his chubby legs clamped around Zach's middle. For the millionth time, Zach wondered how he'd ever let all this go.

"Because I asked him to." Angela's voice drifted from behind. Slowly Zach turned to find his wife—his ex-wife—in the doorway leading to the stairs. The expression on her face matched her tone. Cold.

Why wouldn't it be, asshole? After all the shit you pulled?

"Hi, Angel."

She frowned.

Don't call me that anymore, you bastard. It was a special nickname, given in love. After what you've done, don't you dare call me that.

"You're late," she said, glancing at her watch.

"Sorry. We had a fire."

Those eyes—a light blue—widened. With fear? Word around the station had it that all the guys' wives went bonkers every time there was a fire since the deaths of so many firefighters in the Sinco warehouse.

Jason blanched.

"Where, Dad?" Nicky asked excitedly. "Where was the fire?"

"On Main Street. It was a small one in a restaurant kitchen." He kissed Nicky's head, but his gaze zeroed in on his older, fearful son. "No big deal."

When Angela came fully into the room, the suede skirt she wore swirled around her calves. Beneath the pretty beige blouse, he could see the outline of a lacy bra. "You look nice," he told her.

"Mom has a date." This from Nick.

Zach's head snapped up. "With who?"

"She's got a boyfriend."

"He's not your boyfriend, is he?" Jason asked. His tone bordered on surly, unusual for his demure son.

"Jay . . ." Angela said softly.

"Never mind!" Jason stomped out; she followed him.

Zach and Nicky settled down on the nubby beige couch to watch a show before bedtime. As he stared mindlessly at the cartoon, Zach thought about how everything had changed since that fateful day six months ago.

Though they'd been divorced for two years before the fire, Angela had come to the hospital while he was in intensive care. Suffering extensive burns, a broken arm, and severe smoke inhalation, he'd been on the critical list for days. She'd stayed at his bedside as he faded in and out of consciousness. When he was finally out of danger, she'd withdrawn again. His recuperation had been long and painful. Physically he'd healed. Emotionally, he wondered if the scars would ever go away.

As his son nestled in his lap and chattered on about

the cartoon, Zach remembered how he'd come here to see Angie when he'd gotten out of the hospital and could move around again. It had been a good month after the fire. . . .

I'm sorry. I'm so sorry. Please, give me another chance.

For what?

For us.

Oh, no, Zach, never. I could never do that.

I was wrong, but I've changed, honest. After the fire, all those people dead, knowing it could have been me . . . it changed me, deep down. Please, give me another chance.

No! I can't risk it. What you did hurt so much. . . .

She'd been adamant—and angry at his presumptuousness—so he'd promised not to broach the subject again, to be satisfied with seeing his kids as often as he could and becoming a good father to them.

But, damn it, she had a fucking date. Which she was all dressed up for.

The doorbell rang, interrupting his thoughts. Angela came from the back of the house. Without sparing him or Nicky a glance, she crossed to the door and opened it.

"Hi. Wow, you look great." Deep voice. Sexy timbre to it. Was Angel sleeping with the guy?

"Come on in, Ken." Zach couldn't tell from her tone how she felt about him.

Tall and lean, with sandy brown hair and a goatee, the man entered the house. His eyebrows raised when he spotted Zach. "Hello, Zach."

"Hey, man." He looked to Angela with a silent question.

"You remember Ken Kellerman, don't you, Zach? He's an assistant principal at the school."

Her boss? Shit.

"Yeah. Sure."

Nicky burrowed into Zach and began to suck his thumb.

"Nicky, say hello to Mr. Kellerman." Angela's voice

was chiding. Hmm. Seems like neither of his kids was too keen on Mom's date.

" 'ello."

"Where you going?" Zach asked.

"Dinner and a movie." Kellerman put a hand on Angela's neck. Zach was shocked by how that small gesture socked him in the gut. "Nice of you to baby-sit."

Zach said, "Don't let Angel hear you say a man taking care of his own kids is baby-sitting. She'll skin you alive."

Angela shook back her hair, tumbling long, luscious curls over her shoulders. "We're going." From the couch, she picked up a matching suede jacket and put it on. "I won't be too late."

You'd better not. "Whatever. Have a good time." He cuddled Nicky to his chest. "Nice to see you again, Kellerman."

But the guy only had eyes and ears—and freakin' hands—for Angel. When they left, Zach seethed.

"What's a matter, Daddy?" Nicky asked.

"Nothing, son." He concentrated on the boy. "Want me to read you a book?"

Soon Nicky became engrossed in the newest Harry Potter tale. When he dozed, Zach hefted him up and carried him to his bedroom in the back of the house. After settling Nicky in, Zach knocked on Jason's door. No answer. Another knock. Still no answer. He eased open the door. Jason was sitting at his computer, facing some Internet site.

"How you doing, buddy?"

"Good."

"What you got there?" Zach came fully into the room and sank onto the bed and picked up a baseball glove.

Daddy, wanna play catch?

Can't, buddy. Gotta go.

If Zach remembered correctly, there'd been a cute little redhead waiting for him at the time.

"Talk to me a minute, Jay."

His back to Zach, the boy stared at the computer.

"Get off the computer, son."

Still no answer.

I said get off that fuckin' thing now, or I'll smash it into the floor. Shit, another of his stellar moments.

"Please."

Jason swiveled around to face him. So much hurt smoldered beneath the surface, it almost leveled Zach. "What?"

"You upset about your mother?"

"Maybe."

Though it stuck in his craw, he said, "She's got a life, Jay. That doesn't mean you and I won't still see each other."

The boy stared at him with hollow eyes. This was the worst repercussion of Zach's wildness and self-absorption.

"Look, I know I haven't been a good dad." Nervous, he punched the glove with his fist. "I want another chance."

"Why?"

What to say? Maybe the truth. He sat up straight. "Because of the fire."

"I saw all your pictures in the paper." Jason looked torn. "They said you were a hero, pushing the other guys out of the way."

A lump rose in Zach's throat. "No, not that. But it made me think about things. About what's important to me."

"We aren't important to you. I heard Mom saying that to you all the time when you lived here."

"That was before the fire."

"People don't change that fast. Mrs. Steuben, my English teacher, says lots of people are different for a while after a tragedy, then they go back to their old ways."

Thank you, Mrs. Steuben.

"I won't go back to being like I was, son."

"Okay." The kid didn't believe him for a second. At a chime, Jason turned back to the computer. "I got an instant message."

Zach stood and crossed to his son. Leaning over, he kissed him on the head. "I'm back to stay, Jay. I'll prove it to you."

Jason didn't say anything.

"Don't stay up too late."

Out in the kitchen, Zach decided to warm up some coffee in the microwave. While it was heating, the mug ran over, and out of nowhere, his heart began to beat fast. Suddenly, he was back in the burning warehouse and the plaster was on fire. Its acrid smell—exactly like burned coffee—had hit him just before the the wall caved and buried Zach. He started to sweat. He couldn't breathe, like then.

The nausea came. He turned fast and vomited violently in the sink. Gripping the edge of the counter, he sucked in air as if he'd just gotten a gulp of thick black smoke.

For the six months after Sinco, he'd been having attacks similar to this. They came at odd times, never during a fire or rescue, and usually related to some sensory thing. Or during his sleep. On his own, he'd made an appointment with the department shrink, who was now seeing him regularly. Since the attacks, which Harrison called a form of post-traumatic stress disorder, didn't affect his job, he was still on the line.

Finally he was calm enough to clean up and go into the living room. Something drew him to the stairs. His and Angie's bedroom spanned the top floor of this cozy Cape Cod while the boys slept downstairs. Shakily he climbed the steps, which opened up to the middle of the room. The first thing he noticed was her perfume, soft but sexy. He remembered all the places on her that he'd smelled it when he had the right to touch her. He switched on a light. She'd redone the room since they'd divorced two years ago. Peach walls, gauzy curtains, light oak dressers and a nice wrought-iron headboard transformed the space into a purely feminine boudoir.

Still sweaty from the earlier images, he forced himself to think of something pleasant . . .

Them. On the bed. Angel giggling . . .

Shh, you'll wake the boys.

So, let 'em know I'm humpin' their mom.

Zach . . . oh . . . God . . . yes . . . right there . . .

Like it, baby?

I love it . . . I love you. . . .

Instead of soothing him, the memory made the lump in his throat expand. He'd lost so much. He couldn't even remember now why he'd so cavalierly given her up.

Well, he told himself firmly, it was important to just go on.

Oh, sure asshole. Admit it. You're afraid Jason's right. How long are you gonna be able to take being around her when she doesn't love you anymore?

But then he thought of all those other firefighters who died in the warehouse and never got a second chance to play ball with their kids, never got to make up to their wives for the stupid things they'd done in the past. If nothing else, in memory of them, this change in him was going to last.

He switched off the light and slowly trundled downstairs to wait for his wife to come home from her date.

⌒ THREE

FEELING OLDER THAN dirt, Mitch entered his house through the garage door leading to the kitchen. Just as his shift was ending, there'd been a bad accident on the corner of Glide and Main. His crew had gone and rescued the trapped victims. Mitch had wrenched his back using the Jaws of Life—why the hell hadn't he let one of the younger guys pry the roof off the car?—not to mention that the whole maneuver had taken twice as long to execute because the gas tank had been compromised and the crew had to proceed slowly.

The police had cordoned off the area and kept it secure. Briefly he thought about Detective Megan Hale. He wondered why she'd shown up at the scene—it wasn't her responsibility, though extra cops were often needed at an accident site. Just the same, she'd stayed the whole time to help reroute traffic.

He hadn't seen her since she'd come to the firehouse wanting to interview his guys. She'd done it the next day, but like he'd warned her, she didn't get much out of them.

As he entered his kitchen, he glanced at the clock. Nine A.M. By the time he'd finished the paperwork, it had been shift change. Zach had come on and he and Mitch sat and shot the shit for a while.

Mitch was worried about his brother since Sinco's fire. Zach had been hurt bad—nightmarish burns, a broken wrist, severe lung damage—and his recuperation had taken a long time. Only the fact that he'd been in top shape had made it possible for him to get back to work after just four months of healing and physical therapy. As Mitch poured coffee, sank onto a kitchen chair, and stared out at the lawn, he thought about their conversation. . . .

"How you doing, buddy?" Mitch had asked Zach. Movie-star handsome, even on his worst days, his brother had lost weight and looked tired—his dark eyes had been bloodshot and his face etched with lines that hadn't been there before the Sinco fire. "More dreams?"

"Some." Zach had pretended interest in the bulletin board of the watch room. "Harrison says disturbed sleep is normal." He'd looked at Mitch. "You're the one that's got him worried."

"Why?"

"You haven't had much of a reaction to being trapped and getting hurt as me and Jenny and the other guys."

Mitch had thought about the middle-of-the-night fear that flared like sparks igniting from a fire you thought was out. "Nah, I'm affected. I just deal with it different."

"How?"

"I been running every day. Working out more." He'd ducked his head. "And going to church."

Zach, the ultimate atheist, hadn't mocked him. "Yeah? I been thinking about going back."

Mitch had almost fallen off his chair. Zach hadn't seen the inside of a church since his wedding. "You'd give God a heart attack."

"Fuck you."

Mitch had responded in kind, then said, "Seen Jenny lately?"

"Yeah, sure."

"How she doing?"

"Ask Grady. She talks to him about the fire."

Mitch had thought of his nonrelationship with Cynthia. "At least she's got Grady." Who did he have?

That notion rocketed him back to the present, and to Cynthia, who now stood in the doorway. "Mitch?" She was wearing a satiny robe the color of ripe peaches. It set off her light blond hair. Even in sleepwear, she was dressed to kill.

"Hi."

She glanced at the clock. "You're late."

"I had coffee with Zach."

"Your sister Connie called."

"What did she want?"

"To remind us of Ma's birthday party Sunday."

He sighed. *Shit.*

"You did get someone to work for you, right?"

In the old days, a major temper tantrum would follow his denial.

"I will."

She sat at the table. Her face would give Helen of Troy competition. Wide-spaced blue eyes. High cheekbones. Lush lips. At one time, the whole package could drive him to his knees. "Try, Mitch. Ma will be devastated if you don't come."

Sabina Malvaso, who'd been married to a firefighter, who'd raised five kids—three were smoke eaters—would shrug and tell them to stay safe. Still, it was obvious Cynthia was trying.

"I'll be there." He heard the faint bass of music from above and glanced at the clock. "Which one's home?"

"Trish."

He felt the anger smolder inside him. "We told the principal she wouldn't miss any more school, Cindy."

Cynthia shrugged. "I tried to get her to go."

How had she become so ineffectual with her children, except to bring out the worst in them?

Weary, he stood.

"Mitch, where are you . . . what are you doing?"

"She's going to school." He strode toward the oak staircase that had cost a fortune, but was like the ones in her parents' house. Following it up, he stopped at his daughter's room and heard godawful noise blaring through the door. He knocked. No answer. He pounded. Still none. "Patricia, open this door."

The music lowered. After a moment, the door opened.

The smell of cigarette smoke wafted out. He surveyed the room. Clothes covered the floor in several mounds. A sleeping bag, a stack of shoes, and an upturned wastebasket added to the mess. There wasn't a square inch of space on her desk without junk on it—glasses, piles of CDs, books, magazines. Her computer was on, and the screen showed email.

His daughter wrapped her arms around her waist. Wearing a T-shirt that said *You've been naughty, now go to my room* and long pajama bottoms, she threw back hair the exact color of her mother's. Her pierced eyebrow made him wince every time he looked at it. "Hi, Daddy." She was also as good an actress as Cynthia.

"Hi, princess." He crossed into the room, skirting piles of God knew what; he pushed her cat off her unmade bed and sat on it. "Why aren't you in school?"

She contorted her face. "I got my period."

He shook his head. "Not good enough, Trish."

"How would you know?"

"You signed a contract not to miss any more days."

"Fuck the contract."

"Watch your mouth, young lady."

Turning, she plunked back down at the computer. Damn it, he had to deal with rookies too big for their britches at work. He didn't need this at home. He stood and crossed to the desk. Reaching around her, he flicked the off switch on the power strip.

"Hey, you'll ruin the hard drive."

Dragging her up by the arm, he said, "Better than you ruining your life. You've got ten minutes to get dressed. I'm driving you to school. If you don't stay, or if you cause any trouble, I'm taking this—" He nodded to the computer. "—and all your other toys away from you." He faced her down. "And if I ever smell smoke in here again, you'll be grounded for a solid month. You could burn yourself up hiding it and I don't want my daughter to end up a charred corpse." He locked his gaze with hers. "I've seen them."

Mutinous blue eyes stared back at him. But behind them, he thought he saw something else.

She needs to know you care, Captain Malvaso. She's been given a lot freedom—her mother just lets her run wild, mostly—and sometimes kids view that as lack of love.

The freedom had been because of his job; he wasn't home like regular dads and Cynthia had lost control of both kids years ago. All she did was fight with them. Or throw fits when they did something she didn't like. Mitch's fault was in ignoring it. Well, no more. At least that was one good thing that had come out of the Sinco fiasco. He was going to rescue his children and thought he'd made a good start. Things *had* been better lately with both of them.

On impulse, he kissed his daughter's forehead. "Come on, baby, I've just dealt with a bad car accident and I'm fried. Go along peacefully this time, okay?"

For a minute, she stared at him, then threw herself into his arms. His throat closed up as he remembered how she used to hug him before school, after she won a spelling bee, on Christmas morning. Those hugs had *not* been part of his life for a long time. "Okay. Can we stop for breakfast on the way?"

He drew back. "No. I'll take a rain check for Saturday, though."

"All right." But she stayed close, and he hugged her a little tighter. "Will you tell me a firefighter story on the way to school?"

He had to smile. From the time they were little, in hopes of bringing them into his professional life, Mitch had shared stories about the fire department with them— funny ones, heroic ones, some that were poignant, or stupid, or about pranks played on a rookie. He often told them fire department jokes. Even as they grew up, even when they were getting in trouble, they'd asked for the stories. Mitch always saw it as a kind of verbal hot chocolate, a comfort, a tradition that connected them to him.

Ironically, the tradition had spread. Zach had started to tell these kinds of stories to his own kids. And, once, Jenn confessed that she and Grady shared uplifting fire department stories when things were tense or bad. The oddest part was when the guys at the station house found out about Mitch's storytelling with his kids, they picked up on it, though they often told bawdy and off-color stories he couldn't share with the kids. But sometimes, after a particularly dangerous rescue, or in the early morning when nobody could sleep, they told their favorite heroic ones. During 9/11, the stories became a constant routine.

Promising Trish one on the way to school, Mitch left her standing in front of her closet and went to his bedroom. He hadn't showered after the accident. Maybe if he could grab a quick one before he took Trish to school he might not wreck his car on the drive over. God, he was exhausted.

The hot spray soothed some sore muscles and revived him. Stepping out of the shower, amid the fog, he found Cynthia in the bathroom. She was perched in the way-too-expensive chair in the corner. "Mmm." She eyed his naked body and sipped her coffee. He remembered a time when her come-on would have had him hard in seconds. "You look good for forty-three, darling."

"I feel four hundred and three." He ran a towel over his hair and swiped water off his chest, then rubbed out a circle in the mirror so he could see his face.

Standing, Cynthia approached him. From behind, she scraped nails over his biceps. "Come back. We can spend the morning in bed."

He forced a smile.

She kissed his shoulder. "I'll give you a back rub."

Well, that might be worth it.

"Sounds good," he said noncommittally. He glanced at the modern clock in the corner. It looked like a Picasso painting. "I gotta get dressed."

In the bedroom, as he threw on jeans and a department sweatshirt and Cynthia left to have breakfast, he tried to summon some interest in his wife's seductive suggestion.

Jesus Christ. He used to rush home like a bridegroom

to bed her when they were young and he'd come off a night shift. But their marriage had gone up in flames like kindling lit by years of fighting and neglect. By rights, they shouldn't even be together.

Forcing the knowledge from his mind, he headed downstairs where he found Trish waiting by the door. He herded her into the car, ignoring the fact that her skirt was too short. As they began to drive to school, she said, "Okay, tell me one, Pops."

He thought about which story to tell her.

"One of yours," she said as if she read her mind.

He didn't particularly like bragging about his rescues, or worse, telling when he was in danger, but he was struggling to keep Trish on the same wavelength as he was. And he had to take risks to do it.

"One time, there was this good firefighter who had a really bad sense of direction. He went back into a fully involved fire to help bring out a brother and got trapped on the third floor when some gasoline ignited in the basement and drove the fire up the stairs and shafts. He found the other firefighter, but there was no escape. They wandered down a hall and tried all the doors. They found one that was open. By now, they were weak and fuzzy. And the smoke was so thick, they couldn't even find their way to the window. They stumbled around when an aerial ladder hit that exact window. My men called to them, and they managed to scramble out to the tip."

"You put the ladder up there, Dad?"

"Uh-huh."

"How'd you know where to set it?"

"I didn't, honey." He sighed. "It was a combination of pure luck and some unconscious instinct, I guess. Sometimes firefighters develop that kind of sixth sense. Like when they're in a burning building and could turn left or right. There are countless stories where guys went the way that led to the victim and rescued him."

He smiled.

"What?"

"The firefighter I told you about? He's retired now, but

I get a card every year from him on the anniversary of the rescue, saying it's another bonus year."

"Bonus, like he shouldn't have survived, right?"

"Uh-huh."

Trish smiled and gave him a quick peck on the cheek. "You've led a great life, Dad, saving all those people." Then, she settled down into the seat with her headphones.

Mitch cringed at her words, recalling how he and Jenny had promised each other that they'd *change* their lives when they got out of Sinco alive. Make them more meaningful. Idly, he wondered if she'd given any more thought to having a baby. Six months later, he hadn't done a thing about his situation with Cynthia.

And—remembering the funerals, memorials services and the faces of the widows and children of the colleagues they'd lost—Mitch was ashamed of himself for his inaction.

AT 10:30 A.M., Megan pushed open the front door of Hidden Cove High School, stepped outside, and bumped into solid steel. Or what felt like like solid steel. She stumbled on the concrete sidewalk, was righted by strong hands, and found herself staring into the face of Mitch Malvaso.

The October wind had picked up, disheveling his hair. She could see flecks of gray in it. "Easy, Detective," he said, his voice gravelly.

"Oh. Captain Malvaso. Sorry, I wasn't looking where I was going."

"I was standing in the way." He let go and stepped back.

His face was drawn with fatigue. His eyes were shot through with red. She imagined she looked as bad as he did. She'd had a migraine after she'd gotten home from the accident this morning; she'd puked her guts out, then taken medicine to subdue the pain to a tolerable level.

"What are you doing here?" Mitch asked, glancing at the building. "Was there trouble?"

"No, one of the teachers has a criminology class and

asked me to talk about my experiences." She rolled her eyes. "As a female in the NYPD."

"Big news here in River City."

She smiled.

"It was nice of you to help out," he said.

"How about you? What are you doing here?"

"Playing truant officer."

"I don't understand."

Looking sheepish, he nodded to the building. "When I got home from my shift, my daughter hadn't gone to school." He shrugged. "She's what they call a reluctant learner, though in my book that's like calling a fully involved blaze a campfire."

"So Dad brought her in?"

"Uh-huh." He smiled. It was a nice smile. She liked the way it crinkled his eyes around the edges. "And Dad's standing guard out here to make sure she doesn't bolt as soon as he leaves." His dark brows formed a vee. "She's a good kid down deep. It's just buried under layers of rebellion and teen angst." He rubbed his hand around the back of his neck, as if it hurt. "I hope I survive her adolescence."

Megan thought of her early years and her own father's beleagueredness. *Jesus Christ, Meggie, I'll drag you to school if I have to.*

Mitch glanced at his watch. "Guess I can leave now." They started toward the parking lot together.

"Her dad can get her through these years. I know."

"You do?"

She nodded. "My father was single-handedly responsible for my graduating high school."

"I don't have much in the way of a role model for this kind of thing. My dad died when I was sixteen."

For some reason, she asked, "Yeah? How?"

"He walked into a burning building and never came out."

"Mine, too." The words slipped out before she could halt them.

Mitch stopped at his car and cocked his head. "He was a firefighter?"

"No, I meant he's dead, too. He was a cop. It was a drug bust. Complicated by dirty cops."

"I'm sorry."

"Me, too." Images of his lifeless body ambushed her. She shivered.

"You okay?"

"Yeah." Damn, sometimes the grief snuck up on her like a mugger in the night. "I . . . don't usually talk about his death. It only happened three months ago."

"Maybe you should. Talk about it. My brother's seeing Harrison, the psychologist the police and fire department share."

"What's wrong with your brother?"

"The three of us—I got a sister who's a firefighter, too—we were trapped in the Sinco warehouse six months ago. We were all hurt. Zach almost died."

Megan nodded. "I heard all about that fire. You did lose some colleagues."

His look was stricken.

Again Megan thought of the flyer and the camp she'd dreamed of again last night. This meeting with Malvaso might be kismet. She leaned against his Cherokee. "Captain, do you know about that camp upstate for the kids of slain firefighters and police officers?"

"Sure. On Keuka Lake." He shrugged, the action pulling tight the navy sweatshirt he wore. It looked soft and warm. "Some people from here have volunteered up there."

Terrific. Megan threw back her shoulders; renewed energy pulsed through her veins like a direct shot of caffeine. "You going home to sleep?"

He hesitated. "Maybe." He frowned. "I feel restless, though. Why'd you ask?"

"I, um, wanted to talk about this camp." She studied him. She'd always believed in signs, and bumping into the most popular guy in the Hidden Cove Fire Department—whose father just happened to be killed in the line of duty—had to mean something. "Can I buy you breakfast?"

He smiled over at her. "Why not?"

*   *   *

"ARE YOU ACTUALLY going to eat all that?" Mitch stared down at the half-demolished bacon, eggs, home fries, and pancakes on Megan Hale's Hungry Woman's special. Though she wasn't small, he found it hard to believe she could put away enough food for a lumberjack.

"Uh-huh, why?" She sipped her coffee in between bites and took a swig of tomato juice laced with tabasco.

"Where do you put it?"

Her amber eyes flashed with deep emotion. "My dad used to ask that."

He picked up his fork. "You were close?"

"Yep." She bit into a piece of toast and shoveled some eggs into her mouth. "My mother died when I was five. It was just us two most of my life."

"Losing him had to be hard."

"He was only fifty-five." Her voice caught, stirring something very male inside him. "He'd just made deputy chief."

Mitch shook his head. The loss of a parent at any age was tough. And she sounded crazy about him. "He was proud of you, I'll bet."

Now she chuckled, a curious blend of amusement and regret on her face. It was a nice face—all angles and hollows. "He cried at my graduation from the academy."

"That's nice."

"Tell me about your daughter."

"I'll cry at *her* graduation, I'll tell you that. Not because I'm moved. Because I'm relieved."

"She can't be that bad."

"Actually, she's got a heart of gold. She just covers it up with pounds of makeup and a sassy mouth."

"Why?"

"The sixty-four-thousand-dollar question." He picked at his omelet, not really tasting it. Food had lost its appeal after the fire. Along with a lot of other things. "Did you want to talk about volunteering at the camp upstate, Detective?"

"Not exactly, Captain."

He grinned. "Make it Mitch."

"Megan." She chowed down some more. "The upstate camp is great, but it's four hours from here."

"How do you know it's great?"

"My father and I went up there to volunteer. Dad loved it. He not only worked up there regularly, he gave them tons of money every year. Got other cops to do the same."

"He sounds like a good guy."

She laughed aloud this time. "He was a tough son of a bitch. Criminals cringed when they saw him coming. He got involved in the camp because his brother-in-law was a cop, too, and died in the line of duty. Dad naturally gravitated toward the camp, I guess."

"I see."

Setting down her fork, her eyes got lighter, the color of brandy with the sun shining through the bottle. "It's terrific what they do there. Sports, crafts, gab sessions with kids in the same boat. And lots of adult volunteers to act as role models." She glanced away, fiddled with the lapel of the tan blazer that she wore over a T-shirt the color of hot chocolate. Then she looked back at him. "I was thinking maybe somebody should start one down here."

"*Start* one?"

"A camp. It'd be a great service to the community."

He pushed around his eggs. "That'd be a huge undertaking."

"Would it?"

"And costly."

"Yeah, but with all this interest in the last few years about helping out America's Bravest and Finest, especially since the World Trade Center attacks, I wonder if it might not be easier than you think."

"Why do I sense this isn't an idle question?"

"Because it's not. I had a couple of reasons for coming out to live in Hidden Cove—one is I wanted to get away from the city and its crime."

He watched her, fascinated by the animation that washed over her face.

"But I, um, own some property up on the cove. My

dad bought it when I was a kid because a friend of his—you must know him, Will Rossettie—moved here to work. There's only a cabin on it now, but there's a lot of land and a dock."

"It must be worth a fortune, so close to the city." Mitch thought for a second. "And they're starting to develop all that property on the cove now."

She kept eating. He studied her.

"You want to use it for this camp, don't you?"

"Yep. Once the thought occurred to me, it stuck like flypaper. Then I got Bright Horizon's newsletter advertising the upstate camps, since I volunteered there. I saw the same newsletter in your firehouse. When I met you this morning, and you told me about your dad, it seemed like maybe fate brought us together so we could help these kids."

He glanced at her hand. No ring. "You got any of your own kids?"

"No."

For some reason he asked, "You married?"

"I was. He died."

Mitch waited.

"Four years ago. A kid in a gang took him out with a knife."

Geez, talk about loss. This woman had had her lion's share.

"Anyway, do you think there'd be interest from the fire department and police force to at least investigate putting together a camp like this in Hidden Cove?"

For the first time in months, Mitch felt a lightening in his heart. "I could almost guarantee it. Everybody's looking for a way to channel their energies after the Sinco fire. This would be a perfect opportunity." He frowned. "We got a lot of kids right here in town whose fathers were killed. One mother. Certainly all those kids from New York after the terrorist attacks still need help."

Her smile was sun bright. "What would be the best way to start?"

"Go to the police chief and the fire chief. Get their take on this."

"Good idea."

On impulse, he said, "I'll go with you. As a representative of the fire department."

"Super."

He liked putting that pleasure on her face. "Meanwhile, you should contact the camp on Keuka Lake, too. Maybe set up a visit to discuss how they got started, how they run things."

"Sounds like a plan." Her smile was simultaneously innocent and alluring. She picked up her mug. "To possibilities," she said by way of a toast.

He clinked it with his coffee cup. "To possibilities."

"Thanks for listening, Captain. And for the support."

"You're welcome, Detective."

His cell phone rang before he could take a sip. He flipped it open.

On the other end he heard, "Mitch? Where the hell are you?"

Damn, he'd forgotten all about Cynthia waiting at home for him.

⟜ FOUR

GRADY O'CONNOR SURVEYED the scene unfolding at Sabina Malvaso's birthday party, held in the spacious house of Connie Malvaso Lewis, Jenn's twin sister and lifelong nemesis. Connie was married to Dr. Al Lewis and had three daughters. Filled with awe and a little bit of horror, Grady watched the Malvaso family punt and kick around each other. Their particular dynamics would give a therapist fodder for years.

"Hey, handsome, why the scowl?" He peered down into the pretty face of Angela Scribanni. She'd gone back to her maiden name after her divorce from Zach two years ago. Of all Zach's stupid-ass screwups, driving Angie out of his life was the worst.

Sipping his Molson, Grady nodded to where Connie and Paulie—he was a lawyer and also estranged from the others—talked in the corner. Unlike the other four, Paulie had light hair and hazel eyes. The three Musketeers, Jenny, Zach, and Mitch, were holed up on the other side of the room, acting like they were trading state secrets.

"Look at the five of them," Grady said. "They're never going to change, are they?"

Angela sipped a glass of wine. "I bent over backward

when I was married to Zach to get them to put the past
behind them. I couldn't budge any of them."

He smiled down at the long-haired beauty. These days
she was even prettier, probably because she wasn't worried about Zach chasing other women. Jenny said she had
a new boyfriend. "You bent over backward for Zach, period." He smiled. "You doing okay?"

"I was, until the Sinco fire." She shook her head.
"Zach's been like a dog with a bone, trying to repair the
damage he did. It's good for the boys, but he's driving
me nuts."

"Everybody in the department says he's changed, Angie."

She shrugged slender shoulders. "Maybe. But it's too
late for me." Her blue eyes twinkled at Grady. "Let's talk
about *your* love life, Gray."

For some reason his gaze slid to Jenny. Today she
wore a skirt—a rare occurrence—which clung to her hips
and ended midcalf. The material was red and silky. With
it she'd put on a black spandex top and fringed brown
suede vest. Before they'd left, she'd come to his side of
the house to ask if the outfit was decent enough to wear.
She said she'd gained some weight, but he couldn't tell
where.

"Grady, where'd you go?"

"Nowhere. My love life's in the toilet now that my
arm's healed."

"Yeah, Jenn told me about the parade of girlfriends
who came to take care of you when you had the cast. Did
they really fight over who was going to give you a bath?"

Grady tried not to stiffen. Everybody teased him about
the women in his life. Though he never let it show, except
to Jenny sometimes, he hated the comments. They didn't
know how guilty he felt for not being able to settle down,
for hurting almost every woman he came to care about.
"I'm going to kill Jenny."

Angela laughed aloud, drawing Zach's attention.
Damned if it didn't seem like he'd changed, at least toward Angie. He was eating her up with his eyes.

Mitch made a comment and all three of them started toward Grady and Angela. She said, "I'm out of here," and left before the Malvaso clan reached her.

Zach's scowl was fierce. "Where'd she go?"

"Away from you, buddy."

"Shit."

Jenny took the beer Grady held, sipped it, handed it back to him. "I'm sorry, Zach." She and Zach were only three years apart and used to pick on each other mercilessly. Grady had noticed, though, that since the fire, all three of them had softened. And the bond between them had gotten even stronger. Truth be told, he was jealous of it. For as long as he could remember, it had been the four of them against the world—particularly against Connie and Paul. That he'd missed out on helping at Sinco had been tough for many reasons. Not only hadn't he been able to help, he'd had to stand helplessly by when others tried to rescue Zach.

And the fire had affected Jenny in so many ways. . . . *I want to have a baby . . . I want you to be the donor.*

Zach studied Angela, who stood across the room with Paul and Connie. "Let's not get into this now."

"We wanted to talk to you about something, Grady." This from Mitch, his surrogate big brother and friend.

"Shoot."

"You know Megan Hale?"

"The hot new police detective?"

Mitch cocked his head. "You know her?"

"I've seen her around."

Jenn asked, "You interested?"

"No, babe, I'm not interested. I just noticed is all. She's got a great ass."

"She's got a great idea." Mitch explained about the firefighter's camp Megan Hale was interested in starting in Hidden Cove.

"Jenny and I thought about going upstate to work at the one there the summer after 9/11," Grady commented, handing Jenn back the bottle. She finished off his beer and set it on the table. "But we never managed the time off." He smiled. "I'd be interested in pursing this. It would give us something constructive to do in light of Sinco."

"It'd be a huge undertaking," Mitch said.

"We could do it." This from Zach, which shocked the hell out of Grady. Before the fire, his buddy's altruism was nonexistent. "It'd be a great way to help out."

Mitch and Jenn exchanged a glance. Again, Grady felt left out. He said, "How would we go about it?"

"Megan and I are meeting with the chiefs, Rossettie and Callahan. And she's got a call in to the founder of the upstate camp. Then we'd see where to go."

"Think we could have it running by the summer?" Jenn asked.

Mitch answered. "I don't know. It's October. Maybe we could hold a modified camp by the end of July or August, for a handful of kids, at least. Then increase it each year."

Grady nodded. "That'd be great."

They tossed around ideas for a while, then Paulie approached them. "Hello, Grady."

Giving the middle brother a smile, Grady said, "Paulie." For as long as Grady could remember, Paolo Malvaso had been a sober guy. Since his divorce five years ago, he was even more taciturn.

Paulie faced Mitch. The air seemed to have gone cold around them. "I'd like to speak to you, Mitch, when you have a chance."

Mitch stiffened. "Sure. How about now?"

Paulie glanced at Jenny and Zach. "In private."

"I'm gonna check on the boys," Zach told them and headed to the fancy rec room in the basement of Connie's house.

"Fine." Mitch nodded to Paulie and they stepped to the side.

Jenn glanced at them. "I wonder what that's all about."

"Why don't you ask?"

"Maybe." She looked after where her younger brother had gone. "He's really changed, hasn't he?"

"Yeah." Grady scanned her outfit from head to foot. "You too, babe. When's the last time you wore a skirt?"

"Bite me," she said affectionately. Glancing back to

Paulie and Mitch, she sighed. "Mitch isn't happy, either."

"I know."

"I thought he was going to get out of this thing with Cynthia. But after the fire, nothing happened."

"Sinco changed a lot of people." His heart started to pump fast, like a patient who'd been injected with epinephrine. "Speaking of which, I made a decision about what you asked me."

"Really?" Her eyes got huge and were the color of fall chestnuts. "W—What did you decide?" Her voice quavered, so unlike Jenny that he was momentarily silenced.

Grabbing her arm, he led her down the hallway to one of the dens in Connie's house. There he closed the door.

Inside, she took both of his hands in hers and squeezed them. Hers were cold, like her circulation was bad. "I'm sorry, Gray. This resurrects too much for you. I shouldn't have asked."

"No, it's okay." He gave her a lopsided smile and shrugged. "The answer is yes."

"Yes?" Her jaw dropped. *"Yes?"*

"Uh-huh."

Tears welled in her eyes. She flung herself at him, her arms clasping tightly around his neck. "Oh, God, Grady, I wanted you to say yes so bad, but you waited so long, I was afraid I'd hurt you and I couldn't stand that and . . ." She buried her face in his shoulder.

Geez, this new vulnerability in her stunned him. Jenn Malvaso was a tough cookie—she'd walked into burning buildings without blinking an eye, willingly crawled into compromised cars at accidents, and once finished a rescue with a broken hand. He held her close and smoothed down her hair.

When she pulled back, she stared up at him through spiky lashes. "I'll only ask you once more. You sure this won't hurt you too much? Because of Linda."

There it was again, the ghost that haunted his midnights. Though he was better now, he'd been destroyed by what his wife had done. Not even Jenny knew how bad off he was then, though she was aware of the horrible dreams he still had.

She was still talking. ". . . I mean, I'll raise the kid by myself, like I said. And we don't even have to put your name on the birth certificate. But—"

"Jenny, stop babbling."

"Okay." Straightening, she squared her shoulders like the old Jenn. "I'll make the arrangements. You don't have to do anything except . . ." Her face actually got red, which was crazy, since they talked about sex and guys and women openly.

"Not so fast. I got some conditions."

"Anything."

He laughed at her trust and ruffled her hair. "You better hear them first."

"It doesn't matter. I'll do whatever you say."

"I want to be the kid's father."

"Yeah. That's what I asked you, Gray."

"No, you asked me to be the donor. I don't want that. I want to be the kid's father in the real sense of the word."

Pure pleasure lit her face. It stopped him for minute. "Honest?"

"Yep. I'm never getting married again, after Sheila went off the deep end, and Linda . . ." He didn't complete the thought. Shook it off. "I'm thirty-six. You know how much I wanted that baby Linda was carrying. If I have a chance with you to have one, then I want to be the father." He reached out and cradled her cheek. It felt soft and womanly. "And who better to be its mother?"

"Geez, Gray, this is great. We practically live together, anyway. And a kid needs a father."

"I'm glad you agree."

"Then it's all set." Excitement danced in her dark eyes.

"Not quite."

"What else?"

He hesitated, felt his face heat. "I, um, want to do this the traditional way."

"Do what?"

God, she was so innocent sometimes. "Make a baby."

"The traditional way? As in . . . having sex?"

"Making love," he corrected.

She sputtered, then finally got out, "You're kidding,

right? Pulling my leg like you and the boys used to do."

"Not this time." He grasped her arms, ran his hands up and down her biceps like he was warming them. She was muscular, supple, but womanly. "Look, I don't want to jerk off in a jar to get our child. What would we tell him later, about how he was conceived?"

"Nothing!"

"Besides, it's cold and clinical. I want to make a baby with warmth and affection. With love. I feel more for you than I've ever felt for anybody in my whole life, Jenny. It's part of what went wrong with our marriages."

He could still hear Sheila's tirades about the time he spent with Jenny. And Linda's hysteria. *You don't need me when you got Jenny Malvaso. You fill all each other's emotional needs.*

"I care about you, too, Gray." She toyed with the buttons on the gauzy blue shirt she'd bought him for his birthday. "But not like *that*."

"I know. Me, either. We're friends. But, we could do this the right way." At her skeptical look, he said, "Hey, everything we do together is fun. Why wouldn't sex be?"

"Grady, this isn't a camping trip or a game of racquetball."

"Nope." He arched a flirty brow. "It'll be better."

She glanced down to his belt. "You think you could . . . you know . . . get it up for me? It's not like I turn you on, or anything."

He laughed aloud. "I think I could manage. Given the right circumstances." He brushed back a stray lock of hair. "Come on, Jenny. Let's give it a shot. A little recreational sex will do us good."

"You're not sleeping with anybody else now, are you?"

"Nope, neither are you." He scowled. "And we can't till this is done."

Laying her head on his shoulder, she settled into him. "All right." She always listened to him, and he to her. Ironically, the only times they rejected the other's advice—when they got married—were disasters.

"I do think it's best." He kissed her head. "Let's make a baby, honey."

"Why not?"

For a moment, he was overcome with a swell of emotion for this woman who'd been his best friend all his life. He didn't know what he'd do if he ever lost her. "When?" he asked, his voice gruff.

She drew back. "A little less than a month. I just passed the middle of my cycle.

"Good." He needed to lighten the moment. So he punched the air with his fist as he said, "Thirty days to B-day!"

"B-day?"

"Baby day. The day we make our baby."

ZACH REACHED THE bottom of the steps in Connie's finished basement and stopped when he heard Angie talking with his sister. From his vantage point, behind the door, he could see both of them but they couldn't see him. Feeling a little like a kid eavesdropping on his parents, he nonetheless didn't make his presence known.

Angela rocked Connie's youngest in her lap. Eighteen months old, little Dena squirmed restlessly. "She's beautiful, Connie."

"I can do that, Angie," Connie said standing beside the chair. "She's overtired."

"I love rocking your babies. Sit, though, and tell me how you're doing." Angela smiled at her former sister-in-law.

Zach studied Connie. For as long as he could remember, she'd been unhappy. Her hair was shorter than Jenn's and she'd lightened it. Her build was smaller. But there was a twin-like resemblance anyone would notice. And she was very much like Zach in her personality. Maybe that's why she hated him so much.

"I'm okay." She slicked her hands down her hips, over the dress. "Still haven't lost all the baby fat."

"You look great."

Shaking her head disgustedly, Connie wandered to the couch. "Jenny eats like a pig and never gains an ounce. I *look* at food and my waist expands."

"Jenny hasn't had any kids."

"And she won't at this rate." Connie picked up the colorful afghan that Sabina had made and refolded it. "She dating anybody?"

"Why don't you ask her?"

"As if she'd tell me." Connie's eyes turned hard. "She tells the guys everything. Me, her twin, she mumbles one-syllable words."

"Connie, I won't listen to you bad-mouth Jenn."

"I know. You never did. Somehow you always stayed neutral and never made any of us mad. Just tell me one thing. Is she okay since the fire? I was glued to the TV when they were trapped."

That made Zach feel bad. He knew the families of the firefighters that fought the Sinco fire had a rough time of it.

Rocking back and forth, Angela studied Connie. "It's so obvious you want to be a part of their lives. Why don't you make the first move?"

Sinking onto the sofa, Connie just stared at her.

"All right. None of them are doing very well. Mitch is being stalwart, as usual. But he's different. Jenny keeps to herself these days. She'll only talk to Grady about it. And Zach's having flashbacks and nightmares."

Connie's eyes narrowed on her. "How would you know about the nightmares? You're not . . . oh, Angie, you're not getting back with him after what he did to you?"

"No, Con, I'm not. There's no chance of that happening."

The finality of her tone knifed Zach in the gut.

"Good. He doesn't deserve you."

"Connie, please."

"I don't know how you can take his side. After what he's done."

Shaking her head, Angela kissed Dena's hair. "There aren't sides, honey."

Abruptly Connie stood. "Of course there are. Since we were born, there've been sides. Me and Paulie against the three brave firefighters. And Grady, of course. I'm so sick of—"

Zach couldn't take it anymore. He wanted to turn tail and run from her accusations. But he was done with letting hard situations go, done with not confronting tough issues. And he wanted to be friends with his sister. So he stepped through the doorway. "Connie?"

Whirling around, Connie faced him. He just stood there, his arm braced against the jamb.

"I'm going." Connie tried to brush past him.

He grasped her arm. "Concetta. Please. Talk to me."

"Talk to Angie." She shrugged him off and left.

Angela said, "I'm sorry."

He stuck his hands in the pockets of his navy dress slacks. He'd lost weight since he got out of the hospital, and everything was big. "Nothing I don't deserve. Me, Jenny, and Mitch cut her out all the time." He wandered over to the rocker, ran a knuckle down Dena's cheek. "This is the worst part. I hardly know her kids."

"It's not too late to change that."

"Isn't it?"

She shook her head.

For a minute, he watched her, the woman whom he'd met when she was fifteen, who had slept with him at sixteen, and who married him and had his kid by her eighteenth birthday. He sank onto the couch. Stretching his legs out in front of him, he linked his hands behind his head. "You're a natural, doing that." He nodded to Dena.

"I love babies."

"I wish we'd had more."

Color rose in her cheeks. He knew why. "Don't go there, Zach."

I want another baby, please, she'd begged him when Jason started school.

No, one's enough.

Then later, *You did this on purpose, didn't you?*

No.

I don't believe you.

Please, Zach . . .

She'd begun to cry, and he'd slammed out of the

house. To go to Bridget or Bambi or one of his many girlfriends.

Zach sat up, then hunched over and clasped his hands between his knees. "I know what you're thinking. I remember all those times you asked for another kid."

She stared at him silently.

"You're not even thirty. You can still have more."

Waiting a moment, she finally said, "I may still have more kids, Zach."

He felt like she'd sucker punched him. He tried not to ask but couldn't help himself. "Are you sleeping with this guy Kellerman?"

"That's none of your business."

"Are you *serious* about him?"

"Zach, knock it off. What did you think, that I'd mope about you the rest of my life? That I'd never get married again?"

"No, I was hoping you'd remarry me."

She stood. Clutching Dena close to her chest, she crossed to the Portacrib and settled her niece down into it. Then she turned on him. "I'll never remarry you, Zach, and quite frankly, I resent your thinking I could ever forget what you did. But just in case you're going down that road, let me remind you why I could never trust you again. While I was in labor with Nicky, you were screwing one of your bimbos. While Jason was rushed to the hospital for appendicitis, you were drunk in a downtown bar with another girlfriend. Mitch had to help me get him to emergency. Is that enough? I could go on and on. The scars are numerous and run deep."

He held up his hand and swallowed hard. "It's enough. I haven't forgotten those things, either."

She ran a shaky hand through her hair. "Look, I hope you've really changed, for the boys' sake. But I'm telling you for the last time, there's no chance for us." She folded her arms over her chest. "What's more, if you continue to bring it up, I won't let you into my house again."

Turning, she crossed to the den door and walked out.

His heart heavy, Zach watched her go. And was faced with a horrible possibility: He wasn't going to be able to fix everything.

FIVE

POLICE CHIEF WILL Rossettie and Fire Chief Noah Callahan faced each other like boxers squaring off in the ring. Since they'd both been young officers, their rivalry, and need to best each other, had become legendary. According to Noah, Will had "come out here from the big city" and had "started throwing his weight around." In turn, Rossettie contended that hometown boy Callahan was a hick from the sticks lacking a whit of sophistication. Ten years ago, Will became police chief and five years later, Callahan had been appointed head of the fire department by the mayor.

Mitch knew that, way down deep, they respected each other, and that their antagonism was all smoke and mirrors. He'd heard rumors—he thought from his mother—that when Callahan's wife died, Rossettie had been the first to arrive at the house and didn't leave the fire chief's side for a week.

"All right, Malvaso, shoot." Noah, a wide-shouldered man with boyish charm, a quick wit, and slightly graying hair eased back in his big leather chair behind a monster of a desk, eyeing Mitch but darting surreptitious glances at Megan.

"I think Detective Hale should outline our proposal. It was her idea, after all."

Rossettie chuckled. "Chip off the old block, she is."

All done up in a dark gray suit softened by a pretty pink blouse, Megan smiled at the older man. "Dad would love to hear that."

"She said you knew her father," Mitch commented.

Will's face shadowed. His ruddy complexion and bulk usually made him look younger than his fifty-two years, but grief aged a man quickly. "He was best man in my wedding. I diapered Meggie here."

"Will, please. I'm thirty-six now. And a cop, for God's sake."

Callahan's dark brows formed a vee. "What'd you want to meet with Will and me about, Detective?"

"I . . ." She glanced at Mitch. "We'd like to talk about starting a camp for the children of slain police officers and firefighters here in town. Up on the cove, actually."

Noah looked to Mitch, who nodded his agreement. Only five years apart in age, they'd become friends over the years; Mitch was glad when Noah was appointed fire chief. Noah wanted like hell for Mitch to go the next step in the fire department hierarchy—a battalion chief's position—but Mitch liked the action of being on the line.

"A camp like the one on Keuka Lake?" Callahan asked.

Megan lifted her chin slightly. "Yeah."

"Don't some of our people volunteer up there?"

Mitch nodded. "Uh-huh. Megan and her father did, too. It's where she got the idea to start something like it down here."

"After the Sinco fire, we've got Hidden Cove kids who would attend . . ." Megan's voice trailed off, probably at the bleak look on the chief's face. He'd taken the loss of his men hard. She added, "I know what it's like to lose a parent like they did, Chief."

Mitch had the urge to reach out and squeeze her hand. Will did it first.

"And since Dad loved the upstate camp, I'd like to do something in his memory." She looked to Will. "This would be a nice tribute to him, as well as the firefighters who died here in Hidden Cove."

As Megan outlined her points, Mitch watched the two chiefs exchange glances, nod, scowl at the same things. When she finished, Callahan said, "I agree in principle, Detective. But how would you pull this off?"

"I've got land in the cove that my father left me. Seems appropriate to use that."

"It's the cabin where we go to fish, Noah." Will's statement surprised Mitch.

Callahan whistled. "Beautiful place. The area's big enough for a kids' camp, too. You'd build there?"

"Yep."

Mitch jumped in. Once again, he felt energized by the prospect of the camp, in a way he hadn't in years. "A lot of fire personnel are carpenters, plumbers, and builders. Malvaso Painting could do all the painting. I bet we could get volunteer labor for the entire construction."

Callahan smiled like a proud papa. "Never knew the department not to rise to the occasion."

"My guys'd help, too." Will Rossettie's chest puffed out. "We don't have as much time off as you clowns, but I'd bet my pension we'd get more than our share of volunteers."

Megan hid a grin. Her gaze darted to Mitch. God, her eyes were pretty, lit from within like that. "I think we could staff it with volunteers, too," she said. "We'd probably need a person in charge, but we could basically run the camp through volunteers from the fire department, the police force, and townspeople."

Rossettie grinned. "Maybe Mitello's mother'll agree to cook for the crews."

Mitch laughed. At Megan's questioning look, he said, "Will raves about my mother's cooking. She's known around town for her gourmet Thanksgiving buffet. The fire department guys would jump at the chance to help out if Ma's gonna feed them."

Callahan leaned over and picked up a pen. "Let's get down to brass tacks. First, we need department liaisons. I think we got 'em right here, don't you, Will?"

"Damn straight. I could spare Meggie one day a week to work on this."

"Same for Malvaso." Callahan's brows furrowed. "You got anybody injured or pregnant that you could put on this full time?"

"Not at the moment."

"Me, neither. Keep it in mind."

Will said, "You and me can check into building permits. Both departments are on intimate terms with those jokers over at the town hall."

Callahan scowled. Mitch knew that there had been investigations to determine if the Sinco warehouse had met the fire inspection codes.

"We need a lawyer to lay this all out for us." Noah looked at Mitch. "What about your brother Paulie?"

Mitch stiffened. "I don't know. He's not a big fan of the fire department."

"He lost a daddy to the Red Devil. He oughtta be interested."

"I could give it a shot." Not that he wanted to. He was still pissed at Paulie for scolding him the other day for his kids not spending enough time with their grandmother. Compared to how they used to be, they were a lot more attentive. "I know Jenn and Grady and Zach will want in on this."

At the mention of Zach's name, Callahan turned his head away. Briefly, his hand curled. It wasn't public knowledge in the department, but from things Noah had intimated, and the way he behaved around Zach, Mitch sensed that Noah seriously disliked his brother. Mitch had never been able to find out why, as Callahan didn't talk about it, and Zach clammed up when Mitch asked him about the bad vibes coming from their chief.

Will put in, "Okay. We got any insurance guys to help out . . ."

And so it went. After an hour of brainstorming, they had a detailed plan for getting the project off the ground. The chief checked the clock. "Will and I got a meeting with the mayor." He looked to Megan. "Thanks, Detective, for proposin' this. You're gutsy to instigate it, and generous with that land. It's worth big bucks now that the cove has attracted the attention of the city dwellers."

"The quality of kids' lives is priceless."

Will smiled at her sentiment. "You guys should probably go visit the Keuka Lake place."

Mitch nodded, though he hadn't planned on going up there. But he wanted to, now. He wanted to be integrally involved in this project.

Megan told them, "I got a call in to the director now."

"The departments'll share the cost of the trip." Noah got a nod from Rossettie. He said to Mitch, "You can drive up, right?"

"Yeah, it's only four hours."

"You should drive, Meggie." Will's face lighted with mischief. "This guy's hell on wheels. His group cringed when he used to drive the rig."

"I'll remember that." Her tone was dry.

"Ready to take on the city council, Chief?" Noah asked, rising.

So did Will. "Jesus Christ. I hate these things."

Megan and Mitch walked out, leaving them grumbling.

"They're a pair, aren't they?" Megan said as she and Mitch headed for the elevator.

"Always have been."

"I never saw Will like that."

"Like what?"

"The one-upmanship, I guess. It makes him seem younger."

When they reached the elevator, Mitch pressed the button and they waited for the car. "How did he meet your father?"

"Will's originally from New York. They went through the police academy together. Will moved out here when his wife got sick, but he and Dad never lost touch. My dad was here for days when Will's wife died."

"He the reason you came to Hidden Cove?"

"One of them."

"Was your dad's death the other?"

"Yeah. The electricity of big-city police work was wearing off anyway. When Dad died, that clinched it."

Leaning against the wall, Mitch studied her. The cool police mask that she tried real hard to keep in place slipped when she talked about her father.

"Can I ask you something?" Megan said.

"Sure."

"You don't want your brother working with us, do you?"

"It isn't that. Paulie and I are like oil and water." She stared at him and her honest gaze brought forth his own candor. "He and my other sister Connie hate the fire department."

Oh, my God, no, not you, too, Connie had yelled when Jenn told their mother she was going to the fire academy instead of college.

Mitch had tried to intervene. *Connie, I know you're afraid. . . .*

Paulie had stepped in. *Holy hell, isn't it bad enough we lost Dad? And you risk your life every day. Not Jenny, too.*

When Zach had joined up, it had been the icing on the cake.

"They hate the department because of the risks you take?"

He was pleased she understood. Cynthia had been clueless as to why Mitch, Jenn, and Zach were so estranged from Connie and Paulie. Their relationship held some kind of morbid interest for her, and she used to ask him about Connie and Paulie all the time. "Yeah, mostly. Though it started early. We never really got along."

A sad smile flitted across her face.

"I take it you got no siblings?"

She shook her head. "Wish I did, though. Even if I fought with them."

The elevator pinged and opened; they rode it in silence until they got off on the first floor and exited to the parking lot.

When they reached his Cherokee, Mitch gave her a smile. "Well, call me when you get any information on the camp visit."

"Sure. You need a lot of notice to go up there?"

"I don't think so."

"Good." She headed to her police vehicle. "I'll call you."

BECAUSE OF HER meeting with the chiefs early that day, Megan couldn't stop thinking about her father. So, in her one-room apartment, she stuffed her legs into black spandex, yanked on a T-shirt, and donned her boxing gloves. A punching bag the size of a tree trunk hung in the corner. Sometimes the streetlamp, shedding light through the window, cast it in eerie shadows so it looked like the Headless Horseman. She left it there to remind her that appearances could be deceiving.

Punch. Punch. But her phantom opponent couldn't take away the images of her dad.

"Stop it!" she told herself. "Think of something else."

Lance.

Not exactly stress free. Punch. Punch. Punch. Harder, sending pain up her arm.

Her husband's craggy face superimposed over the bag. She'd met him when she joined the NYPD. An experienced cop, he'd been paired with her in a program to give new recruits a taste of many facets of police work.

"Son of a bitch," he'd said when he'd gotten his first glimpse of her. "A cherry. And a looker at that." Sarcasm dripped from his mouth. "Must be my lucky day."

She'd been intrigued by the twinkle in his deep blue eyes and the cleft that claimed his chin, and couldn't stop staring at him that first night in the car on a stakeout. Later, when she'd watched him scoop a baby out of harm's way in a subway accident, then disarm a mugger, she'd been impressed. It took her two years to catch his attention as a woman. And then she'd gotten him to notice her only because they'd been drinking at The Dragnet on Eighty-fifth Street after a retirement party.

"Oh, hell," he'd said when she'd come on to him in the parking lot. "I been trying not to do this for . . . how long has it been, little girl, since you joined the department?"

She'd smiled a very grown-up-woman smile. "Twenty-five months."

Against his better judgment, she knew, he'd grabbed her and kissed her right there in the dark parking lot. She lost her heart after that. He'd tried to tell her he was a bad bet, twice divorced, too old for her at fifteen years her senior, far too cynical. Even though he went home with her that night—the sex had been so good it was criminal—he still warned her to run the other way.

She hadn't listened. Her father had liked him in that peculiar *Band of Brothers* way, and that was all the approval she needed.

Sure, her dad had been royally pissed when she'd come to him three years after she and Lance were married. "Daddy, I . . ." Hiccups. Crying. Megan, who rarely cried.

"What is it, baby?" Patrick had asked.

"I found out that Lance . . . there's another woman . . . oh, Daddy."

The infidelity had driven her and her husband apart, of course. But it had sobered Lance, too. After months of separation, she'd finally agreed to meet with him.

"I'm sorry. Forgive me. I love you, Meggie." All the significant men in her life called her Meggie.

"Fuck it, Lance. If you think I'm going to forgive you for humping that bimbo, you're crazy."

"Just give me another chance. I didn't know how important you were to me until I lost you."

After weeks of crawling—the best damned groveling she'd ever seen—she'd forgiven him. On her father's advice—"Meggie, life's too short. You're crazy about him"—she'd taken Lance DeBreque back into her life.

A few months later—she'd just turned thirty-two and he was only forty-seven—at the height of a blissful honeymoon-type reconciliation, a punk on Tenth Avenue had taken him out with a knife.

Megan couldn't bear to think of her big and brawny husband, flawed though he was, lying waxen and cold in that coffin. To escape the macabre images, and the crummy little studio she rented, she found an NYPD sweatshirt, stuffed her things into a fanny pack, and headed outside to run. The unseasonably chilly October air slapped her in the face as she made her way down Hanson Street, over to the park, and started to circle it. The cold seeped into her bones, and she stumbled on stray rocks. Seemed she couldn't outrun the images; they accompanied on her trek around the big circle with the copse of trees inside it. On her fifth lap, she noticed something flare in the center of the park, inside the trees. She went another hundred yards and caught sight of it again.

Fingering her pack, she felt for her small revolver. Carrying it everywhere was a habit left over from living in the big city; she was glad now that she'd brought it along.

She jogged toward where she'd seen the flame. Quiet, she crept up to the trees. As she closed in, she smelled the sweet scent of pot. Then she heard, "Come on, Bobby. Live a little."

"My dad said he'd kill me if I did it again."

"Come on."

Shit. Teenagers. What were they doing out this late on a school night? Where the hell were their parents?

Megan left the gun in its pouch and burst into the trees. "All right, guys, as they say in the movies, freeze!"

MITCH SAT ACROSS from Cynthia on a stiff-backed chair in the holding room of the Hidden Cove Police Department and waited for their son, Bobby, to come in. He stared at the dingy gray walls, feeling as if they were closing in on him—like everything else these days.

"So much for all the therapy," Cynthia said cuttingly. She crossed her legs and folded her hands in her lap, stunning in classic slacks and sweater, even at this time of night and under these circumstances. "My father warned you it wouldn't work."

Actually, it was in another of her tantrums that she told him her parents' reaction when Mitch, who'd seen his son's downslide a little too late, had insisted they get help for Bobby. The boy had been way too surly and rebellious for a then-fifteen-year-old. He remembered Cynthia's reaction. *Daddy says you coddle him. Christ, Mitch, you care more about what those two kids do than what I do.* She'd thrown a book she'd been reading against the fireplace. *I'm sick of being ignored.*

Stone-faced, Mitch had found solace in his old friend, withdrawal. He'd gone ahead and and gotten Bobby connected with a counselor. In the meantime—especially since the Sinco fire—he'd managed to spend more time with the boy and they'd had some good long talks. Bobby had promised Mitch his foray into drugs was over.

"What are we going to do with him now?" Cynthia asked.

"You got me. I thought we had a handle on *him*, at least."

The door flung open and he stood to greet his son. Instead of Bobby, though, in walked Megan Hale. "Megan?"

Cynthia's head snapped up. Coolly, she studied the detective. Megan looked about eighteen, dressed in some kind of leg things Trish often wore, an oversize NYPD sweatshirt, and sneakers. "Hi, Mitch." She faced Cynthia. "I'm Megan Hale."

"Our new detective?" Cynthia scanned Megan's clothes.

"Sorry about the rags. I was out running when I found your son and his buddies in the middle of the park." Pointedly, she glanced at the clock. "At eleven o'clock on a school night."

Though he knew she was right, Mitch felt the sting of her words. She thought they were neglectful parents.

They were. How the *hell* had the kid gotten out without Cynthia knowing about it?

"Let's sit down." Megan hooked a chair with her foot and straddled it. "I found five boys in the park over on Hanson Street. I was running and saw a fire spark in the trees so I went to investigate."

Ludicrously, Mitch wondered why she was running so late at night. Her face looked pinched and she was pale.

"I smelled the pot before I reached them."

"And?" Cynthia asked.

"The kids were talking about smoking grass. Encouraging your son to do it." She shot a quick look at Mitch. "He said his dad would kill him if he did."

"Was he smoking?" Cynthia wanted to know.

"I don't think so. Neither was one of the other boys. Three of them were stoned. But Bobby being there with them is incriminating."

Cynthia asked, "Did he or did he not smoke an illegal substance?"

Straightening, Megan gave her a hard look. "I said I don't think so. But I gather he has in the past. And we don't know what he would have done if I hadn't come along."

His wife's stare turned haughty. "Is he being charged with anything?"

"No, not right now. Chief Rossettie said to give him a warning and release him to you."

Cynthia visibly relaxed. Mitch shook his head at the familiar pattern. When she could, his wife avoided the real issues. If Bobby wasn't being arrested, she wouldn't have to deal with the problem. Just like she was denying there was anything wrong with their marriage. Or if there was, that they could fix things since Sinco.

"Mrs. Malvaso, the issue of drug use needs to be addressed with Bobby."

"It has been, Detective."

"He's headed for trouble."

"How long have you been in town?"

"A few weeks."

"Then I don't see how you can make that assumption."

Mitch cringed inwardly at her tone and the carelessness behind her words. "Cindy, why don't you go on home? I'll wait for Bobby. The three of us will talk when we get there."

"Don't you have to go back to the station?"

"No, I got a replacement for the night."

"Fine." She stood and nodded to Megan. "Detective," she said and strode out.

Mitch watched her go. Once again, he felt the rush of despair. This marriage was never going to work. Yet, tonight was living proof of her inability to keep his kids on the right path. *He* had to be around to do that. If she got custody of Trish and Bobby, they would never survive living alone with her. He'd been over it a hundred times in his mind. His job hours were erratic, courts favored women . . . in the best scenario, the kids would be with Cindy at least part of the time. And he knew deep in his father's heart Bobby would backslide big-time even living with his mother part-time without Mitch to act as a buffer.

He turned to find Megan staring at him. "Mitch, I don't mean to butt in, but your son's in trouble. Just because he didn't get caught tonight doesn't mean there isn't a problem."

Her understanding of the situation—and the sympathy in her amber eyes—loosened the band around his chest. It felt so good to have someone else understand his son's situation. "There's a problem. I know that."

Angling her head, Megan glanced after Cynthia. "His mother doesn't seem to think so."

"His mother's real good at denial."

"He needs help."

"He's gotten help." At her questioning look, Mitch ran a restless hand through his hair. "He'd been smoking marijuana for two years before I found out about it."

She just stared at him.

Mitch drew in a deep breath and shook his head. "My hours are crazy. Firefighters aren't home like most fathers. I missed the signs because I wasn't there." And because he and Cynthia were fighting like cats and dogs whenever Mitch was home and he hadn't had the emotional energy to deal with the kids.

Megan's look stayed neutral. They both knew his explanation was paltry.

"I know that's not an excuse. When I realized what was happening, I intervened. Bobby saw a counselor for a year." He felt the jolt of parental inadequacy. "I thought the therapy had been successful."

"How did he get out tonight?"

"I don't know." He plucked at his white uniform shirt. "I came here from the station. Cindy said she thought he was studying in his room." Shaking his head, he added, "It's such a cliché."

"I'm sorry. Is he still seeing the counselor?"

"No, we stopped because he seemed to be on the straight and narrow."

"He should go back."

"I know. That won't go over big with him or his mother."

Megan cocked her head.

"Long story." Cynthia hated any kind of counseling. It was why they'd never sought help for their marriage. She'd been so spoiled as a child and teenager, she wouldn't even consider admitting that problems in their relationship were partially her fault. And going to a counselor showed weakness in her estimation, and her parents'. So Mitch had insisted on it for his son, but not for himself.

Uncomfortable, Mitch stood. "I'll do something, though. I'm not giving up on my son."

"Good." Megan stood and rubbed her eyes with her thumb and forefinger.

"You all right?"

She blinked hard. "Yeah, sure."

He gave her a skeptical look.

"I'm tired is all. I'm okay."

She didn't look okay. On impulse, he asked, "What were you doing running so late at night?"

"Trying to outdistance the demons."

He chuckled in understanding. "Let me know if it works," he said.

She smiled weakly. "I'll go get Bobby."

PEERING OVER AT his son's shaved head and the hoop that adorned his left ear—and his ragged black Metallica sweatshirt—Mitch wondered once again how he'd fathered not one, but two teenagers who looked like they just walked out of an MTV video. He himself couldn't be straighter.

But then he watched Bobby dig into a hot fudge sundae like he was five again, and the little boy peeked out from inside the punk façade. "Dontcha like yours, Dad?"

"Hmm?"

"You aren't eating."

Mitch glanced down at his own dessert. The last thing he wanted tonight was ice cream. But he'd brought Bobby to a town diner because this ritual with his kid always soothed troubled waters.

Daddy says you coddle him. If he was afraid of you, he'd be better behaved. Cynthia's stale accusation made him at least try to sound stern.

"I like the sundae just fine." He sampled a scoop of the gooey chocolate. It was still warm. "But I'm pissed as hell at you, kid."

Blue eyes just like his mother's stared over at him. The comment was a low blow; the counselor had told Mitch that Bobby needed to please him—almost as much as he needed to thwart his mother—but Mitch didn't know what else to do right now.

"Sorry, Dad."

Mitch downed another taste of ice cream. "How'd you get out?"

Bobby turned back to his dessert, shoveling in big spoonfuls. "She went to bed. I booked."

"All right, *why'd* you go out? You had to know we'd be mad."

"I wasn't wasted." Defensiveness, and maybe some embarrassment, colored his tone.

"So Detective Hale said."

"She's not so bad."

"No?" This was new. Usually the kid was quick with epithets for the police that far outshone Mitch's own generation's use of *pig*.

"Uh-uh. She believed me that I wasn't smokin'."

"She could have arrested you for aiding and abetting."

Bobby swallowed hard. The bravado gone, he shivered. "I know. She said so."

"And she will next time. Just because you never got caught by the police when you were doing drugs before doesn't mean it isn't well-known around town what you were into."

"Much to Her Highness's embarrassment." The kid's anger at his mother was like smoldering fire—just waiting to flare. "Wait till Grandma and Grandpa find out."

Cynthia's parents' overtly critical comments about their grandchildren's behavior seemed to egg the kids on.

"Is that why you did it? To shame your mother?"

"I dunno." He clanked the sundae dish with his spoon. "Anyway, I wasn't doin' *drugs*."

"Marijuana is a mood-altering substance and it's against the law to use it."

The boy's shoulders sagged and he pushed away the half-finished dessert.

Mitch dragged it back. "Let's eat and talk about something else."

You're too easy on him. He needs a firm hand.

Mitch dug back into his own sundae and soon Bobby followed suit. "Let me say one more thing. How about going back to the counselor you saw for a while?"

"Aw, Dad, I don't want to do that."

Mitch sighed.

"Please, give me one more chance."

What to do? God, parenting was hard. "All right. We'll let it go for now. But we'll talk about it again in a few weeks. If there's been no trouble again . . ."

Bobby clasped his arm. "Thanks, Dad."

Mitch changed the subject. "Written any new songs lately?"

He hesitated. "One."

"Something I haven't heard?"

Bobby cleared his throat and licked his lips. "Yeah."

"How come? I thought I got a private performance for all of them." He'd made it a point to show interest in his son's music.

No response.

"Bobby? What is it?"

"The song's about the Sinco fire."

The spoon stopped halfway to Mitch's mouth and his heart started to pound. "Really?"

"I wrote it because of the six month anniversary. It's from the view of a kid who lost a parent in the fire."

Reaching out, Mitch squeezed his son's arm. "Were you worried about me dying, Bobby?"

His son just stared at him. Then he said, "You should have seen how you looked in the hospital, Dad. I'll never forget it."

"I'm sorry if that upset you." But he wasn't really. Not if it could bring this kind of connection with his boy.

"I wanted to talk to you about it. You know, how it felt being trapped. Seein' other people die."

"Why didn't you?"

"I was afraid it would make you feel bad."

"I told you once you could tell me anything. Ask me anything."

"You don't always tell the truth."

No response from Mitch this time. Instead he remembered the conversation Bobby was most likely referring to. . . .

"Dad, she's a bitch."

"Do *not* call you mother that again."

The kid had been going through his "colored hair" phase. On that day, it was dyed an electric blue. "Why do you stay with her? You're a nice guy."

He'd known he couldn't tell Bobby that though he and Cynthia were attempting to work things out, Mitch was mostly trying to salvage the marriage for him and Trish. So he'd said instead, "Relationships are complicated, son."

He faced his son squarely, though he'd hedged shamefully then. "You mean I don't tell you the truth about your mother and me?"

The kid snorted.

"She's changed. Since the fire."

"That's what she'd like you to believe."

"Aren't you getting along any better?"

He scooped up some fudge with his finger and put it to his mouth. "She told me I had to take my Marilyn Manson poster off the wall tonight."

Mitch knew Cynthia objected to the controversial punk rocker who fascinated Bobby. Was that what had driven him out into the night?

"She said if it wasn't gone, she'd rip it down when I went to school tomorrow."

Fine way to keep the kid from being truant.

"I'll talk to her."

"I took it down."

"What'd you put up in its place to piss her off?"

Bobby glanced at him and smirked. "Korn." Oh, great, a rock group noted for its obscene lyrics.

Mitch sighed. "All right, let's go home and you can play that song for me."

They drove through the deserted streets, the silence broken only by the radio; every two songs they'd switch stations. Another compromise he'd made with his son. Cynthia wouldn't let Bobby ever listen to "that trash," a.k.a. his own kind of music, in her car.

The house was dark and Mitch prayed she was asleep when they entered through the garage. For more than one reason. Quietly, he and Bobby made their way to the basement door and trundled downstairs. Mitch had installed tons of insulation, refinished the walls and floor, closed off all the heat vents and put in baseboard heaters so the kids could do their thing down here without disturbing Cynthia.

Bobby had set up his guitar and amps in a corner of the basement. He picked up his beloved Gibson. Mitch dropped down on an overstuffed chair and struggled not to close his eyes. Stretching out his legs, he watched Bobby tune up.

Before he started to sing, the kid asked, "You sure you want to hear this?"

"Yeah, of course."

"Dad—"

"Play it, Bobby."

The guitar emitted mournful notes—one string played at a time. Then Bobby's deep voice crooned into the mike, "Daddy, what is that cloud of dust? Mommy, what does it mean for us? Daddy, where did you go? On that evening you never came home . . ."

Mitch swallowed hard. He listened to the rest of the lyrics and allowed his son's deep bass to conjure the awful images. They transported him into another time, another place. . . .

When Bobby finished, he looked over at his father. "Oh, shit."

Mitch tilted his head. "It was . . ."

But Bobby was in front of him. "Dad, you're cryin'."

Embarrassed, Mitch raised his hands to his cheeks. "I am?"

"I'm sorry."

He shook his head. "The sign of a great song. It's moving."

Bobby dropped down to his knees, bracing his hands on the arms of the chair. "Was it awful, Dad?"

"It was awful."

"Do you still think about it?"

"Yes."

"Sorry this reminded you."

"No, it's okay. I can't forget it anyway." He shook his head. "You should record that. Send it somewhere."

"Nah."

"I think so. *You* think about it." He checked the clock, anxious to escape this avalanche of feeling. "Now, get to bed. We'll talk tomorrow about your punishment for tonight."

"Okay."

They stood.

Bobby was his height, almost six feet and, somewhere along the line, had become broad shouldered. The boy was a man in so many ways. He shocked Mitch by lunging into his arms. "I got you, Dad," Bobby said, holding on tight.

Mitch hugged back, hard. "I got you, too, kid."

"I'm sorry."

He clasped his son to his chest, like he used to when Bobby was little; the connection soothed the ravages of his soul. "For sneaking out?"

"Yeah, that. But mostly because of the fire. Because you saw your buddies die." He drew back but kept hold of Mitch's shoulders for a minute. "You're a real hero, Dad."

Mitch shook his head. How many people had said that to him since the fire? Problem was, Mitch didn't feel like a hero.

As they climbed the steps one behind the other, Mitch felt instead like a half-assed firefighter, who had to leave his shift tonight because of personal problems, a luke-warm father whose son sneaked out of the house because of a fight with his mother, and a shitty husband who dreaded going upstairs to his wife.

Definitely not hero material.

SIX

"YUMMY! JENN SAID, sidling up to Grady at the black, industrial-size stove where he stood making dinner. Her mouth watered as the aroma of seafood filled the air. "What is it?"

"O'Connor's Special." He batted her hand away as she snitched a small piece of cleaned, uncooked asparagus. "No tasting."

Popping the forbidden vegetable into her mouth, Jenn picked up *The Firehouse Cookbook* from the long expanse of counter that ran the length of one wall. "Uh-oh, Zach will never eat seafood."

"Wanna bet?"

She snorted.

"Why's he on tonight, anyway?" Grady asked casually. Too casually.

He knew she used to love it when her two brothers were on duty with her. It happened regularly with Mitch, as he was part of the Rescue Squad, which served side-by-side with Quint 7. She only worked with Zach when one of them was subbing on the other's group. But since the fire at Sinco, Jenn hated it when they all worked together, fearful that she might watch her brothers die.

"The cap's kid had induction into Honor Society." She swatted Grady's butt to lighten the mood. "You were in that in high school, weren't you?"

Grady grunted and stirred a cheesy-smelling sauce. Everybody teased him because of how smart he was; in school he'd gotten straight A's and, unlike her and her brothers, had gone to college, majoring in biology. Instead of choosing a job in industry, though, he'd surprised them all by whipping through paramedic training and joining the fire department. In a medical emergency, the crew was glad for his brilliance.

She sauntered to the scarred oak table where one of his ubiquitous books lay open. *War and Peace*. "This good?"

"It's great. You should try reading something other than *Firehouse* magazine."

Jenn rolled her eyes. Dropping into a chair, she leafed through the book, casting surreptitious glances at Grady. She was worried about him. He'd come to her half of the house last night when she'd gotten home from yet another dead-end date.

Grady had had their Dalmatian, Bucky, with him. The dog had been found as a puppy abandoned in the aerial bucket of the Quint one day and Jenny had taken him home. Grady and the dog had plunked down on her queen-size bed and he'd scanned the room while she stood in front of a large mirror attached to a maple dresser and took off her jewelry. He seemed to be seeing the dark green walls, wood trim, and hardwood floors for the first time. "This where we're going to do it?" he asked, petting Bucky.

Facing away from him, but with a clear view of him in the mirror, she removed her jacket and started unbuttoning her blouse. "Do what?"

"Make a baby."

She shrugged, though her heart beat a little faster at the thought. "Sure, if you want."

"I think I want to do it in my place."

"Whatever."

Sprawled out on the green-and-blue geometric print

comforter, he picked up a throw pillow from her bed and bunched it in big strong fingers. He was wearing only gray fleece shorts. His bare chest was sprinkled with hair darker than that on his head. "Think it'll take more than once?"

"I don't know." She caught him staring at her. She'd gotten down to her bra, and was unzipping her jeans. He watched. Though she'd never been shy around him before—he'd seen her in her underwear many times and in bathing suits that revealed more—tonight, his intense gaze made her shiver. "What are you looking at?"

"How come you didn't wear your fancy stuff tonight?"

She glanced down at the serviceable white bra. "Nobody was gonna see it, buddy."

He arched a brow.

Breaking eye contact, she picked up a huge Syracuse football jersey and pulled it over her head, removing the bra when she was covered. It was a trick she'd cultivated when she shared a house with three brothers—undressing beneath her clothes. Playfully, she tossed the bra at Grady, and he caught it in his hand.

"You haven't forgotten?" she teased. "No sex for me with anybody else until this kid's in the oven."

He'd stared at the bra, obviously not amused, before he dropped it on the nightstand by her bed. "Then what, Jenny?"

"What do you mean?" She shucked off her jeans and panties, and pulled on black boxers. Barefoot she padded to the bed, dropped down on her knees and gave Bucky a hug. "How you doing, boy?"

The dog barked and lapped at her face.

Grady stared at her. "You gonna sleep with other guys when you're pregnant?"

Jenn sat beside him, cross-legged. "I hadn't thought that far."

His face shadowed. She scooted over, displaced the pillow, and cuddled into him. She'd done it a hundred times before, especially since the Sinco fire, but never heard his heart pound like this under her ear. "Are you having second thoughts about the baby thing? It's okay if you are."

"No, I'm just considering all the angles of it." He stroked her arm. "I, um, don't think I want you sleeping with anybody until you have the baby."

"Only if you don't, either."

"Okay."

Pulling back she sat up. "Gray, I was kidding. I don't imagine I'll feel much like sex when I'm fat and ugly. But that doesn't mean you can't."

His smile was sad as he tucked a strand of hair behind her ear. "You'll be beautiful."

"What's wrong?" She checked the clock. One A.M. "Why are you up so late?"

Though he'd been sober since he came in, his face turned even bleaker—like a medic who'd lost a patient. He glanced away from her, reached out and scratched the dog's head.

"Did you have a nightmare?"

He nodded.

"About us in the fire?"

"No."

"Linda?"

"Yeah." He sighed. "Sheila was in it, too. Probably because I saw her today. She was drunk again." Grady's fiancée had gone downhill fast after Grady had broken off with her.

This topic burned Jenn as no other did. Though most people thought Grady was pretty well adjusted and was quite a ladies' man, Jenn knew he suffered terrible guilt over his fiancée's downslide and his wife's suicide. She shuddered whenever she thought of Linda being seven months pregnant. Grady had rambled on dozens of times about how cool it was to feel the baby move inside his wife's belly. When they both died, he'd been shattered. That was when he became convinced he hurt women he really cared about, and would always be that way. So he played the field and never got serious about any one woman.

Controlling her anger, Jenn asked softly, "What about

Linda? Did you dream about her because of the baby stuff? With me?"

"I don't know."

"Geez, Gray, maybe this isn't such a hot idea."

Facing her again, he'd put his fingers on her mouth. "No, it is. I'm looking forward to it, like I haven't looked forward to anything in a long time." His hand traveled to her stomach and pressed gently. He smiled, then pulled her back down beside him and she stretched out on the bed.

She nosed his bare chest—he smelled wonderful—and said, "All right. But if you change your mind . . ."

"I won't." He kissed the top of her head.

Because she knew he needed it, she whispered, "Stay." They occasionally slept together, moreso since the fire.

He reached out to switch off the light. The room plunged into darkness. "Yeah, I want to. . . ."

Grady crossed to the table and sank down beside her, dragging her back from memories of last night. Briefly, his gaze scanned the kitchen, then he pulled another book out of a backpack on the floor. "I like this one better than Tolstoy." Today, his face was alight with mischief and the sadness of last night was gone. The light blue of his shirt made his eyes the color of the sky.

She glanced down at the book, *How to Get Pregnant,* and chuckled. "I think we can figure that one out by ourselves."

"It has details. Like when you're ovulating, how to tell. There's a simple way to . . ."

Her brother Mitch walked into the room; he always seemed a bit intimidating in his white captain's shirt. Grady hastily slid the book into his pack.

"What smells so good?" Mitch asked.

"Shrimp and scallops O'Connor."

"Is it ready yet?"

"Um, almost," Jenn said.

He eyed her and Grady. "What are you two up to? You got that look on your faces that always spelled trouble when you were kids."

She smiled intimately at Grady. "I'll never tell."

Grady stood. "Chow's on. Call everybody, Captain."

Once dinner got under way, the conversation turned to firefighting, as it often did. Jenn thought of the stories Mitch told his kids.

"Did everybody hear about the incident in the mall parking lot yesterday morning?" Snyder asked. "Group Two's Rescue Squad went."

Jenn said, "I didn't. What happened?"

"A little sedan was tipped on its side. They were getting ready to send a guy into the vehicle to stabilize the victim when they saw the pool of blood in the car. The smoke eater who'd have gone inside would have had to crawl into it. So the Cap thought of something else to try. They stabilized the guy's head while he was in the car with tape and a cervical collar. Then all the guys got together and picked up the car and set it right. They were able to open the door and remove him without exposure to his blood."

"Smart thinking," Mitch commented.

"Did they test him?" Grady asked.

Snyder nodded. "Yep."

"He was HIV positive, wasn't he?"

"Uh-huh."

"Hell, I hate goin' on those calls." This from Hector Pike, a firefighter on their group.

They were halfway through the meal, still trading EMS stories, when the PA began to crackle.

Grady, who'd spent a lot of time cooking, said, "Shit, I knew it."

"Domestic dispute on Forman Street. Report of a stabbing. Midi 7, go into service."

"Tough luck, O'Connor," LoTurco said as he reached for the steaming pasta.

"We'll save you some," Thomas promised, shoveling more succulent shrimp onto his plate.

The dispatcher continued, "Firefighters are instructed not to enter the building before the police arrive."

Just as Jenn threw back her chair, she saw Zach and Mitch exchange a glance.

"I can go," Zach said to the Quint 7 substitute officer.

Zach was studying for his paramedic license, whereas Jenn was just an EMT. Emergency medical technicians had less training than paramedics but more than first responders, a certification that all firefighters held.

Everybody stilled. The HIV story had spooked them.

"No, you won't. This is mine and Grady's." Jenn headed for the bay. "Just save us some food," she called out as she left the kitchen.

Grady grabbed the computer report from the office as they hurried to the two-person medical truck. Kicking off her shoes, she stuffed her feet into her bunker boots, drew up her pants, and snatched her turnout coat from the hook on the wall. By then, Zach and Mitch had come out to the bay. Grady was revving up the Midi when Mitch head-locked her. "Be careful."

Zach opened her door. "Really, Jenn."

Hiding her exasperation, she kissed Zach's cheek. "I will."

He slammed the door just before they spun off.

Inside the truck, Jenny picked up the radio. "Midi en route to scene, over," she said into it.

"Over. Repeat, do not go into the building without the police."

They glanced at each other as sirens screeched like banshee wails. Grady took a turn, throwing her up against the door. She righted herself and picked up the computer printout. "Top-floor neighbor called in the disturbance. Apparently she heard yelling downstairs. She went around outside to look in the window and saw a guy with a knife."

"Oh, joy," he said and increased the pressure on the gas pedal. His face was flushed, like she imagined hers was, with adrenaline starting to kick in.

The police had not arrived when they reached the non-descript brown house set back off Forman Street and shaded by maple trees. Twilight had fallen, and a fine mist cast an eerie gloom over the landscape. Once the sirens stopped, it was church quiet. "On the scene," she told dispatch into the radio. "No police yet."

"Over. Do not go into the house."

"Yeah, we got it, Chas."

Grady leaned back in the truck and drummed his fingers on the steering wheel, staring at the house. "What was that all about back at the station with your brothers?"

"They worry about me, now." She studied the house. There were outlines of people crossing in front of the windows and she wondered what was going on in there.

He waited a minute before he said, "I do, too, Jenn."

"I know. I worry about all you three. I never did before." She tried to quell the hot annoyance—and the even hotter anger—that flared inside her. "It's another effect of all those guys getting killed at Sinco."

He nodded.

"The shrink we saw said it's normal."

Shrugging, he reached over and squeezed her arm. "Just be careful."

"Right back at you," she said saucily.

Flashing red lights and the staccato blasts of the police siren heralded the 911 truck that pulled up behind the rig; accompanying it were two black-and-whites. "The cavalry's here," Grady quipped as he climbed out of the Midi.

"Yep," Jenn said and followed him.

GRADY WINCED AT all the blood. It pooled on the floor and spattered the walls. He thought of the story Snyder had told just minutes ago. Detective Hale—with the nice ass and the great idea about a camp—seemed oblivious to the sweet, sickening scent and its potential danger; she raised her gun, as did the other two officers. Automatically Grady stepped in front of Jenn to shield her from the gory sight.

"Hold on," Hale ordered them, panning the room with her Beretta. Off to the right, the woman on the floor wasn't moving. The man in the corner moaned.

Grady said, "This must have just happened. We saw them going back and forth in front of the window when we arrived."

Hale grunted. "Stay back."

Grady waited, unwilling to risk his life or Jenny's if

the scene was still dangerous. Slowly, Hale approached the man. A ten-inch-long butcher knife lay about three feet from his hand.

Stepping between the guy and the knife, training her weapon on him, she said to one of the officers, "Bag it."

Jenn eased out from behind Grady. She fumbled in the ALS—advanced life support—bag and tossed the cops arm covers, gloves, and masks. A uniformed officer donned the precautionary gear and crossed to Hale.

Finally, Grady said, "Detective Hale, the woman needs care." His voice was calm, like it got in a crisis.

"All right, do your thing." Megan kept her gun pointed at the man. "But try to disturb as little as possible. This is a crime scene."

As the officers bagged the weapon, Grady headed toward the still and silent woman. "Jenny, check the guy out. Then I'm going to need help here."

After giving Hale the gear to protect herself, Jenn donned mask, gloves, and goggles, as did Grady. He bent down and took the woman's pulse; it was thready. Dark red blood oozed out of cuts on her arm and made puddles on the floor. Reaching into his bag, he'd just found the gauze when he heard from across the room, "What the fuck . . ."

He glanced over to see Jenn go sprawling backward on her ass. In seconds, Megan Hale dropped to her knees; the guy's arm flailed and hit her. Braced, she stayed upright and shoved her gun to the man's head. "Go ahead, you son of a bitch. Try that again and you'll be in pieces all over this goddamned floor."

Mumbling incoherently, the guy lay back.

"You okay, Jenny?" he asked.

She righted herself. "Yep." He noticed blood turning her blue HFD shirt rusty in places. Damn it. No matter how hard they tried, they couldn't avoid contact with blood.

Ignoring it, Grady tended to the woman, but was dimly aware of Detective Hale calling the crime scene investigators, questioning the guy, and reading him the Miranda rights, after which he said, "Goddamned cunt deserved it."

That nailed the asshole, Grady thought.

Jenn crossed to him and the woman. "He's okay. Drunk as hell with a nasty bump on his head. Several superficial wounds. She must have turned the knife on him somehow, or there's another one around here."

The woman had a long gash on her forearm; she'd lost a lot of blood. Grady had packed the wound with gauze. They could stem the flow now, but her survival depended on how much blood she'd lost before they could get inside. "Elevate her arm and put pressure on the brachial artery while I hold the packing."

Through the goggles, familiar amusement danced in Jenn's dark eyes. She knew the drill, but Grady turned into an autocrat in crisis situations. "Yes, sir."

"Bite me," he mumbled.

As he held down the bandaging, he glanced across the room. The police found a second knife by the door; they bagged it and now were leading the handcuffed man out. Hale told them, "I'll meet the crime scene team here and then come back to the station house. Meanwhile, fingerprint him and book him. Have the backup unit bring in the witness." She approached Grady and Jenn. She, too, had blood on her shirt and gray blazer.

"How close is the ambulance?" Grady asked, anxious to get the victim to the hospital. They'd done all they could.

Hale talked into a radio. "A minute or so."

"Good." He peered over at Jenn and scowled. She was blinking rapidly. "You okay, Jenny?"

"Uh-huh."

Squatting so they were eye level, the cop's look was bland. "He hit her in the face."

Grady's heart started to beat faster. "Where? I can't see it."

Jenn answered. "Under the mask. I'm all right."

"Promise?"

It had been a kid thing. When they were ten, they'd made a pact to always tell each other the truth, no matter what. Those promises had covered not divulging the whereabouts of a secret cave they'd found, what she'd done with a boy on a date, his concerns about not wanting to go to college, and her ex-husband's alcoholism. They were things she'd never even shared with her brothers.

"I promise."

Hale frowned at the byplay but didn't ask about it.

More sirens blared outside, then the noise came to a screeching halt. In minutes, two men rushed through the door and close behind them more police officers. Grady recognized the medics, as well as the cops.

"Status?" the ambulance attendant, Macon, asked.

"BP, eighty over sixty. Pulse thready. Bleeding slowed but not stopped."

Grady held the packing in place and Jenn kept the victim's arm elevated and the pressure on her artery until she'd been transferred to a stretcher and the ambulance corps took over. They all followed the guys outside.

Tugging off her mask, arm covers, and gloves, as did Grady and Jenn, Hale held out her hand. "Megan Hale."

Jenn shook first and introduced herself, then Grady did the same.

"I met your brother Mitch," Hale said to Jenn. Then to them both, "Good job here tonight."

"Thanks." Jenn nodded to Megan's bloody shirt. "You'd better get out of those clothes. Exposure to his blood is dangerous." As they'd heard earlier, HIV was always a threat, like fire hiding in walls ready to spring on them.

Hale looked down, surprised. "Jesus." She eyed Jenn. "You, too."

Jenn glanced down at her uniform. "I'll shower and change when I get back to the firehouse."

Megan scowled. "I don't have clean clothes at head-quarters. I just took a load of dirty stuff home. I'll have to go back to my place. . . ." She checked her watch. "But I wanted to question the witness right away."

"I have extra shirts at the station house. It's not far from here." She eyed Megan's five-six curvaceous frame. "You're shorter than me, but they'll do."

Again, Megan looked down at the blood. "All right. I'll follow you over."

Once they got in the truck, Grady grinned. "Sure one of your T-shirts will fit her, Genevieve? She's pretty stacked."

"Fuck you."

Grady chuckled.

They radioed their situation and headed to the fire station.

After a minute, Jenn asked, "So, you think she's pretty?"

"Who?"

"Detective Hale."

"Yeah. Great eyes."

"Oh, sure, you were looking at her eyes."

He took a curve a little too fast, sending her toppling into him. The connection felt good. "Hey, babe, I thought you got over that flat-as-a-board hangup."

She righted herself. "You guys won't let me."

"Big brother prerogative," he said smugly.

"Like I said, fuck you."

He winked at her and his eyes danced with mischief. "Hey, yeah, you're gonna do that. I can't wait!"

MITCH AND ZACH paced the watch room, waiting for the Midi to return. "We're about as subtle as a neon sign," Mitch said. "She'll have a fit we're out here."

"I know." Zach snatched a clipboard off the desk. "Let's pretend we're doing something." He scowled. "I'm almost a paramedic. I could have gone with Grady."

"Jenn's an EMT. She's always partnered with Grady for EMS calls. You're subbing on the Quint. She'd have been pissed."

Zach's eyes were troubled. "I worry about her now."

"Me, too." Mitch playfully socked his brother's arm. "Shit, I even worry about your sorry ass."

Zach smiled weakly.

The bay door creaked as it went up. "Here they come." Expertly, Grady backed the Midi into the huge garage.

Mitch was surprised to see another set of headlights in the fire station drive and spotted a white Jeep behind the rig.

Leaving the watch room with Zach, he headed for the Midi. He stopped short when Jenn jumped out and he saw the blood on his sister. "Christ, what the hell happened?" Closer, he caught a glimpse of her temple. "Holy hell." He looked to Grady. "What went down?"

"I got shoved," Jenn said simply.

And Zach exploded. "Goddamn son of a bitch." He grabbed Grady's arm. "Where the hell were you when this happened to her?"

Grady stiffened. Though they'd been childhood blood brothers and teenage conspirators, sometimes Zach and Grady went head-to-head about things. "Chill, Malvaso. I was working on the victim. Jenny got shoved by the stabber."

"The *stabber* shoved her? Shit, she's covered with blood."

"Not hers."

Mitch stepped between them. His brother was over-reacting, and they all knew it. "Back off, Zach."

"I'm fine." Jenny soothed Zach's arm, but there was exasperation in her voice, like a mother tending to an unreasonable child.

Zach's gaze lifted from her shirt to her face. He reached up and fingered the bruise. She flinched but didn't back away.

"Zach, I'm *fine,* really."

Mitch grabbed Zach's arm and drew him back. "Why don't you go patch her up?"

Briefly Zach closed his eyes. "All right. Come on, honey."

Mitch saw Jenn give a *please understand* look to Grady. After a moment, he nodded and followed them inside.

"What was that all about?"

Pivoting, Mitch turned and saw that Megan Hale had entered the bay. "Hell, you, too?"

She glanced down. "He got a few swipes in, but I

didn't get leveled." She patted her side. "Probably because I got a gun."

"You need to get out of that shirt."

"It's why I'm here. Your sister said I could borrow something of hers."

It won't fit you.

"We've got things here." He nodded. "She'll be busy for a while trying to calm Zach down."

"They hooked up?" At his questioning look, she added, "Is that why he's so upset?"

"No, he's her brother, *my* brother."

"Ah, the one you told me about."

"Yeah. Come on, I'll get you something to wear." He led her to a locker in the back of the bay. From inside, he pulled out a navy HCFD T-shirt and handed it to her. "You wanna take a shower?"

"No, I don't have time. There's a lot going on at the station. I've got to talk to the witness, and I need to be there when they finish booking the guy. Then I've got to meet with the CSIs. I'll just wash up and be on my way." She held up the shirt. "Yours?"

"Mmm." At least that'd fit over her breasts. Geez. For the first time since . . . he couldn't remember, he got hard looking at a woman's breasts.

Stifling the thought, he led her down a hallway, through the common room to the bunk room. "The head's in through there."

"Thanks."

Mitch watched the graceful sway of her hips as she disappeared into the john, then he returned to the kitchen. Jenny was seated, with Grady flanking her and a grim-faced Zach tending to her wound. The air crackled with the electric tension of hurt feelings and suppressed fear.

"I gotta shower before you put the stuff on," Jenn said irritably. "Just clean it, will you?"

Grady bit out, "Shut up, Jenny."

Zach grumbled under his breath and swore. When he finished doctoring her, Jenny threw back the chair and stalked off. The three men stared at each other.

"Look, guys," Mitch said placatingly, "Jenn can take care of herself."

"Yeah? Tell that to all the—" Zach cut himself off. "Damn it, I'm gonna go work out."

Grady waited till Zach left. "He's on edge."

"It's tough." Mitch nodded to where Jenn had exited. "She okay?"

"Sure. It's just a bruise." He didn't sound sure, but the injury looked minor to Mitch.

"Anything else going on that I should know about?"

Grady sank onto a chair. He'd cleaned up at the sink, but he seemed exhausted. "She has bad dreams sometimes."

"You keeping an eye on that?" Mitch would never forget when he first discovered Jenn and Grady sometimes slept together. For a long time, he didn't believe it wasn't sexual. They'd had words about it, so mostly they didn't bring it up.

"Don't start," Grady snapped.

He held up his hands, arrest style. "I'm not."

Grady cleared his throat. "Shit, we're all a mess."

Mitch crossed to the stove, picked up a plate they'd kept warm from dinner and brought it to Grady. "Here, eat. Maybe we'll have it together by the time she comes out."

"Maybe." Grady dug in.

After drawing himself coffee and joining Grady at the table, Mitch dropped down next to him. "So, what's happening in your life? I sure could use some good news."

Grady choked on his own dinner. "Nothing much." He wouldn't meet Mitch's eyes, which was odd. "What's going on about the camp? Anything more on that?"

JENN STALKED INTO the bathroom and threw the lock on the door, something automatic that she always did, being the only female on duty. "Damn it!" She went to the mirror and stared at herself. She didn't look that bad—a chestnut size bruise by her left temple, raised a bit. Bloodshot eyes from fatigue. Well, she *was* pale.

Someone came out of a stall. Megan Hale.

"Oh, shit, I forgot about your shirt."

"That's all right. I got something from your brother." She plucked at the navy cotton. "It's big, but it'll do."

Still staring ahead, Jenn caught Megan's gaze in the mirror. "It doesn't look that bad, does it?"

Megan came up close and examined her. "It's fine."

A couple of inches shorter than Jenn, Megan was completely different in looks with her blond hair cut longer in the back than the sides, with wispy bangs. And she *was* stacked. Like Grady said. For the life of her, Jenn couldn't see why that comment bothered her tonight. She knew she was no beauty queen. She'd never cared before.

She wondered if Grady would want to date Megan Hale. He'd always had a thing for big-eyed blonds. Both Linda and Sheila had those looks. It used to amuse Jenn. Her gaze strayed to the detective's hands. "You married, Megan?"

"Nope. You?"

"No."

"Were you ever?"

"Yeah. Divorce." Jenn ducked her head. "You?"

"Widow."

"Sorry."

They sounded like little girls on the playground, feeling each other out.

Megan washed her hands, then picked up the blazer she'd left on a chair. "I've got to get back to the station." She took a few steps toward the door.

"Wait a sec."

Megan stopped and pivoted around.

"I think this children's camp is a great idea. We all want to help."

"Yeah, Mitch told me. I hope it's a go."

"He says you're donating the land. That's generous of you."

"It's something I can do."

Jenn's eyes narrowed on the other woman. "Why do you want to?"

"My father died three months ago. He was a cop and

he loved the upstate camp; we used to volunteer at it every summer." The other woman's eyes were stricken with fresh pain. Jenny had seen the same kind of thing a lot in other eyes since the Sinco fire.

"Oh, Megan, I'm sorry. Mitch didn't tell me that."

She shrugged.

"You been in Hidden Cove long?"

"A few weeks."

On impulse, Jenn asked, "Wanna go have a beer sometime?"

"Yeah, sure. I—"

Megan's cell phone rang, interrupting the sweet camaraderie. She flipped it open. "Hale." She waited. "*What?* Shit, I'll be right there."

"What happened?" Jenn asked when Megan clicked off.

"The stabbing victim? She just died at the hospital."

THERE WAS A *dead body lying on either side of him in the Sinco warehouse. Zach opened his mouth to scream, but nothing would come out. Then one of the bodies turned into Jenny. She was staring at him with lifeless eyes.*

Suddenly Zach was on the street, and Angie's body was on the sidewalk. He passed it, arm in arm with Tammy, the young clerk from Starbucks he was screwing. Angie's face contorted. "Don't, oh, please, Zach, don't do this to us."

"Noooo . . ."

"Zach, wake up."

He couldn't. He kept seeing the dead firefighters, then they turned into Jenny, then Angie. "No, no, no."

"Here, let me try."

He was shaken, hard.

"Zach . . . Zach . . ."

Finally his eyes opened. Jenny perched on one side of the cot, Grady on the other. Reality dawned: the dark bunk room, lit only by the moon sneaking in through the slats of the blinds; the HCFD standard nightwear—T-shirt and gym shorts—they had on; Jenny's hair was down and messy. Grady looked . . . worried.

"What's going on?" Zach got out. He sounded like he'd fought a fire without an airpack.

"You had a nightmare." Jenny's voice was raw with worry.

Zach dropped back into the pillows. "Christ." He scanned the dim confines of the bunk room. The Rescue Squad was out. Only Group One were in bed, and the others either slept through the shouts or had zonked back out.

"Was it about Sinco?" Jenn asked.

"Sort of." He grasped her hand, held it like he used to when they were kids and he'd creep into her bed because he was scared of the dark. "You were hurt."

"Oh, Zach."

Grady, who'd been his best friend since day one, stood but stayed near the cot. "You gotta get some help, buddy."

"I am."

"The department shrink?"

"Yeah."

"How often?"

"Not often enough, I guess. It mostly happens when I'm asleep and once in a while when it gets a funny trigger when I'm awake." Zach sat up. "Look, I'm sorry I woke you." He stared at them both. "And I'm sorry about earlier."

"Forget it," Grady told him. "Just get some rest."

Jenny leaned over and kissed his cheek. " 'Night."

He waited until they'd both dozed off, then he slipped out of bed. Donning the HCFD sweats he kept on the end of the bed, he trudged out to the kitchen. It was 5 A.M. Almost time to get up. He'd put the coffee on and wait for the shift change.

After assembling the pot, he watched it drip. He couldn't get Angie out of his mind. The dream had been so real. Of course, she *had* caught him with Tammy. And she'd pleaded with him to tell her he wasn't cheating, just like she'd begged him in the dream.

Feeling as exhausted as if he'd hauled hose for hours,

he crossed to the phone and picked it up. He dialed his
. . . correction, her . . . number. He'd wake her up, but—

"Hello." The voice on the other end was sleep slurred
and sexy. He felt a brief stirring of arousal, though since
the fire, he'd been about as interested in sex as a eunuch.

He said into the receiver, "I always loved how your
voice sounded in the morning."

Angie chuckled. She must be really sleepy if she
wasn't mad at his sexual innuendo. "You woke me up."

"I'm sorry."

"It's okay. I have to get up for school in half an hour."

"Please. Talk to me. Just for a little while." Geez, Zach
Malvaso, begging. Who would have thought?

"What's wrong?"

"I . . . just need to talk to you."

"You had a nightmare."

"Yeah. You were in it . . . dead."

She sighed. "Zach, I'm safe."

"Jenny, too."

"Did something happen tonight? To bring this on?"

"Jenny got hurt in a call. She's okay." He waited. "We
lost a stabbing victim."

"That was always the hardest for you, even before the
Sinco fire."

"Talk to me," he repeated. "Like you did when I was
in the hospital. Tell me good things."

He pictured the way she'd settle back—he could hear
the rustle of the sheets, could feel the heat of her, see her
mussed and sleepy, smell the lotion she put on before she
went to bed every night. The images were so intense, he
had to stand and pour a cup of coffee.

"Jason got a big part in the middle school play."

"Yeah, what is it?"

"*Guys and Dolls*. He's Nathan Detroit, the gambler."
Zach listened as she told him the storyline of the musical.
Angie loved plays and had passed that interest on to their
sons.

"Remember when we went to see *Phantom* in New
York?" he asked.

"Yes. I couldn't believe you'd gotten tickets for my birthday."

Sometimes, he'd done nice things for her.

"I wish I'd taken you to more shows."

"Zach, don't, it doesn't help."

"I have so many regrets, Angel."

"The important thing to do now is just move on."

"Like you are."

Gently, she said, "Yes, Zach, like I am. You have to, too."

"You don't believe I've changed."

"No, I believe you've changed. I just don't know if it's permanent. Regardless, too much has happened between us to go back."

"So you said." He was being unfair. "I'm sorry, I don't mean to keep raggin' on you."

"You're hurting now, I know that."

"Tell me more."

"Nicky made a cute poster yesterday . . ." He let the soft cadence of her voice slide over him. ". . . I saw your mother last night, she was with Will Rossettie . . . I'm getting my master's degree on Saturday. . . ."

He zeroed in on the last comment. "Would you like the boys to be there?"

"It's a long ceremony."

"What time is it?"

"Four in the afternoon."

"We got a painting job in the morning, but I'll be done by noon. I could bring them. If they get restless, I can take them out."

"Zach, don't do this to get back in my life."

"I want to do something nice for you. Maybe I can make up for . . ." He didn't finish. Both of them knew he couldn't possibly atone for all the shit he'd pulled.

"All right." She hesitated. "Zach, Ken's coming."

Son of a bitch. Had she slept with the guy?

"Zach?"

"It's okay. If we see Kellerman, I'll be civil to him."

"I guess we could try it."

"Well, I'd better let you get ready for school."

"Are you going to be all right?"

"Yeah. Give my love to the boys. I've got them tomorrow, right?"

"Uh-huh."

"Look, thanks for talkin' to me."

"I'm sorry you're going through this."

"Thanks."

After he hung up, he sat sipping his coffee in the empty kitchen of the firehouse. Accompanied only by the sound of the fridge turning on and the smell of strong coffee, he thought about all he'd lost.

It made him incredibly sad.

 SEVEN

IT WAS THE third week of October before they got to visit the camp. As Mitch steered the car up Route 17, he stole a quick peek over at Megan Hale. He was driving fast as Will had warned he would, but safely. It didn't seem to faze her. He supposed she'd been in nerve-grating car chases, so this was a mild experience. For some reason, the danger of those chases, and other situations a cop routinely experienced, didn't sit well with him today.

"I'm sorry this was such short notice," she said, catching his gaze.

"No problem."

Damn it, Mitch. I had plans for us tonight. There's the gallery opening. . . .

Mitch had said nothing to his wife.

Cynthia mumbled under her breath, *Always the fire department.* At least her reaction was better than her temper reaching flashover like it used to whenever his job took him away from the social life that was so important to her.

"You sure?" Megan asked. "You're scowling."

He shot her another glance. She was dressed today in one of the suits she seemed to favor—a green linen-y

thing that looked soft to the touch. With it she'd matched
a light green blouse. She looked pretty. The colors reminded him of the shades of green in fire.

He'd dressed more casually than she, in jeans and a
cotton pullover sweater. "I'm sure." He nodded toward
the CDs Bobby had carefully stacked in a holder. "Want
to listen to some music?"

"Sure. What do you like?"

"Pick anything."

Giving him a half smile, she riffled through the discs.
"Oh, wow. What are you doing with these?" She held up
a handful of CDs.

"What are they?"

"Indie labels."

He couldn't resist. "I got CDs about the Indianapolis
Five Hundred?"

She chuckled. "Indie as in independent artists."

Grinning, he took a quick glance at her. "I know what
indie means in the music industry. The discs belong to
Bobby. My son idolizes groundbreakers, particularly the
women."

She popped in a CD. Mellow tones of a familiar tune
about what happened all summer long emanated from the
player. "I love this song. This artist."

Mitch said mischievously, "Yeah, she's a nice person,
too."

"You know Emm Gryner?"

"Uh-huh." He smiled at the memory. "Bobby thinks
she's the best thing since the Beatles. She gave living-
room shows when she first started out. We had one."

The little-girl look on her face was cute. "Emm Gryner
came to your *house*?"

Much to Cynthia's dismay. His wife had worried like
hell that the twenty friends Bobby and Trish had invited
would ruin her carpets. To Mitch, who routinely saw rugs
charred to a crisp, a little dirt was inconsequential. At
times like those, his and Cindy's differences seemed in-
surmountable.

"Mitch?"

"Yeah. Little Emm . . ." He pictured the tiny Filipino/

Canadian woman with the face of an angel and the voice of a superstar. ". . . set up her keyboard in the family room, brought her electric guitar and blasted us all out of the house. It was fun."

"Wow," Megan said again.

"Bobby was beside himself. He was like a kid again. Threw himself at her when she pulled in the driveway and got out of her car. Took her to his room. Had her sign his guitar. He still talks about it."

"I would, too. I *love* the way she sings."

"You should mention it to him sometime. He'll flip when he realizes another adult knows about her."

Megan studied the CDs, her face lighting like a starburst. "Dar Williams. Ani DiFranco. They're all my favorites."

Mitch shook his head. And listened as she played the vocalists' best songs and bubbled on about them. It ate up almost half of the four-hour trip.

Midway to the camp, they stopped for lunch. The diner she suggested was cozy and Mitch found himself enjoying her company. "This is a great place."

"My dad and I used to stop here every time we came up to Keuka Lake."

He sipped his coffee. "When was the last time?"

Her dark blond eyebrows knitted. "Last summer."

"Really? I . . ." He halted the mug halfway to his mouth. "Megan, it didn't click before. I'm sorry. This trip must be hard for you."

Her eyes became overcast, like the clouds coming out on a sunny day and spoiling the sky. "Yeah." She took a long swig of soda from her straw. "I still can't believe he's gone."

Without thinking, he reached out and covered her hand that was lying on the table. "I won't spout clichés. Losing someone you love is a bitch. And it's only been three months."

"Almost four." She bit her lip. That gesture of vulnerability spoke to him. "I know it'll get better. It did with Lance."

He squeezed her hand before he let go. "Your husband?"

Sighing, she nodded.

"You must still miss him."

"I miss being close with a man. Not just physically, but in sync. Like how he knew by just looking at me what my day had been like, or where I stood on a topic, or even what I liked to drink. Those little intimacies."

"I miss that, too." The words were out before he could censor them. Shit!

She cocked her head. "I don't understand. You've been married a long time."

"That doesn't mean . . ." He shook his head. "Forget it."

Understanding flickered on her face. Suddenly he was embarrassed for her to know about his floundering marriage. It made him feel inadequate.

Luckily, their food arrived. While they ate, they talked about Bright Horizon. "We're meeting the chairman at the lake, right?" he asked.

"Uh-huh. He's down there today for the Women's Oncology Camp."

"Isn't it late for a camp?"

"Some are held in the fall. I think this is the last one. I'm glad we got to go to the actual campgrounds. It's closer to us than Rochester, where Bright Horizon's headquarters are."

Mitch watched her eat. The special was hot meatloaf. She'd gotten the man-size portion with extra mashed potatoes, devouring the food like one of his burly cohorts.

"And you get to see the camp," she said, heaping a mound of spuds on her fork. "For ideas."

"Yeah." He bit off a chunk of his BLT. "You really think we'll be able to pull this off?"

Her whole face brightened. It was then that he realized what an investment she had in this endeavor. He wanted, more than he could rationalize, to help her make it a reality.

"Of course." She looked at him quizzically. "Don't you, Mitch?"

"You know what? I do. We'll start small, build up."
He frowned.

"What?"

"You sticking around Hidden Cove?"

She glanced out the window at the parking lot. "Yeah. Will's the closest thing to family I have. And I need a change. I think Hidden Cove's just the right place for me." She looked back to him with pretty amber eyes sparkling in the sun that came through the glass. "Like I was meant to come here."

"Hmm." For some reason, the thought made him uneasy, akin to the feeling he got when he knew fire was hiding inside a wall ready to spark out. He couldn't figure out where the concern came from.

THE CLOSER THEY got to Branchport, New York, the more Megan felt her muscles tighten. She'd been distracted by Mitch Malvaso's easygoing manner and unexpectedly dry wit, and hadn't let herself think about where they were headed. But when they made the turnoff at the end of Lake Road and reached the sign with the Bright Horizon logo—different-colored balloons held by a clown—she was ambushed by memories. A pang shot to the back of her neck and there was a familiar clutch in her stomach.

"You okay?" Mitch asked from beside her.

"Sure, I'm fine."

"You look pale."

"I'm fine." She glanced at him. *He* looked great in the ruby-red sweater and tight-fitting jeans. His boyish tell-me expression made her shrug. "Okay, it's . . . tough." The camp, which spread out over acres on the left side of the road, brought back too many associations. She gripped her hands together in her lap. "Seeing it again, for the first time since . . ."

Mitch bypassed the entrance, drove about twenty yards down and pulled off the road to the shoulder, where it was safe. "What are you doing?" she asked.

Putting the car in park, he raised his hand and slid it

across the Cherokee's bench seat. His fingers hovered behind her neck, making her nervous. "Being a friend." He nodded back to the camp. "Wanna talk about it?"

"The camp's a great place. So much for kids to do. I loved working with them." Memories paraded before her like film clips from a favorite movie. "Dad was super with the youngest ones—seven. He knew how rough-and-tumble to be with them and when to be tender."

"With you, too?"

"What?"

"Did he know when to be rough? Tender?"

"Yeah, particularly when Lance . . ." She trailed off. "Never mind."

"When Lance died?"

"Oh, yeah." She wasn't going to say that. She was going to say, "when he cheated on me."

I miss that, too.

You've been married a long time.

That doesn't mean . . . Forget it. . . .

Mitch's eyes nailed her with a knowing stare. "Did you have a happy marriage, Megan?"

"Mostly." She traced the outline of the window, feeling the ridge of rubber around its perimeter. "We had some bad spots. Dad gave us both good advice."

For a moment, he stared straight ahead. "I wish my father were alive."

"To give you advice."

"Yep."

"About what, Mitch?"

Shrugging, he shook his head. "Everything." He nodded his head back to the camp. "Ready, partner?"

"Yeah, as ready as I'll ever be."

He squeezed her shoulder gently. "You don't have to be tough with me, Megan."

"I am tough."

"All the time?"

"I try to be."

"Well, cut yourself some slack on this one, Detective. I promise I won't tell the guys at the station house if you shed a few tears."

Grinning, she felt her muscles ease. "You're a nice guy, Captain."

He drew back his arm and gripped the steering wheel. His hand was big and sprinkled with dark brown hair. Out of nowhere, she saw an image of that hand on pale female skin. Hers.

It made her say, "Your wife's a lucky woman."

"Not hardly." He put the car in reverse, made a turn, and headed toward the camp.

THE RESIDENTIAL CAMP on Keuka Lake was a beauty. Particularly now, in the fall, when there was nothing quite like outdoors in upstate New York. Whorls of yellow, red, and green surrounded the thirteen and a half acres, set right on the water. They parked by a huge pavilion with a high, peaked roof and cavernous interior. It was some kind of meeting place. Down a sloping, grassy piece of land Mitch saw tennis, volleyball, and basketball courts— he'd love to have those at their new camp. Facing the lake were several cabins and another bigger building, which Megan said was a dining hall.

Today, a mild Indian summer afternoon where the sun shone brightly but the air was crisp, several women walked around the grounds, women with breast cancer consoling each other, finding support. Mitch was simultaneously warmed by the sight and saddened by their plight. As a veteran firefighter, he knew only too well how tenuous life was.

Instead of going down to the camp proper for a closer look, he and Megan headed to the other side of the road where the offices were housed. Climbing another slight incline, they knocked on the door of a small building just across from the swimming pool. An outdoor chapel-like area lay just ahead.

"Come on in," a gruff voice called out. The chairman, a bear of a guy named Hank Fisher, stood and came toward them as they entered. "Meggie," he said and hugged her hard. He welcomed Mitch heartily.

Meggie. What Rossettie called her.

They exchanged pleasantries, sat down, then Fisher said, "So, you want to do something like this down by you?"

Megan smiled. Tension was still there, around her mouth and eyes, but she seemed happy to see this guy. "On a much smaller scale. We have about ten kids who had a parent killed in a fire in our town, and there are some in neighboring areas where children lost parents from other catastrophes. They won't all come, so we're hoping to have one cabin for girls, one for boys open next summer." She frowned. "And of course, any from the WTC attacks that won't make the trip up here."

"Sounds good to me." Fisher ran a hand over his white brush cut and settled more comfortably on one of the couches. "We had a small group when we first started, too. It grew into this over the last twenty years."

Revved up now, Megan cut to the chase. "We need to get the steps in order. Quite literally, we're building this from the ground up. How do we start, Hank?"

"Money." He shrugged. "Gotta have the cash base. So begin with fund-raising. And hire an accountant who'll get things in order for you there. It's one area you shouldn't hand out to just anybody. Legal guy could be pro bono, though. Meanwhile, you can be looking into the permits: from the health department to run a camp, from the American Camping Association to accredit the place. Building permits, too."

Mitch nodded, inspired by the man's enthusiasm and support.

"Then, decide what activities you want to offer, make a list of what you need to run them, and figure out the staff. Finally, you set a budget."

"How do we get the money?" Mitch asked.

"Talk to special-interest groups, like the Kiwanis. Run ads in the papers. Get the town government to donate. Write grant proposals. Have fund-raisers. The dance marathon we have at a local college raises several thousand dollars a year." He scratched his chin. "Somebody good at fund-raising and PR would be a real help."

Mitch's sister Connie came to mind. She did a lot of

charitable work for the hospital where her husband practiced medicine. But Mitch couldn't imagine her taking an interest in this camp. She hated fire fighting.

"It sounds so simple." Megan sighed. "I know it's not."

Hank laughed. "It's not, but it's doable." He leaned forward, warming up to the discussion. "If you got the fire in your gut to do it."

"I do," they said simultaneously.

"What will be our biggest costs?" Mitch asked.

"Well, fixed things like insurance. Transportation, though that might not be an issue for you this year. Once your camp gets going you'll need buses because you'll attract from a wider area. We get kids from all over the country." He thought for a minute. "Obviously, building materials."

"We can get a lot of those donated," Mitch said. "Along with firefighter and police manpower to put up the buildings."

"Can you give us a basic idea of what facilities we should have to start up?" Megan asked.

"Yeah. Come on, we'll tour the grounds and discuss it along the way so Mitch can have a visual. Then we'll come back here and I'll show you some of the paperwork I kept from when we started."

He got up and led them out of his office to a reception area. "This is where we run Bright Horizon Camps down here, though our headquarters are in Rochester. We have a large staff up there now, but you won't need anything that big right away."

"What would you recommend?" Mitch asked.

"A paid person in charge, to coordinate everything. A secretary. As you grow, you can add more—we split the duties up into a program director, a volunteer coordinator, and a recreation director."

They left the administrative building, bypassed the pool, and crossed the road to an A-frame; the sign by it read Infirmary. "Because we have camps for kids with cancer, HIV, and sickle-cell anemia, our medical facilities here are important. You won't require all that, but you'll need a nurse, at least. And a small treatment room. A few beds in case kids get sick. That could be volunteer staffed for now. Same for a social worker or psychologist, though truthfully, our kids come here to get away from their cancer, or the fact that their parents died, not get therapy for it."

They left the infirmary and reached the grounds proper; Mitch saw a group of women laughing under a tree and wondered at the resiliency of the human spirit, how people could enjoy a simple afternoon when they had a life-threatening illness. Passing the outdoor courts on the way down to the lake, Fisher said, "You'll need physical activities: swimming, sports like archery, volleyball, and basketball—Meggie's favorite if I recall."

"What's that?" Mitch asked as what looked like an obstacle course came into view.

Megan chuckled. "An adventure course." A session was in progress.

One woman held a rope which was suspended from a tree, the object obviously being to clear a distance and get past a marker. Another group huddled around a horizontal log suspended about ten feet off the ground; women were boosting each other up.

Megan laughed. "You should have seen me do the log bar the first time. The guys had trouble hoisting me up; their hands kept slipping down my legs."

He glanced briefly at her legs. "I'd have liked to see that."

They kept walking, by a huge circle made of tires that was a go-kart track, and a small miniature golf course. "You'll need equipment for outdoor activities, though again, you might be able to get some of that donated, too." They reached the lake and Fisher stared out over the water thoughtfully. "As a matter of fact, we just got a grant to update our boats and other water equipment. We're going for all new stuff. You can have what's still usable of our old stuff; it'll last you a few years at least."

Megan caught Mitch's gaze. The pleasure on her face made his gut clench. "That'd be great."

Heading back up, they passed several small cabins: one for arts and crafts, a costume room, a petting zoo. "This is a big part of our program, especially for kids who are too sick to be active," Fisher told them.

"That won't be a problem for us," Megan said.

"It might," Mitch put in. "Not all kids like sports. I know Jamie Baker's little ones are into art and drama. If they came to our camp, we'd need something to interest them."

"We have a variety of arts and crafts, drama, and music opportunities. There's a talent show, too, that both counselors and kids participate in."

Mitch rolled his eyes. "Count me out." He thought a minute. "But my son's into music. He might be able to help with those programs."

Fisher smiled. "That's what happens. You'll think of a lot of people's talents you can use and draft them to work with you. The camp will take shape fast."

They came upon the large building Megan identified as the dining hall. "This is where we cook and eat breakfast; the other two meals we have down at the water pavilion." He nodded to the right. "You'll need a kitchen staff, not too many for ten to twenty kids, though."

"My ma could do that with her hands tied behind her back," Mitch said.

Everybody laughed.

By the time they finished the tour, Mitch was a bit overwhelmed. "This is quite an endeavor," he said.

"That it is. Just remember, we started out small, and grew into all this. You'll do a fraction of it at first and build from there."

Mitch asked a few more questions, then Fisher suggested they head back to the office to take a look at the initial paperwork on the camp and get some promo literature, brochures, and volunteer applications they might want to see. Someone came up to talk to Hank, so Mitch and Megan stepped off to the side. Megan stared out over the lake, her shoulders tense again. "You okay?" he asked.

She nodded.

He touched her arm. "You want some time alone here?"

"Yeah." Her voice was raw. "I would."

"I'll go back to the offices with Hank. Get the stuff he has for us. Take your time."

Still facing away from him, she nodded.

He moved in closer, got a whiff of some flowery scent, like honeysuckle. "I could stay with you," he whispered.

"No, it's okay."

So he left her alone, staring out at the lake, by herself. It tugged at his heart and stirred something inside him. He tried to ignore it as he walked up the hill with Hank.

MEGAN HAD BEEN all right on the drive up. Mitch had successfully distracted her and the talk with Hank Fisher had energized her. But as they'd walked around, and she'd come face-to-face with the real places that were connected with her memories, the loss of her father became a tangible presence. It accompanied her now as she went on a cathartic pilgrimage. First, she trekked down to the dock, out to its end. She could see her dad there, so vividly, she had to close her eyes to withstand the emotion. One time in particular stood out. . . .

"Geez, Meggie, you never learn." As he said the words, he'd scooped her up into his arms and carried her toward this very dock. He was a big and brawny guy, able to easily wield her not-so-slight weight.

"Put me down. This is child abuse."

"You're past thirty. No judge in the world will convict me."

He tromped over the wooden decking.

Hugging him around the neck like she used to do when she was little—he smelled of the outdoors and Old Spice aftershave—she giggled at his nonsense. "Okay, okay, I'm sorry I said you were over the hill when you missed that basket. You're not, Dad, you're—"

They reached the end of the dock. She was fully clothed in shorts and a long-sleeved shirt, as it was cool that day.

"Oh, for God's sake, you're not going to—"

He did. He tossed her like a sack of potatoes off the dock into the water. Soggy and sputtering, she came up to the sounds of the laughter of all the kids in her cabin.

"I'll get you for this. . . ."

She could still see him holding his stomach, guffawing, his brown eyes full of glee just like the kids.

Megan opened her eyes and stared out at the water. The images were gone, just like he was.

Turning away, intending to go find Hank and Mitch, she headed up the slope. A few women greeted her as they walked by. She wandered off to the far side of the property, past the cabins, and stopped. Once, at midnight, when she couldn't sleep, she'd found her dad out here.

He was by the huge oak tree, his back to her, locked in a big-time embrace with a woman. She thought about leaving him to his privacy, but couldn't resist busting his chops.

Clearing her throat loudly, she said, "Hi, Daddy."

Her father took his sweet old time finishing the kiss, then, tucking the head of his companion to his chest—she was a woman he liked and respected and looked forward to seeing here every summer—he peeked over his shoulder. "Get an eyeful, Meggie?"

"You should be ashamed of yourself. Out here in public."

He chuckled. "No way. Now go back to bed, little girl, and let me finish what I started."

Laughing, she'd walked away.

She chuckled now, too, but felt her shoulders tense and her chest tighten. She rubbed the back of her neck. How could good memories hurt so much? Hurrying past the activity huts and pavilion, she crossed the road and approached the pool. Memories of him were there, too—doing half gainers off the diving board, racing with Hank Fisher in the relays, his big, powerful arms cutting through the water. He was so robust. All it took was one nine-millimeter shell through his chest. . . .

I'm sorry, Detective Hale. The bullet hit an artery. If we'd found him sooner . . .

Megan blinked back tears. Life was so precarious. She'd learned that with Lance first, and now with her dad. Her head started to hurt, as she wondered if she was living her own life fully now, or was she grieving too much. Today, it was as bad as it had been three months ago when her father had died.

She guessed she'd made a mistake coming up here so soon. But the visit was for a good cause, and it strengthened her resolve to get the camp project off the ground in Hidden Cove. The kids of slain cops and firefighters needed it.

Today, she *felt* how much.

MITCH COULD SENSE something was wrong with Megan when they drove away from the camp at five o'clock. "You're not okay, are you?" he asked.

Rubbing the back of her neck like she'd gotten whiplash, she said, "Just a little sad."

"Take anything for that headache?"

"How do you know I have a headache?"

"I'm an expert in the signs. Firefighters get them all the time from the smoke."

"I've got one coming on. I'm going to take something now." She began digging in her bag. "I always carry it with me." She pulled out a blister pack. "Shit."

"What's wrong?"

"This one's empty." She rummaged through her purse. "Maybe there's another in here. I've had more headaches than usual, lately, and have been popping these babies regularly."

"No problem, we'll stop somewhere."

"Can't." She dumped the contents of her purse in her lap. Rifled through the menagerie. He was amused to see what she carried in it. Her gun, some crackers, a bottle of water, an address book, cosmetics. "Son of a bitch. It's not here." But she went through her stuff again, this time a little frantically.

"Why can't we just pick up some ibuprofen?"

Tense, she massaged her temples. "It won't touch this. If it's a migraine, I gotta have Zomig."

"There's over-the-counter medicine now for migraines."

She gave him a baleful look. "It won't be enough."

Heading through the town of Branchport, he watched for a drugstore. "Let's try. Anything else help?"

"Food might. Something plain." She glanced at the crackers. "The doctor said to get rid of the tight neck muscles." She rolled her shoulders.

Determined to help her, he pulled into a drugstore parking lot. "Stay here, close your eyes, and rest. I'll go get some over-the-counter stuff."

"Mitch, you don't have to . . ." But he was out the door before she finished. He ducked inside, spoke to the pharmacist, and within five minutes, came back with nonprescription medicine. "Here," he said, sliding into the car. "Take three."

She did, and then he tugged on her arm. "Turn around."

"What?"

"I'm going to rub your neck."

"Mitch, really, you don't need to."

"Megan, I know how debilitating migraines are. My mother used to get them. Let me help."

"All right."

She angled herself sideways in the car.

"Take your jacket off."

She did.

He lifted his hands and began kneading her neck. "Jesus, I've tied Boy Scout knots looser than this."

"Of course you were."

"What?"

"A Boy Scout."

"That's me, good old Mitch."

"You sound like . . ." Her head dropped forward. "God, oh, that feels great."

His hands slid down the deltoid muscle. Kneaded harder.

"Oh, Mitch."

He chuckled. Mostly when women said that to men, they were in a different position. Out of nowhere, he was blindsided by an image of Megan under him, clutching his shoulders, her long, curvy body wrapped around him, murmuring the same words. And moaning. Forcefully, he pushed the image away. He was a married man and shouldn't be thinking about sex with other women.

He might not if his marriage hadn't burned itself out years ago. Though Cindy swore she wanted to rekindle whatever smoldering embers were left, his instincts were telling him that it was too little, too late.

Promise me, when this is over you'll do something about it. You'll make your life better.

Even when his hands began to hurt, he kept up the massage. Finally Megan straightened. "That's enough. Your fingers are going to fall off." She turned to face front again and lay back on the seat. "Thanks."

"Close your eyes now, for a bit. How about some food?"

"Love some."

"What?"

"Anything."

After a few blocks, he pulled up to an Italian place called *Ciao's*. "This okay?"

She opened her eyes. "Great." She smiled over at him, and gave him a grateful, thanks-for-understanding look. It did funny things to his insides. "I'm starved."

"Surprise, surprise." He got out of the car and followed her inside.

The interior was dimly lit with candles in straw-bottomed wine bottles on each table. There were a smattering of people eating dinner. A round-bosomed receptionist that everybody referred to as Mama seated them at a corner table. Megan shifted restlessly. "Something wrong?" he asked.

"Should we be eating somewhere this expensive?"

He glanced at the menu. "It doesn't cost that much. The departments can handle these prices."

She pondered the choices. "I don't know what half of these things are."

"Hush your mouth. My mother would be horrified."

Chuckling, she said, "What would be good?"

"They got my favorite—gnocchi in a light pink sauce.

A hot antipasto to start with. Maybe round it off some spumoni."

"Gnocchi—that's potato noodles, right?"

"Yep, though they can't be as good as my mother's, a lot of Italian places do a passable job."

"Okay, I'll have the same."

He smiled at her. She smiled back. The candlelight flickered over her clear skin; it was still pale, almost porcelain. The waitress brought them a bottle of San Pellegrino water with lemon, and Mitch poured. He raised his glass. "To a successful day."

Toasting, she looked thoughtful. "Yeah, the good news is Hank thinks we can do it. The bad is that it's gonna take a shitload of work." She sighed.

"We'll do it, *Meggie.*"

She blushed.

"I noticed Will called you that, too."

"Throwback to my childhood. Hank picked it up from Dad."

"It's cute."

"Cops aren't cute."

He never thought they were before, either, but right now, sitting across from him, her eyes dancing with enthusiasm, she fit the bill.

The meal was tasty, the conversation even better. Mitch regaled her with stories about him and Jenn and Zach's exploits when they were young, and about how he used to tell his kids firefighter stories instead of fairy tales at bedtime. She talked a bit about her early police days. Sadness clouded her eyes when she mentioned Lance; it . . . affected Mitch for some reason. He was sorry to leave the restaurant—after she ate her spumoni and half of his. Once in the Cherokee, they headed down the country road leading to Route 17 by eight-thirty.

Megan lazed back in the seat and closed her eyes. "God, I could go to sleep."

"Like the pigs do."

"What?"

"My mother used to say the pigs eat and go to sleep." She chuckled. "I'd like to meet your mother."

"You will. I know she'll volunteer for the cooking at the camp."

"Hmmm."

He let her drift off, switching the radio on to some mellow jazz. Headlights from oncoming cars illuminated her face, which was no longer pale. Her body stretched out in the front seat, comfortable and relaxed. Settling in, he was running over in his mind what they would do next for the camp when he saw some of those headlights headed right for him.

"What the fuck—" He jerked the wheel to the right.

The Cherokee hit the shoulder of the road and skidded off bumpily into a field; it careened along about twenty feet then jarred to a stop.

Megan jolted awake in the seat, and Mitch's hand shot out to keep her secured as they lurched forward.

THE FLASHING OF police lights combined with the stark terror of a near accident made Megan's head hurt again. Shit, she'd just about circumvented the damn migraine and now this. At least nobody had been injured. The driver of the truck had fallen asleep at the wheel and crossed into Mitch's lane. The guy had landed up ahead in a ditch, stuck but unharmed.

She was sitting in the Cherokee when Mitch returned to the vehicle. He slid inside and looked over at her. "Damn, that was close."

"At least we weren't hurt."

He took a second glance at her. "You're pale again."

"I'm okay."

"The headache back?"

"A bit." She leaned against the seat. "I'll be fine. I'll just close my eyes again. What time is it?"

"Almost ten."

Megan thought of his wife and kids waiting for him. "I'm sorry we'll be so late."

"Me, too."

"You should call home."

"I did." He pulled out onto the road. "I told Bobby we'd be delayed."

"Not your wife?"

"She went to the new art gallery's opening in town."

She peered over at him. "So, you did have plans."

His grin was devilish. "Hey, look on the bright side, I got spared the pain of trying to appreciate 'art' that looks like drunk amoebas swimming helter-skelter."

She chuckled and closed her eyes again. It wasn't too bad now, so if she could just relax . . .

They'd been on the road only ten minutes when the pavement turned erratic from construction; Megan felt her stomach pitch as they hurtled over the bumps and tried to avoid potholes. She sucked in a deep breath. For every thud of the tires, every bump they hit, every streetlamp that burned brightly, Megan's migraine symptoms worsened. Pounding pain started behind her right eye, like thousands of tiny pickaxes were hammering at her skull.

When they hit a patch of torn-up tar, and bounced precariously for several yards, her stomach lurched. She sat up quickly. "Mitch, pull over." She put her hand to her mouth.

With just a quick glance, he checked the rearview mirror, slowed down, and swerved as far off onto the wide shoulder as he could. She bolted out of the car, made it a few feet, and fell to her knees. Where she vomited violently.

As usual that only made the biting, clawing pain streak from her eyes to her neck and back again. Her stomach emptied finally, but she couldn't get up. Her chest heaved with the effort to contain the agony in her head. Then she realized Mitch was at her side. He reached out to touch her hair, and she stiffened. "Don't. I-It hurts." She buried her face in her hands. "Movement and lights kill."

"Jesus."

When she could, she opened her eyes.

He said, "You'll never be able to ride with the bumpy road and streetlamps."

"Just let me sit a minute." She eased onto her fanny, removed her jacket, and took deep breaths.

Hesitating, he got up and went to the car. When he returned, he held a bottle of water and a cloth that he'd wet. She took the cloth and put it to her face, on her eyes, then on her neck. It, and being ill, eased her stomach, so she rinsed out her mouth and tried to stand. Wobbly, she gripped his arm. "I'm sorry."

"Shush. Lean on me."

Resting on his arm and shoulder, she let him lead her to the car and practically lift her inside. Reaching over her, he grasped the belt and buckled her in. But the jar of the door closing made her stomach jerk. God, she hated this lack of control. The weakness.

He got in the other side. "Megan, what can I do?"

"Just drive."

They'd only gone a mile when he had to pull over and she retched again. This time, it was the dry heaves, since nothing was left in her stomach; he held her head and crooned softly to her.

After the third repetition of the process, he got them back into the car, drove off the highway, and into the parking lot of a small but well-known motel chain.

She said, "I'm sorry. I just can't control this."

"It's okay. We'll spend the night here. Will the pain go away if you sleep?"

"If I can get to sleep, it will."

He exited the car, softly closed the door and went inside.

Megan covered her face to block out the parking lot lights. She wanted to die.

BECAUSE MEGAN WAS so weak, Mitch had to carry her into the room. By the time he got the door open, she was deadweight in his arms. Remembering what she said about the light, he didn't switch any on, but took her to one of the two double beds.

Sorry, sir, we have no adjoining rooms.

Reluctant to leave her alone in this condition, he made a split-second decision to get one room, two beds. He didn't know her well enough to decide that, but what choice did he have? He hoped she saw that in the morning.

"I'm sorry," she mumbled as he lay her on the mattress farthest away from the door and out of the path of light from the bathroom.

"Shh, it's okay."

He stretched her out and stared down at her. She lay still as death. Gingerly, he removed her shoes. At least she'd taken her jacket off earlier. When she didn't say anything, he walked over to the door, closed it and went to the bathroom. Running the cold water, he soaked a washcloth with it. He came back and leaned over to put it on her neck. She sighed. "Thanks. That feels good."

"Don't talk." He straightened, but when he let go of the cloth, it fell away. He propped it against the back of her neck with a pillow. Then he returned to the bathroom, got another cold compress, came back, pulled up a chair and put it on her forehead. She sighed, and after a few minutes, dozed.

He alternated the compresses for a while, then when he was sure she was asleep, he went out to the Cherokee. He phoned home first. Thankfully, no one picked up. He left a message that it had taken longer than he'd anticipated to get the accident straightened out and he wasn't going to make it back tonight. Partly the truth. Then he grabbed a gym bag he kept in the truck, returned to the room and checked her again; she was sleeping lightly, still moaning some. In the bathroom, he took a scalding shower, donned sweatpants, and came out to the room.

Where he found her crying. She seemed half asleep.

At a loss, he went right to the bed. She was whimpering. It stunned him, given how tough she always came across before this trip. Sitting beside her, he didn't know what to do. Her eyes opened.

"Does it hurt, Meg?"

"It's a lot better." Her voice was sandpapery. ". . . Hate this . . . feel so vulnerable." She mumbled the words into the pillow as if she wasn't even awake.

"I'm sorry."

"Stay . . . with me . . . hold me . . ." She spoke haltingly, and he wondered if she even knew what she was saying or who she was talking to.

Aw, what the hell . . .

He circled the bed and as lightly as he could, he lay down on the mattress. Behind her seemed a safer bet.

He drew her close.

She cuddled back into him. He held her until he felt her breathing even out. Soon she was in a deep sleep. For a minute he just stayed close, enjoying the feel of her. Then it hit him. Holy hell, what was he doing?

Helping a colleague.

It took the strength of Hercules to pull away from this colleague. But she whimpered again, said, "No . . . ," and burrowed back into him.

So he stayed right where he was. After a while, he felt himself relax and his eyes closed.

He awoke to gray dawn. And a warm, womanly body cuddled into him. Which was unfamiliar. But nice. Her hair smelled lemony. He inched as close as he could get. "Mmm."

He thought he heard an "Mmm" in response. Then he felt her snuggle even closer.

His body reacted to the press of hers against his.

"Mitch?"

His eyes popped open. That wasn't Cindy's voice. It wasn't Cindy he was holding—not that they ever cuddled like this through the night anymore. So it wasn't his wife's body his was at attention for.

Oh, my God.

"Megan?" He let go immediately.

Somewhat gingerly, she eased away and turned to face him. Her hair was a mess, her clothes destroyed. One of the buttons on her blouse had come undone. The glimpse of the upper swell of her breasts drove up the fire in his belly. He forced himself to look at her face; there were no lines of strain around her mouth and eyes, and her shoulders were relaxed.

And she was looking at him with a whole rainbow of emotions flitting across her pretty features. Confusion. Understanding. A little bit of chagrin.

Reaching out, he rubbed her forehead with his thumb and finger. "Better?"

"Yeah, a lot." Briefly she closed her eyes. "I'm embarrassed."

"For being sick?"

"If I recall, I puked all over the place. I couldn't walk . . ."

And you cried. "Meg, you were ill." He looked around. "It's why I got one room. I was afraid to leave you alone."

She let out a frustrated breath. "That was probably a good idea. One time when I had a really bad one, I fell and hit my head on the sink. I don't know how long I was out." She shuddered. "I hate being alone during one of these."

He cleared his throat. "So you said."

Giving him a puzzled look, she asked, "I did?"

He nodded. "It's why I'm in this bed."

"Oh, God, did I beg?"

For a brief flash, he had a vision of her begging, but not for comfort. For something much much sweeter. His body hardened further at the thought. "No," he managed. "You didn't." He ran a thumb under her eye. "You cried, a bit, though."

"That is *so* not me."

"I won't tell," he teased.

"Thanks." She looked at him as if he hung the moon. It was probably the sexiest thing he'd ever seen.

Easing away from him, then, she got out of bed. And groaned.

He propped his head up on a crooked elbow. "What's wrong?"

"I feel like I got hit by a truck."

"We almost did."

"I remember." She sighed. "I meant that after one of these, every muscle in my body is sore."

"Do you see a doctor, Megan? Last night was pretty brutal."

"I've seen everybody. I have medicine I need to take when I get even an inkling of one of these coming on. It precludes the attack."

"Now I understand why you were so upset when you realized your blister pack was empty."

"I never forget it. I still don't know how this happened." She looked down. "Damn, I'm a mess."

He rolled off the bed and reached for his duffel bag. "I've got extra stuff in here. And there's toothbrushes from the motel in the bathroom."

"Oh, good." She took the duffel, pulled out one of his shirts, and held it up to her chest. "This is becoming a habit."

He knew his grin was little boyish. "I don't mind."

She smiled. "Well, I'll go shower. And change." She headed to the bathroom. When she got to the door, she glanced over her shoulder. "Thanks again, Mitch. If I can ever repay the favor . . ."

Nodding, he winked at her. "I'll keep that in mind, *Meggie*."

When the door closed, he tried, really hard, not to think of all kinds of repayment. He flopped back down on the bed and, linking his hands behind his head, just stared at the bathroom.

EIGHT

JENN SWERVED THE Midi off the road, scouting for a defensive spot to park the rig. The Rescue Squad vehicle followed right behind her, and cordoned her truck off. People didn't realize how often firefighters were hurt by careless drivers, or worse, gawkers, especially in predinner rush-hour traffic like this. It was the one thing that sparked Grady's temper quicker than matches to tinder. Another company, Engine 17, had just arrived on the scene of the two-vehicle accident. Wails from police sirens and ambulances sounded in the distance.

She and Grady bounded out of the truck and headed for Mitch, who, as captain and highest ranking officer of the three companies, was in charge. Two cars were tangled in the middle of the busy intersection: A Camaro had been T-boned by an Accord, stopping all four-way traffic.

The din of cars idling and horns beeping surrounded them as Mitch called out, "Assess the mechanism of injury, O'Connor."

Like a doctor used to taking charge, Grady made a quick study of the scene. His face was grave when he came back to report. "One patient in each car. The Camaro victim will have hard impact on the left side of the body, possible spine injuries. Patient in the Accord could have chest injuries, maybe head trauma from snapping forward. Jenny should go to the Camaro; I'll take the Accord. We'll both need help."

Grady and Jenn hustled to their respective assignments. Giving orders for Engine 15 to assist Grady, Mitch spoke briefly with the lieutenant on that crew, then joined his sister at the Camaro. He tried the driver's door, she the other side.

"This one needs extrication," Mitch yelled to his crew. They were already setting up the Hurst equipment.

Grady had opened the Accord door and had climbed in the front seat. Two black-and-whites had also reached the site and the cops bounded out to direct traffic around the accident. One approached Mitch and Jenn.

"I gotta get inside, Mitch," she said.

"We'll cut you in."

Before speaking to the cops, Mitch himself taped the front passenger window and razored it out, then loosened it with an ax. The glass came off in one rectangular sheet, shattered, but intact, though slivers fell inside. Meanwhile, Jenn whipped off her turnout coat and, with a boost from her brother, climbed through the opening; he passed her the advanced life support bag carried on the Rescue Squad. Mitch started barking orders to his crew amidst the buzz of voices outside, but Jenn blocked everything out.

With the air bag pinning his chest, the victim lay back against the seat, his eyes closed. His left side was kissing the driver's door. He was about fifty, with slightly graying hair and tanned skin.

She recognized him immediately. Stan Steele, Town Council president and, if the Hidden Cove grapevine was accurate, the heir apparent for mayor of their home sweet home.

"Councilman Steele, can you hear me?"

His eyes opened. "Yes."

"Don't move. I'm going to assess the damage here." She'd do a quick ABC examination—airway, breath, circulation—first.

"What's going on?" he asked.

"Well, sir, you were in an accident, and now you're trapped in your car." She checked his airways. He was breathing fine. "The Rescue Squad's going to get you out, but meantime I'm making sure you're all right." She took out a stethoscope. His heart was a steady thud in his chest.

Again he closed his eyes. There were lines of pain around them, accented by his tan.

She picked up a neck brace. "I'm gonna put this collar on you, Councilman. Just stay still."

"Do I have a spine injury?"

"I don't know. This is precautionary."

He winced as she circled his neck with the collar.

"You're lucky you have your seat belt on," she said to distract him.

He chuckled, his blue eyes giving a brief twinkle. "It's the law, ma'am."

She smiled, remembering now. Steele was a bachelor, and women in Hidden Cove went gaga over him.

From outside she heard, "Here, Jenn. Cover him and yourself; we're ready to take the front window."

Jenn snagged the protective blanket and shook it out over the councilman. "We have to rip this baby apart in order to get you outta here. This thing will keep the glass off us."

"You getting under that blanket with me, sweetheart?"

Chuckling herself, she said, "You betcha." Hmm, this would be a story to tell. Even in pain he was gorgeous; his looks were similar to Grady's, only the councilman's hair was dark. She checked his skin condition and pupil dilation before she covered him.

"This won't take too long, Councilman Steele."

"Make it Stan. I'm always on a first-name basis when I share a blanket with a woman."

A woman! Oh, brother. "Okay."

"Your name?"

"Jenn Malvaso."

"I know Mitch. You're his sister?"

Huddled now under the thermal, it was intimate. She could hear him breathing. See trickles of sweat run down his face. "Yep, he's everybody's favorite fireman," she said with no rancor. And to make small talk so he wouldn't think about what was happening outside the blanket.

"Yeah, he is. Noah Callahan speaks highly of him."

After only a minute or so, Mitch's voice came through their cocoon. "Okay, Jenny, we're done here." Slowly she eased off the blanket. Mitch was on the hood of the car, disposing of the air bag. Then, he dragged the glass-laden blanket off them. The sound of a generator split the air. Steele jumped.

"It's just the Jaws of Life, Stan."

Other crew members were popping the four poles that held the car together, and then one of them would tear back the roof.

From the hood of the car, Mitch nodded to the councilman. "Hey, Steele, fancy meetin' you here."

"Malvaso."

"Noah's on his way. He got wind of this and wants to make sure we're treating you right."

Steele shook his head. "I don't even know what happened."

"Try not to move," Jenn ordered.

"All right." He addressed Mitch. "I was stopped at a light, it changed, then I was halfway across the intersection."

Jenn checked his blood pressure again. It was a little high, 159/94. She wondered how Grady was doing.

Finally, a grinding sound rent the air, and the roof was ripped back. "Arrgh, makes my teeth hurt."

"How are your arm and leg?" she asked.

"Let's just say I'm trying not to embarrass myself by bawling like a baby."

"Just us firefighters here, Councilman. No need to be brave."

"My constituents might not agree."

LoTurco, from the Rescue Squad, handed her chest gear, which would stabilize the patient in case of chest injury; he held a backboard. He was mumbling to Mitch, but Jenn couldn't make out what he was saying. She did note more sirens, signaling the arrival of additional rescue personnel. She showed Steele the harness. "I'm just going to secure your chest with this."

She fitted the vest as carefully as she could around him, but still, he moaned in pain.

"Now, this is the tricky part. We've got to get you on the backboard." Which was being lowered from the roof that was no longer there. LoTurco jumped in the backseat to assist Jenn on the other side. "We'll start from the top and slide it down, then pull you up without jarring your neck."

"Sounds complicated."

"Piece of cake. But it might hurt."

"Go ahead."

The maneuver took ten minutes, with numerous push-pulls, tugs and the careful easing of the board behind the victim. By the time they were done, Jenny's arms stung with the strain. She stood and reached down to lift the secured patient out of the car with LoTurco. On the ground, Mitch and another crew member took the backboard from them. Chief Callahan was there, standing beside Grady. The other patient had apparently gone on the ambulance and Engine 17 firefighters were across the way.

The second ambulance crew then accepted the patient from the firefighters. Only when extrication was complete did they officially take over.

When Steele was supine, on a stretcher, Noah stood over him. "Councilman, you okay?"

He wasn't; he was in pain. "Great. This pretty lady took good care of me."

Jenn rolled her eyes. "Just doing my job."

With his uninjured side, he reached for her hand. "And you do it well." Squeezing her fingers, he smiled. "I'll be in touch," he said.

As they wheeled Steele away, with Callahan by his side, Grady came up behind her and put a hand on her shoulder. "Good job, Malvaso."

"Thanks." Briefly she covered his hand with hers. "Your guy all right?"

"Yeah, though there's concern for the bleeding."

"Jesus, she's a bitch," Ed Snyder, another member of the Rescue Squad, grumbled as he joined them.

"Who?" Jenn asked.

"Brennan. Jumped all over me when I tried to give her a hand with the stretcher."

Grady shrugged. "She's a good firefighter. She was on top of things."

Snyder snorted nastily. "Yeah, well, it's common knowledge that she likes to be on top. . . ."

"Who does?" Everybody stilled at Noah Callahan's appearance.

Snyder averted his eyes guiltily from Brennan. "Ah, nobody, Chief."

Callahan glanced to where Casey Brennan, a female firefighter from 17, stood by herself near her rig. He eyeballed Snyder. "Come with me a minute, Ed."

They left and Grady sighed. "When will Snyder learn to keep his big mouth shut. He can't make those remarks about women in the department."

Surprised by his strong remark, Jenn looked around to see if they had an audience. No one was near them. She leaned in close. "They say it's true about her."

"What? That she sleeps around or she's a bitch?"

"Both."

"Doesn't give Snyder the right to bad-mouth her."

"You are such a pussycat."

"Casey's okay."

Jenn studied the woman. She was tall and muscled. Black as night hair fell carelessly around her face. "You think she's pretty?"

"Christ, Jenny, what's with you? First Hale, now Brennan."

"What about Hale?" This from Mitch, who'd just come up to them.

"Jenny asked if I thought she was pretty."

Mitch cleared his throat and turned away. How odd. Usually he'd rag on Grady about the women in his life.

"How'd your trip to Keuka Lake with her go?" Jenn asked.

"Great. We're meeting with the chiefs this week. Let's get back and I'll tell you about it." He grinned. "Oh, and I think you got an admirer, sis."

"Me?"

"Yeah. Councilman Steele was smitten. He was already grilling Noah about you before they took him off."

"Steele, the ladies man." Grady shook his head. "Stay away from him, Jenn."

"I think he's a doll."

Grady frowned.

Mitch grinned.

Then they headed for the trucks.

BADGES WAS A police/firefighter hangout of the first order. Tucked away behind one of the bridges of Hidden Cove, it was run by two brothers, one a former member of America's Finest, one an America's Bravest. Zach loved the place. The interior was dark and cool and the proprietors catered to their clientele like mothers to their children.

Mementos surrounded them; pictures of police and fire academy graduating classes, photos of rescues and shootouts dating back decades, firefighting posters people had contributed. Zach stared at an advertisement for a golf tournament to raise money for the 9/11 victims.

And there were always firefighters and cops here. Stories about the department were bandied around like family histories.

That was why he'd come here tonight, when the walls had started to close in on him; he knew there'd be camaraderie and some tales told. He sat on a stool at the long mahogany bar and listened to LoTurco tell one. Often the stories centered around a topic. Tonight it was *foam*.

"No shit, my pa said this really happened. It was years ago, when he was still on the line. A tanker turned over on the highway. The gas tank blew and fire shot out every place. A firefighter took a hose in with foam and sprayed the pool of gas. While they were in the middle of it, the fire ignited again. They put it out. The fucker sprang to life *again*. Three times before they got it out."

Another smoke eater said, "I got caught, too. One time, the foam was defective and wouldn't douse the Red Devil. I was in the bitchin' fire so long it singed off my eyebrows."

A third guy spoke up. "Leo Stapleton"—the author of the classic firefighting book *Thirty Years on the Line*— "told a story once about how he was in a gasoline spill and the press arrived. One reporter came up to interview him with a cigarette in his hand. They were standing in the middle of a puddle of gasoline. . . ."

"Oh, God, I just remembered another . . ."

Soothed by the stories of bravery, Zach let the sound of their voices calm him.

Grady arrived just as the guys finished up with their storytelling.

"Hey, buddy," Zach said, "What are you doing here?"

"Needed some space is all."

"Want a beer?"

"Yep."

Zach ordered one for his friend and another for himself. They shot the shit for a while, then Zach said, "Hey, I heard the councilman took a shine to Jenny today."

Grady shook his head and frowned. "Yeah, I guess."

"You miffed?" Zach asked.

"Why would I be miffed?"

"It's no secret you look out for her as much as me and Mitch, since Sinco."

Grady sipped his beer. "Jenny's a big girl. She can date whomever she wants."

"Give it up, O'Connor. I see right through you."

For a minute Grady looked torn. "Maybe I don't like it." He scanned the bar. "Hey look, Brennan's here. All by her lonesome in the corner."

Zach tracked his gaze. He didn't know Brennan well, but had heard about her and worked some subbing jobs with her, where they fought a few fires. She was as good a smoke eater as he was. "I heard tell about that one."

"Fuck, that pisses me off. Everybody's so quick to

judge her, so quick to believe all the nasty rumors."

"Yeah, you're right. Even if they're true, they're nobody's business."

Snagging his beer, Grady stood. "I'm gonna go tell her she did a good job today."

"Good luck." When Grady left, Zach felt in his pocket for a cigarette. He took them out, then remembered as of last summer you couldn't smoke in bars anymore. He knew he shouldn't be smoking anyway, but sometimes it calmed him enough to keep the demons at bay. Harrison said there was a lot of symbolism to why so many smoke eaters indulged in the ugly habit. He noticed that Brennan had also lit up in the past. At the jukebox, somebody put on some country-and-western music.

Zach tuned into the music and scoped out the bar; he saw the front door open and Noah Callahan walked in. *Shit.* Just what Zach needed.

Callahan didn't see Zach until he was on top of him. The chief's face—remarkably unlined for forty-seven—hardened. "Malvaso," Callahan said, stopping.

"Chief."

Callahan glanced around as if looking for an escape. When he didn't immediately find one, he transferred his gaze back to Zach. "How you doin'?"

"Great."

"How are the episodes?"

Everybody knew Zach had experienced PTSD since the Sinco fire. At one time it might have bothered him. "Getting better. I'm still seeing Harrison."

"Good." The chief's eyes narrowed on him. "Nothing's happening on the line though, right?"

"No. Stupid things set them off, like a smell. The nightmares are the worst part of this whole thing."

"All right. Just checkin'."

Grady returned. "Hi, Chief."

The atmosphere warmed up as if a tropical breeze blew in. "Hey, O'Connor. Hear you did a great job today. Both victims are in stable condition."

"How's the councilman?" Zach asked.

Merely flicking a glance at Zach, Noah said, "Stan's fine. Asked a million questions about your sister."

Grady sighed. "So I heard." He angled his head across the room. "Brennan did great today, too."

"Well then, I'll go tell her." He nodded to both men and took off. Like a prisoner who'd just gotten a pardon.

"What the hell did you do to torque him off?" Grady asked when the chief was out of earshot. "He freezes up like an ice cube whenever you're around."

As far as Zach knew, there were only three people who were aware of the reason for Noah's blistering contempt. And one of them was dead.

"I sinned, Gray. Big-time. He's got reason to hate me."

Grady studied Zach. "You know buddy, this new self-effacing you boggles my mind."

"What's this self-effacing shit?"

"Nothing. Forget it." Grady sat and noticed the pack of cigarettes out on the bar. "Zach, those things'll kill you."

"Maybe." Watching Callahan hover over Brennan's table, he finished, "Probably make a lot of people in this town happier than shit if they did."

"Zaccaria?"

"Forget I said that. I'm just being maudlin."

But Zach knew forgetting was a tall order. Some things ran too deep, some actions were too far-reaching.

He stared at Callahan. Like sleeping with the chief's wife.

THERE WAS A light on upstairs in Jenny's half of the house when Grady let himself into his side. Restless, he was thinking about Zach, and how the guy seemed to be sinking lower into . . . sadness. Just like Brennan.

Now *she* was a piece of work, Grady thought, dropping his keys on the foyer table and hanging up his jacket. As he crossed through his living room, entered Jenny's part of the duplex through the French doors, and made his way upstairs to her bedroom, he recalled his conversation with his colleague. . . .

Hi, Brennan.

She'd looked up and for a minute, he saw in her navy

blue eyes the same sadness as was in Zach's. She'd said gruffly, *O'Connor.*

You did a good job today.

Yeah, thanks. You, too. She took a drag on her Marlboro.

He didn't know why he asked, but he added, *Want some company? You could hang out with me and Zach.*

She indicated her beer. *Nah, this is all the company I need.*

He took the hint. *Sure. Fine.* And turned to leave.

O'Connor? she called out after him.

He glanced over his shoulder. *Yeah?*

Thanks for asking, though.

Poor girl. Some monkey was on her back big-time.

Then he'd come face-to-face with his own monkey. Just as he was going to join Zach at the bar, his ex-fiancée, Sheila, walked in. Grady detoured into the john, not wanting to face her, but not before he saw her weaving and leaning heavily on her date. She was still on the downslide—drinking excessively, flitting from man to man. Because of Grady. Because he couldn't be what she wanted him to be. It cut as deep as a finely honed scalpel.

Jenn wasn't in her bedroom, but he heard splashes coming from the bathroom adjacent to it. He called out, "Jenny?"

"In here."

He sidled up to the door, but didn't peek inside. "You decent?"

"I'm wearing bubbles."

He chuckled. "Can I come in?"

"Uh-huh."

Standing in the doorway, he watched her. Eyes closed, head back, she was totally immersed in big, flaky soap bubbles.

"Decadent," he said, folding his arms over his chest. She looked cute in the tub.

"Hey, it's your fault."

"That it is." He'd bought her the tub three years ago when they'd fought a particularly nasty fire and come home so sore they could hardly stand it. And they almost hadn't made it out of the burning house; the close call had scared them. She'd always wanted a Jacuzzi and swore that night she'd scrimp for one. The next day he'd bought her the six-foot-long, three-foot-high tub. He'd had it installed when they were working, and when they'd come home to find it, she'd gotten tears in her eyes.

"Gray, where'd you go?"

He crossed to the toilet, dropped the lid, and sat down. "Just thinking about when I bought this baby."

Her dark eyes were full of warmth. "I loved that you did that for me."

Touched, he smiled. Then he raised his eyebrows sexily. "Sure has added spice to my love life." When he entertained a woman, and Jenn made herself scarce, he used the tub for other purposes than bathing.

"Spare me." Lifting a slender leg, she ran over it with a loofah. "How's Zach?"

For a minute he was distracted by the long expanse of shin poking out of the water. Finally he answered. "Not good, honey. We need to spend more time with him."

"Did he say something?"

"Same old, same old. He's really down." Grady dipped a hand in the tub and scooped out some bubbles. He blew on them and they poofed out in the air.

"Mitch said Zach's seeing Harrison twice a week now."

Grady nodded.

"Who else was there?"

"Callahan. He told me Steele has the hots for you." For some reason, that didn't sit well tonight. Zach had been right about his reaction. Maybe it was because he'd heard the guy liked to acquire women and he didn't want Jenny to become part of his collection.

"Noah Callahan said the councilman had the *hots* for me?"

"In so many words."

"That's crazy. Stan's got his pick of choice meat in Hidden Cove."

Stan? "Oh, I don't know. You're pretty prime beef, Malvaso."

She giggled. Like a girl. His gut clenched in a totally foreign reaction to her laughter. It made him say, "Sheila was there."

Jenny's dark eyes turned molten. "Son of a bitch."

"It's okay, I ducked into the bathroom to avoid her."

"No wonder. She practically scratched your eyes out the last time you saw her." Jenn shook her head. "I hate that woman, and Linda, for what they did to you."

He didn't respond.

"Was she drunk?"

"She looked it."

"That's her own stuff, Gray. You're not responsible for what happened after you broke up with her."

"So you say." He searched for something else to to talk about. "Brennan was there, too."

Jenn had grabbed a bar of soap and was washing her arm. Momentarily, she halted the action. "Yeah? You talk to her?"

"I tried. I went over and she blew me off."

"Hrrmph."

"I feel sorry for her. She's a loner, which is her choice, but she seems sad, like Zach."

"Everybody says she's tough as nails."

"Well, they say that about you, too, and you're really a softie."

"Hmm. I'll tell you, this bath stuff Mitch brought me back from New York when he went to that conference makes my skin soft."

Her comment made *his* mouth go dry. He wanted, a lot, to touch that skin. So he reached over and stroked her shoulder. Muscled and supple, it was nonetheless velvety as duck's down. "Feels good to me," he said.

Maybe because of the gruffness of his voice, she shot him a puzzled look.

Jesus, what was he doing?

To defuse the charged atmosphere, he stood, placed his hand on her head—and dunked her under.

She came up sputtering. "You creep, I'll get you for that."

He laughed as he left the bathroom. " 'Night, Genevieve," he sang out.

But it was a long time before the sensation of touching her bare shoulder left his fingers. And it bothered him. He and Jenny were best of friends and never once reacted to each other sexually. But since they decided to make a baby together, he'd been on edge sometimes when he was around her.

That night, he dreamed about his wife; she was screaming at him that he was terrible with intimacy, with love. Then Jenn came into the dream, bare-shouldered. She stood by Linda and said, "She's right, Gray. Be careful."

"OH, GOD, HE is so freakin' sexy."

"I know. Sometimes I can't stand looking at him."

But she did; Jenn sat on the nubby beige couch in her duplex, shoveling moo goo gai pan out of a carton and into her mouth, and mooned over Pierce Brosnan as he flirted with Rene Russo in *The Thomas Crown Affair*.

Megan Hale, also sprawled on the sofa, stuffed her face like Jenn hadn't ever seen *anybody* eat. "This was a great idea."

At the end of her shift, Jenn had bumped into Megan as they were both exiting headquarters. They'd stopped and chatted, then Jenn had impulsively asked if Megan was free that night. Grady had a date later on and Jenn was at loose ends. Apparently so was Megan because she readily agreed to come to Jenn's house for some Chinese take-out and a chick flick.

"That the kind of guy you like?" Jenn asked, the sweet taste in her mouth pleasant.

"Does anybody not?"

"Was your husband dark haired?"

"Yeah, blue eyed, too. He was a lot bigger, though."

"Well, there's big, and there's big."

Again they giggled.

"You two talking dirty already?"

Jenn glanced behind her and said, "Shh, I'm busy," but her gaze held for a minute on Grady, who had just come up from the basement where he'd been working out before getting ready for his date. He was dripping with sweat, his face flushed an appealing red, and his muscles glistened—he wore no shirt and they were defined more now that they were slick. From the corner of her eye, Jenn saw Megan take a long second look.

Grady wiped his face with a towel. "Hi, Megan."

"Grady."

"Having a good time?"

Megan's eyes lit. She was really pretty as her hair fell forward and she nodded to the TV. "How could we not?"

"Is that Brosnan? Jenny thinks he's Adonis."

"He is."

Rolling his eyes, Grady said, "I'm outta here."

When he left, they continued to eat and watch TV. But Jenn was distracted; even Pierce couldn't keep her attention. She kept picturing Grady's muscles, thinking about how things between them felt different these days. Especially the other night, when she'd been taking a bath and he'd touched her skin—differently, and then yesterday, when they'd been working out together. Grady had pulled one of those world-class muscles.

"What's wrong?" she'd asked when he'd finished stretching and had moaned.

"I wrenched my shoulder."

"You should take a Jacuzzi."

"Maybe."

"Want me to rub your back?"

He'd given her an odd look, as if he had to *decide* to let her. "Yeah, why not? I'm pretty sweaty, though."

What a strange remark, she remembered thinking. A self-conscious one. They were often sweaty, given the things they did together. He'd stretched out on the mat and she'd wiped his back with a towel.

Then she'd straddled his butt. He'd stiffened. "What's wrong?"

For a few seconds, he didn't say anything. Then he teased, "You gaining weight?"

"Up yours," she said and began to massage him.

He moaned, loudly, when she kneaded his deltoid muscle.

"Feel good?"

"Mmm. You got great hands, Malvaso."

She grinned. "That's what all the guys say."

He had a nice back, wide, muscular from hours spent staying in shape—necessary to a firefighter. It was sprinkled with freckles that sometimes peeked out on his face, too. She worked the whole area. When she got to his waist, his shorts slipped and an inch or two of skin below his waist was exposed. For a minute, her heartbeat speeded up.

"Jenn? What's wrong?"

"N—" She cleared her throat. "Nothing."

"You stopped."

She swallowed hard, and shook herself. Geez, this was Grady. What the hell was she thinking?

Still she'd wrapped up the session quickly, dumbfounded by her very feminine reaction to him. They'd always been immune to the male/female stuff with each other. They were best of friends. Must be all the baby talk. . . .

Megan interrupted her thoughts. "Jenn, you okay?"

"Yeah, I was just thinking about Grady."

Megan stopped eating. "You two have an odd relationship."

"Do we?"

"Yeah. You aren't related, but you seem closer than brother and sister." Then she added, "And closer than most married people."

Jenn picked up an egg roll. "We are. We've been friends since we were five. He's close to Zach and Mitch, too," she added defensively.

"He's a doll."

"Mitch?"

Megan shifted in her seat. "Um, no, I meant Grady."

"Yeah, women think so." She stared at Megan, who was a nice person. Jenn tried to make herself say, *Grady thinks you're attractive, too, you should go out with him,* but she couldn't get the words out of her mouth. Instead, she nodded to the TV. "Oh, God, here's the dance scene in that dress."

Appropriately distracted, Megan turned her attention to the screen.

Ten minutes later, Grady came back into her living room.

He wore a steel-blue gauzy shirt tucked into beltless navy jeans. His damp-from-the-shower hair was combed off his face and he'd shaved.

He smelled like heaven.

"I'm going," he said, then looked at the TV. "Oh, geez, this the scene on the stairs?"

Megan grinned. "Yep."

Standing next to the couch on Jenn's end, Grady absently reached out and put his hand on her shoulder, his eyes focused on the TV. "Looks like it would hurt to me."

"What's a little pain?" Megan joked.

Grady squeezed Jenn's shoulder. "I'm off."

"Don't try any stair tricks with Sally," she warned, but her tone wasn't as teasing as she meant it to be. The picture that assaulted her, of Grady naked and tumbling on steps with the pretty high school teacher, didn't sit right.

Instead of answering, he leaned over, kissed her hair, said, "Not one of my fantasies, babe," winked at Megan, added, "Save me some of that cake I saw on your kitchen table," and left.

Megan sighed. "Lucky lady."

"Rene Russo?"

She crunched the last of her food. "Nope, I meant Grady's date."

Jenn's heart clutched again in her chest. "Yeah, they all think so, too," she said, but it didn't amuse her like it used to.

GRADY AWOKE EARLY the next morning and lay in bed, thinking about his date last night. It hadn't gone well. Sally Hines was pretty enough, and fun to be with with. They'd slept together in the past. But when she came on to him after dinner and the movie, he kept picturing Pierce Brosnan on the steps with Rene Russo, and thinking of Jenny drooling over the guy.

Like water on fire, the image doused all interest in sex with Sally.

Linking his hands behind his head, he thought about his and Jenn's upcoming . . . assignation. He'd wanted to do something romantic—candles, a movie, even a Jacuzzi bath together—to put them both in the mood, though he had a feeling it wouldn't take a hell of a lot for him. For some reason, he couldn't wait to get his hands on her. Which was odd, given they'd been friends for years and never been attracted to each other before. Maybe he was looking forward to this because he liked Jenny more than he liked any other woman in the world.

That had always been a problem for both Sheila and Linda. God, he'd really blown those relationships. He simply couldn't . . . like them as much as Jenn. He couldn't confide in them, whereas he told Jenny everything. He was still ridden with guilt, and in the intervening years since Linda had died, he hadn't been able to find anyone who truly interested him. He'd had a string of bad relationships, then he gave up and just started dating casually. With casual sex.

Which he couldn't get up for last night.

He heard banging downstairs. Jenny must be awake.

Getting out of bed, he tugged on sweats and made his way to his kitchen. She was in his half of the house, rummaging through drawers. She had on a shrunken Penn State jersey—where he'd gone to college—and boxers. Her hair hadn't been combed and he noticed it was getting longer. She wore it pulled back at work. "What are you doing up so early . . . and banging around in my kitchen?"

She turned and stared at him; her gaze dropped to his bare chest for a little too long. "Um . . . nothing."

"Nothing?"

"Oh. I was looking for that sharp paring knife you borrowed. I got a cantaloupe from the store and was going to cut it up." She looked a bit embarrassed, then raised her chin. "I was making you breakfast."

He grinned. "Great."

She turned back to the drawer. "Here it is."

"Is that coffee I smell?"

"Yeah. Come on over."

Their kitchens were back-to-back and he followed her through the French doors, the foyer, and into her kitchen. She crossed to the counter and he grabbed some coffee. Sitting down at her breakfast bar, he watched her crisp movements at the sink. She didn't like to cook, but when she did she went about it with ruthless efficiency. Right now she was making short work of the cantaloupe. Barefoot, her long legs seemed to go on forever. She said, "I'm surprised you're up so early."

"Why?"

She hesitated. "You weren't home when I went to bed."

"Hmm."

"What time did you get in?"

He chuckled. "Checking up on me, Genevieve?"

Her head snapped around. "No!" She went back to the fruit. "Just curious."

Surprised at her vehemence, he murmured, "About midnight."

"Did you have fun?"

"It was okay."

"You like Sally."

"Yeah." He paused. "Truthfully, I was a little bored."

Jenn was quiet a minute. "No staircase activity?" she asked, her voice hoarse.

He laughed. "Maybe."

Her shoulders stiffened. He was just about to tell her he was teasing when she said, "Ouch! Jesus. Son of a bitch."

"What's wrong?"

She reached for paper towels. "I sliced my thumb."

He was out of the chair like a shot. By the time he reached the sink, she had the towel on the cut . . . and there was blood all over the cantaloupe. He knew thumb wounds bled profusely but the sight of Jenny's blood knocked him off balance for a minute. "Let me see."

She held out her hand, wincing when he pulled off the towel. Blood oozed from her thumb. He grabbed another towel, wet it, and wrapped her back up. Then he raised her arm over her head. "Keep it above your heart."

"All right." The action hiked up her too-small shirt, exposing her midriff, where the boxers slipped. She was dusky all over and always looked like she had a tan. He dragged his eyes away from her waist, but they focused on her breasts—full, round, and unfettered beneath the soft cotton.

"Gray?"

He swallowed hard. "Hmm?"

"Did you sleep with Sally?"

"No." He looked into her eyes. They were swimming with something he couldn't interpret. "We said we wouldn't, because of the baby thing."

"Did you want to?"

What the hell kind of question was that? He didn't like the direction of this conversation. So he said, "Guys always want to, babe."

"Oh."

"Look, I'm gonna go get the first aid stuff. Keep your arm up." He fled to his bathroom.

By the time he'd doctored her hand, it was too late to eat. They headed for their respective showers, and he dressed distractedly. He was downstairs fast and waiting in her kitchen again. Sipping more coffee, he glanced at the clock, then crossed to the bottom of her steps. "Jenn," he called out, "Get a move on. It's late."

No answer. Then he heard her swearing.

"Jenny?"

"I'm coming." More swearing.

He took the stairs two at a time. When he reached her open bedroom door, he stopped in his tracks. Her back to him, she was in front of her dresser. She wore the navy uniform pants and boots. But she was naked from the waist up. Well, almost naked. She had a bra on. Well, almost on. Her hands were around her back, trying to fasten it. She swore again.

"What's the matter?"

She clutched the front of the bra. "I, um, fuck, I can't clasp the bra. My thumb's sore, and the hooks hit right on the cut."

"Oh."

She sighed. "I'd wear a sports bra, but they're all in the wash."

"Want some help?"

"I guess."

He crossed to her. As soon as his hands went to her bare skin, as soon as they lifted to grab the ends of her bra, he felt his body tighten. She had a beautiful back, with a mole right below where her hair fell, which now swirled out around her shoulders. He had the urge to kiss the mole, sweep her hair back and put his lips on her neck.

Christ, she'd probably slug him.

He clasped the bra quickly. "All done."

"That was easy. Years of practice, I guess."

"Nah, I'm better at taking them off."

Those beautiful shoulders slumped. "I'll bet."

His hands went to her arms and he rubbed up and down. "What's wrong, Jenn?"

"Nothing, I'm just grumpy because this cut's going to be a pain in the ass for a while."

They stayed where they were, the atmosphere charged like a fire about to erupt. Then she said, "Hand me my shirt; I've got to get dressed."

He stepped back and picked up the navy T-shirt. "I'll wait downstairs."

NINE

ON HER WAY to the academy gym for a game of pickup basketball, Megan passed MediaBlitz. Located on Main Street, it was a surprisingly large media store that carried everything from current popular music to guitars, videos, and even some sheet music. She'd browsed around it often in the six weeks she'd been in Hidden Cove. Swerving over to the curb, she left her truck and, amidst the heavy downpour of October rain, hurried inside. Soft strains of music were everywhere—booths set up for listening off to the side of the store were soundproof, but hints of the tunes came through. At ten on Saturday morning, in a deluge worthy of Noah's ark, it wasn't yet crowded.

Megan zeroed in on the folk rock section.

Emm Gryner's nice, too . . . she came to our house . . . it was fun. . . .

Don't think about it, she told herself. *Don't think about Mitch and the trip to Bright Horizon Camp last week.*

Good at blocking like any cop worthy of her star, Megan reached the back of the store, successfully keeping her mind blank. A woman with a mission, she was plowing through the CDs when she heard, "Detective Hale?"

Pivoting, she found Bobby Malvaso behind her. She

hid a grin—he was so different from his dad with his shaved head, earring and tattoo on his forearm. "Hello, Bobby."

The boy held out his hand. "Nice to see you again." He gave her a shy grin. "Under better circumstances." Maybe he and his dad weren't so different.

"Yeah." She nodded to the music. "What are you looking for?" she asked.

"Looking for? Oh . . ." He shook his head. "I work here."

"I see." He was just sixteen. "Not too much, I hope."

"Nah, Dad said Saturdays only." He rolled his eyes. "My mother wanted me to work with Malvaso Painting because it pays better, but Dad won for a change."

"Your dad told me you like the indie artists."

"Emm Gryner rocks."

"I agree."

His dark eyes widened. "You know her music?"

"Got a whole collection of Gryner, DiFranco, and Williams."

"No shit?" He actually reddened. "Sorry. Dar Williams has a new CD out."

"Really?" She nodded to the stacks. "Help me find it."

When he came close, she noticed he was taller than she, though slightly built. Not like Mitch's substantial frame and world-class muscles.

Which had pressed against her, all night long, just a few days ago.

Don't think about it.

"Detective Hale?"

"Yeah?"

"You spaced out."

"Sorry." *I was thinking how good your father felt in bed.* Damn it. She took the CD from him. "I've heard a couple of these songs."

"*Mortal City*'s the best."

"Yeah?"

"Wanna hear it?"

She had time before the game, which started at eleven. "I would." He led her to a booth and opened the door.

Inside, he shoved the CD into the slot and put on his favorite tune. It filled the small booth.

"I love her voice. Some people don't because it's high, but I think it's cool."

Megan nodded. "I like her words."

"Yeah. You know *The Christians and the Pagans*?"

"Uh-huh, it's one of my favorites. Music can preach tolerance better than churches sometimes."

He grinned. Megan grinned. And they listened to three more songs.

She bought that Williams CD and an old Ani DiFranco she didn't own. Bobby promised to let her know when the new Emm Gryner disc came in.

Polite—again like his dad—he walked her to the door and pulled it open. "This was fun, Detective."

She held out her hand and shook his. "Yeah, Bobby, it was. A lot of fun. Maybe we can do it again."

"That'd be mad-cool."

She hesitated, wondering if she should . . . oh, hell. "I know you're a musician. I'd like to hear you play some time."

He rolled his eyes. "My mother says it's just godawful noise."

"That's not what your dad says."

"Now my dad has taste."

She winked at him. "And a neat son." When he blushed again, she said, "See ya," and stepped outside.

On the way to the gym, Megan thought about the boy who obviously adored his dad and seemed estranged from his mother. Megan recalled the night she brought him into the station. Cynthia Malvaso didn't even wait to see her son. She'd swept out of the holding room like a queen leaving the ghetto and it was up to Mitch to deal with the situation. She'd also looked at Megan as if she'd just crawled out from under a rock, while the lovely Mrs. Malvaso dressed as chic as a *Vogue* model.

Not your business.

But she wondered . . .

I miss that, too . . . his mother's real good at denial . . . Dad won for a change. . . .

Megan drove through a big puddle and it splashed water onto the windshield. The car skidded on the wet pavement.

Don't think about it. Just drive, she told herself. Squinting through the rain, she headed for the gym.

When she reached the academy on the outskirts of town, she parked and hurried inside; no one had arrived yet. Glad for the solitude, she didn't bother removing her sweats and headed right for the cage of balls set out for them to use. The gym was fairly new, having been built for the combination police/fire academy institution that trained personnel from Hidden Cove and surrounding areas. A shared facility, it was evidence of the departments' emphasis on physical fitness. On weekends and nights, the place was open to all cops and firefighters. Megan had seen the Saturday morning pickup games advertised but hadn't played yet. Today, when she got up and it was raining, she decided to come and join the fun. She hoped others showed up.

For several minutes, she ran up and down the court, dribbling the ball, then began to shoot.

Look at the three pointer, her father had proudly said when he'd watched her play in college. *That's my girl.*

God, she didn't want to think about her dad. Remembering brought on the excruciating pain she'd experienced on the trip to Bright Horizon.

Well, not all of it was painful. She could still feel Mitch's arms around her the next morning. Still feel him pressed against her. She'd blocked the memory for days, but today, alone in the cavernous gym, she couldn't stop the images.

Bouncing the ball on the floor, she muttered, "Okay, so I admit it."

She was attracted to him. Big deal.

Thud, thud. Another shot, which she missed.

Was he attracted to her? He'd been aroused; she'd felt him hard against her.

Normal reaction in the morning, she told herself as she went in for a quick and dirty layup. *He's a man, for God's sake.*

But it had felt so good. To be cocooned by him, to experience the rush of excitement that had been missing from her life for so long and made her feel alive after years of emotional coasting.

"Arrgh . . ." She ran to the other end of the court, made a layup, ran back, made another. Sweat beaded on her forehead and dampened her shirt.

The activity didn't banish the images. Breathless after several laps, she went to the foul-shot line. She'd have to concentrate here. On her toes, she sent the ball spinning, and missed by a mile.

Fuck it, this whole thing was awful.

Because Mitch Malvaso was a married man.

She sucked in a breath. And deflated. Abandoning her warm-up, she crossed to the side of the gym, leaned against the bleachers and slid to the floor. She remembered what had happened to *her* marriage like it was yesterday.

Lance had stood in the doorway to their bedroom, looking so handsome with his curly brown hair and snapping eyes. That day, though, those eyes were sad. *Meggie, I gotta tell you something. . . .*

She'd been ambushed. Never suspected a thing. *Okay. Promise me you'll hear me out.*

Why wouldn't I?

Promise me.

I'll hear you out.

I've been . . . I didn't mean to . . . Oh, hell, I slept with somebody else. . . .

The room had actually dimmed. She remembered the odd sensation, the disorientation, the shock. She could still feel the gut-wrenching pain that shot through her then, an emotional bullet released by her husband's infidelity.

How many times? she'd asked Lance.

A half dozen maybe.

Oh God, she remembered thinking. *It hadn't even been just once when he was drunk, or mad at her. . . .*

She'd put her head down in her hands. Deep, angry sobs had erupted from her; they wouldn't stop. She'd loved him so much. Thought he loved her the same way. . . .

Now, seated on the gym floor, she put her head down again, the weight of his unfaithfulness like a leaden vest on her chest. Eyes closed, she drew in a deep breath. After all that pain, here she was on the other end, attracted—a lot—to a married man.

"Megan? Is that you?"

Her heart clenched at the familiar voice. She opened her eyes to see players had arrived. Mitch was making his way to her. Shit. She pounded the ball with her fist. Son of a bitch. He was dressed in navy gym shorts and an HCFD navy T-shirt. His bare legs were corded with muscles. His chest—she remembered every detail of it—strained the cotton material. In high-tops and white socks, he looked young and so sexy she wanted to weep like she had back then when Lance delivered the devastating news.

Reaching her, Mitch crouched down. "Are you sick again?" His voice lowered to an intimate pitch. "Do you have another headache?"

The words caused myriad sensations to flood her. Her face reddened at the thought.

"Meg?"

"No, no. I came to play basketball and nobody was here yet so I just sat down to wait."

Shadows came over them.

"Hey, Megan, hi."

Peering behind Mitch, she saw Jenn and Zach Malvaso and Grady O'Connor. "Hi, Jenn." Megan greeted the others as she stood, forcing Mitch to do the same. "You here to play?"

Always the leader, Mitch answered. "Yeah, we had a painting job scheduled and got rained out, so we could come."

"Oh, that's great." More people were arriving. "Looks like some of my guys are here."

They turned to see several cops enter. One of them called out, "Hey, Hale, what're you doin' with the enemy? Get over here."

She was puzzled.

"Cops against smoke eaters," Jenn explained. "Sorry, Megan."

"Sorry? Why?"

" 'Cause we're gonna whip your ass, girl."

"Don't bet on it." She circled around them and hustled over to her group. God, she had to get away from Mitch.

Jesus, how had this happened?

AS HE WARMED up running laps around the perimeter of the gym, Mitch was in a sour mood. He'd been a bear on the way over, given Cynthia's tirade this morning. More often now, she reverted to her old ways and today was one of those times, though thank God she hadn't lost it completely.

Like a kid sneaking away from his parents—he despised the comparison—he'd tried getting out of the house before she woke up. She'd come downstairs just after he'd had breakfast with Bobby and was about to leave.

"Where are you going?" she'd asked. "It's raining out."

"To play basketball at the academy."

She came into the room just as Bobby got up from the table. " 'Morning," the kid mumbled. And headed out.

"Wait a second." She snagged Bobby's arm. "I want the garage cleaned out today."

Bobby said, "So clean it."

"Watch it, young man," Cynthia told him. "You won't be going anywhere."

"Cynthia, he has to work at the store."

"At that ridiculous, low-paying job?"

"He likes it."

Bobby's color had risen. "Don't talk about me as if I'm not here."

He and his son had had a great morning until then, watching the birds flit and flurry out the window. "Go on, Bobby. I'll talk to your mother."

His mother had folded her arms over her chest after Bobby left. "You undermine my authority with him. My parents think so, too."

"Jesus, Cindy, it isn't about who wins. It's about getting along."

"I want the garage cleaned."

"Fine, Bobby and I'll do it when he gets out of work this afternoon."

"I don't want you going off to play with the boys."

"Why?"

"Because you're never here."

"That's a bit of an exaggeration."

"Last week, you went up to Keuka Lake for this camp thing—your latest excuse to spend as little time as possible at home. You didn't come back till the next morning."

He glanced at his watch. "I gotta go."

She'd grabbed his arm. "Mitch, how are we going to work on this relationship if you're not here?"

Exasperated, he'd said, "We've been working on it, Cindy, and it's gone nowhere."

"Because you're not trying."

"I am." But he'd known, as he faced her in the kitchen, he didn't want to try anymore. They were both kidding themselves.

"Well, try harder. Your kids need their father at home."

Bingo. She hit his Achilles' heel. And she knew it. Briefly, he wondered if she was intentionally trying to keep him home by using the kids as hostages. God, what a thought.

"All right, I'll try harder." He'd watched her, the woman he once loved so much he couldn't think straight. "You, too."

"Meaning?"

"You've got to be nicer to Bobby."

"Maybe if you were nicer to me."

"Meaning?" he parroted.

"You and I haven't had sex in weeks."

Christ, she couldn't be saying what it sounded like. If he'd hop in the sack more willingly, she'd what, be nicer to her own son? If she'd meant to bribe him, it had backfired. He'd been so disgusted, he'd stalked out.

Mitch finished his warm-up laps and trekked to the

middle of the court. He'd purposely kept his gaze down, so he didn't look at the other players. At Megan. But she was in sight range now, and when he took a good long look at her, he almost swallowed his tongue.

Her clothes certainly weren't siren material. She wore only shiny black shorts and a white HCPD T-shirt. But what they revealed could tempt *him* to throw himself off the cliffs like Odysseus's men. Lean legs, muscled arms, and curves to die for. He'd only seen her in suits, and of course his T-shirt twice, but they'd both been baggy on her. He remembered vividly what she looked like when she'd come out of the bathroom that morning.

Her attractiveness hadn't escaped the attention of her colleagues—one sergeant in particular, Rick Ruscio, who everybody compared to Bosco, the *Third Watch* character. He was a lot like the hotheaded, bigoted cop. He said, "Hey, you sure do fill out those shorts, Detective."

Jenn came up to her. "Ignore him, Megan. He's so stupid he doesn't know you could fire him for that remark."

Ruscio mumbled for Jenn to fuck off, Grady yanked on his shirt and told him to shut up, and Megan tossed her head in his direction. "I don't need help with Ruscio. Showing him up on the court will be enough."

The players circled around the two people, one from each team, who would jump for the ball when it was tossed between them. There were five players for the police and only four for the firefighters. Mitch, as always, was point guard, meaning he'd direct the team.

"What position do you play, Hale?" one of the guys asked.

"Guard."

"Ever play point?"

"Once or twice. I can handle it."

Mitch wondered if she could. She didn't know he, his sister and brother, and Grady had played together since they were little. They could really burn up the court.

"Give her a shot," Ruscio said. "I wanna see what she's got."

Just then Will Rossettie hurried in. "Sorry I'm late."

"Our ref finally arrives." This from Mitch.

Will hustled to the center of the court, looking fit and younger than his fifty-two years. "Meggie? You finally made it to one of these."

"Uh-huh." Her grin was the Cheshire cat's.

Will whispered in her ear. Mitch exchanged a quick look with his team. Something was going on here.

Sliding in between Grady and Ruscio, Will blew his whistle and tossed a ball up in the air. Grady leaped up and easily tipped the ball to Jenn, who threw it to Zach, who dribbled to the end of the court where his brother was waiting. Mitch sunk an easy layup.

Megan hustled down. A beat cop took the ball out and threw it to her. As Mitch passed her heading down the court, she said, "Nice play, Captain."

He couldn't resist teasing her. "Show your stuff, Meggie."

She did. At first she dribbled nice and easy to half-court. When she reached their end, she tossed the ball to one of the forwards on the left. As they were playing zone defense, Mitch watched from under the basket; she zipped with the speed of light to the top of the key, caught the pass, pivoted, and sank an outside shot, before any of his guys could cover her.

"Nice shot," he yelled around cupped hands.

She gave him a half grin and hustled to the other end of the court. Mitch took the ball down. He went fast and dribbled to the left where Grady waited. From practically the sidelines, Grady took a three pointer and it swished right through the net.

"Shit," one of the cops yelled.

Megan dribbled to the end of the court again, but this time they were ready for her. Jenny, a little taller, was all over her. Megan managed to pass off the ball off, but her teammate missed.

Zach intercepted it and made a fast break to his end and scored.

Fire lit Megan's eyes. Mitch had to bite his lip to keep from smiling. God, she was cute—sweaty, mischievous, youthful. She dribbled the ball down the court then, fast as summer lightning, cut inside, and was headed right for the basket. Mitch blocked her way. Without slowing down, she ducked to his left, circled around him, and scored.

Hmmm.

Again Mitch controlled the ball all the way down the court. He was waiting for Jenn to set up, and checking out Zach's position, when a streak of black and white came out of nowhere . . . and stole the ball! Right away from him! Megan made the breakaway, easily scoring again for her team.

Mitch made a T with his hands. "Time."

"Chicken," she mumbled as she passed him.

He chuckled. "Just bein' smart. Didn't know we had a ringer."

In the huddle, Mitch suggested they switch to a man-to-man defense and double-team Megan. "Jenny, you take her with Grady."

Jenn said, "You and Zach should do it. You're faster. And she's like the wind."

Over the next hour, they held her to twelve points and the score was tied when Rossettie called one more minute of play. Megan was dribbling down the court like an NBA pro. Mitch saw the glint in her eye. Instead of staying back, he ran up to her. Arms out in classic blocking position, he moved in close and edged her with his side. She edged back, pounding the floor with the ball, pushing them both down the court. He kept zigzagging with her, trying to hold her back, but she circled around him, or ducked to the side, or simply bulldozed through. Still she couldn't get off a pass or a shot.

Near the basket, she tried to dribble around him. He skidded backward and stopped; she managed to get by him, but he pivoted, planting his feet firmly in front of her. He was about a half a foot taller than her, and had at least fifty pounds on her. She had to stop.

She didn't. Instead, expecting him to move, or not seeing his quick maneuver, she plowed right into him and went down, hitting the floor with a thud, landing flat out on her back.

"Oh, fuck." Mitch flew to her. He reached her just as Grady did. She was moving and her eyes were open.

All business now, Grady leaned over her. "You okay, Hale?"

"Yeah, I—" she tried to get up.

He held her down. "No, don't move. Let me check you out." Grabbing her wrist, he took her pulse. Asked her a few questions. Checked her eyes. All the while, Mitch's heart beat like a drum.

"I'm okay, O'Connor. I just got the wind knocked out of me."

Finally Grady nodded. "You seem fine." He stood and held out a hand.

Taking it, Megan sprang to her feet and looked to Rossettie. "Foul, right?"

"Yep."

Still reeling from worry, Mitch didn't say anything.

Zach protested. "She charged."

"I think it was an illegal block." Will raised his eyes innocently. "Two shots. You make one, the good guys win."

"I will," she said, sashaying to the line.

Mitch stood, shaking his head. He tried, unsuccessfully, to reconcile the tough cookie before him with the woman he'd held all night long because she didn't want to be alone and in pain.

Megan poised on the line, fitted the ball to her hands, went up on tiptoes, and sunk the shot without even hitting the backboard or the rim. She scored with one graceful swish of the net.

Ruscio charged her and scooped her up. "I take back every bad thing I ever said about you, Hale. You're the best."

And that, Mitch thought as he walked off the court, was beginning to be a huge problem for him.

AS MEGAN PULLED open the door to Badges, she wondered if Mitch would be here. She hadn't meant to eavesdrop, she really hadn't, but when somebody had suggested they all come here for lunch after the game, and the rest had jumped at the chance, Mitch had begged off. Megan had been stretching behind a stack of mats at the end of the bleachers where they couldn't see her when Mitch's brother and sister approached him.

"Come on, Mitch, go with us," Zach had coaxed. "You never do anything for yourself."

"I came here this morning," he said, and under his breath added, "at great cost."

Jenn had sounded angry. "You deserve a little fun. It's pouring rain, and you got nothing else to do."

Mitch sighed wearily. "I promised Cynthia I'd come home and clean the garage."

His sister snorted. "She's a bitch."

"Jenny, don't." His tone was weary.

Megan could tell this wasn't a new argument. She felt bad listening in, but she couldn't leave without being noticed and she didn't want to embarrass Mitch.

"Doesn't she want you to have any downtime?" Jenn sounded like a little girl.

"You guys go."

It was quiet, then Zach suggested, "How about we have a quick lunch and I'll come back to the house and help out? We'll get the garage cleaned in half the time."

Mitch didn't answer right away, then he said, "What the hell? I'll call and tell her."

Jenn swore. "Don't, she'll talk you out of it."

"I'll come, honey, I promise."

Megan had waited till they left then headed for the locker room. It bothered her, more than it should, to think of Mitch in an unhappy situation.

She saw him seated at a large table when she walked through the door of Badges and crossed to the dining area. Maybe his life wasn't so bad, after all, if indeed he came. Maybe his wife had been understanding.

God, he looked good. He'd changed into jeans and a thermal shirt the color of cherries. His dark-as-midnight hair was combed back and damp from his shower, accenting his strong Italian features.

"Hey, it's the ringer," he called out when he noticed

her. "Come on, hotshot, I'll buy you a beer."

She grinned and took a seat opposite him. His smile was warm, and his gaze friendly. She noticed that for a second, it dropped down to the navy cotton sweater she wore, then he snagged the waitress. "What'll ya have?"

"A Corona." She plopped down and opened the menu. "I need red meat."

Grady, next to her, smiled. "After that performance, you can afford the cholesterol." He lifted his own beer in salute. "Where'd you play?"

"In college."

"Where?" Jenn asked, leaning over so she could talk around Grady.

"John Jay. I went when I decided to be a cop. My dad insisted."

"Your dad a cop?" one of the uniforms asked.

"He was." She caught Mitch's sympathetic gaze. "He died in the line."

The young rookie blushed. "Geez, Megan, I'm sorry, I forgot. It's why you're so hot about the camp."

"How's that going?" Ruscio asked.

As Megan talked about their trip, she was hard-pressed not to think of the intimacies she and Mitch had shared. When someone asked him a question, and he answered, his voice was gruff. She wondered if it got like that during sex.

After they ordered, one of the cops lazed back in his chair and said, "Somebody finish telling the story about Malvaso."

"Nah, let's drop it." This from Zach.

"Did I interrupt something?" Megan asked.

"No, we're telling stories again." Mitch looked at her. She remembered he'd told her about their habit of doing that.

"Sorry I stopped it."

Mitch's eyes twinkled. She liked seeing this side of him—younger, less world-weary, teasing. "This was one of 'my brother's a hero' stories."

"Oh, yeah," Zach said, "I got my ass chewed out was what happened."

Megan smiled at the byplay. "What'd you do?"

Mitch shook his head. "We were called to the cove. Zach was subbing on Engine 3, which covers part of the lakefront. It was one of those freezing November days. A little boy and his sister were on a dock with a black lab. The dog knocked the little boy into the lake. When we got there, we saw his red coat, bobbing in the water. He was too far to reach with poles and a rope wouldn't do any good at that point. The cap sent somebody back to the rig for the blow-up boat." Mitch looked at Zach.

"Hell, they were never gonna make it in time." Zach shook his head. "So I jumped in."

"After the officer specifically told him not to," Grady added.

"I used to be a lifeguard, for Christ's sake."

Mitch continued the story. "Yep, he whipped off his turnout coat, kicked off his boots, and dropped his drawers before anybody could stop him."

"Did you get the kid?"

"Uh-huh."

"Did he live?"

"Yeah." Zach's dark eyes shadowed. He was really good-looking, though she found Mitch more attractive. "But he was brain damaged."

Mitch smiled sadly. "Not extensively, though. He can function. His parents are thrilled he's alive."

"Zach still visits him," Jenny said.

"You do?"

"Yeah. He lives down by the cove. When I'm that way, I stop in."

"The family thinks Zach walks on water."

"The cap didn't. He put a reprimand in my file and I was on piss-poor duty for a month. Inspections, cleaning toilets."

Jenn socked her brother's arm. "He also got an award from the city."

They all laughed.

Megan was warmed by the story and by the camaraderie among them all. She wanted to be part of it.

When the waitress came and said their lunch was taking longer than expected, Jenn asked, "Anybody want to play pool?"

"I do." Megan needed to get away from the table for a minute. Grady reached out and touched Jenn's arm. There was that easiness between them again, that tangible closeness. "Be careful, babe. I'll bet she's a shark."

Jenn kissed him on the nose. "I can hold my own. I beat you, all the time. Holler when the food comes."

She and Megan headed for the table. Jenn won the toss to break, and took the first shot. "Seven in the corner." She sank the ball easily. Chalking her stick, she said, "Glad you came with us."

"Me, too. You do this often?"

"Yeah. Mitch doesn't come much, though."

Careful. "He seems busy."

"He's too nice a guy." Jenn nodded to the balls. "Six in far left." Again she made the shot.

Megan caught a glimpse of Mitch, gesturing, laughing, probably telling another story. "Everybody loves Mitch, don't they?"

"Yeah. I just wish . . ." She shook her head. "Never mind."

But Megan knew what his sister was going to say. Again, it tugged on her heart. Finally, Jenn missed and Megan picked up her cue. She settled into the game and tried not to think about her opponent's brother.

When the food arrived, they went back to the table. Mitch's eyes were alight with good humor and just plain fun.

Jenn dropped down and stole a french fry from Grady's plate. "She killed me."

"Told you," Grady said.

"Who taught you to play pool?" Mitch asked.

"My husband."

Ruscio choked on his beer. "I didn't know you were married."

"Widowed. A cop. He died on duty, too."

Grady reached over and squeezed her arm. She noticed Jenn's eyes focus on the gesture. "You've had a lot of loss."

She just nodded and looked to Mitch.

"Yeah, she has." He shook his head briefly at Grady. "So, Gray, I heard you picked up the new car." Jenn had told Megan she and Grady were car buffs.

Grateful for the reprieve, Megan ate her mile-high beef on kimmelwick. When she finished, she left the table to go to the ladies' room. Pushing open the heavy door, she was thinking about Mitch. Inside, she found a young girl standing before the mirror. Crying. Rain-drenched from head to toe, tears streamed down her face. When she saw Megan, she swiped at her cheeks.

"Are you all right?" Megan asked.

Unnaturally red hair dripped out fat drops of water when she nodded. Megan saw then she had an eyebrow ring, which always made her cringe, it looked so painful.

"You don't look all right."

The girl just stared at Megan in the mirror.

Edging onto the corner of the vanity—informality worked best with kids—Megan cocked her head. "This place is a bar, even though it serves food. Is there a reason you're here alone?"

"I . . . I walked over to find my father."

"You walked here in this downpour?"

"Uh-huh."

Suddenly Megan had a thought that made her stomach queasy. "Who's your dad, honey?"

At the endearment, the girl's eyes teared again. "Mitch Malvaso."

Damn it.

Megan noticed Mitch's daughter was shivering. Quickly, she reached over and grabbed some paper towels. "Here, dry off as best you can, then I'll take you to your dad."

The girl accepted the paper towels and wiped her face and hair. Her thin sweater was soaking wet. "I don't want to . . . will you get him? I'll embarrass him if I come in there when he's with his buddies."

"I can't believe he'd care about that. Trish, right?"

"Yeah, sure, he wouldn't care, like, under *normal* circumstances but . . ."

"Are you in trouble?"

"No, he is. My mother's gone ballistic . . . she—"

Abruptly, Megan stood. She didn't want Trish to go any further. "I'll go get your dad."

"Okay."

"Wait right here." She squeezed Trish's arm as she left.

Megan quickly made her way to the table. As unobtrusively as she could, she got Mitch's attention. "Could I see you a minute?"

His dark brows arched and he rose. Setting down his napkin, he stood and circled the table.

Megan snagged her jacket from the back of her chair, then drew Mitch off to the side.

"What's going on?"

"Your daughter's here. I found her in the ladies' room, soaking wet and crying."

"What?"

"She asked me to come get you."

"Is she hurt?"

"No, no. She's . . . apparently your wife's upset. . . ."

His face crumbled. "Oh, no."

Heading through the bar, they reached the ladies' room. Mitch yanked open the door and hurried inside. As soon as Trish saw him, she hurled herself into his arms. "Oh, Daddy."

He held on tight. "Shh, it's okay. Tell me what's going on."

Trish sobbed into his chest.

Megan coughed. "Look, I'll leave you two alone." She set her coat on the vanity. "She's wet to the bone, Mitch. Put this on her."

Just as Megan was leaving, she heard, "Daddy, Mom's freaking, I didn't know what to do."

"It's not your fault, baby, it's . . ."

Closing the door, Megan didn't hear the rest. But she didn't have to. She knew Mitch was already blaming himself.

*   *   *

INSIDE THE CHEROKEE, with the heat blasting, Mitch reached over and took his daughter's hand. She hadn't said anything since they left the bar. "Trish, I'm so sorry."

"Why does she get like this, Daddy?"

"She hasn't thrown one of these tantrums in a while." Since the Sinco fire, which she said changed her. "It's my fault."

His daughter leveled a very adult, very disgusted gaze on him. "It's not. Big fucking deal, you had lunch with your friends."

"Don't use that word, Trish. I told her I'd come home. In any case, it's not your problem."

"I hate this."

"I know, baby."

Mitch kept his emotions contained for the five-minute drive to his house, but he felt like a volcano about to erupt. Bundled in Megan's coat—shit, she had to witness this scene—Trish was silent, too.

When he pulled in the driveway, he saw immediately why his daughter was upset. The garage door was up, and outside on the lawn, with rain drenching everything, were the contents of the garage: tools, brooms, paint cans, several drop cloths, bikes, and dozens of other things. They were getting soaked, and cardboard boxes were already soggy.

Looked like Cynthia had cleaned out the garage herself.

She was still inside; he could hear her banging things around.

"Do me a favor, honey?"

"Uh-huh."

"Go in through the front door and upstairs. Now. I want to deal with this alone."

"Okay." She opened the car door. "Daddy?"

He was just staring at the ménage before him. "Hmm?"

"Bobby will be home from work soon. He'll wild out if he . . ."

"I know. I'll take care of this before he sees it."

Kissing him on the cheek, Trish left and Mitch

bounded out of the car. Damn it, how dare she do this to his children? No wonder they acted out.

You should have gone home.

He strode into the garage.

And sucked in a breath.

The place was almost empty. Stuff had been tossed out the back door, too. But what dumbfounded him was that Cindy was attacking his workbench with a sledgehammer. Big dents marred the surface of the carefully crafted bench.

It had been his father's, one Angelo Malvaso had lovingly made and Mitch had sentimentally kept. It was also one the few things Mitch had left of his dad's. Cynthia knew all that.

He quelled his temper—and the sinking pain in his chest. He'd deal with that later. Calmly, he walked over and grabbed the sledgehammer mid-swing, easily wresting it from his wife.

She turned. Her eyes were wild, her hair askew. And there were tear tracks on her face.

"What's going on, Cynthia?"

"I'm cleaning the garage."

"I told you Zach would help Bobby and me do it this afternoon."

"Now you don't have to."

"If you're trying to make a point, you have."

"Not yet." She crossed to a shelf that held his painting supplies—brushes, rollers, turpentine. In one swift move, she swept her arm across the shelf so everything clattered and clanged to the floor. A can popped open, spreading thick black paint on the cement. She went for the other shelf, but he grabbed her wrist before she could do more damage. When she tried to pull away, he encircled her chest with his other hand. "Stop this right now."

"You son of a bitch!"

"Cindy, I only had lunch with the guys."

"You said you'd come back." She struggled against him.

"I'm sorry you're upset."

"No, you're not."

"Come on, let's go inside and talk about this."

"No." She started kicking backward, caught him in the shin.

"Jesus." He lifted her then. Dragging her inside, though she still kept kicking, he tried to calm her. "Stop it now."

She only struggled more.

Somehow he managed to get her upstairs and into their room, where he threw her on the bed. "What the fuck is *wrong* with you? You've lost it completely."

"I'm angry." She buried her face in the pillows. "I hate when you ignore me. My mother says I'm crazy to put up with it."

He didn't deny the charge. But, trying to achieve some kind of peace, he repeated, "Look, I'm sorry you're upset."

"When you get with that goddamned fire department, you forget all about us."

Us, as in kids. "I never forget about the kids."

"Oh, just me, then."

He watched her. Very quietly, he said, "Take a glance in the mirror, Cindy, and see if you can figure out why I don't want to be here. You look like a child who's just had a temper tantrum." He crossed to the door. "Stay here. Get yourself together. I mean it. Don't come downstairs until you've got a grip."

He opened the door, but she was behind him and slapped it shut with her hand. "Don't go," she said silkily, sidling her body up to his.

Oh, God.

"Stay. Here. With me. Let's make up in bed. Like we used to."

He felt his stomach pitch.

Slowly, he turned around.

She was already opening her blouse.

He stared at her hands, but instead of seeing her well-manicured fingernails undoing buttons, he saw Trish, clasping on to Megan's coat, her nails bitten to the bone, her hair plastered to her head. Instead of hearing Cindy's pleas, he heard Bobby ask, *Why do you put up with this, Dad?*

"No, Cindy," he snapped angrily. "I'm not going to bed with you. Not unless things change between us. It only confuses the situation between us, and truthfully, I don't even want to anymore." There, he'd said it aloud, instead of just avoiding the issue, spurred on by thoughts of what she'd done to his kids today. "Now, I'm going to right things in the garage. Then I'm taking my traumatized daughter, and her brother, who will feel like shit if he see what you've done, out to get something to eat." He opened the door, but turned to face her. "Don't even think about trashing this room, or anything else in the house. I'm only going to put up with so much."

He slammed the door on the way out.

TEN

LIKE MINNESOTA FATS, Jenn chalked her cue and studied the break she'd just made on the pool table. "I can't believe she beat me."

Grady leaned against the wall of Badges and enjoyed the rare occurrence of Jenny Malvaso stumped by another woman. For as long as he'd known her, she could run athletic rings around every female in the department or elsewhere.

"She killed you at basketball, too," he said, purposefully adding fuel to the fire.

It didn't singe her. "She killed you, too. And Mitch. Nobody's given him competition since he sank the winning shot the last game his senior year in high school." Jenn called the pocket, bent over, and lined up the cue. She looked cute today in loose-fitting jeans and one of his sweatshirts.

She sank five shots before she missed.

"Pretty good there, babe," he said, readying his own cue, eyeing the table.

As she passed him to pick up her beer, she slapped his fanny. It felt good. He scowled. Anytime she touched him lately, it felt good. Too good.

Leaning over, he drew back his cue, and just as he thrust it forward, she said softly, "I got my period a few days ago."

The ball went two feet off its mark.

Grady straightened. "Dirty trick," he said, yet he couldn't help but smile.

Sitting on a stool, Jenn's dark eyes danced. She was relaxed but there was something about her expression—more than mischief—that made him drop the cue and cross to her. Her face full of emotion, she peered up at him. Her skin was so pretty and utterly flawless.

He ran his knuckles down her cheek. "You did, huh?"

She held his gaze. "Yep. Right on schedule. So, about two weeks, I guess?" He didn't say anything. "Till B-day," she added uncertainly.

He wanted to kiss her. Right there at Badges, he wanted to cover that sexy mouth of hers and kiss her. Tenderly. Passionately.

"Gray?" She reached out and grasped his arm. "What is it?"

"Nothing, I—"

He was saved from explaining his uncharacteristic response by a commotion in the corner. "Give me another goddamned drink," someone yelled.

Manny shook his head. "No way, Ace. You're cut off."

"It's only three o'clock in the goddamned afternoon."

"You got here when we opened."

Jenn shook her head. "Who is it?"

"I don't know."

"Think Manny needs help?"

Grady's gaze strayed to the front of the bar just as the door opened. In stalked a woman—Casey Brennan, the female firefighter on Engine 17 that nobody particularly liked. She strode up to the bar owner and patron.

"I'll handle this, Manny. Thanks for calling me."

"What the fuck? Why'd you call my little girl?"

Grady looked away. "We shouldn't be eavesdropping." They both turned back to the pool table. But since it was the middle of a Saturday afternoon, and the place was all

but empty, angry words filled the air like smoke, insinu-
ating everywhere.

"Come on, Dad, I'll take you home."

"Don't wanna go home."

"Well, you can't stay here all day."

"Why the hell not?"

Casey sat down. "Dad, please. Don't make a scene."

Grady pretended interest in the play, but his heart
wasn't in it. Poor Brennan. She was probably embarrassed. Jenn cooperated, too, but as the minutes wore on,
the argument got louder—from the father's side. Brennan's voice stayed low and soothing.

Finally, the old man barked, "Shit, I'll go just to shut
you up."

Grady caught the startle reflex from Brennan. She re-
coiled as if she'd been hit.

The man struggled to his feet. He steadied himself on
the table, and Casey got up to grasp his arm. She was a
big girl, but her father was bigger in height and bulk.
When she put his arm around her, she staggered back into
the chair.

Grady dropped the cue and crossed to them. Without
saying anything, he looped the man's other arm around
his own neck. The guy mumbled something, but too much
alcohol had drained the fight out of him, and he was
woozy besides. Brennan didn't say anything to Grady, just
looked at him with eyes like storm clouds. He shrugged,
and she said, "Just help me get him to the car."

It was a long trek, one she never would have been able
to make alone. On the way, "Dad" knocked over three
chairs when he weaved into a table and clipped a picture
off the wall. It fell to the floor with a glass-breaking shat-
ter.

Thankfully the rain had stopped. The three of them
made their way to a big black truck; when they reached
the passenger side, the guy tried to shrug them off. "I can
drive my own fuckin' truck."

"No, Ace, you can't." Brennan's voice was raw. She
opened the door and looked to Grady.

He nodded and helped boost her father inside. She slammed the door and faced him. "Uh, thanks." Her face red.

"No problem. Listen, Jenn and I were just leaving. I rode over with her. Why don't I follow you home with your car, and you can drop me off at my place."

"I'd never ask a stranger to do that."

He gave her a grin, one Jenn called his in-your-pants smile. "You didn't ask." He nodded to the yellow Camaro in the parking lot. "That yours?"

"Uh-huh."

"I'd like to let it rip."

She gave him what passed for a smile. "I don't know. . . ."

Her father banged on the door.

"Okay," she said fishing her keys out of her pocket.

He took them. "Hang on for a second. I gotta tell Jenny."

Grady jogged back to the bar, thinking what an enigma Brennan was.

THEIR DOG AT her side, Jenn lay in Grady's bed and tried to concentrate on the book she had spread out on her lap. "Ovulation occurs anywhere from ten to fourteen days after menstruation. Doctors suggest you use an ovulation testing kit. . . ." She tossed the book down, wondering what happened to just making love when the mood hit and coming up pregnant. Technology had made a damn science out of having a baby.

Pressing her hand into her stomach, she sighed. A baby. Grady's baby. The thought warmed her more than a 100-degree day. Would it be a boy or a girl? A ballerina or a football player? A grin spread across her face. She wanted a boy, she decided, who looked just like Grady. Mile-wide shoulders, pecs to die for, and the prettiest blue eyes the color of the Caribbean Sea. His lashes were dark blond and lush. . . .

Hell, what was she doing? This wasn't normal. It wasn't good! She knew in her bones that any kind of real sexual interest between her and her best friend would just gum up the works. She wasn't gonna let it happen.

Restless, she stretched out on her stomach and checked the clock on the wall. It was a huge, beautiful teak clock fanning out like the sun. Grady said it was like waking up to a sunrise everyday. That particular sunrise now said 5 P.M.

And the man who belonged in this room, with its bed like a lake and teak furniture he'd ordered from Sweden, was not home.

She'd been puzzled, then . . . miffed that he was taking Brennan's car home.

"Why the hell you doing that?" she'd asked in the bar when Grady had told her what he was up to.

She'd angered him. He always got those little grooves between his eyes when he was mad at her. "I'm helping out somebody we work with," he said, handing her his 'Vette's keys. "Here, drive the silver bullet back to our place."

"Yeah, sure . . ."

Bucky nosed her. "Come on up, boy." She patted the mattress, and the Dalmatian leaped eagerly onto the bed. "Where is he, do you think?"

The dog nuzzled her neck and licked her face then settled at her side. Absently, she petted him. "Stupid question. He's probably doin' her right now." Sure, he said he wouldn't screw anybody until after baby day, but Brennan was a piranha who ate men alive whenever the mood struck her. Grady wouldn't be able to resist her. Would he even try? The thought turned Jenn's stomach queasy, so she banished it and picked the book back up.

"The woman should lie flat on her back, with her knees raised for twenty minutes after copulation."

Oh, this sounded like fun.

But it would be, she knew. Grady had to be a terrific lover. Women hounded him after he slept with them and she'd bet they weren't coming back for his sweet talk. "I wonder what he kisses like?" she said to Bucky.

They'd kissed before, when they were thirteen. She told him she was worried about kissing a guy for the first time and he said he'd practice with her. The first few attempts, they'd fallen over laughing on the floor. But he did teach her. "Open your mouth a little . . . run your tongue . . ."

Where was Grady running his tongue now?

This was nuts.

She grabbed Grady's phone. Valco had asked her to a party he was having for the guys over at Engine 14. Maybe she'd call and get directions. Looked like Grady wasn't going to be home anytime soon.

She'd just jotted down the route to Valco's house when she heard a car pull into the driveway. Telling herself not to, she eased off Grady's bed and went to the window. Hmm, a snazzy yellow Camaro. Grady would love that. Cars were an interest of theirs.

One that Brennan obviously shared with him, too.

Jenn watched for a while, but Grady didn't get out.

"Shit," she said, playing with the mini blinds. "What's he doing?"

Wandering back to the bed, she flopped down and picked up the book. "It's recommended the male not ejaculate within twenty-four hours of the attempt to conceive." She grunted. "No nookie for you, buddy." She chuckled. "Not even chokin' the chicken." She glanced toward the window. He never answered her when she asked if he thought Brennan was pretty. Zach did. He'd told her that.

Of course, once, Zach would sleep with anything in a skirt so . . . she wondered if Zach ever did Brennan? She didn't like that thought much, either.

"Hi."

Jenn looked up and her heart took a tiny little lurch. Grady's face was flushed and his eyes bright. His hair was a mess.

She couldn't help herself. "Well, looks like I don't have to ask what took you so long."

He crossed to the dresser and removed the contents of his pockets, placing them on the top. "What do you mean?"

Gripping the book that told her how to let this man get

her pregnant, she shifted on the bed. "Wasn't it awkward, with the old man in the house, or did he pass out?"

"You mean Ace? He doesn't live with her." Grady drew the sweatshirt over his head. His back was to her.

"How convenient."

Bare chested, he faced her. "What's going on with you tonight, Jenny?"

She held up the book. "We're gonna do this in a couple of weeks. I don't like the idea of you fucking Brennan before that. No telling what she's picked up along the way."

Grady's face flushed a deep red. His eyes narrowed on her. "For the record, we went for a walk through her neighborhood. She talked some about her father. I talked about mine." Grady's dad had been an alcoholic. "In any case, these digs are really beneath you. She's a female in the department and instead of bashing her like the guys— not that I believe a tenth of what they say—you should be sticking up for her." He nodded to the bathroom. "Now, I'm going to take a shower. I thought we might get a pizza, but if you're gonna grill me, I don't want to be with you tonight."

Stalking into the bathroom, he slammed the door shut.

Jenn closed her eyes. Damn it, he was right. What was wrong with her? She looked down at the book. It was this baby thing. It was making her act stupid, and making her and Grady fight. They *never* fought. She had rows galore with Mitch and Zach, but she and Grady almost never exchanged a cross word.

What if this baby thing wasn't right for them to do? What if it ruined their almost perfect relationship? Grady was the most important person in the world to her. She didn't know what she'd do if she lost him.

He came out of the bathroom five minutes later. A lush blue towel wrapped around his waist and a smaller one circled his neck. His eyebrows arched when he saw her. "Still here?"

"Yeah." She glanced down at the book. "I'm sorry."

He stared at her a minute then went to the dresser. "Okay." He pulled out clothes.

"Gray?"

"Huh?"

"Can we talk a minute?"

"Sure." Pivoting he came to the bed. He sat down and absently ran a towel over his head, then down his chest. He missed a bead of water and Jenn had the absurd urge to lick it off, actually to follow it with her tongue down his breastbone. "Jenn?"

She raised her eyes to his face. He'd shaved. He had a little nick on the side of his neck. Before she could stop herself, she reached out and ran a finger over the small cut. "Hurt?"

His breathing speeded up. His eyes locked with hers. They stared at each other, then Grady bolted off the bed, grabbed his clothes, and strode to the bathroom. "I'm gonna get dressed first."

What was that all about?

A few minutes later, he came out in jeans and a navy-blue T-shirt tucked into them. He was barefoot and his hair was combed back. Instead of sitting on the bed, he took a chair several feet away from her. "So shoot."

"I, um, something's going on here, Grady. And I don't really like it."

"What?"

"Promise you won't laugh."

"I won't laugh."

She held up the book. "I think it has to do with this."

"With making a baby?"

"Uh-huh."

"W—" He cleared his throat. "What do you mean?"

Restless, she got off the bed and walked around the room. His place was spotless. She crossed to the dresser where a picture of him and her sat. It was taken two years ago on the cap's boat, and they were laughing like kids.

"I, um, I'm feeling some different stuff lately." She kept her back to him, thinking about the time he did up her bra. Nodding out the window, she said, "This thing with Brennan. It feels like jealousy."

When he didn't say anything, she turned. He was lying back in his chair, his eyes closed, his hands clasped over his middle. His features were taut, as if he was in pain.

"Gray?" Oh, God, this *was* going to hurt them. Their relationship. She flew across the room and dropped down in front of him. "I embarrassed you. I'm sorry. Forget what I said. It's stupid, probably just—"

"I ran into the bathroom because I got hard when you touched my chin."

Her jaw gaped and her gaze dropped to his fly. The snug jeans revealed an impressive bulge, but was he . . . for her? She sat back on her heels and stared up at him. "Jesus, I never expected this."

"Me, either."

Both of them were grim faced. Tentatively she reached up and placed her hand on his knee. He covered it with his own. "Gray, we . . . I'm . . . this male/female stuff doesn't work very well for us. All those bad relationships we've had."

He stared down at her. "You're afraid I'll hurt you, aren't you? Like I did everybody else."

"No! I've got two bad marriages behind me so I got no right to talk. But if I'm already a jealous shrew, and you're so self-doubting, what will . . . making love do to us?"

"I'm not sure."

"I don't want to spoil what we have."

"God, Jenny, I couldn't live without you. You're the only thing that got me through those rough times."

"I feel the same way."

She nodded to the bed. "This could ruin things." She sighed and put her head on his knees. His hand went immediately to her hair. "I could find somebody else."

"Oh, yeah, well, that makes this better." His words were harsh.

"I mean a donor. Go back to artificial insemination."

"I want this kid to be mine."

"Then you could be the donor."

"I suppose your original plan was best." He kept stroking her hair. "Maybe you should make those arrangements with the doctor instead of . . ." He didn't finish.

"All right." His touch felt so good. "You can date

Brennan, do whatever you want with her. I still won't . . . you know, until at least I see if I'm pregnant."

"Let's not discuss that right now."

"Okay."

They stayed as they were. "Hungry?" he finally asked.

She eased back and stood. "Yeah, let's go get a jumbo pizza with everything." She held out her hand. He took it and brought it to his mouth and kissed it so gently tears moistened her eyes. "It'll be okay, Jenny, I promise."

"That's good enough for me."

Standing, he drew her to him. His hug was hard and extra long. It made Jenny feel safe. In her heart, she knew they'd made the right decision to do this with science instead of their bodies, to not endanger the most important relationship in the world to them. She just wished she didn't feel so bad about it.

ELEVEN

CLASPING A MANILA envelope in his hand, Mitch hurried out of the firehouse and through the connecting door that led to headquarters. Tired, he rolled his shoulders. He'd been sleeping like shit and felt like he'd hauled hose for hours. He and Megan were meeting with the chiefs about the camp tonight, but he was not looking forward to it.

He hadn't seen her since Cynthia's blowup about the garage and he was embarrassed. *You're pathetic,* he told himself. *You're forty-three years old and you let your wife run roughshod over you.* Well, he was sick of it, which was why he'd made an appointment to see the department psychologist this week. Things couldn't go on like this.

It had nothing to do with Megan.

Did it?

Preoccupied, he didn't see his brother coming toward him until Paulie was upon him. Here was another failure. Since Sinco, Mitch had regretted their estrangement more than ever, but like a lot of things, he let it go. He felt even worse now that Zach had told him Connie and Paulie were beside themselves when he and Jenny and Zach were hurt at that fatal fire.

They met at the desk in the reception area of headquarters. It was the end of the workday and the staff had gone home, so they were alone.

"Hey, Paolo, how are you?"

His brother's light brown eyes were flinty. "Just fine, Mitello."

"What are you doing here?"

"I had a meeting with Callahan."

Mitch's brows arched. "Really, why?"

"I ran into him at the country club last week and he asked if I'd be interested in working on Project Kids-Camp."

The notion made Mitch shift from one foot to the other. "I see."

"Don't worry, I said no."

"Worry?"

"I told Noah you wouldn't want me to interfere with fire department business."

"Why'd you tell him that?"

Paulie shrugged shoulders encased in fine Italian wool. "Come on, Mitch, you never wanted me and Connie to have anything to do with that part of your life." He angled his head. "Or any other, for that matter."

"That's not true."

"Well, it's the way I see it. So does Concetta."

"But—"

Paulie glanced at his Rolex. Instead of it being an impatient gesture, it was a nervous one. "Look, we sound like kids again. Let's just keep the status quo. You three go your way, and Connie and I will go ours. At least we each have *some* family." With that Paulie pivoted and strode away.

His brother's accusations sparked Mitch's guilt. As he walked through the reception area and waited for the elevator to the fourth floor, he shook his head. He seemed to be fucking everything up. There were a lot of incidents in the past that estranged him and Paulie. How many of them were Mitch's fault? Things were especially bad five years ago when Paulie got divorced. Had he been any help at all to his brother then?

"Hello, Captain."

Turning, he saw Megan had come into headquarters and crossed the reception area. For a moment, he felt flushed by heat—similar to the sensation of walking into a burning building. She had on a dress; he'd never seen her wear one. It was simple—a black long-sleeved sheath, scooped neck, hitting just above the knee. It hugged every curve and indentation on her very . . . nice body. With it she wore dark stockings and—shit—heels. Jamming his hands in his pockets, he said, "Wow!"

She blushed.

Without thinking, he asked, "You got a date?"

She averted her eyes. "Uh-huh."

His stomach dropped to his knees. *This* was not good.

"With Will." She smiled and he noticed she was wearing raspberry-colored lipstick. "It's his birthday and I'm taking him out for dinner after the meeting."

A sense of relief flooded Mitch. Nope, this wasn't good at all.

The elevator pinged, and the door opened. They stepped inside. Oh, hell. She had perfume on. Something sexy, sinful. Suddenly he remembered what it felt like to hold her all night. He cleared his throat and leaned back against the elevator wall, grasping onto the rail.

"So, what were you scowling about?"

Mitch shook his head. "My brother Paulie was here. We're like cats and dogs, still. It's not right." Then he added, "A lot of things aren't."

Her look was knowing. She'd seen up close and personal the shambles his marriage was.

He had to bring it up. "Thanks for what you did with Trish."

"I'm sorry she was upset."

"Me, too." Suddenly, he wanted to tell her the whole story, about Cindy, about the changes in him since Sinco. But he wouldn't. He couldn't encourage a closeness he already felt for a woman other than his wife.

Thankful when the elevator opened, Mitch allowed Megan to go first. She headed out—and right into the arms of Stan Steele. "Oh," she said as he grasped onto her. She'd raised her hands, and they rested on the politician's arms.

"Steady there, beautiful." Steele's words were silky.

"Hello, Councilman," she said.

"Megan, I told you to call me Stan."

Dropping her arms, she stepped back. "Stan."

He eyed her like the big bad wolf. "You look terrific. Surely you didn't work in that lovely outfit."

"No. I'm going out." She glanced at Mitch. "We have a meeting before with the chiefs."

"Yes, I know." Steele's gaze darted to Mitch, too. "Malvaso."

"Steele." They sounded like two high school boys vying for a cheerleader's attention.

Steele's smile got even more oily. "How's your sister these days?"

"Just peachy."

"She's a great firefighter. Saved my life."

Too bad. "Jenny's something."

"Mmm. I think so, too."

"Mitch, we have to go. The chiefs said six."

"Sure." Mitch resisted the urge to move in and put his arm on her back.

Steele said good-bye, and Mitch and Megan walked down the corridor to the fire chief's office. "Stay away from him, Meg."

"Excuse me?"

"He was eating you up with his eyes."

"Me? Mitch, really, I'm not some femme fatale."

"Yeah, well look in the mirror." His voice was gruff as they reached the chief's office at the end of the corridor. "He's a snake. Don't let yourself be one of his—"

"Son of a bitch, Callahan. I won't listen to this shit." The door of the Chief's office was ajar. Everyone had gone home up here, too. And Will was yelling loudly.

"Calm down, Will. I wasn't suggestin' anything."

"Like hell."

"Fuck it, Rossettie. Face the facts. They handed in one motel bill. What am I supposed to think?"

Megan stilled. Mitch froze.

Their gazes locked.

"Megan isn't a home wrecker."

"Mitch is the most honorable man I know." This from Callahan. "Nothing like his brother."

Megan's face went ashen.

This time, Mitch did move in close and squeeze her arm. "Meg, I'm sorry."

Megan swallowed back her revulsion. And her guilt. Will Rossettie was the closest thing she had to family. And any leak that she slept around would ruin her credibility.

But she *had* spent the night with the man beside her who looked as sheepish as she must. The *married* man.

"I never thought—" he said, nodding to the door. "About one bill."

"Me, either."

"Because it was innocent."

She couldn't meet his gaze. Her thoughts lately told her she wasn't so guilt-free. And she knew by now his marriage had problems.

"Let's face this head on." He knocked on the open door.

Grumbling. Some more swearing. "Come in." Callahan's voice was weary.

Megan and Mitch entered the office. Rossettie was at the window, dressed in a suit, his back to them, and Callahan leaned on the edge of his desk. The fire chief's usually calm demeanor was gone. He batted the paper he held against his leg. His eyes were flaming.

Mitch said, "We overheard you yelling at each other."

Rossettie circled around. He focused on Megan. "I don't believe anything was amiss, Meggie. Especially after . . ."

He knew about Lance's infidelity. God, she didn't want anyone else to find out. "There *was* nothing amiss."

Noah straightened. "Sit, you two."

Megan and Mitch took chairs in front of the desk.

"Will? Join us?"

"I don't wanna sit. You got me too stirred up."

Sighing, Noah held up the paper. "This is the expense

report. One motel room." He glanced at Will. "And no room bill on the police submission."

Megan started to speak, but Mitch put out his hand to stop her. "It was my decision."

Noah's brow furrowed. "What do you mean?"

"Megan had a migraine headache. She didn't have her medicine with her, and was really out of it with pain. I realized we couldn't drive home. The small motel we pulled into didn't have adjoining rooms, so I booked one because I was afraid to leave her alone."

She looked to Will. "You know how sick I get with those."

"Yeah." He crossed the room and stood behind her. Gently, he put his hands on her shoulders and faced Noah. "I told you there was a good explanation for this."

Shifting in his chair, Noah studied them. Finally, he said, "I apologize if I jumped the gun, but I don't apologize for wantin' to keep some integrity in our departments."

"You think I don't?" Will growled.

"Will, I just don't want rumors and innuendo flyin' around. I hate that kind of thing."

"What was he supposed to do, leave her alone sick? She's a basket case when she gets those things."

"No, of course not." Noah faced Megan. "I'm sorry if I offended you."

"It's all right. I share your concern about propriety. And I don't want my reputation in tatters over something innocent."

Mitch straightened, his body tense and unyielding. "Did anybody else see this expense report? I wouldn't want Megan hurt by this."

"My secretary. And the financial secretary."

"I hope they don't gossip." This from Will.

Silence.

Noah finally said, "All right, let's drop this and get down to business. I'd like to get the camp off the ground."

They settled in, Will taking a seat right next to her, in touching distance, like a protective father.

"So, what's the verdict?" Noah asked.

Megan gave a weak smile, aware of the tension emanating from Mitch. "Hank Fisher thinks we can do it. He's not only given us a clear plan to follow, but offered the still usable lakefront equipment he's replacing."

"Tell us what he thinks about how to get it goin'."

"The first thing we need to do is get some money. Bright Horizon started on a shoestring, and we're going to be a lot smaller, so he thinks we don't need even that much."

Leaning over, Will squeezed her arm. "We got five K to start with already."

"Really? Where?"

"From the Police Union and the Fire Department Benevolent Fund."

Noah put in, "And I just talked with Stan Steele. He says the council's a hundred percent behind this; they'll donate all the money from their annual Thanksgiving Ball to the camp. Sometimes it's topped twenty K. It usually goes to a charity anyway, but hasn't been earmarked yet."

"Wow!"

Mitch relaxed back into his chair. "We need somebody in charge of fund-raising. Right away, Fisher says. And an accountant." He thought for a minute. "I think I should ask Connie, my sister. She's raised tons of money for the hospital where her husband works, and other charitable organizations. And she has a business degree."

They discussed other methods of getting money—grants, contacting various organizations that did good deeds.

"What's next?" Noah asked when they'd exhausted that subject of cash.

Megan answered. "We need permits and campground accreditation."

Will nodded. "Our secretaries can do that."

"We need a lawyer, too," Megan added.

Noah looked uneasy. "I talked to Paulie, Mitch."

"I know, I saw him on the way in."

"He said no."

"Yeah, he told me."

Silence.

Paulie and I are like oil and water. . . . He and my other sister Connie hate the fire department.

"I'll talk to him again," Mitch offered. "I think I might be able to convince him to join us."

"Great!"

"What about building the place?" Will asked.

Mitch seemed in his element about this. His dark eyes snapped with excitement. "Snyder's brother is an architect. He said he'd ask him to design the camp—both what we need the first summer and additions."

Megan smiled. "I like thinking about the future of it—expanding it. Bright Horizon was absolutely beautiful."

Will reached for her hand and squeezed it tightly. "Ours will be, too, Meggie. Your dad would be proud of you."

Her eyes moistened.

Mitch's voice was gruff when he said, "Between Malvaso Painting and McKenna's construction company, we should be able to build a few cabins and pavilion no problem. I hope we can start in February."

As they wound down, they decided to call a meeting next week at the academy for all people from both departments interested in participating.

"I'll do a memo to send out to them," Megan said. "How many people?"

"Let's see, there's two hundred smoke eaters and about a hundred cops. Add in staff, maybe four hundred."

"Great."

They stood. Noah faced them fully. "I'd like to say again I wasn't lookin' to offend anybody with my concern about your trip to Keuka Lake."

"You had cause." Mitch was innately fair and had so much integrity. "Forget about it."

Megan smiled. "I agree." She'd forget about that one night, too.

Will told her he'd meet her downstairs, he had a few things to say to Noah, so she and Mitch left together. They didn't talk until they reached the elevator and stepped inside.

Mitch held up a big manila envelope and a small white

one he carried. "I, um, have something for you. Two things actually."

"What?"

"A note from my son. His school talent show is tomorrow night. He's singing. He said you wanted to hear him sometime, and thought you might want to come."

"I would, thanks."

"Thank *you*. For showing an interest in him."

"I am interested."

"I know, and so does he."

She nodded to the larger envelope. "What's that?"

Pulling out papers, he looked a bit embarrassed. "Some information on migraines I printed off from the Internet."

She quelled her first response, which was to say, *You did that for me?* Instead she shrugged. "Oh, Mitch, I've read all the stuff available on migraines. Nothing's helped."

"Really?" He smiled. "Have you read about reflexology?"

"No, what's that?"

"Grady told me about it. He's a paramedic. It's foot massage therapy." They reached the first floor of headquarters and exited to the lobby. "Here, look."

She read the front of the thick packet. Smiling, she peered up at him. "This has to be a hoax. Foot massage cures headaches?"

"Don't laugh, there are hundreds of testimonials. People swear by it. Left their emails to contact them. There's also medical documentation. It has something to do with the nerves going from the foot to the head."

"I can't believe it."

"It's true. Read the intro paragraph and see."

She scanned it. "Yeah, that's what they say."

Jamming his hands in his pockets, he stared at her. "You got a guy to rub your feet, Meggie?"

"Yeah, of course. Scores."

He just watched her. Then he said, "I'm sorry. About what the chief implied earlier."

"It wasn't your fault." She clenched the folder. "You were trying to help me and got hurt by it."

"I should have thought it through." He shrugged. "I guess I'm not very good at covering things up."

Something made her ask, "No practice?"

"Never." He said it meaningfully. "Not once."

Megan got the message. He didn't cheat on his wife.

Well, good. Having been on the other end, she knew how horrible it was when your husband was unfaithful to you.

And never, ever would Megan be the other woman.

Empty coffee cups and juice boxes
Pushed off to the side,
Off to the side.
And caffeine is in my blood,
Not so wise.

Mitch listened to the soulful tone of his son's lyrics and weeping notes of the guitar Bobby played for the Hidden Cove High School talent show; he wanted to bawl like a baby. He didn't think he'd ever heard anything so sad.

I always hate Sunday mornings like this.
Because I want to cry for the week that
I have missed.

How to separate the writer from the speaker? Was Bobby depressed? Did he actually feel this hollowness?

I'm sick of my friends.
Thought they'd be there to the end.
Now I'm not so sure anymore.

Had Mitch seen any of Bobby's friends around the house lately? Did Bobby have anybody to talk to?

It's not wise to let your parents sit by
As you cry again.
But what are you supposed to do
when there's nothing left to say?

Oh, God.

Be perfect,
Be fearless,
Have fear.
Be perfect,
Be flawless.
Just be perfect!

For a minute, when the song ended, the audience was hushed. Then they erupted, with fervor—a row stood, then another, then another.

Despite his horror over the song's message, if indeed this was how Bobby felt, Mitch leaped to his feet and clapped heartily. The ovation went on for ten seconds . . . twenty seconds . . . thirty. Only at the end did Mitch realize his cheeks were wet. He scanned the audience. Several people were crying.

Trish was also on her feet, whistling with fingers in her mouth.

And Cynthia remained seated, in between them.

What the hell?

When everybody sat back down, he looked at his wife. Her sculpted cheeks were red, her eyes narrowed. Her hands were clasped in her lap, her knuckles white. He and Trish exchanged a worried glance, but focused on the rest of the acts.

Bobby won the talent show and got another standing ovation. Everyone herded out to the foyer on their way to the cafeteria for a reception. In the mob, Bobby was nowhere to be found. After a couple of tense moments in the foyer, Trish mumbled something about being *hard to please* and went to find her brother. Mitch pulled Cynthia into the side hall.

"What the hell's wrong with you?"

She was so angry she could barely speak. "Do you have any idea what he just did to us?"

"To *us*? He made me very proud."

"That's so you. He embarrassed us in front of the whole high school staff and students. People will be saying we expect too much of him, we don't understand him. We'll probably get calls from concerned teachers. And *counselors*!"

"It was a song, Cynthia."

She lasered him with a piercing stare. "Then why were you crying? If you didn't think it was personal, you wouldn't have been so affected."

Since her statement was true, since he couldn't answer the taunt, he tried reasoning with her. "All right, if it's how Bobby's feeling, shouldn't we be more concerned with his mental health than if he embarrassed us, which I don't think he did?"

"You're something else. You always take his side. You always defend him."

"Cindy, he didn't do anything wrong."

She looked away, over his shoulder, and frowned. From behind, he heard, "Mitch. Mrs. Malvaso."

Oh, just what he needed.

He pivoted to see Megan standing in the hallway. She wore a gray skirt and top, over which she'd donned a red leather jacket. Her eyes were full of emotion.

Cynthia's tone was frigid. "Hello, Detective."

"Hi, Megan."

"I just wanted to say how wonderful Bobby's song was. I cried."

Me, too. "Thanks."

She smiled at Cynthia who just glared at her.

"He should be out now, in the cafeteria," Mitch told her. "Stay and tell him what you thought."

"I'll go find him." Still nothing from Cynthia. Megan nodded to her. "Nice to see you again, Mrs. Malvaso." She left hurriedly.

Pivoting, he said, "That was swell. You were rude, Cynthia."

"Why is she here, anyway?"

He shrugged, feeling guilty. Now was not the time to tell his wife Bobby asked Megan to come. "She's done some work at the high school and knows all the kids, I'd guess."

"She could dress a little more appropriately. A ranking police officer shouldn't wear red leather."

Megan looked dynamite to Mitch, and despite the circumstances, set off tiny explosions in his body. "Is that really an issue here?"

As she'd done often before the Sinco fire, Cynthia turned her head away. Oh, fine, the silent treatment. Why did women *do* that? Did they know men *hated* it with a passion?

"I'm gonna go find Bobby."

"Fine, I'm leaving." She had met him here, so they had two cars.

"You could congratulate him."

"I will not encourage this kind of morbid sentimentality."

Mitch walked away. He couldn't trust himself to say anything more. And he was damn glad he was seeing Harrison Friday. His life—his marriage—felt, tonight, like it was going up in flames and there was nothing he could do to stop the fire.

MEGAN WAS TREMBLING. It was obvious Cynthia Malvaso was pissed. She just hoped Mitch's wife hadn't found out about the single motel room. Why else would she treat Megan like a pariah? What else could be wrong with her tonight, when her son was so startlingly successful? Across the room, she saw Bobby talking to his sister. Making her way through the crowd, she approached them.

"Don't go with him up to The Hill, Trish. He's a jerk."

The Hill was where all the kids parked.

Megan greeted them. "Hi, there."

Trish faced Megan. "Hi, Detective."

"Trish."

She smiled at Bobby. "Hello, superstar."

Bobby's grin was huge. "You came."

"And I'm glad I did. You were awesome."

"Yeah, not bad for a kid brother." Trish glanced at her watch. "I'm bouncin'. Tell Dad I went out with Ray."

"Trish, don't—"

She kissed Bobby's cheek, said, "Ciao, Detective," and

left, her clogs battering on the vinyl. Megan noticed her
skirt was short and her shirt tight underneath her light
jacket.

Bobby scowled after her.

"Something wrong?"

"She's got a sucky boyfriend. He's a powder keg."

Megan frowned. "Meaning?"

"He's got a temper."

"Not a good companion, then."

Bobby shook off his mood and faced her with glowing
eyes. "So, you liked it?"

"You made me cry."

"Trish said Dad cried, too."

"How could he not?"

Bobby's gaze was far away. "I'll bet she didn't."

"Who?"

"Nobody." He shook his head. "Dad's a softie."

Yeah, I know.

Megan really wanted to change the subject. "So, how
many other songs have you written?"

"About thirty. I'm going to sing in a coffee shop in
December."

"Great, I won't miss it."

Bobby glanced past her shoulder. "Here he comes."

Mitch approached Bobby. "Hey, kid."

Bobby smiled, so warmly, so affectionately, it made
something inside Megan shift. She hadn't thought much
about having children, but the expression on Bobby's
face, for his dad, was so special it made her stomach contract.

Mitch gave Bobby a huge, hard bear hug. "I was so
proud of you, son. You're really good."

"Thanks, Dad."

Mitch drew back. "Pretty sad stuff, though."

Darting a glance at Megan, Bobby rolled his eyes. "Oh,
no, here goes."

"Here goes what?" she asked.

"Dad'll worry about the sad lyrics for days."

Playfully Mitch punched his son's arm. "Yep. We gotta
talk. Maybe it's time to start that counseling again."

"Maybe."

Mitch looked over at Megan, his eyes taking her in briefly. "Thanks for coming."

"My pleasure."

He stared at her a little too long. Then he checked out the cafeteria. "Where's Trish?"

"Ray picked her up."

A vee formed with Mitch's brows. "Connelly?"

Shifting nervously, Bobby nodded. "Uh-huh."

"Where'd they go?"

"I don't know."

Uh-oh. Bobby lied. He knew where Trish went. So did Megan.

Hmm. What should she do about this? Betray the kids by telling Mitch? Or let the girl endanger herself?

Maybe there was a middle ground. "Well, I'm off. I have some paperwork at the office to finish."

Glancing at his watch, Mitch said, "This late?"

"Yeah." She addressed Bobby. "You were wonderful, Bobby." She held out her hand.

He bypassed it and shocked Megan by giving her a hug. "Thanks. It meant a lot that you came."

She swallowed hard, touched by the spontaneous gesture, and hugged back. "I wouldn't have missed it." Drawing away, she smiled. "Besides, I'm gonna get to say 'I knew you when.' "

"Hope so."

She faced Mitch. It was a mistake. There was a look on his face, so profound, so . . . grateful . . . that she wanted to throw herself into *his* arms.

"Good night, Mitch."

"Good night, Meg."

She turned so she didn't have to face the Malvaso men again. Son of a bitch. They were both staking out territory in her heart.

And it wasn't good.

THE HILL WASN'T crowded tonight. Since the weather was getting cold, kids weren't parking much. As Megan

drove up the paved incline, she tried to remember necking
with boys in cars. It seemed so long ago, but the memories
came eventually. One boy in particular whom her dad had
disapproved of. Damn, there was even a time Patrick Hale
caught her, half dressed, with Johnny. Mitch Malvaso had
reason to worry. Yet, she'd survived, as would Trish.

She reached the top of the hill just as a car whizzed
by her. Going fast. Dangerously fast. She was thinking
about chasing him down when she saw Trish on the side
of the road. Smoking.

Megan pulled over. Slid down the window. "Trish, it's
me, Detective Hale."

In the moonlight, Megan could see Trish's clothes were
disheveled, her hair a mess and lipstick smeared. Some
hot and heavy activity had gone on up here. "What's going on?"

Trish took a last drag on the cigarette and tossed it to
the ground. "The fucking asshole tried . . ." Her bravado
faded and tears welled in her eyes. Immediately, Megan
got out of the car. She took Trish by the shoulders. "What
did he do?"

The girl looked up at her with innocence in those
highly made-up eyes. "He tried to do stuff I didn't want
him to."

"*Did* he? Do stuff you didn't want him to?"

She shook her head. "He would have, but I kneed him
in the nuts."

"Are you sure? Because if he did, I can pick him up."

"Jesus Christ, my mother would have a fit."

"Excuse me?"

"She got pissed at Bobby's song, probably because it
embarrassed her to have everybody hear it."

Ah, so that's what Mitch's wife was angry about. Not
anything she'd found out. Hell, what a witch to be angry
at Bobby. Megan forced herself to focus on Trish.

"Still, if this guy did anything to you against your
will . . ."

"He didn't." She looked away. "I let him, you know,
do some stuff. Not a lot. But then I wanted to stop. When

it seemed like he might not, I stopped him myself, like Dad told me to."

Megan bit back a smile. She would've liked to hear that conversation. "All right. Come on, get in, I'll take you home."

Trish hesitated. "Daddy'll know, then."

"Honey, I have to tell him anyway."

At Trish's stricken look, she squeezed the girl's shoulder. "But if we clean you up some, and tell him the truth, and if you promise not to go out with that jerk again, he'll be okay, won't he?"

"Yeah. Mom'll flip. But I don't give a shit." Her voice indicated otherwise, but Megan ignored it.

"Let's go, girl."

In the car, Trish chattered on while she took the water Megan had in her bag, cleaned her face, and applied a bit more makeup. Her mother should talk to her about wearing so much. And that eyebrow ring . . . God, why did kids *do* that to themselves?

When she'd finished with her face, and was rebuttoning her blouse, she glanced over at Megan. "Better?"

"Yes."

She scanned Megan. "Mag jacket, Detective."

"Thanks."

"You dress good."

Ah, a high compliment from a teenager.

"You ever get in trouble like me when you were young?"

A hard choice, one adults faced when dealing with kids: how much to tell of their own misspent youth, as a show of understanding, but without encouraging bad behavior. "Yep. And it hurt my dad, too."

"You got a great dad?"

She swallowed hard. "I did."

"When'd he die?"

"A few months ago."

"Wow." Then, in a gesture reminiscent of Mitch, she reached over and squeezed Megan's arm. "I'm sorry."

Megan's throat got tight.

They chatted until they pulled into the driveway of

Mitch's home. It was a lovely house with peaks and ga-
bles and interesting architecture in a nice part of the city.

"Guess I gotta face the music, huh?"

"You do."

"Will you come in with me?"

"I would, but there's no need. You got a greeting
party." She nodded out the window through which they
could see Mitch striding down the sidewalk.

HIS HEART IN his throat, Mitch had hurried out of the
house. He'd been watching for Trish, having had a bad
feeling when Bobby said she went out with Ray. When
he'd seen Megan's police vehicle pull into the driveway,
his pulse began to thrum. If something had happened to
Trish . . . why else would Megan be at his house this late?

The door opened and his daughter got out. *Thank you,
God.*

Reaching the car, he scooped her up and just hugged
her.

"I'm okay, Daddy."

He forced himself to calm down. "All right." But it
was a few seconds before he let her go. "What happened?
Why are you with Megan?"

Trish bit her lip. And in typical Trish style, she said,
"Detective Hale can tell you. I'm going in. Come up to
my room." She literally fled into the house.

Since Cindy was asleep, he let Trish go and crossed to
the truck. He peeked in. "Meg?"

"Hi."

He slid inside and closed the door. "What happened?
Trish said you'd tell me."

Sighing, Megan gave him a sympathetic look. "I found
her on The Hill, walking on the roadside, smoking."

"What was she doing up there?"

"Well . . ."

He hit his head. "She went parking with Connelly,
didn't she?"

"Yes."

"Son of a bitch. He's an asshole."

Megan nodded to the house. "I think she knows that now."

"Why, what happened?"

"He wanted to go further—physically—than she wanted to, and so she kneed him but good and got out of the car. He tore away and left her there."

"I'll kill the bastard."

Reaching out, she clasped his arm. "I know you must want to. I would, too. But Trish handled it."

"Are you sure? How do you know he didn't . . ." He threw his head back and fisted his hands. "Fuck!"

"She says he didn't. I asked a lot of questions and I believe her." She hesitated. "You should talk to her, too, though."

"You can bet I will."

"She's more concerned about worrying you."

"She's a good kid, Meg."

"I believe that. I parked on hills a few times myself, Mitch."

"Yeah, me, too."

Maybe it was the mention of necking, of flirting with sex in the confines of a car, but suddenly the atmosphere became charged with an emotional current so strong it jolted Mitch. Unable to stop himself, he reached out and grabbed Megan's hand. Held it between his two. "Thanks for taking care of my little girl, Detective."

She cleared her throat. "Hey, I owe you, Captain."

He traced one of her fingers with one of his, down its length, up to its nail. Her skin was as soft as a baby's.

Then he encircled her wrist. Rubbed her pulse point. Felt it leap. His was dancing the tango, too. "I'd better go," he said hoarsely.

She closed her eyes and expelled a breath. "You'd better."

It killed him to break the contact, but he did. He released her hand and, without looking at her, afraid she'd see what was on his face, what was in his mind, mirrored in her eyes, he opened the door, got out, and shut it quietly.

Without looking back, he headed to the house to take care of his daughter.

~~ TWELVE

ALL WEEK, GRADY was proud of how he'd handled the situation with Jenny and their feelings of sexual attraction. They'd purposely spent a lot of time together, uncomplicated by any male/female stuff, as she'd called it. They'd voiced thanks that they'd dodged that bullet, even joked a bit about it; he felt better—he *did*—that they'd decided not to take any risks with their relationship to satisfy some stupid sexual curiosity.

He was sitting at the table in the firehouse kitchen, sipping coffee after a training session on terrorism, thinking of how things were going well. Their captain, Bob Drake, was reading a firefighter/cop equipment magazine, which had a funny stories insert. "Holy shit, this is hysterical," Drake quipped.

"Read it," Hector Pike said as he cleaned the refrigerator.

"Okay. The first one is a cop story." He cleared his throat. "A police lieutenant was called to a domestic violence scene along with the firefighters. The cop ended up bringing the couple to the station house. The guy was arrested, and the woman questioned by the cop. When the cop was done with the questions, he said he needed documentation of her bruise and a female cop would escort her into a private room and take a Polaroid. He thought everything went fine, until later when he was looking at the report, he saw the picture. It was of the woman's breasts. The lieutenant called in the female cop. 'What the hell is this?' he asked.

"The young woman cop said, in all sincerity, 'You said to get a picture of her boob.' "

Everybody laughed. The humor felt good. "Are there any more?" Grady asked.

They told a second story, about firefighters. Grady cracked up along with his crew. They were all still laughing when a flower delivery guy came in. He deposited a huge, green papered arrangement on the table.

"Who are these for?" Grady asked.

"A Jenn Malvaso," the guy said and left.

Grady's good humor hissed out of him like a balloon losing air. "Arena's Florist." He knew it was the most expensive place in town. A man sent those flowers when he was really in the doghouse, or out to impress the pants off somebody. Hell, he'd used it a time or two.

"Who they from?" Drake asked.

"I haven't got X-ray vision," Grady snapped. Then he added, "Somebody should tell Jenny they're here."

"What are here?" Entering the kitchen from the bay, Jenn came to the table, looking sweaty and dirty from their training. There was a smudge on her cheek. "Who are these for?"

Grady crossed his arms over his chest. "You."

Group One's other member, Norm Nedwecki came into the kitchen. "Lookee here," Norm said. "Jenny got a beau?"

"Not that I know of." Grady's tone was a little more edgy than he liked.

She shot him a puzzled look, took the card, and ripped it open. Her face flushed. Then she scanned the guys. They were all facing her, waiting. Stashing the card in her pocket, she started to back away. "I gotta shower."

"Who they from, Malvaso?" Norm asked.

Her chin came up. "None of your business."

Grady caught Hector's eye. He signaled the other guys. "Get her." Two of them rushed to her sides. Each grabbed an arm, effectively trapping her. Her eyes glinted pure fire as Grady approached her. "You don't want to do this, O'Connor."

"Oh, yeah, sweetheart, I do." He reached for her pocket. Her booted foot came out and kicked his shin.

"Son of a bitch." As he rubbed his leg, he nodded to Drake, who circled around her and snagged the card out of her pocket.

"Give that back to me. I mean it, you guys, it's none of your business."

But Drake was already reading. " 'To the gorgeous firefighter who kept me company under a blanket a week ago. How about dinner? And I have tickets to *Chicago* Friday night. You're off. I checked.' It's signed *Stan*."

Jenny swore ripely while the guys howled and made jokes about the glamour girl going out with Stan the Man. Grady tried to see the humor in it, managed a few snorts, though they weren't heartfelt. When they let her go, Jenn snatched the card away from Drake. "All right, you morons, you can start acting like adults again." She stalked off to the bathroom. Grady knew this little razzing was far from over. The guys would rag on her for days. So would he . . . or he would have in the past. He didn't find much to smile about in it this time. He crossed to the coffeepot, pretending to be amused.

"He's a real Don Juan, from what I hear." This from Norm.

Drake put in, "My wife says he's *yummy*. What the hell kind of word is that?"

"Better warn our girl off him," Hector told Grady.

Leaning against the counter, Grady stared at the door where Jenny had exited. "You think?"

"If you don't want Jenny to be another notch in his belt."

Grady's stomach clenched. Jesus.

He went looking for her a half hour later. She was checking supplies in the Midi. "Is it safe to come close?" he asked, his hands up, arrest style.

Her eyes were amused. "Yeah, sorry about that. How's the shin?"

"You could kiss and make it better." Shit. Where had that come from?

Hesitating only a split second, she said, "I think I'll pass." She focused on the ALS bag and riffled through the bandages.

Casually, he leaned against the truck. "So, you going out with him?"

She shrugged.

"You don't like plays much. Last time I took you to New York, you fell asleep right after intermission."

"That was *Death of a Salesman,* Gray." She didn't look at him. "It might be fun."

"Yeah?" He folded his arms over his chest. "They say he's a shark."

"I can handle myself. Besides, what holds true for Brennan does for Stan, don't you think? We shouldn't take rumors about either of them at face value."

"I guess."

She faced him fully. "Do you want me not to go, Gray?"

"Do you want to go?"

"I asked you first."

"Sure, if you want to go out with an octopus, go ahead."

Temper sparked in her eyes. "Well, maybe I will then."

He pushed away from the truck. "Fine," he snapped out. "Go," and walked away.

Now, he felt even sicker. Fuck it, let her do what she wanted. *It might be fun.* Hell!

ON FRIDAY NIGHT, Grady wandered into Jenn's bedroom just as she was securing a belt around her waist in front of the mirror. "Holy shit, where'd you get that?" Her outfit made him want to punch something. The jumpsuit was a deep red—great with her hair and eyes—hitting every curve she had. He moved in closer. She fastened on a gold necklace with a ruby-studded heart dangling right between her breasts, which were accented by the scooped cut of the neck.

"I bought it last night." She slipped into fuck-me heels. "Like it?"

He took a long gulp of the Molson he carried, then locked his gaze with hers in the mirror. "It's the kind of thing a woman wears when she wants to get laid."

She rolled her eyes. "I just liked it. I thought it looked good on me." She wasn't really paying attention. She was fussing with a purse, which she never carried. Of course, there was no room in the outfit for a wallet or anything else. The clothes fit her like a wet suit.

Shaking his head, he crossed to the bed and flopped down. He drank his beer and watched her. Now she was putting on makeup. "Why you wearing war paint?"

She chuckled. "I don't know. I want to look good, I guess." She scowled. "You shouldn't be drinking beer if you're going to work tonight on the basement."

He shrugged.

"Why don't you call somebody up and go out instead?"

"I don't feel like it." He sounded, even to his own ears, like a surly child.

"Are Zach and Mitch coming to help?"

"Zach is. Mitch has something with Cindy."

"Hmm." She clipped on pretty sparkly earrings. They called attention to her ears, which he'd never particularly noticed before.

"Anybody home?" Zach's voice came from downstairs.

"Up here," Grady called out. "Speak of the devil."

Her brother appeared in the doorway and stilled. Then he let out a wolf whistle. "Wow, sis, you look like a million bucks."

"Grady says I look like I want to get laid."

"That, too." He crossed to the bed and sank down next to Grady. "Who's the lucky guy?"

"Stan Steele."

Zach scowled. "Yikes. Watch it with that one. He's got a reputation for stringing women along."

"I'm a big girl. I can take care of myself."

The doorbell rang and Grady shot off the bed. "I'll get it."

"Gray, I—"

But he was out the door before she could stop him. Gripping his beer, he trundled down the steps, covered the foyer in five angry steps and yanked open the door.

The illustrious councilman perched on the stoop. Dressed in an expensive suit, his hair slicked back, he held a red rose in his hand. Pretty trite gesture, if you asked Grady. *He'd* be more original.

"Hello." Steele checked the house number. "Is this Jenn Malvaso's place?"

Grady stepped back. "Yeah, she's ready. Come on in."

When Steele came inside, Grady held out his hand. "Grady O'Connor. I live on the other side of the duplex."

"Oh." Steele looked puzzled but he accepted the handshake. "Well, nice to meet you." He stared at Grady. "You were there the night of my accident, too, weren't you?"

"Yeah, I'm a paramedic. I was working in the other car."

"Thanks for all you did."

Shit, he was going to have to be nice. "No problem."

Zach came barreling down the steps. "Hi, I'm Jenn's brother, Zach."

An amused smile flitted across Steele's pretty face. "Yeah? You guys chaperoning her?"

"Ignore them," Jenn said, also coming down the stairs and speaking from the side. "I'm ready."

Steele ignored them, all right. He only had eyes— which looked like they might pop out of his head—for Jenn. Grady's hand clenched at the scorching look the guy gave her. "Well, I'm . . . speechless."

"Yeah, she cleans up pretty good, doesn't she?" This from Zach.

"You look beautiful," Steele said in an I-want-sex tone. He stepped forward and handed her the rose.

Jenny blushed. Jesus, she was going to fall for this crap.

"It's lovely." She turned to Grady. "Here, put it in water, okay? We need to get going so we make can the show."

"Yeah, sure. I'll put it in water." He took the rose.

"Well, have a good time." Zach winked at her. "Don't keep her out too late, Steele."

Steele laughed and Jenny rolled her eyes. "Can it, little brother."

Grady said nothing. The door closed behind them and he took another swig of his beer, stared at the rose—and promptly crushed it into useless petals, which he let fall to the floor.

"She's dead meat," Zach said. "He'll take her to some quiet restaurant in the city, wine and dine her, go to a show, then try to get her to stay overnight in New York."

"Well, you'd know the drill, I guess."

There was absolute silence. Grady looked up from the floor. His friend's face was ashen.

"Geez, Zaccaria, I'm sorry." He ran a hand through his hair. "I'm rattled about Jenny going out with that guy. I didn't mean to slam you."

Collecting himself, Zach shrugged. "It's true." He jammed his hands in his pockets. "Nobody else believes I've changed, so what does it matter?"

"Nothing better with Angie?"

"Angie's hot and heavy with another guy who isn't walking all over her."

Grady shook his head. "It must be tough."

Zach scowled at the petals on the floor. "That really worry you?"

"Some."

Zach studied him. "Anything going on you want to talk about? You seem preoccupied lately. Quiet. Melancholy."

"Hey, I'm always thinking. Remember how you used to tease me about that?"

"Yeah." He shrugged. "It's different now. Everything is, though, to me, since Sinco."

Grady stared at Jenny's front door. "Yeah, everything's different to me, too."

JENN TRIED TO participate. On her front stoop, under a light Grady must have left on, she let herself be drawn into Stan's arms, let him run his hands up and down her back and even settle on her hips. When his mouth lowered, she closed her eyes.

It was a nice kiss, warm, affectionate. They'd had a nice time tonight, finding several areas of common interest. Stan was an interesting guy. And a sensitive one.

"Hmm," he said pulling back. "Sure I can't interest you in coming over to my place?" He glanced up at the duplex's second story. "I wouldn't want to risk my life by asking to come in here."

She followed his gaze. There was a light on in her bedroom, and in Grady's. Jesus. All affection, warmth, and interest in Stan drained out of her. "Grady's like another brother. They think they have to watch out for me."

"Maybe they do." His hands dropped to her bottom and squeezed.

She stepped back. "I'll go in now."

An amused flicker came to his eyes. They were blue, but not as dark or intense as Grady's. "All right. Will you go out with me again?"

She wondered if the councilman would want to see her if she was pregnant. Which she could be soon, if the artificial insemination worked the first time. "Sure."

"I'll call you."

Jenn let herself in and checked the clock. Two A.M. What the hell was Grady doing up? Should she go see? No, she was feeling vulnerable tonight, and had been all week, though she'd hidden it from him. In her heart, she knew their decision last week was the right one—God, she couldn't risk losing his friendship—but that nagging feeling of attraction just wouldn't go away. Best just to sneak in without his knowing. She headed to her room.

And there he was. Again, he was stretched out on her bed, holding a book in his lap; he'd put on his glasses, which he only needed when his eyes were tired. Riding low on his hips were black sweats; he wore nothing else.

"What are you doing up?" she asked.

"I couldn't sleep."

"Were you waiting for me?"

"No." Removing his glasses, setting them on the table, he glanced at his watch. "It is late, though."

She turned back to the dresser. "Sorry, Dad."

"Very funny."

"What did you do tonight?"

"Zach and I got the old paneling down."

Slipping off her necklace, she removed the belt and reached for the back of her outfit. The zipper seemed stuck. She struggled with it.

"Here, let me help." He was off the bed and behind her before she could say no, she didn't think it was a good idea for him to touch her right now. He looked sexy lazing on her bed, and they'd agreed not to notice those things.

His hands went to her shoulders and rested there for a minute. Leaning over, he buried his nose in her hair. "You smell good."

Her breath hitched. "Thanks."

He stayed where he was.

She caught his gaze in the mirror. "Gray?"

As if coming out of a daze, he eased away and she felt his fingers on her back. He tugged on the zipper. Then his knuckles brushed her skin, over her bra. She shivered; he raised gooseflesh all down her spine. "Your skin is so soft," he whispered. "It feels like expensive silk."

She didn't think she could talk.

He parted the material of her jumpsuit. "What the hell is this?" he barked.

She was startled by his tone. "What?"

"You wore a red lacy bra." None too gently, he yanked the zipper all the way down. "And panties to match."

"So?"

"You only wear this stuff . . ." He seemed to stutter. ". . . That date you had a while ago and I waited up, you said you wore your white underwear because you weren't gonna do anything. Because of the baby."

She stilled. Why *had* she worn this? She remembered thinking about Grady when she'd chosen her underwear tonight and how he'd snapped her bra for her that morning; and she did recall the conversation they'd had a few weeks ago.

Forcefully, he gripped her arms. "You haven't forgotten about the baby next week, have you?"

Shaking her head, she wouldn't meet his gaze in the mirror.

His fingers tightened on her arms and he stepped closer again. "I saw him kiss you."

Her head came up. "Were you spying on me?"

"Maybe." He ran his hands down her side, to her hips. "He touched you here. Like a lover would." His fingers flexed on her sides. "Did you want to fuck him?"

"Grady!"

"I wanna know."

"No!" She tried to pull away. He held her fast. Drew her back against him. Oh, God, he was aroused. Fully, heavily, gloriously aroused. "Gray." She breathed his name.

"How was the kiss?"

"Stop this."

He yanked her even closer. "How *was* it?"

Sighing, she felt control slip away from her. "Okay."

"Just okay?"

She leaned back, let him slide his arms around her waist. "No fireworks, if that's what you mean."

"Good." He lowered his head. Kissed her bare shoulder where the suit had slipped. "I can give you fireworks, Jenny."

Closing her eyes because the sight of them together in the mirror drove her wild, she struggled for sanity. Somewhere, in the dim recesses of her mind—which was suddenly clouded with the feel and smell of her best friend—she remembered their fear of blowing their friendship and how it wasn't worth the risk of experimenting sexually with each other.

"We agreed that wasn't a good idea."

"Right now, I don't give a shit what we agreed on." She watched this time, as his nose pushed at the material of the outfit. It fell off one shoulder. "I want you, Jenny."

"We said we were going to be sensible about this."

"Screw sensible." He nipped at the red lacy strap with his teeth and she jerked into him.

"I don't think . . ."

But his hands came up, pushed the jumpsuit to her waist, and cupped her breasts. She filled him perfectly. Gently, he caressed her. She moaned.

"Jenny." His voice was scraping, parched.

Still, she tried. "Grady, I'm scared—" But one of his big, masculine hands drifted lower, pushed the suit completely off, and covered her midriff. She sucked in a breath when he went even lower and cupped her. No longer could she remember her objections, that this was the boy she'd known since they were five. Simply, he was a man she wanted with utter desperation. Acute, raw desire shot through her, like water surging through a hose, charging it with an unstoppable current. When he slid his hand inside the lacy ridge of the panties, the desire erupted. She thrust her hips forward with his very first intimate touch of her. "Grady."

His mouth was on her ear. His tongue traced it. "Jenny, love." His words were slurred, like a drunk's.

Closing her eyes, she felt his fingers slid through her curls and find her. He rubbed her there, up and down and she groaned. Moaned. The sounds escaping from her became one long sexual chorus. Suddenly, the exquisite sensation was gone. Her eyes flew open. "You're close," he said, sliding down the red lace so she was fully exposed. "Kick these off."

Sexually drugged by his ministrations, she obeyed him. Meanwhile he disposed of her bra and she spilled into his hands. "Spread your legs." She closed her eyes as she did that, too. "No, no, open your eyes." She was powerless to deny him. "Now watch me touch you." One hand fondled her breast, the other slid down to cup her again. There was so much heat, she thrust forward—to douse it? To make it burn hotter? His knuckles grazed her up and down. "Harder?" he asked, nipping at her ear. Every single nerve ending sizzled inside her.

"Yes, oh, God, yes."

He increased the pressure. In only seconds she was about to burst into hot, dangerous flames. But again, the tender, violent pressure stopped. "Ohhhhh," she said and then he thrust two fingers inside her, keeping his thumb on the most sensitive spot.

She came, so fast and so intensely that consciousness dimmed. She was aware only of his fingers ramming inside her, stoking the fire, burning her up like the sun.

When sanity returned, she opened her eyes and saw that his hand was still on her. Its pressure and slight movement sent aftershocks through her. Then he began massaging her. His face was flushed, his eyes sparking in the mirror like blue flames. He said, simply, "Again."

THEY STUMBLED TO the bed. Jenn's mind was muddled in the aftermath of two climaxes, and Grady was about to die with need. Pressing her down on the mattress, he shucked his sweats; she stretched out; he covered her with his body and took her mouth. Their first real kiss wasn't gentle—it was fast. Hard. Furious. He was barely sane as he devoured her, his teeth closing over her bottom lip, nipping it. Need thrummed inside him like an explosion waiting to happen. When she kissed him back, invaded his mouth with her tongue, it detonated.

Suddenly, he was on his back. And she was straddling him. He wanted her hands on him, her mouth all over his body. But she continued to only kiss him. His fingers fisted in her hair, keeping her fastened to him. Then her lips found his chest; when she tongued his nipples, he arced forward off the mattress. Her laugh was a seductress's; he gripped her arms, roughly. But when her hand went to his erection and closed around it, his mind blanked. All he could do was feel . . . slow, strong . . . up and down . . . hard . . . harder . . .

And then her mouth was there. Circling the tip . . . licking the shaft . . . and finally, finally taking him in fully.

He let it go on until he thought he'd burst into a thousand pieces. But he needed to be inside her the first time, so he flipped her over and plunged into her.

At the primitive connection with Jenny, his Jenny, he came with volcanic force.

3 A.M.

"Sit up in the middle of the bed and cross your legs."

Since she was high on him, like a sexual junkie who couldn't get enough, she did as she was told. He rose, went to her dresser, and came back with something. From behind, he knelt on the mattress and slid up to her.

"Close your eyes."

Again, no argument. But when she felt something cover her eyes, tie at the back . . . a blindfold? Jesus . . . she started.

"Shh," he said into her ear. "It's me, remember."

Him, Grady, oh, God . . .

He encompassed her; his chest fitted against her back, his arms encircled her. She could smell him, feel him, his hard thighs imprisoning hers.

Then his hands were everywhere. She didn't know she could get aroused so quickly again, but the mental images that danced behind the blindfold went straight to her core.

When he fondled her breasts, he whispered, "I've teased you about being small. But these are perfect." He played with one nipple. "Just perfect."

Arching into his palm, she moaned. When he took her hand and placed it between her legs, she stilled. "Gray?"

"It's okay, just a bit, I want to see you do this." His breath was silky in her ear. "For me."

She touched herself. Just a bit. Hearing his breath come fast, feeling him harden impossibly against her, she smiled, and continued the gentle rubbing until he took her hand away and replaced it with his own. "My turn," he said hoarsely.

4 A.M.

They'd gotten drinks, and he thought it odd she brought in a glass of ice. But the only talking they did was naughty sex talk, so they sipped their beer in silence, holding hands on the bed, not thinking, either, about what they were doing.

He was surprised when she took his glass from him

and eased him down to the bed. Pleased when she pressed him back into the pillows and switched off the light. Thrilled when she opened his legs and went down on him again.

God . . . the sensation spiraled in him, hot, heavy, and thick with passion. . . .

But he practically ricocheted off the bed when, after bringing him to the brink, as ecstasy clawed to get out, he felt something shockingly cold against his balls.

It catapulted him into oblivion.

10 A.M.

"How can you be hard again?"

"Never happened like this before," he said groggily.

They'd slept, and awakened cuddled into each other.

Once again her hand found him. It didn't take long to bring him totally awake. Suddenly she was at the end of the bed, flat on her back, her knees draped over the edge, her feet on the floor.

"Open for me, baby." He could have done it for her. But his face was intense and he seemed to want the dominance.

She did as he ordered. He stood between her legs, then, slipped one hand under her buttocks and lifted them high, throwing her weight onto her shoulders. She gasped at the vulnerable position, at the exciting sensation.

He buried himself in her. She moaned. He positioned her legs over his shoulders, then held them there as he began to thrust harder.

"Jesus," she said. The friction against her was almost intolerable. "I can't, Gray, it's too much, I . . ." She writhed on the bed.

"Oh, yeah, you can, Jenny. Come again, for me. . . ."

1 P.M.

She was half on her side, half on her stomach. His hand clasped her breast; hers gripped his shoulder.

They'd made love again, and he was still inside her,

from behind. Never in his life had he felt so joined to someone. His mouth on her neck, he inhaled her, tasted her. He could barely see straight, his eyes blurred with fatigue and sexual drunkenness.

She said, "Gray."

"Jenny, my Jenny . . ."

He reached down and pulled up covers. Clasping her to him, he fell into a deep sleep.

The images came then. . . .

Linda, screaming at him, just before he was leaving to take Jenny to the doctor because she'd been ill. "You're terrible at this, you know."

"Terrible at what?"

"Loving me. It's all your fault."

"What is, Linda?"

"We can't make this work. We're never going to make this work. Maybe it's your father, leaving you so young. Maybe it's because you're so fucking handsome."

He started to walk away. She pulled him back with her next words. "Maybe it's Jenny Malvaso."

"What the hell do you mean by that?"

"She's too important to you. You'd give up your life for her. Sacrifice our marriage for her."

"No, Linda, she's sick. I just need to take her to the doctor."

"Fine, go to her. But don't think it's going to be any different with her. You destroyed Sheila. You're destroying me. You'll hurt Jenny, too, just like you do every woman you come near. . . . And you'll kill her baby, like you killed mine. . . ."

"Grady, wake up."

"No, no, no . . ."

"Grady."

He reached out for purchase. Something shook him awake. Jenny was holding him. He glanced out the window to get his bearings. Holy hell, it was getting dark again. He looked around. The bed was destroyed. His hands tightened on her; he realized they were both naked.

It was then he remembered what had happened last night.

Jesus Christ, what had they done?

THIRTEEN

THE FIRST MEETING to launch Project KidsCamp with police and fire personnel was held in the gym of the academy, which had been set up with folding chairs on the wood floor. Mitch had told Jenn they expected about two hundred people. She sat off to the side, alone, and waited for the meeting to begin; it was delayed because the fire chief and the police chief were at a bad car accident. Forcefully, Jenn tried to quell the panic inside her. But it kept pushing to get out, like water against a dam, and she had to struggle not to succumb.

A magazine dropped in her lap. She looked up to see two of her group members, Hector and Norm, sneering down at her. "Gimme a break, guys."

"Ms. Gorgeous Firefighter has to keep up her looks," Norm teased. "Can't go to pot while you're dating Stan the Man."

Feigning a smile, she said, "Up yours."

They laughed and took seats behind her. To keep herself in check, she glanced down at the rag. *Glamour*. Geez, these guys weren't letting up. When she'd come to work yesterday after three days off, she'd found the wall of her locker covered with newspaper articles about Stan

Steele. She'd joked with her crew—God, you couldn't let these clowns know anything bothered you or you were dead in the water—but she hadn't found their razzing funny.

Neither had Grady, when he'd rushed in late, hurried to his locker, which was next to hers, and seen the prank. His blue eyes were bloodshot as they narrowed on the photos. His linebacker shoulders, encased in the light blue uniform shirt, had stiffened. Their slump told her he was exhausted. She'd made a few casual comments, he'd grunted, and opened his own locker. As she stood there, not knowing what to say, he'd stuffed in his gear, slammed the door shut, and walked away without really talking to her.

He'd been treating her like Typhoid Mary since Saturday. After he'd blown her away with his lovemaking. Today, in the cavernous gym, her heart clenched and her body tightened just at the thought. Leafing through the magazine, pretending to study the anorexic models, she saw Grady instead, driving into her with the force of a conquering hero . . . on his knees, his face buried in her lap . . . behind her in the mirror, caressing her, whispering naughty things.

And then it had all stopped, snatched away by a nightmare about his past, which got him in its clutches and wouldn't release him.

"What's wrong?" she'd asked when he finally came awake.

His eyes were wild, and he was covered in sweat. "She said I'm going to hurt you."

"Who said?"

"Linda."

"Linda's dead, Grady."

"I killed her. And our baby." His hand went to Jenn's stomach. "She said I'll destroy you and the baby we make." His gaze flew to her face. "Like I did her. And Sheila."

"Gray, no, stop. You just had a nightmare."

He'd grown more agitated, gripped her arms so hard, he left bruises. "We can't do this, Jenny."

Because her heart started galloping with fear, she tried to ease the moment with humor. "We already did it, Gray. And it was wonderful."

He shook her. "No, no, it was stupid. Dangerous."

"Grady . . ."

Pushing her away, he leaped out of bed and rummaged madly through the tangle of sheets and pillows on the floor for his sweatpants. His movements were erratic, like a man who'd been ill and was disoriented, as he stuffed his legs in his pants and pulled them up. He faced her. "Get dressed."

"What?"

"Get dressed. I don't want to see you like that."

The words had sliced through her, cutting her insides to ribbons. She was pretty shaky from the cataclysmic sex they'd had, too. Quickly, she'd taken the sheet and wrapped herself in it. Poor armor against what was to come.

"Okay, okay," he said, pacing, raking his hand through his hair. "We did this. But it was a mistake."

"How can you say that?" Her voice was raw with suppressed emotion.

"Because it's true." He stopped. Turned. Studied her face. "See, I'm already hurting you. It's in your eyes."

There had been something convoluted in his thinking, but his words hurt so much she couldn't figure out what, exactly. Now she realized he *was* hurting her, only because he rejected her.

"We'll go back to how we were. We can stop this now from going further."

She'd swallowed hard. "What if I don't want to?"

"You *have* to." His voice rose a notch. "You *have* to, Jenny. I can't lose you."

"You won't lose me, Gray."

Again he began to pace, his tawny looks reminding her of a jungle tiger, caught in a trap. "Oh, yes I will. I'm hurting you now. I hurt every woman I care about."

When he stopped at the end of the bed, she came up on her knees and crawled over to him. Holding up the sheet with one hand, grasping his arm with the other, she kept her voice even. "You're upset. Let's not decide anything now. We'll just . . ."

"No!" He'd never yelled at her like that. "No! We've got to fix this right away, while we still can. You've got to promise me, you'll forget about us, together like that. We won't do it again, and we'll pretend it never happened."

"Gray, you're talking crazy. I can't forget about this."

"You have to."

She was about to protest again when he added, "You have to, Jenny. Even if you don't want to, you have to do this for me."

"For you?"

He gripped both her wrists. "I never told you something."

"What?"

"After Linda was found . . . in the car . . . in the garage . . . dead, with my baby—I knew I'd never feel that baby kick again, feel it turn over in her stomach. You know how much I loved that."

"I know you did."

"When I realized it was my fault, I gathered up all the pills in the house. I was going to take them."

"Gray, no, tell me you didn't."

"I did. I wanted to die. But I kept thinking about you, and what you'd feel if I killed myself. So I didn't take them. And then you were there. Do you remember you didn't leave my side for days?"

"I remember." She'd practically had to dress him; she forced him to eat; she slept with him every night for weeks.

"I would have died without you, Jenny." His grip tightened. "I'd die now if you left me."

"But I won't . . . why do you think I'll leave you now?"

"Because sex screws things up with me and women. It always has. I end up hurting any woman I'm romantically involved with. You and I will burn ourselves out. And then . . . you'll hate me, too."

"No . . . I could never hate you."

"I'm not willing to take the chance."

Raising her chin, she said, "I am."

"Please, don't say that. It isn't too late. It's only been one night. . . ."

She started to tell him it was already too late for her when she saw the sheen of tears in his beloved blue eyes. It silenced her. "Please, Jenny, please, do it my way. I can't lose you. . . ." The moisture leaked from his eyes and coursed down his sculpted cheeks. She'd seen him cry before, when his dad died, when her dad died, of course when Linda and the baby died. Like then, she couldn't stand it.

Gently, as a mother might, or a sister, she'd reached up, hugged him to her.

And promised him she'd forget about what had happened and would always be his friend. . . .

In the three days since, he'd been out of the duplex most of the time, and avoided her when he was home. They hadn't driven to work together, like they usually did. For her part, she walked around on eggshells, unsure of her footing, not wanting to say the wrong thing. She was beginning to think he was right that sex with a woman ruined things for him.

A deep male voice brought her out of the rumination. "What's in the magazine that could put a scowl on that lovely face?"

She looked up. "Oh, Stan, hi."

The guys behind her snickered like twelve-year-old boys.

She stood, stepped into the aisle and away from her crew, then held up the magazine, scrambling for an excuse for her mood. "These models drive me crazy, they're so skinny."

His blue eyes warmed. "I prefer a little meat on my women," he said silkily. Reaching out, he squeezed her waist. "Like you."

She backed up a step, right into someone. Turning, she saw Grady was behind her; he'd clasped her arms to steady her. His face was blank, and he dropped his hands as soon as he could. The white gauzy shirt he wore with jeans made him look pale tonight, instead of sexy like it usually did. "Sorry, didn't mean to interrupt. I was looking for Zach."

"Um, I think he's . . ." but she was speaking to his retreating back. She closed her eyes to tolerate the rush of loss she felt.

"Jenn?"

She pivoted around. "Hmm?"

"I said I have to go up front. But I was wondering if I could buy you a drink afterward."

She wanted to vomit at the idea of having a drink with another man. But as she watched Grady walk stiffly around the back of the gym to find her brother, she remembered her promise to him.

I'll forget about this . . . we'll both date others . . . our relationship will be back like was it before you know it. . . .

And so for Grady, she pasted on a smile like the models in the magazine. "Sure, Stan, I'll have a drink with you."

LISTLESSLY, ZACH FOUND a seat in the academy gym, not paying attention to where he was going. He was still picturing his boys, as he'd left them, climbing into the car with Angie and Ken Kellerman. Nicky had raced back, crying, "I wanna stay with you, Daddy."

Zach had scooped up his son for a big hug. "It's okay. Mom made dinner plans. She didn't know I'd be stopping over."

"Don't care," the child said, burying his face in Zach's neck. Zach had hugged him tight. "You have to go, buddy. How about if I come by tomorrow night and take you and Jason to McDonald's then?"

" 'Kay . . ."

Zach sighed and tried to get his mind off what he'd lost. Tried not to think about the fact that it should have been him taking his family out for an impromptu dinner. The department psychologist, Harrison, had said it was important to think about the future, but what kind of future did he have without them? Stretching out his legs, Zach accidentally knocked over a bag that was propped up against a chair in front of him. The contents spilled out.

Just as Zach leaned over to gather up the stuff that had fallen out, so did the person next to him. They butted heads.

"Shit."

"Ouch." Zach sprang back and rubbed his skull.

"Shit, Malvaso, watch it."

He stared into the annoyed face of Casey Brennan. "Sorry, Brennan. I was just trying to fix the mess I made."

As if her mind were elsewhere, she said, "Well, good luck. It's not so easy."

He watched her bend over. Her hair was a mass of inky black waves. It had a tousled look. The red sweater she wore accented its darkness. She stuffed the bag with several things that had scattered under the chairs in front of them. He saw thread and material. There were a couple of books. "Fuck, I can't reach that one."

"Stay out of the way and I'll get it."

"No, I . . ."

But Zach leaned over, carefully avoiding Brennan's hard head, and rescued the book. Spiral-bound, it was thick, and green, and dog-eared. He had a quick view of the title, only catching the large multicolored word BADGEBOOK before she snatched it from his hand. "I'm not gonna steal it, Brennan."

Her look was fulminating. "Leave me alone, Malvaso." She stood, hugged the package to her as if it were a cashier's check for a million bucks, and stormed out of the row and down the aisle. Angling his body, he watched her go stand in the back, still clutching the package.

Hell, she was crazier than he was.

"What was that all about?" Grady dropped down into a chair on the other side of him. "You say something to piss her off?"

"Obviously. Damned if I know what. I was just . . ." His voice trailed off as he glanced at Grady's face. "Holy hell, what happened to you?"

Sighing, Grady shook his head. "You don't want to know."

Zach stared at his best friend since grammar school. Though he'd had some tough breaks, Grady O'Connor seemed to roll with all of the punches life had thrown at him. He was the sanest man Zach knew, though Jenny had hinted he suffered a lot of guilt over his bad relationships with women. And to lose his wife and baby like that . . . Still, Grady had always seemed *together*. It was clear that something was really wrong now, though. Zach could see it in the strain around his eyes and the battered look in them. "Gray, what's wrong?"

"Nothing I can talk about."

"You sick?"

"No."

Fear, quick and potent, zinged through Zach. Grady and Jenny were closer than even he and Grady were, or he and his sister. "Is something wrong with Jenny?"

Closing his eyes, Grady shook his head. "Jenny's fine. It's me. It's personal."

Zach waited a bit. Admittedly, in the past, he'd been jealous of Grady and Jenn's closeness. But something was too wrong now to let petty stuff interfere. Finally, he said, "You talk to Jenny about it? She can help."

"Jenny can't help with this." He slouched down in the seat and folded his arms over his chest. "Let's change the subject, okay?"

"You sure?"

Grady nodded.

Zach sat back. "Jenny here?"

"Over on the other side."

"Why aren't you sitting with her?"

"Lover boy was putting the moves on her."

Zach caught sight of Jenny staring up at Stan Steele. The guy's hand was on her shoulder. "How was Friday night?"

"What do you mean?" Grady snapped.

"Shit, you really are bummed. I meant Jenny's date with Stanley."

Grady's gaze tracked Zach's. His jaw hardened to

granite. "I don't want to talk about that, either."

O-kay, he'd try something else. "I called you all day Saturday. We were going to finish the basement paneling. There was no answer. Where were you?"

Abruptly, Grady stood, barked, "Quit grillin' me, will you?" and stalked away.

Zach shook his head, feeling as if he'd landed in Oz. He knew he could be insensitive sometimes, but he was pretty sure he hadn't said anything offensive to Brennan and he didn't know what the hell had just happened with O'Connor.

Thinking things couldn't get any more confusing, he saw his brother Paulie and sister Connie walk into the gym. Holy hell!

MITCH TOOK GREAT pleasure in seeing his sister and brother arrive for the meeting. He would have gone over to them, thanked them for considering his offer to be part of Project KidsCamp, but just then both chiefs showed up and Callahan hurried to the mike.

After apologizing for being late, Noah smiled. "I'd like to welcome you all here. Let me say it's a downright joy to have gotten such interest in this project. We're gonna give you an overview of the setup of this camp and where we need help, talk some about the upstate camp, then get down to the nitty-gritty of volunteer lists and time lines."

There was a rumble of agreement through the crowd. Mitch bet half the off-duty cops and smoke eaters in Hidden Cove were here. Damned if this wasn't going to work.

Briefly, Callahan introduced the front table to the crowd. Mitch sat at the opposite end from Megan; in between them were Will Rossettie, Stan Steele, and the chief. Purposefully Mitch didn't go near Megan, nor had he talked to her before the meeting began. And he hadn't seen her since last week when she'd rescued Trish.

But he could recall, like it had just happened, the intimacy of that night together in her car. Her hand had felt slender, female, in his. Her scent had surrounded him. It was at that moment that he realized he was in big trouble.

He'd tried denying his attraction to her, tried minimizing it as just something physical—hell, she was gorgeous and he was only human. But that night, he'd realized he was attracted to her as a person, not just as a woman.

But he was a married man, and even though he wasn't happy in his relationship with Cindy, he was in no position to let himself get close to Megan. So he'd not contacted her, seen or heard from her, since then. And he took some steps to get help. He'd had a session with Jack Harrison as soon as he could get one. That first appointment hadn't been easy.

Tall, muscular, with a full head of dark hair and genuine concern in his eyes, the shrink was so open, everybody broke down and talked to him. Even Bobby, who'd consented to see him, liked him.

Harrison said easily, "So, Mitch, you back here because of the Sinco fire?"

Mitch had nodded. "In a way. Remember I told you I'd promised Jenny I'd change my life if we all got out of there?"

"Yep. You said you wanted to work on your marriage and take your kids in hand."

"Well, the kids are better. I'm spending more time with them, and they seem to be responding. And of course, Bobby's seeing you."

"Yep. And he's talking, which is good."

"I'm glad."

"And Cynthia? How are things with her?"

"Not good. She says she's changed, but life's slipping back into the same old, same old."

"That often happens after the stun of a tragedy wears off. How are you feeling about her?"

"Like I don't want to try anymore."

"Why?"

"It's not going to work."

"Have you told her?"

"I've tried. She refuses to listen." He felt embarrassment well inside him, but he needed help, damn it, and concealing things from a therapist you freely chose to see was stupid. "We've, um, stopped sleeping together. I can't do it anymore."

"Have you thought about separating for a while?"

"I can't see a way to leave her without putting the kids in a bad spot. Bobby would go on a rampage if I left him alone with her, and Trish would just do more stupid things to act out." He stared over Harrison's shoulder at a print on the wall. A Manwaring original, it showed firefighters in a bucket, battling a fully involved blaze. Damn, his whole personal life felt like that—putting out one fire after another. "And it gets more complicated than that." He ran a hand through his hair. "Something else has happened."

The therapist waited.

"I met someone."

Still Harrison said nothing.

"A woman. I like her. I'm attracted to her. I think about her a lot."

"How far has it gone?"

"It hasn't. We've behaved honorably." He told Harrison about the progression of his and Megan's relationship. "But it's not going anywhere. I can't see a way to divorce Cindy."

"Mitch, why don't you bring Cynthia in here? She can't be happy with the situation, either; she has to know you're seriously unhappy if you won't sleep with her. We can talk about the disintegration of the marriage, discuss whether it can or cannot be fixed, then see where you two really are."

"I've already asked. She won't come."

"Try again . . ."

So he had.

And as he'd predicted, Cynthia had refused. She wasn't going to any therapist, she said, and she'd argued about Bobby seeing one again. She said what they needed was more time together, for Mitch to pay more attention to her and they'd be fine, for him to treat her like he used to. In return, she'd promised to take more of an interest in his activities, and even help out with the camp.

So again he'd been stalemated. He didn't quite know

where to go from here. He was considering talking to his brother about his legal options, especially since Paulie had responded so well to his overture about working for the camp.

After the last meeting with the chief, Mitch had gone to his brother's upscale office in the swankest building in downtown Hidden Cove and asked to talk to him. Dressed in a navy power suit, Paulie had been intimidating behind his desk.

Mitch had just been himself. "I want you to reconsider Noah's offer to be legal counsel for Project KidsCamp."

"You must really be stuck, if you'd stoop to asking me a favor."

Mitch shook his head. "How did it get like this, Paolo? So hostile?"

"It's always been this way. You made your choices."

Though Mitch didn't believe the estrangement from Paulie and Connie was all his fault, right then, he didn't care. He was so tired of old resentments and grudges. He just wanted to go forward. He'd told Paulie as much.

And, miraculously, Paulie had agreed to give it a shot. He'd also agreed to be the legal rep for the camp.

Concetta had come around, too, making Mitch wonder just how long they'd wanted to be a part of his life. He'd stopped by her house after he'd left Paulie. In her state-of-the-art kitchen, she'd angled her head toward her big brother, baby on her hip, and said, "Jenny and Zach know you're here asking me this?"

"No, why?"

"They won't want me."

"Of course they will."

"Not Jenny."

"She will, Connie. And it's for a good cause."

Connie swallowed hard. "I remember when Daddy died in that fire. I was ten. You were only sixteen, but you took his place."

He'd crossed to her then and taken the baby from her. With his free arm, he'd hugged her. "I made mistakes, Connie. So have you. But this Sinco thing was a wake-up call to firefighters. Let's try not to make any more."

Wistfully, she'd put her head on his chest. "The fire changed me, too. I was so worried."

"Then you'll be head of our fund-raising? This size thing will be a piece of cake, compared to what you've done for the hospital."

"Yes, I'll do it. So long as I don't have to work directly with Zaccaria."

"Connie, he's . . ."

"Mitello, please. There's stuff you don't know. That I don't want you to know. But I won't work with him."

"All right . . ."

Chief Callahan's words brought Mitch back to the present. ". . . Megan Hale, the brains behind this project."

Everybody clapped and whistled. There were a few catcalls. Smiling brightly, Megan approached the mike. Tonight she wore a tailored suede-looking suit in a coppery color that would accent her eyes. It clung to her in soft ripples as she moved to the podium. Desire coursed through Mitch's system like a shot of cognac.

But he wouldn't cheat on his wife.

I haven't had any practice at this.

None?

Not one single time.

He knew *Megan* knew what he meant. He'd wanted to ask her if she'd ever cheated on her husband, but he hadn't. In the end, it was something he didn't need to know. It was hard enough staying away from her.

Now, he concentrated on what she was saying.

When she called him up to help her explain where they needed volunteers—in fund-raising, building, camp staffing, and program development—he stood a decent distance from her.

When she asked him to explain how they would take names tonight and form committees to meet in a few days, she stayed back from him.

But when she smiled shyly at the end of their talk, and thanked him for all he'd done to make tonight happen, he felt like somebody had taken a sledgehammer to his heart. He wanted to touch her so badly his hands shook with the force of restraining himself.

⁓ FOURTEEN

MEGAN DOWNED A Zomig and drank from the water
fountain in the fire department headquarters hallway before she entered the chief's conference room. The first
steering committee meeting was tonight, and about twenty
people were getting together to plan a time line and map
out programs, then divide up into subcommittees. Mitch
had said he thought they should include the community
at this point, so several laypeople would be on this board,
too.

Mitch. She hadn't spoken personally with him since
that night over a week ago in the car in his driveway, and
they'd only had one brief meeting to plan tonight, which
was all business. She looked down at her hand; against
her will, she traced the path his big, masculine fingers had
followed when he'd touched her. Sometimes, her skin still
tingled with the memories of the brush of his fingers over
hers. The contact had affected him, too.

I'd better go.
You'd better.
They both knew what they were saying, just like the
last time they were at headquarters.
I haven't had any practice at this.

None?

Not one single time.

Sighing, she rubbed her temples. This was not a good thing to think about when she was trying to ward off a headache that had ambushed her because of the meeting tonight.

How exactly had this happened? How had this man, this *married* man, infiltrated her life so much?

Son of a bitch. She headed down the hall when she saw a group of people exiting the elevators. She met them at the entrance to the chief's conference room.

Zach Malvaso. Grady O'Connor. A woman she hadn't met but who looked familiar. Must be Jenn's twin, Connie. And of course, Mitch. He was dressed in knife-creased black slacks and a blue-and-black checked shirt. When he stepped aside, she saw Cynthia Malvaso behind him, talking with another man Megan recognized as Paul, the estranged brother.

Well, good. Bringing his wife, *including* his wife in their project, was just what they both needed. Mitch's smile was warm when he turned it on her. "Hello, Megan. You know my wife, Cynthia."

"Yes, hello, Cynthia."

"Detective." The woman's eyes were a beautiful blue, but they were cold and flat. Tonight, she wore a teal tunic and off-white trousers. She examined Megan's outfit, too. Megan had put on a pair of gray slacks, a long-sleeved T-shirt, and her red leather jacket. Certainly not Mrs. Malvaso's taste, which obviously ran to Ann Taylor and Talbots.

Megan greeted everyone else and they went inside. She scanned the room for a place to sit away from the Malvasos, who took chairs at one end of the table. Jenn Malvaso was at the opposite end; they must not have seen her. Megan watched as Jenn caught sight of her family and her whole face tightened. Something about her look made Megan head for her. "This seat taken?" she asked Jenn.

"No." Jenn's smile was perfunctory. "Sit, I'd like the

company." She glanced at her family. "Geez, Cynthia did come."

"What do you mean?"

"Mitch said she wanted to be a community volunteer on the steering committee. I was shocked."

"How nice. All in the family."

Someone pulled out the chair next to Jenn. Stan Steele, again. "Mind if I sit here, ladies?"

Megan sighed. Why the hell not?

Both Megan and Jenn greeted the councilman warmly.

"We'll get this meeting under way," Will Rossettie announced when everyone was seated. He glanced at Megan. "Meggie, you and Mitch ready?"

Megan nodded. "I've got the committee list right here. Except for the community volunteers." Which was why she hadn't known Cynthia Malvaso would be here.

"I've got that list." A cute little woman who Megan recognized as the chief's secretary stood. "Noah compiled it."

They passed out their respective papers.

The chief continued. "We'll break into small groups in a minute. Before that, I'd like to thank everybody for volunteering, particularly our community people. You'll be doing a lot of the preliminary work." Will picked up a remote. "If you'll look at the screen, I'll show you our time frame."

Megan focused on the time line she'd been instrumental in creating. In November, they would set up committees and take part in the Harvest Ball and two other fund-raising projects. December was the deadline for people to volunteer for the various committees, as well as finalizing the architectural plans. Building would begin as soon as the weather cooperated, probably March unless they got a warm spell and they could dig in February. The physical camp had to be done by May or June to get the inspections and permits completed if they wanted to run a camp in July or August. Meanwhile, groups would meet to set up the program and orchestrate the volunteers during the weeklong camp itself. Fund-raising would be continuous.

Megan smiled at the reality before her on the screen. She glanced down at the end of the table and caught Mitch's gaze. He threw a *We did it* grin back at her. Cynthia Malvaso leaned over and touched his arm possessively. She whispered something to him that chased his smile away.

Megan was grateful when the chief asked them to separate into committees.

She and Mitch would supervise everything; tonight they were to meet with the building committee—headed up by Zach and McKenna, who owned a construction company, and the program committee, which had been given to Jenn and Grady. Connie Malvaso Lewis would head the fund-raising; the chiefs would oversee volunteers. She noticed that Cynthia Malvaso was part of fund-raising. Mitch's brother Paul, at this point, would work alone.

The committee separated into groups scattered around the large room. She and Mitch met at the center of the room. He looked good tonight. He'd combed his hair back off his face, accenting his strong, Italian features. Dark, knowing eyes scrutinized her. "You got a headache again, don't you?" was the first thing he said.

"Nope. It's gone." She patted her purse. "I took a Zomig."

"Did you try the foot massage?"

She drew in a deep breath. "Um, no."

He colored as if he knew he shouldn't have asked the personal question, as if it just slipped out. "So, do we split up, or go to building and program together?"

"I think we should split—"

Zach called out, "Mitch, Megan, come over. Snyder's brother wants some input into the sketches." One of the firefighter's brothers had volunteered to do the architectural plans.

They headed for the building committee. A small, blond man with keen eyes stood by an easel with a large sketch of the property on the cove already drawn to scale. He was introduced to them as Clay Snyder. Megan and Mitch stood behind him, close enough so she could smell his aftershave. It was spicy. And so sexy she had to close her eyes to get a grip.

"So," Snyder said, "I understand we're going to draw out a full-blown camp, and decide afterward what to build for the upcoming summer."

Megan nodded. "That's the plan."

"So, shoot," the architect said. "Let's start with the waterfront and work our way back."

"All right." Megan focused on the drawing. "Bright Horizon has a pavilion and boathouse on the water. The docks and swimming beach are off that. I think it worked well." She looked to Mitch.

He smiled. "Seemed good to me."

Quickly Snyder drew a pavilion on the water and a boathouse off to the side. He sketched in a couple of docks. "This is just for placement. And I suggest you make the pavilion as big as you'll want it eventually. We'll design the other buildings so you can add onto them." He finished drawing. "Next?"

"I think the cabins should be close to the water," Mitch put in. "Don't you, Meg?"

Meg. Only he called her that.

"Uh-huh. Boys on one side, girls on the other. We're starting with one cabin each."

"How many will we have eventually?" Clay asked.

"Probably three for boys, three for girls, if the camp grows. Age groups at Bright Horizon are seven through eleven, nine through thirteen, and fourteen and over." Megan smiled. "I can't believe we'll ever get big enough for that."

"Do counselors have their own cabins?" Snyder asked.

"No, they bunk with the kids. Everybody does, even paid staff."

"The chairman and camp director have their own cottage, don't they?" Zach asked.

"Yes." Her gaze locked with Mitch's for a moment. "They're married."

Mitch's eyes burned briefly. Her insides turned to mush.

Someone joked about keeping things in the family.

The design continued. Six cabins, two to be built for this summer. One hut for music, arts and crafts, and woodworking, to be eventually expanded to a hut for each area. A boathouse.

"Outdoor activities?" the architect asked.

Zach said, "We'll have to wait for the program's brainstorming for that." He turned to the side. "Hey, Jenny, don't forget a basketball court."

Again, Megan noticed Jenn's smile was strained. "I won't forget," she called out from her table.

"Let's just stick with the buildings, then, for now," the architect said.

In the end, they decided to use the existing cabin as a kitchen/infirmary, and build a covered portico for eating if it rained. Later they could add a dining hall.

After an hour, they took a break to wait for the program committee to finish and give the architect their input. Mitch turned away from Megan quickly and crossed to the fund-raising group, where he sat down with his wife and put his arm on the back of her chair.

Megan watched them steadily. The sight of them together was a needed reminder, especially after the heated look he gave her when they mentioned the upstate camp founder and program director were married.

"CHECK MY LIST one last time, will you, Grady?"

Biting his tongue at the young secretary's ploy to get his attention, Grady took the clipboard from her. "Sure, Babs." Babs, what the hell kind of name was that?

A pert blond, she sidled in close, letting her breast graze his arm. He could only imagine what Jenny was thinking. She'd been tense all night. Hell, she'd been as taut as a rope about to snap for almost a week. Tonight, Friday, it would be a week since he touched her.

Don't think about that, he told himself, forcing his concentration to the list of activities. He bent his head and got a wiff of sexy perfume. It did nothing for him, whereas Jenny's bath splash, when he'd smelled it as she took a seat at the table, had made him rock hard.

He heard a chair scrape back and looked up. "I'm taking a break," Jenn said. "Wanna come, Gray?"

"No thanks. Babs and I need to finish this up to give to building."

"I'm ready for a break, too," Grady heard someone say. Steele again. Jesus, he was practically stalking Jenny. How the hell had he gotten so integral to this project anyway?

"Sure." She smiled up at him. "I guess I'm on my own."

They left, and Grady could barely sit still. He tried to focus on the list. Go-carts. Basketball. Putting green. A host of water activities: kayaking, paddleboats, a tour boat, small inboard boats. Mitch and Megan had gotten all that water equipment from Bright Horizon. Good. Grady thought about the age groups they'd need to plan for. They'd decided to house overnight only children older than seven, but they were going to provide a day camp for kids six and under. They'd have to cut that off somewhere. Couldn't have babies around the camp.

Babies.

Today was B-day, but there would be no baby for him and Jenny. Not after what they did last week. He had to push it out of his mind. He couldn't stand thinking about her like that—straddling him, kissing her way down his spine to his butt, licking the back of his knees. It killed him to recall what he'd given up.

Killed. Now there was the operative word. His hand clenched as he remembered the feel of his unborn child. . . .

He concentrated on the list. Music. Drama. Art . . .

About ten minutes later, everybody in their group took a break. Zach came over to Grady, who was seated alone at the table. "You guys done?"

Grady looked up. "Just about."

"Where's Jenny?" her brother asked.

"She took a break."

"She left." This from Mitch who approached them. "She said she didn't feel well and she was going home."

Grady's chest tightened. "If she's sick she shouldn't be driving."

"She's not. I'm taking her car. Steele drove her back to her place."

A pencil in Grady's hand snapped in two.

"Easy, tiger," Mitch joked. "Jenny's a big girl. She knows how to handle a guy on the make."

He pictured Jenny handling *him*. Touching his chest. Kissing his stomach. Taking him in her mouth. The *ice,* for God's sake. He threw back his chair. "I've had it."

Zach's brows arched. "We need to go over the program."

He thrust the list at Zach. "Here's what we decided. Babs can clarify anything you don't understand." He stalked out of the room, leaving his friends openmouthed at his abrupt departure.

Somehow he found his way to his car. His mind was a jumble, his heart filled with conflicting emotions. He needed to see Jenny so badly he hurt with it. He'd been treating her like shit, avoiding her, ignoring her. He couldn't bear to look into her eyes. At her face. She wasn't happy with his decision; he hated that, but his mind was stuck and he couldn't figure a way out of this. He was positive he was right about no romantic involvement between them; it was a stupid idea. Look how cruelly he was behaving. They'd made a terrible mistake. He was just trying to backpedal to where they'd been.

We can't forget about this, Gray.

He had to have her in his life, though. He had to. Recklessly, he drove home. What if she was there with Steele? No, she wouldn't be. She was suffering over *him*. She wouldn't fuck another guy so soon.

She would later on, though, when this was all over. How could he bear knowing that, maybe even hearing about it once they got past this hump? The blare of a horn told him he was not paying attention to his driving. He'd gone over the white line on the road. He glanced down at the speedometer. Eighty. Shit. He slowed, drove more carefully. Her car wasn't in the garage, of course. Steele's car wasn't there, either.

Thank God.

He let himself into his half of the house. Dropping his leather jacket on a chair, tossing his keys on top, he didn't stop when they slid to the floor. Hurrying, he crossed to the French doors that connected their houses. He'd been locking them from his side.

Nice, O'Connor. Very nice. It probably hurt her. A lot. Stepping into the foyer, he heard noise in the living room. Thank God she wasn't in her bedroom. He crossed to the doorway.

She was lying on the couch, which was made up as a bed. Shit. She couldn't sleep up there, either. A fire blazed away and she was on her side, facing it. Bucky, their dog, slept peacefully near the hearth. In the firelight, Grady saw Jenn wore plain red cotton pajamas and white socks. Her hair was obscuring her face, its shiny strands glowing in the light.

"Jenny?"

Her hand fisted in the pillowcase, but she didn't look at him. "I'm okay, Grady. Go to bed."

"Mitch said you were sick."

"I'm not. It was an excuse to get out of there. Then he wouldn't let me drive."

"Steele took you home."

"Please, just go away."

He couldn't. He came further into the room. When he approached the couch, she turned over and faced the back of it. His chest felt so tight he thought it might burst. At a loss for how to lessen the pressure, he knelt down and began stroking her hair. For a while he didn't say anything. Then he whispered, "I'm so sorry."

She just shook her head.

"I knew I'd hurt you."

Again, nothing. Then he saw her shoulders shake, heard the sobs she was struggling to muffle. Reaching over, he tried to turn her to face him.

"No, don't." Her voice was raw, constricting his heart even more.

With force, he pulled her around. She wouldn't look at him, instead covered her face with her hands as she cried. He stood, then bent over, lifted her, and sank down on the couch, cuddling her to him. "Jenny."

She sobbed into his chest, grasping his shirt.

He'd done this. He'd made this strong, independent woman, whom he'd seen cry only a handful of times, come apart. This was what he did to women he loved.

Finally she quieted. Drew back. Looked at him. In the firelight, her face was red, her eyes swollen. "I'm sorry. This is so girly."

He kissed her nose. "You're entitled. I put my fist through one of the walls down in the cellar two nights ago."

She lifted his hand and kissed his bruised knuckles. "I can't bear it being like this between us."

"Me, either. I've been afraid to talk to you about it, afraid to come near you, really."

She snuggled into him. "I'll do it your way, Gray, I will. But it can't be like this. You can't avoid me, ignore me. I can't stand it."

He hugged her close. "I'm sorry. I keep making so many mistakes."

"Just promise me you won't push me away anymore."

He was surprised that she didn't ask him to reconsider his decision. "I won't."

Finally he felt her relax.

"You haven't been sleeping, have you?" he asked, drawing circles on her back.

"No."

"You always get emotional with no sleep."

"I've heard you prowling around."

"I can't zonk for more than a couple of hours."

She sighed.

Without really thinking, without censoring what he was doing, he kicked off his shoes and stretched out on the couch, bringing her with him. Reaching to the back of the sofa, he tugged off an afghan Sabina had made and covered them.

Like Eve to Adam, Jenn nestled into him. He hugged her close and closed his eyes. Tomorrow he'd think about what they were going to do.

*   *   *

THINGS WERE BETTER between Grady and Jenn the next week. They were excruciatingly kind to each other. They spent time together. They rode to work in the same car. Though they avoided touching, and didn't spend the night together again, it seemed like things were on track.

Until they were called to a bad car accident on Jay Street one night at 3 A.M. When they arrived at the scene, Mitch was already there, as was another Midi. Her brother approached their rig. "Go back to the firehouse, guys. I got Midi Five."

Grady frowned. "Why?"

Mitch threw Jenn a concerned look, then grasped Grady's shoulder. "Because the victim in the car is your ex-fiancée, Sheila Madigan, Gray. She's drunk and drove her car right off the road." He drew in a deep breath. "It doesn't look good."

≈ FIFTEEN

LATER THAT WEEK, Mitch was on duty, sitting in the firehouse living room watching a show about 9/11 heroism that they'd taped right after the horrific day. He'd put this particular video in because all week, things around here had been morose, since Sheila's accident, mostly because of Grady's reaction, and Jenn's mood. And the situation at home was still bad. These videos about heroism and rescues soothed his soul, not unlike the stories he told his kids.

This particular episode was entitled *Lucky Six*. He smiled. It traced the experiences of FDNY's Ladder Company Six and their rescue efforts and proved that miracles *did* happen.

A Captain Jonas came on and began the story. Then he was a voice-over for pictures of each of the firefighters in their house. Not used to working the towers, Jonas said, they heard the news about the WTC and within minutes were at the scene. There was a video shot of the north tower. Jonas's voice again. "We climbed Stairway B of the north tower, stopping to catch our breath and take water from evacuees along the way. At the twenty-seventh floor, we heard a rumble and knew the south tower had collapsed. I ordered my group to start back down."

Another picture came on; this time it was a black woman. Halfway down in the company of other people, the firefighters had met Josephine Harris, a Brooklyn grandmother. She was exhausted from her trek down from the seventy-third floor. They assisted her until her legs gave out. They stopped at a landing with her. She told them to leave her and save themselves. They refused and stayed with her. "Everything started moving and shaking around us," Jonas said. "We thought we were goners. When that calmed down, we spied a door on the second floor and pried it open." There was the miracle—a two-floor section of the staircase was still standing; the men put Harris in a harness and slid her down. Then they waited. A second miracle . . . they were rescued a short time after. They found out later the others they were with when they stopped to help Josephine were killed. Their group was spared *because* they stayed with her to help.

Mitch felt heartened by the story, as he did every time he saw it. He was watching the next upbeat tale when the PA system blasted out its staticky call. "Elevator accident at the Federal Building, 403 Main Street. Rescue Squad, Quint and Midi Seven, Engine Seventeen go into service."

Mitch bounded off the couch, hoping for a piece of those 9/11 miracles in whatever they'd be facing now. He met up with his sister at the entrance to the bay. She was jumping into her bunker boots. In seconds more firefighters arrived, one of them their brother Zach. For a minute, Mitch felt a sting of fear. The three of them didn't work too much together, and with the upcoming nine-month anniversary of the Sinco fire, this was . . . ominous.

"Sure you want to drive, sis?" Zach said as he suited up.

"Yep."

"Grady usually does."

Mitch noticed Jenn's eyes darkened at the mention of their friend. "Yeah, well, he's not here, is he, so I'm driver."

They piled into the Midi; as Mitch opened the cab of the Rescue vehicle, he heard his brother say, "Just jerking your chain, Jenn."

"Fuck you," came his sister's retort.

"What's gotten into her?" LoTurco asked as they pulled out of the bay.

"Maybe you guys busting her chops about Steele?"

The men had been merciless since her date with the councilman, especially since they'd heard about him taking her home from the camp meeting a week ago. They'd left pictures of him pinned to her pillow, bought her a book on being "first lady," and kept up the glamour razzing with makeup and other toiletries till Jenny lost it last night and really lit into them.

"Nah," Snyder put in from the backseat. "She's worried about O'Connor."

"We all are."

Mitch wanted to change the subject. Something was happening to his friend and he guessed what it was, in part anyway. When Sheila had been hurt, it resurrected all kinds of guilt in the guy. She was still in a coma, and Grady had taken some furlough to keep vigil, and to *get his head on straight,* Jenn said. Mitch didn't know what all was bothering Grady, but he suspected his sister knew, though she wouldn't talk about it. Sometimes, those two were closer than Siamese twins.

The rigs arrived at the Federal Building in minutes. The structure was brand new and was scheduled to open next month. Zach and Jenn swerved in right behind them. A rookie met them at the door, and they hurried through the lobby of the first floor to where Battalion Chief Ron Jackson had set up Incident Command.

He looked relieved when he spotted Mitch. "Glad you're here, Malvaso," the BC said. "We got a humdinger."

"What happened?"

"An elevator problem was discovered on the final inspection for this building when the feds brought in their own guy. Two repairmen were trying to fix it—seems the shaft was too high in the hoistway and needed to be lowered further into the drill shaft hole." He referred to a drawing of the elevator insides and pointed out what he meant. "The flange support unexpectedly broke loose and severed the hydraulic line." He paused dramatically. "One car dropped and went right through the first floor. A support beam's lodged between the first floor and the pit."

"Somebody hurt?" Zach asked, hefting out the ALS bag.

"Yeah. But it gets worse. It's a two-car elevator. The second cab is suspended in its shaft and needs to be shored up. Engine Seventeen's doing that right now. But we can't wait to go down . . . far as we can tell, the car pinned one guy and knocked the other out."

"We'll go through the pit door," Mitch said.

"Can't. Another beam came loose and jammed the door to the pit from the inside."

Catching his drift, Mitch turned to LoTurco. "Get the rappelling equipment."

LoTurco headed out and Mitch faced his group, which had assembled behind him. "I'll go down." He nodded to his sister, the logical choice to go with him since she was an EMT. "Jenny, while I assess the situation, you get ready to come next if I need you."

Jackson walked with Mitch to the elevator. "It's dangerous, Malvaso. You're gonna have to work from the second shaft. We're stabilizing the cab overhead now, but it could fall right on you."

"I know." He refused to think about the danger, about something happening to him, just as he had at Sinco. As he donned the harness and ropes, though, his mind flashed to Bobby and Trish, and for a second to Meg, but when he was ready, he blocked them out.

After he was anchored, he lowered himself from the first floor to the top of the cab, then rappelled the rest of the way. This was a deep basement, several courses more than normal. He could see the car hover ominously over the empty shaft where he landed.

Two men were on the floor of the shaft. The first was lying flat on his back and semiconscious. The second lay immobile, crushed by the elevator car. He spoke into the radio. "We need a medic right away. Send Jenny. Then we'll need air bags and cribbing to shore up the collapsed car. Snyder and Tuck have experience with this, so get them here when the other car's stabilized." More softly, he said, "My guess is the second group will be a recovery operation, Ron, not a rescue. The guy didn't stand a chance."

"Got you," Jackson said.

Mitch checked the air and the ventilation—both seemed good—and waited for Jenny. He tried not to glance at the cab overhead, but his heart pounded in his chest at the possibility of it falling. Noise from firefighters working to shore it up filtered down.

As he saw his sister appear, swinging from a rope like *Tarzan*'s Jane, he thought about what he'd promised her at the Sinco fire. Her descent was slow. She reached the top of the car and planted her feet there.

"Good girl," he said, smiling. "Come the rest of the way. You'll be in the second shaft, honey. So be careful."

Instead of finishing the descent, she bent over and put her hands on her knees.

"Jenn, you all right?"

"I feel a little woozy."

"From the rappelling? You've done it before."

"I know." A pause. "Give me a second."

This was odd. But she finally came down on the rope and her feet touched the ground. Swallowing hard, she tugged open the top of her shirt. "Wow! It's hot down here."

It wasn't. And she was breathing hard, gasping almost. Then her eyes began to glaze over and she slumped into him.

Holding his sister, Mitch said into the radio, "Jackson, get Zach down here."

MEGAN SMILED AT the drawings of the camp that the architect had just delivered after getting input from last week's meeting. She couldn't wait until Mitch saw them. As soon as she had the thought, she quelled it. Instead she beamed up at Will. "These are terrific."

When Noah walked in, Will said, "Wait until you see these."

Noah sighed, looking harried. "I could use some good news."

"Something wrong?"

"This inspection stuff. Ever since Sinco . . ." He put his hand on his hip. "Damn. A page." He picked it up, glanced at the message and immediately went for his cell phone. "An emergency." He waited. "Callahan here. What's goin' on, Jackson?" Another pause. "Oh, no."

Megan frowned.

Will stiffened.

They expected trouble and got it.

"I'll be right there." He clicked off. "I gotta go." He headed for the door.

By tacit agreement, Megan and Will followed.

"It's the new Federal Building," Callahan said as he strode quickly down the hall. "An elevator car fell on two workers who were trying to repair the shaft. The Rescue Squad went down. There's a casualty."

Megan's heart thumped against the wall of her chest. The Rescue Squad. Mitch. "Is it a firefighter?"

"No, one of the repairmen. But there are smoke eaters and paramedics down there."

Will swore as they reached the elevator and they got in.

Megan thought about the weight of the cab they rode down in. It could crush and kill anyone in its way. They reached the lobby of the police headquarters.

They all took their own vehicles and raced to the scene. In minutes they were there, out of the cars and into the building. Noah led the way as they hurried to Incident Command.

"Jackson, give me an update."

"It just got worse, Chief." He nodded to the open elevator doors. We sent Malvaso—Mitch—rappelling down there, and then his sister. Something happened to her, so he called for Zach. We're waiting before we send down teams to shore up the collapsed elevator until the second suspended elevator is completely stabilized." He hesitated meaningfully. "All three Malvasos are down there."

"The elevator's *not* stabilized yet?" the chief asked.

"Not completely."

"Shit."

Megan sucked in a breath. "Why did you send Mitch and Jenny down before it was safe?"

The chiefs exchanged glances. "It's the way it's done, Meggie," Will told her. "The highest ranking officer went down and then a medic."

The BC put in, "We didn't think there'd be a problem with the stabilization, but it's taken longer than expected."

"What's wrong with Jenn Malvaso?" Callahan asked.

"Got me. Zach's treating one of the workmen now. The other bought it."

Megan blinked hard. Visions of the second cab catapulting through the hoistway onto her friends—and a man she'd come to care too much about—stunned her. Oh, my God!

She sat through interminable minutes until someone yelled, "The cab's stable."

Shouts went up from the others. The BC spoke into the radio.

"They're ready to pull up the medics and the victim, too," Jackson told the group standing by.

It took minutes to get the victim—who'd been strapped to a backboard—up the shaft. Then, Jenny came out.

Mitch did not.

Jackson was on the radio again. "Guys are coming, Malvaso. Cribbing and air bags, too." He turned to the four firefighters waiting the command. "Go ahead."

Clapping a hand over her mouth, Megan turned away. Though it seemed safe in the shaft now, she thought she might be ill acknowledging the danger Mitch had been in all this time.

JENN WAS STRETCHED out on the floor of the new Federal Building trying to regain her equilibrium when Grady rushed through the front door. Oh, great. They'd just begun to get on track with their relationship when Sheila drove her car into a guardrail. Now he'd be worried about *her*.

And she didn't even know what had happened.

He rushed to her side. "Jenny, Christ, are you all right?"

"Yeah, I am."

"What happened? I went to the firehouse. When you were out, I called Noah's office. Babs said there was an elevator accident, and somebody was killed."

"A repairman. It happened before we even got here."

"I'm sorry." He studied the harness she'd been brought up on; it was undone but hung loosely around her. "How'd you get hurt? *Where* are you hurt?"

"I'm not. I don't know what happened. For some reason, the rappelling made me light-headed. On the way down I got dizzy. I stopped on top of the cab thinking it would pass. But then I went the rest of the way and fainted."

"Did they check you out?"

"Zach did, while we waiting for the backboard and stuff to come down." She shook her head. "It was scary until they stabilized the other car."

"What?"

"The other car wasn't stable. They had to shore it up."

"And you went down there?"

"Uh-huh, the guy who was alive needed immediate care."

Grady rubbed his eyes with his thumb and forefinger. She could see the strain around his mouth. He'd been suffering over Sheila and didn't need this.

"How's Sheila?"

He waited a beat before he answered. "She came out of the coma today. I got to talk to her."

"How did that go?"

He didn't say anything.

"Gray." She touched his arm. "What happened?"

When he looked at her, his blue eyes were so bleak it broke her heart. "Same old, same old. This was my fault. I broke up with her because we wanted different things in life. Jesus, Jenn, it was kids and living sanely instead of jet-setting all over." He ran a hand through his hair. "Anyway, she said if I'd stuck with her, she'd be all right."

"You know that's not true."

"Do I?"

"You used to." She paused and clasped his hand. "And you were just starting to feel better about us."

"I—"

"There she is." Zach knelt beside her. He said a quick hello to Grady, then took Jenny's pulse. "It's still high." He brushed back her hair. "Mitch said you turned as white as a ghost and fainted."

"It wasn't that bad."

Creases formed on Zach's brow. "Jenn, you couldn't do your job. That's not you."

"The rappelling . . ."

Grady's eyes narrowed on her. "That never bothered you before. I don't remember you ever almost fainting."

"I do." Zach chuckled. "When you were a teenager, and it was that time of month. Remember I found out how weak you got the first few days and teased the hell out of you about such a girly reaction."

Jenn smiled.

Zach was called away, and Grady settled in next to her. "Do you have your period, Jenny?"

She stilled. "Um, no."

"When's it due?"

"A couple of days ago. So that's probably the cause of all this. It'll come today. It's probably started now and that's why I got weak." She glanced quickly at Grady's face, which had drained of color. "Gray, did you hear? I'm all right."

His eyes were dark. "I heard, Jenny. I heard that your period's late."

A NOVEMBER WIND had blown in by the time the rescue had been completed and Megan left the building. She'd stuck around, to make sure everyone was all right. Jenny. Zach. Mitch.

Her stomach was still queasy over what had happened, what *could* have happened, and by the time she got to her car, her hands were trembling. Delayed reaction to a crisis, she knew.

Everything's okay, she kept telling herself. He came out of it fine. She fumbled with the lock and dropped her keys.

"Meg?"

She spun around. "Oh, you startled me." His face bore traces of grime and his turnout coat was unbuttoned. He'd taken off his helmet and the wind ruffled his dark hair.

"You all right?" he asked.

She drew in a deep breath. "Me? You're the one who was down there. Where that car could have fallen on you. You could have been . . ." She clapped a hand over her mouth and whirled back around. "Oh, God."

Mitch waited a moment. Then he moved in close. Put his hands on her arms and drew her back against him. His breath fanned her ear. "I'm all right, Meggie."

She bit her lip. He *was* all right. And she didn't warrant his tenderness. "I don't know why I'm so upset. I'm a cop. I deal with these situations all the time."

He drew her even closer, and by God, she let him. One arm came around her, crossed over her collarbone; his hand rested on her shoulder, his head against hers. "Don't you? Know why you're upset?"

She didn't answer.

"Meg."

She shook her head.

"Look at me."

"No." She swallowed hard. "Please, let me go. I'll be better. Stronger the next time I see you."

His arm tightened. It felt so good to be close to him like this. But, God, she had to remember their situation. Mitch was married. Like Lance had been married. When he cheated on her. She would *not* do this.

"Please, Mitch. Don't say anything more."

His hesitation was long and meaningful. "All right." He stepped back. She heard keys jingle so he must have bent over and picked them up. "Here." He reached around and put them in her hand. Closed her fingers over them. Squeezed. Before he stepped totally away, she felt the soft brush of his lips on her hair.

Then she heard the heavy footsteps of his bunker boots as he tromped back into the building.

SIXTEEN

THE MORNING AFTER the elevator incident, Mitch slept in at the firehouse, had breakfast with the next shift, and returned home about nine. It was harder and harder to come back here, well, not here, but back to Cynthia. Especially after . . .

Let me go. I'll be better. Stronger the next time I see you. . . . Please, Mitch. Don't say anything more. . . .

He hadn't, of course; he'd respected her wishes. Respected *her* even more for her morals. She would *not* get involved with a married man, wouldn't even confess her feelings. And he knew she had feelings for him. He'd known it for days, given how well they got along, how much they had in common. And watching her with his kids, watching her work for this camp had solidified it all for him.

After pouring coffee, he crossed to the window and stared out across his yard at the trees—bare now of the fall foliage; their branches swayed a bit in the wind. It was almost Thanksgiving. Where would he be next year at this time?

"Well, you finally decided to come home."

He pivoted and faced his wife. She was dressed in a

neat pair of slacks and a blue sweater. Already she wore makeup and had her hair done up. "Don't start on me, Cindy. I had a bad night."

After a brief hesitation, she went to the counter and poured coffee for herself, then took a seat at the table, absently opening a magazine that lay there. "What happened?"

"An elevator accident. We had to rappel into the shaft."

Staring down, she leafed through the pages. "You've done that before. How high up were you?"

"Only the first floor."

"What was the problem, then?"

I could have gotten smeared all over the concrete floor if the other elevator had fallen. "The other car—it was unstable; it could have come down. The situation was . . . tense."

She looked up, and for a brief second, he wished she'd pull through here, sympathize with the danger he'd been in, try at least to understand him.

Finally she said, "If you'd take that battalion chief's job Noah wants you to have, you wouldn't routinely be in this kind of danger."

He cocked his head. "Do you worry about me, Cindy?"

"Of course."

"No, really, like shaking, stuttering, unable to sit still worrying."

"No." She leaned back in the chair, poised like a queen holding court. "You told me when we first got married, in order to be a firefighter's wife, I had to suppress that kind of thing."

Well, he had told her that.

"Do you really want me be an anxious mess because you choose to put your life on the line every day?"

"No."

Still . . .

Me? You're the one who was down there. Where that car could have fallen on you. You could have been . . . Megan had clapped a hand over her mouth and spun back around. *Oh, God . . .*

Mitch knew he wasn't being fair. Megan had been

there, seen it unfolding. Still the comparison popped into his head.

"Take the test, Mitch. Become a battalion chief. You won't be in harm's way. We'll have more prestige. More money."

"You don't need more money, Cindy. Your father gives you whatever I can't afford."

"You never seemed to mind."

In truth, he hadn't. He personally didn't care about material things, but if she did, her father providing them was fine with Mitch.

"My parents think it's a good idea. Daddy and I were just talking about that."

"But caring about prestige is so shallow."

She stiffened. "Of course, I'm shallow next to the big, altruistic firefighter."

His first impulse was to flee, say he needed a shower and get away from her. It was his standard MO, whenever things got tough. But he thought about Bobby's song that night at the talent show, he thought about Trish intentionally dating a bad boy, and yes, he thought about Megan's real concern for him.

Carefully, he placed his cup on the counter. "I've had enough, Cynthia. Our relationship isn't working for me, and I'm not putting up with it anymore. You have two choices. Come to see Jack Harrison with me, talk this out, see if we're salvageable, or if this relationship has crashed and burned. Who knows. You might find *you* want to break up."

"I won't be just another divorcée."

Not *I don't want to lose you*. Not *we've been married twenty some years*.

"You may not have a choice."

"I don't like ultimatums. I refuse to go listen to some *fire department* shrink tell me what a wonderful man you are. What a horrible wife I am. I'm still pissed that Bobby's seeing him."

"Then we'll go to someone else."

She shook her head.

"Is that what you're afraid of? Somebody telling you you're selfish? And shallow?"

Folding her arms over her chest, she raised her chin. "I am what I've always been. Who I've always been. The woman you fell in love with."

"We're not *okay*, Cindy."

"I am."

"Well, I'm not."

"What would you do Mitch, leave me?" She said it so incredulously that for a minute, he thought it had to be a ridiculous idea.

"I could do that."

"You'd never leave your children."

Bingo! God, was she really banking on that? Was she holding it over his head? What kind of woman was she?

"No, you're right, there. I'd never leave Bobby and Trish alone with you. They wouldn't survive." He edged in close. "But I'll tell you something. I *will* take steps. First, I'm moving into the basement. Today. I won't sleep in the same bed with you anymore. And I'm going to get both psychological help and legal advice."

"Go ahead. You'll never go through with a divorce."

"I could have *died* last night, Cindy. I almost did die in the Sinco fire. Life's too—"

"Oh, spare me. You've decided to change your life after a couple of close calls. That's so melodramatic. So . . . trite."

He closed his eyes to block out the sight of her, standing before him in her designer clothes, with her expensive manicure and haircut, telling him that potentially fatal experiences were trite. "I feel sorry for you, Cynthia. Really I do. But I'm not buying into this anymore." He brushed past her. She snagged his sleeve.

When he turned, he saw a brief flash of vulnerability on her face. "Is there someone else?"

"What do you mean?"

"Another woman? Are you screwing some bimbo you think could make you happy?" Her eyes narrowed. "It fits, you know. Cutting off sex with me, now moving out of our bedroom."

"I'm not screwing anyone, Cindy." With that he turned away.

His heart thudded in his chest as he took the steps two at a time to his bedroom. Once he got there, he stopped. God, was he doing the right thing? They'd been married so long. She was the mother of his children.

The incompetent, sometimes cruel mother of his children.

He removed two suitcases from the closet and filled them with clothes . . . doing it methodically so he didn't feel the pain. He went to the garage, got boxes, then stuffed the rest of his belongings in them. Cynthia was gone, by then. He'd heard her leave not long after he began packing.

It was when he was getting the last of his things that he found an album at the bottom of the dresser. It looked old and he didn't remember it. Inside were pictures of him and Cindy when they were young and first married . . . on their honeymoon, eyes shining with desire and something else, expectation . . . him in bed, he was sure after some lovemaking that at one time had been sensational . . . at her parents house in the Hamptons, in bathing suits, holding drinks, laughing. . . .

His heart constricted as he leafed through their early days together, traced the face that had once enthralled him. So much lost. So much forgotten. There was none of that happy anticipation of a wonderful future in either of their expressions anymore. The disillusionment, the disappointment at what his life had become threatened to overwhelm him.

He put his head down and buried his face in his hands.

MITCH WAS WAITING in the kitchen when Bobby and Trish came in from school. His heart was heavy—he felt like he did when they found a corpse in a fire—but he had things to do, and he'd do them. Thank God Cynthia had not returned. He'd called the battalion chief and told him he wouldn't be in and to get a sub.

"She thinks you're hot," Trish teased her brother as they barreled through the door.

"Oh, please."

Their youthful bantering reminded him of when they were young and would come home from elementary school. Because of his schedule, he'd often get to wait for them at the bus stop. They'd clamber off the bus and throw themselves into his arms, bubbling on about their day. Where had the time gone? And what had he done with it?

They saw him at the table. As if she'd read his mind, Trish crossed to him, threw her arms around his neck and kissed him on the cheek. "Hi, Daddycakes."

His throat worked convulsively. It was what she'd called him when she was little. "Hi, princess."

Bobby stood back. "What's wrong?"

The kid could read him so easily. "I have to talk to you two."

Trish and Bobby exchanged worried glances.

"Sit."

Trish took a chair adjacent to him. Bobby said, "No, I'd rather . . . what's going on, Dad?"

No use postponing this. He'd jump right in, hoping he didn't drown. "You know your mom and I haven't been getting along for quite some time. You guys have both talked to me about it."

Immediately, Bobby crossed the room to stand in back of Trish. He put his hand on her shoulder. Mitch saw her grasp it. They knew bad news was coming. And their faces were fraught with worry, and something else. Fear.

Bobby said, "Don't move out and leave us here with her, Dad. Please."

Emotion vised Mitch's chest. He managed to get out, "I'd never do that, Bobby. I promise."

His son's shoulders relaxed. Trish's didn't. "What are you going to do, Daddy?"

"I'll be sleeping in the basement for now. I'm going to keep seeing the department psychologist, and go to a lawyer. Things can't go on the way they've been between your mother and me." He went with his gut. "Nor between your mother and you two. I know it's been bad."

"It's been a fucking nightmare," Bobby said, his uncharacteristic swearing surprising Mitch. "She treats you like shit, and me like I'm the reincarnation of Satan. She's only nice to Trish when they do girl things together."

"Bobby . . ." Mitch didn't know what to say. It was all true. So he told them what was in his heart. "I love you both. You're the most important thing in life to me. I promise I'll never abandon you."

"We're the most important thing in your life?" Trish asked.

Jesus. "Of course."

"Mom says it's the fire department. That you care more about that than us."

"Oh, baby, and you believed her?"

His daughter looked so young, so vulnerable, he stood and pulled her out of her chair. She hugged him tightly. His gaze sought Bobby's. There was a simmering anger in his son's look.

Bobby said, "It's bullshit, Dad. I didn't believe her."

Mitch smiled, then held out his hand. "Come here, buddy."

Without a second's hesitation, Bobby stepped to him and hugged them both in an awkward but meaningful embrace. Mitch felt his eyes sting. He promised himself he'd never ever let these kids down again.

And now he knew what he always suspected—part of that vow most likely would include leaving their mother. And taking them with him.

JENN RETURNED HOME from her shift after a good night's sleep, which she'd desperately needed. Zach had pronounced her fit, so they'd let her go back to the firehouse after the elevator accident. They'd had no runs, though; she'd gone to bed and was asleep by ten.

Grady had protested her returning to work last night. He'd put up such a fuss Mitch had to take him aside and talk to him. Then he'd stormed out of the Federal Building. She'd thought he might show up at the fire station, but he hadn't.

Intuitively, she knew he wasn't home when she stepped inside. The house was so still. She wondered if he'd come home at all last night. *Damn,* she thought, going to the kitchen to make coffee. Things had been on track, after a rocky patch. Not that they were the way she preferred. She wanted him as a friend *and* lover. Christ, whenever she was around him anymore, her blood heated. But if he didn't want her that way, or couldn't accept the change in their relationship, she'd take the status quo. Then Sheila had gotten hurt, and he'd been thrown off course again, so even going back to just friends wasn't working.

And now her period was late. Placing her hand on her stomach, she was afraid to hope for a baby. Grady would not be happy if she was pregnant, she was sure. It would throw him into another tailspin. Chiding herself, she ducked into the downstairs powder room off the back of the kitchen to check again.

And there was evidence. Some spotting on her panties. Okay, so she wasn't pregnant. She was getting her period. It would be fine. She forced herself not to be disappointed. This would be the best for Grady.

She was just leaving the john when Grady appeared in her kitchen doorway. He looked like hell. His face was bristly with yesterday's whiskers, his clothes—from last night—were a wrinkled mess. His hair was disheveled. But it was his eyes that got to her. They were so bleak she wanted to die.

"Did you get your period?" His voice sounded as if he'd smoked Marlboros all night.

"Um, yeah, I think so."

A muscle leaped in his throat. "What do you mean, you think so?"

Feeling her eyes mist, she turned away. *No, I will not cry over this.* Heading for the stove, she did her best to sound casual. "I have some spotting. I'm sure I'm getting it."

"Just spotting? That doesn't mean anything. You could still be pregnant."

"I'll get it."

"You're days late. What if you don't get it?"

"I will. It's probably just the stress of what's been going on between us."

"You've been stressed before. Has it ever delayed your period?"

"Yeah, sure." It hadn't, but she was on unfamiliar ground and didn't know how to navigate the territory.

Suddenly she was yanked around.

"Oh." Spots swam before her eyes and her head spun. She felt like she did when her SCBA ran out of air. She grabbed Grady's arm to steady herself.

"Jenny, what . . ." He clasped her shoulders, then dragged her to him and enveloped her in his strong arms. "Geez, baby, what's going on?"

Feeling weak, and frustrated, and not a little scared, she buried her face in his chest. "I was dizzy, that's all."

"Dizzy?"

She nodded.

"And stress hasn't affected your cycle before, has it?"

She shook her head, fearing she would cry. She'd wanted a baby since the Sinco fire. At one time Grady had wanted it, too.

But he didn't now. So if carrying his child was going to make him unhappy, she wouldn't wish for it, either. *Please, God,* she prayed. *Don't let me be pregnant. For him. Let this mean I'm getting my period.*

Somewhere she found the strength to pull back and compose herself. She looked up at him and saw so much love, so much concern, so much affection on his face, she was humbled by it. And she knew she could live with just that for the rest of her life. She touched his face reverently. "Gray, it's okay. Let's not get ahead of ourselves. This is a good sign. I spot sometimes before I get my period. I think it's coming."

"You do?" He sounded so hopeful it broke her heart. But she'd be damned if she'd let it show.

"Yeah."

"All right." He brushed back her hair and kissed her nose. "I'm sorry. I know I'm making this rough on you."

"I don't care. I just want you to feel better about things. For us to be back to where we were."

"After we know for sure. I promise, things will be better."

"Okay."

"You could do an early pregnancy test. We could find out today. You can get results the first day of a missed period."

"I don't want to do it now, Gray."

"Why?"

Because I should be doing it with hope that I'm pregnant. Not to prove I'm not.

"Some women I've known have done a pregnancy test right away, and it was negative, and then a week later it was positive." She sighed. "I'll do it Saturday if I don't get my period by then. Like I said, I think it's coming anyway."

"All right." He drew away. Ran a hand over his face. "Can I have some coffee?"

"Yeah, sit. I'll get it for you."

Looking unutterably weary, he took a chair at the table. "Saturday's the Harvest Ball, isn't it?" he asked.

Uh-oh. "Um, yeah."

"Do I have to wear a monkey suit?"

"I'm afraid so."

He smiled at her, nicely distracted, now. "Hell."

"You'll look like a million bucks."

"Renting one will cost almost that much."

"Get a funky one. I love the different shirts and ties."

"Sure, you can pick it out for me." He watched her. "You got a dress?"

"Yes. I bought a new one."

"What time do we have to go?"

She took a seat adjacent to him. "Gray . . ."

He sipped his coffee. "Yeah?"

"I . . ." Hell, she didn't want to deal with this now. He was like a spark waiting to ignite and she dreaded tossing this match.

He cocked his head. "Ah, I get it. You're going with Steele, aren't you?"

"Yes. He asked a while ago."

"Have you been dating him all along?" Grady's voice had gotten tight again.

"We've had some drinks after work."

"I thought you were with your family those nights."

She felt defensive. "I never said that."

"I just assumed."

Fuck, how did she handle this? One of them had to act sanely. "It's not serious. I like Stan, but he's too slick for my taste."

"Then don't go to the ball with him."

"I have to, Gray." She covered his hand. "I'd rather go with you."

He shook his head. "Jesus, Jenny. What if you don't get your period by then? You could be—"

She'd had enough. "Stop badgering me. This whole thing is not my fault, Gray!" She was appalled that her voice shook and she felt tears threaten again.

He startled, then swore vilely and pulled her from her chair into his lap. "Ah, honey, of course it's not. I'm sorry. I hate making you sad like this." More swearing. "Jesus, Jenny, how did we get to this point?"

"I wanted a baby." She mumbled it into his shirt. "I wanted you as the father."

He shook his head. "Christ, be careful what you wish for. . . ."

ZACH WATCHED MITCH walk into Badges and knew immediately something was wrong. His brother's face was ragged and his gait stiff. Since Mitch was always Mr. Laid-Back-and-Easy, Zach worried. "Hey, Mitello."

"Hi, Zaccaria." He looked around the bar. "Oh, fuck."

Zach tracked his gaze. In the back of the bar, Megan Hale sat at a table with Will Rossettie. She had her head down and Will had his hand on her back. Obviously, the woman was upset.

"What's going on?" Zach asked.

After a long hard stare across the room, Mitch took the stool next to Zach. "My whole life's going down the toilet. It's why I called you."

"You said you took the kids out to dinner but they were going to a concert tonight and you were at loose ends."

"Yep." He ordered a beer.

"Tell me what's going on."

Mitch recounted what had happened with him and Cynthia today. "I . . . Jesus, Zach, our relationship has been on the skids for years. At first I stayed in it because I took vows and I didn't want to give up without a fight. Lately, though, I stayed for the kids. Now I find out they're petrified I'd leave them with her. I feel like I should have done something long ago."

"Hindsight's always twenty-twenty." Zach knew that only too well.

Mitch stared at his beer. "This is so big, I don't even know where to begin."

"Far as I can see, you only got one problem. How to keep your kids."

"Yeah, that simplifies it, doesn't it?"

"And they're older, so they'll have a say."

"I guess."

Zach added, "Cynthia might not even want them."

"Holy hell, I never thought of that."

"You're too nice a guy to think of that."

Mitch's gaze drifted past Zach's shoulder. He noticed his brother kept glancing toward Megan Hale. Hmm.

"Mitch?"

"Cynthia might try to get them for spite."

"Maybe. But look on the bright side. Trish and Bobby have had plenty of practice acting out. They could make her life miserable if she tried to keep them against their will."

Mitch laughed at that. Zach was glad he could make him feel better.

"I guess I need a lawyer. Divorce sucks, doesn't it, Zach?"

Zach shook his head. "Yeah."

Mitch watched him. "How are you doing, buddy?"

"I'm hanging in there."

"Any more attacks?"

"Not recently. I been reading about PTSD. I don't have the classic symptoms. Fighting fires and doing rescues like that elevator thing don't trigger it."

"I know. It's why you're still working."

"Yeah." Restlessly, Zach ran his hand through his hair. "I'm depressed though, you know?"

"Can I do anything?"

"Being around you and Jenn helps. Let's change the subject. Did I tell you I'm looking to buy a house in the city?"

"No, where?"

"One of those big old ones on Park Avenue. I found one that needs a ton of work, but it's huge and I could take in a tenant if I fix it up right. I'm not sure about the money, though, if I can afford the down payment."

Mitch looked at him. He looked at Mitch.

"Are you thinking what I'm thinking?" Zach asked.

"Would there be room for Bobby and Trish?"

"Yeah, and Jason and Nicky when they visited."

Mitch smiled, Zach smiled, and suddenly the world seemed a little brighter.

Will Rossettie broke up their good mood. "Sorry to interrupt, guys, but I gotta leave. I have to be somewhere by eight." He glanced across the room. "And Meggie's a wreck."

At Will's description, Mitch's face blanched and he looked guilty. "About . . . what?"

Something *was* going on here.

"Today's her father's birthday."

"Shit."

"And she won't leave. She says she doesn't want to go home to an empty house. I can come back, but I have to take care of something first." Will faced Mitch, his look that of a concerned father. "I know you've gotten to be friends with her. After the trip to Keuka Lake."

Mitch nodded.

"Want to keep an eye on her for me?"

"Yeah," Mitch said earnestly. "I want to keep an eye on her."

"Thanks, Mitch." Will gave one last look across the room and left.

Mitch stood and threw some money on the bar. "Sorry about this. We'll talk more, okay?"

"Yep." Zach checked his watch. "I think I'll swing by Angie's. See if the boys want to go out for a snack." He glanced over at Megan. "We got *a lot* more to talk about, buddy."

Mitch sighed. "We do. Not now, though."

"Soon." Zach hugged his brother, drew back. "It's gonna work out."

Mitch smiled and walked away toward Megan Hale.

MEGAN LOOKED UP from her beer and was startled to see Mitch standing at her table. "Can I sit down?" he asked.

"That's probably not a good idea."

Ignoring her protest, he slid into the booth across from her. "Will told me what today is."

She glanced away. God, she didn't want to talk about this. "Look, Mitch, I know you have good intentions, but I'm feeling pretty raw, and I don't want to . . ." Suddenly her eyes filled with tears. "Shit." She bolted up out of the booth, headed outside, and as the wind whipped around her, she stumbled to her car. In the dark and cold night, she felt so alone and angry and confused, she wanted to punch something. The bag, she thought. She'd go home and take out her mood on the punching bag. She reached for her purse to get the keys, only to find she didn't *have* her purse. Shit. Shit. Shit. She'd left it in the booth.

"Here it is." Pivoting around, she found Mitch behind her. He had on jeans and a leather jacket with the collar turned up. He looked so good and strong and safe she wanted to throw herself into his arms. Instead she grabbed her purse from him.

"Thanks." She rummaged inside for the keys. "Son of a bitch." Her heart was pounding and her hands shook. "Where the *hell* are they?"

She heard a jangle—not from her purse. She looked up to find Mitch, holding her keys.

"They're right here. I thought you might try to make a quick getaway." He turned, then circled the car and opened the passenger door, keeping the keys in his hand.

"What are you doing?" she asked frantically.

"Get in. I'm not letting you drive like this."

"Mitch, I'm fine. I can take care of myself."

"I know you can. But you're not driving when you're so upset. I shouldn't have let you go last night; I worried like hell about you being on the road when you were so upset."

She stared across the hood of the car at him.

"Get in, Meg. You can call Will on his cell phone so he doesn't cancel his plans, and tell him I'm taking care of you."

"You *can't* take care of me."

He arched an arrogant brow. "Yeah?" Oh, God, he could be so sexy. "Watch me."

For a minute she was immobilized. Then she circled the car and climbed inside. He slammed the door, went around to the driver's side, and slid in behind the wheel. He started the engine and pulled out without another word. "Put your belt on."

Sputtering, she did.

"Call Will."

"Mitch . . ."

He drew his cell phone out of his pocket. "Do I have to call information to get his number?"

"Damn it, Mitch."

He grinned. In the dim light of the lamps from the parking lot, she saw him freakin' *grin*.

"This isn't funny."

"I do know how to get my way when I want to, Meggie."

She sighed. "All right, I'll phone him."

Megan made the call then gave Mitch directions. When they swerved into the driveway of the old house where she rented a room, she was suddenly embarrassed by it. He lived in a beautiful home in a nice part of town. "It's just a studio apartment," she said, "I haven't had time to find anything else."

"I don't care about those things, Meg." He exited the car and came around her side. When he opened her door, she scowled. "What are you doing?"

"I'm coming in."

"No, Mitch. You're not. You can call a cab from out here."

He jangled the keys. "I got the house key. I'll try all the doors till I find which one is yours, and let myself in."

"When the hell did you get so autocratic?"

"I don't know." Again, the boyish grin.

But this really wasn't funny. She remembered last night and the stark fear she'd experienced when he was in danger. It had forced her to admit her feelings for this man, to herself, and indirectly to him outside the Federal Building. Climbing out of the car, she peered up at him. "Last night, I said I'd be stronger the next time I saw you."

His face softened so much, she had to close her eyes to block out his expression. "I remember."

"I'm not strong enough, Mitch. Not tonight."

"All right, then I'll be strong for both of us."

"Mitch."

"Come on, Meg. I want to be with you. Just for a bit."

In the end she relented and let him into her place, hugely afraid she was letting him into her life. All the way up the two flights of steps, down the corridor, and to her room, she thought about Lance, and how he'd been unfaithful. How hurt she'd been that her husband had slept with another woman. By the time they were inside, she felt tougher.

At least the place was clean and she'd folded up the sofa bed. Still, the dingy walls and drab furniture were embarrassing. All of her own stuff was in storage. "Sit," she said. "Want a beer?"

He took off his jacket and tossed it on a chair. "Yes, ma'am."

She shed her coat, got them Coors Lights, and they sat on the couch sipping from the bottles.

"Want to talk about it?" he finally asked.

"About Dad?"

"Uh-huh."

She shrugged. "He loved his birthday. He would have been fifty-six. We used to do special things every year on this day. Dress up and go to Coney Island. Have a date for Elaine's. Ride the ferry to . . ." She drew in a breath, remembering the feel of the wind in her face, the smell of her father's aftershave next to her. "I miss him so much. . . ."

Tears leaked from her eyes. Placing the beer down, she wiped them away; Mitch held out a handkerchief. She took it. "I'm sorry."

"For missing your father?"

"No, for being so weak."

"Meg, this is the first time you haven't been with your dad on his birthday in how many years?"

"For as long as I can remember."

"Cry it out. You'll feel better."

As if they'd been given permission, the tears came like water bursting from a hydrant. Dropping the handkerchief, she buried her face in her hands and let the sorrow, the sadness, flow out of her. After a bit, she felt strong hands grasp her arms, tug her over, and then encircle her in an embrace so warm and safe it made her cry harder. He smoothed down her hair. "It's okay, Meggie. It's okay."

She didn't know how much longer she cried in his embrace. She only knew that when she was spent, she *did* feel better. After drawing back and mopping her face, she let herself look at him. "Thanks." She shook her head. "You seem to always see me at my worst."

"No, never that."

She rolled her eyes. "I do feel better."

His gaze intense, he brushed his knuckles down her cheek. Suddenly the atmosphere changed. It went from tender and comforting to tense and charged. He stared into her eyes. His were deep brown, the color of rich earth, and his lashes were so thick. "Meg," he said simply.

She shook her head. "Mitch, this isn't . . . we can't . . . No matter what I implied last night, we can't . . ."

"I know we can't. But I have to tell you something." Again, she shook her head.

"I won't have you thinking badly of me," he told her.

She was puzzled and gave him a questioning gaze.

He said simply, "Because of my feelings for you."

Bang. Boom. Somebody had voiced it. This was *not* good.

"We shouldn't talk about it."

"We have to. I want to tell you about my marriage. About me and Cynthia. It'll sound like a cliché, but please believe me, every word is true."

"I don't want to hear about you and your wife, Mitch."

He told her anyway. "We've been unhappy for years. I know you've picked up on it, by what I've said, by what my kids have done and said."

No, no, she didn't want to hear this. She couldn't. So she conjured Lance again. Pictured him, sitting on Lila Jenkins's couch.

Was that what he'd said to his girlfriend? *Megan and I have been unhappy for a long time.* They hadn't been.

"We're so different, and it's come to a head."

She's so young, Lila. Not at all what I want in a woman.

"I'm going to take steps . . ."

I'm going to tell Megan, leave her . . .

Had Lance said what Mitch was saying to get the other woman into bed? Was that what Mitch was doing?

Suddenly she couldn't stand it, couldn't tolerate the thought of being like Lila Jenkins. She stood abruptly and held up her palm. "Stop it, Mitch!" He hesitated and she rushed on, "I don't want to know this."

"Why, Meg?"

She looked down at him, down at the married man she was falling in love with. "Because Lance cheated on me."

Mitch just looked at Megan. It was the last thing he expected. Why would any man cheat on her? "I don't know what to say."

She began to pace, her long legs, encased in tight jeans,

eating up the floor space; she kept quiet, didn't even look at him.

When she didn't respond, he shook his head. "You've talked like you were so happy with Lance." He shifted in his seat, uncomfortable with this news. "Did you divorce?"

Shaking her head, she wrapped her arms around her waist but continued to pace. "No, but we separated for a while. He didn't want a divorce, said it was just a *thing*, that he'd made a mistake. He was sorry and he promised he'd spend the rest of his life proving it."

"You took him back?"

"Eventually, though he groveled a lot beforehand. And he did prove he loved me. We were blissfully happy until he died a few months later." She stopped and faced him. "I loved him so much, Mitch. I didn't know he was unhappy. I don't really think he was. It was just something he did, something very stupid and very wrong."

"I'm sorry that happened to you."

She moved in close to him, knelt down, and shocked the hell out of him by taking his hand in both of hers. "I was so hurt, I wanted to die."

"I can imagine."

"I can't do that to another woman, Mitch."

He watched her, wondering how far to go, wondering how not to inflict any more pain on this beautiful, moral woman who'd already been hurt too much. "I see where you're coming from, Meg. But my problems with Cynthia have nothing to do with you."

"How do you know that?"

"They've been going on a lot longer than six weeks."

"Still, it isn't right."

"To have these feelings?"

"Yes. And to voice them. To act on them."

"All right, we won't act on them. We'll continue as we have, until things are settled between me and Cynthia. Nothing will change between you and me in the interim."

She looked skeptical.

"Trust me."

She swallowed hard.

"Please."

"All right."

"I do have to say one thing, though."

"Mitch . . ."

"No, I do." He cradled her face in his hands. "I'm not your husband, Meg. What I feel for you is not just a *thing*. And it's not a mistake."

She opened her mouth to protest. He quelled it with his thumb on her lips.

"Shh. Hear me out. I didn't seek this out with you, but it's happened and I don't regret it. I'd be dissolving my marriage, whether or not you'd come to Hidden Cove. For the kids, if for nothing else."

Her shoulders relaxed. "All right."

"But I need to say out loud that I *do* have feelings for you."

"I—"

"No, don't say anything. If it's to protest, it won't do any good. If it's to tell me you feel the same, which I think you do, I won't be able to leave if you say the words." He kissed her nose. "Which I'm going to do, right now."

She leaned back and he stood. Without another word, he circled around her, got his jacket, and donned it. At the door, he turned to face her. By then she'd risen, too, and watched him from across the room.

"I'm a man of my word, Meg. And I want to do the right thing here. But know this. I aim to have you. When this is all over, by God, I will."

Opening the door, he left her, feeling a calm, and a sureness, that he hadn't felt in a long time. His step was lighter as he descended the stairs and whipped out his cell phone to call a cab.

SEVENTEEN

SITTING IN HIS 'Vette, waiting for Jenny to come out of the store, Grady clutched the purple-and-white package with e.p.t. on the front; he stared down at the early pregnancy test they'd picked up after work. Damn, why hadn't Jenny done it days ago? She hadn't gotten her period and now she was really late. She'd had a little spotting, but none which would constitute a period. Still, she'd insisted on waiting until today. Why?

Stupid question, jerk. You've been Jekyll and Hyde for weeks; she's afraid of you. Afraid of what you'll do if this is positive. She'd been simply postponing it.

Looking out at the trees swaying in the November wind, he shook his head, angry as hell at himself. He had to get his shit together. Whether this test was positive or not, he was taking action. He'd called Harrison and made an appointment for right after Thanksgiving. He would have gone in sooner but the department psychologist was on vacation next week. He *should* have sought therapy years ago, but Jenny had been his friend, counselor, and lifeline for so long he hadn't needed a shrink. Since she couldn't fulfill that role now, he had to have help.

He'd been careful with her all week. He'd succeeded

at being his old self again—to a degree—but every time he looked at her stomach, he thought about how this maybe-baby had gotten there, and he got scared all over again. Still, he'd coddled her whenever she'd let him and talked to her like he used to. The only thing he hadn't done was sleep in the same bed with her at night. He didn't trust himself.

She'd had other signs that she was pregnant. She'd been tired, falling asleep early—thankfully they'd been on days at work so she could rest when the fatigue hit her at night. And certain foods had turned her stomach. She'd had no more dizzy spells, though, or he wouldn't have let her on the line. Quelling the panic inside him, he looked up when she opened the car door. She hung her dress in the back and slid into the front seat. "Wow, it's getting cold."

He smiled. "You should have worn your winter coat."

She smiled back, so warily, it made his chest tight. She was waiting for Hyde to surface. She had been all week. Her gaze dropped to his hand. "What are you doing?"

"Reading the directions while I waited for you."

Her faced drained of color.

"This says we could have found out a while ago."

She reached out and placed her hand over his on the package. "I know. I *did* think my period would come any day. When it didn't, I was afraid."

Staring down at the test kit, which held the key to their future, he felt his breath catch. "I know."

"It's probably going to be positive."

"Yeah, I realize that."

"I—I'm sorry."

Torn, he watched the sadness darken her beautiful brown eyes. "Don't say that, honey. I know you want a baby."

"That was before . . ."

"Before I wigged out."

"You've got cause, Gray."

His heart swelled with love for this generous, giving woman who cared so much for him. It made him sane and conversely conjured every nightmare inside him.

What if he lost her? "You are so special," he said, soothing down her hair.

"So are you."

He wanted to kiss her, felt the need so badly he had to shake himself. "Let's go see what we're dealing with."

They drove home in silence. He parked in the garage and they went in through his side of the house. Once in the kitchen, she clutched her dress to her like a shield. "I'll go hang this up." Her voice quavered.

Taking the dress from her, he squeezed her shoulder. "I'll do it." He hung it in the hall closet. "No more delays." He led her to the downstairs powder room. When he handed her the package, her hand shook so badly she dropped it. "Jenny, love, it's okay."

She drew in a breath. "I'm so scared."

"Of me."

"No, of what this will do to us."

"Well, you have every right to feel that way after the asshole I've been."

"Gray."

"Honey, let's just *do* it." He opened the package and held out the cup. "You get a urine sample. I'll do the honors with the little white wand."

She nodded and slipped inside. In a few minutes, she opened the door. By now, her face was chalk white. The cup was on the vanity. She stepped back, but when he moved toward the sink, she sidled in close, looping her arm through his, laying her head on his biceps. The tenderness of the gesture, that it said so clearly she needed his support, fortified him. He took the wand and stuck it in the cup.

They had to wait two minutes for the results. Leaning against the wall, he pulled her around and encompassed her in a hug. "Want me to tell a baby story?" he asked. "I heard a great one the other day."

She shook her head. They often told firefighter stories, like Mitch did with his kids, to cheer themselves up when things were tense.

Jenn said, "Do you really want to talk about *babies* now?"

"Yeah, this is nice."

He recounted how Engine 5 went over to the high school and just seconds before they got there, a girl had her kid in a bathroom as small as this one; she gave birth on the toilet.

"The guys thought the baby was dead," Grady said. "But then they looked into the commode and there was this little thing swimming in the toilet, face up."

"Jesus. Really?"

"Yep, the cold water saved her somehow."

They cut the cord and pulled the baby out of the toilet, suctioned her, and kept her warm until she was taken to the neonatal center.

Jenn held on to him, then said so softly it broke his heart, "Somebody worthy will adopt that baby, be happy about her."

Was she thinking of them? Of his attitude?

He straightened. "Time to find out about our own baby, Jenny." Though he knew in his heart what the result was going to be.

With one arm still encircling her, he moved to the vanity and picked up the wand. There was a pinkish/purple line in the large round window.

Jenny was pregnant with his child.

"Oh, God." He felt her slump against him, but he couldn't move.

When he heard her muffled sobs, it mobilized him. He tugged her fully into his arms, cradled her head, and kissed her hair. Tears moistened his own eyes, and curiously, he didn't know if they were tears of joy or fear. Weary of his ambivalence, he hugged her closer.

When she drew back and peered up at him, her eyes were sparkling with so much—fear, yes, but a joy so deep it humbled him. "I'm—"

He placed his fingers on her mouth. "Don't say you're sorry. We can't be sorry about this."

"You didn't want it."

"Oh, honey, I'm so fucked up right now, I don't know what I want. But I won't spoil this. I won't."

"Gray."

He cuddled her next to his heart. The mother of his child. His best friend. And the most precious lover he'd ever had. They had a lot to deal with, but he savored the moment. In many ways, was sobered by it. Time to behave better. Time, definitely, to get his act together.

"I've got an appointment with Harrison as soon as he gets back from vacation, Jenny. And I'm going to keep seeing him until I get my head on straight. I promise, I'll do that. For you."

She clung to him. Hugged him hard. But she didn't cry again. After a long while, he drew back and stared down at her. "Come on. Let's get Mom down for a nap."

"I can't." She hesitated. "The ball tonight?"

"Shit, I forgot." His heart started to beat faster. The mother of his kid was going with another man.

Your fault, asshole. If you'd handled this whole thing better, she wouldn't be dating someone else.

Okay, so he'd deal with it. "The ball doesn't start until nine."

"We're having dinner."

"Oh."

"I wish I could cancel the date."

"I do, too." He glanced at his watch. "When's he picking you up."

"Six."

"You don't have much time then." His smile was genuine. "I'll spoil you tomorrow."

"We have to work tomorrow."

Gently, he brushed his knuckles down her cheek. "Honey, you can't work tomorrow. You have to go off the line right away."

"Oh, God, what was I thinking?" She glanced up at the ceiling. "If I tell the brass, my brothers will know."

"Yeah, they will."

"Grady, they'll be . . . I don't think they're going to handle this very well."

He sighed thinking of how Mitch had grilled him when he found out Grady and Jenn often slept together. How Zach had erupted more than once about Grady not watching out for her.

A strong primitive urge to protect this woman, and the baby she carried, welled inside him. "You'll call in sick tomorrow. Then our group's off for a few days, and you and I have furlough for Thanksgiving. That's time enough to tell your family."

"Gray, are you okay with this?"

"Hell, no. I don't want you out with another man tonight."

"No, I mean the baby thing."

"Honestly, there's so many conflicting emotions inside me, I don't have a clue what I'm feeling." He drew her close again. "Except that I love you, Jenn. I've loved you since we were kids, right through all the shit that's happened. And I love you even more now."

Her eyes filled. "Oh, Grady." She buried her face in his chest and said, "I love you, too."

MITCH WAS WAITING in the living room, among the Aubusson carpet and Stickley furniture that his wife valued so much, when Cynthia came down the steps. She wore white silk, low cut with thin straps and a hemline to the floor; he bet the dress would have cost him a week's salary. Her trust fund had paid for it, but still, it seemed like a foolish extravagance. As did thousand-dollar chairs.

"I'm ready," she said stiffly.

At a loss for what to say to her—they'd hardly spoken all week—he nodded. "Fine."

"You could tell me I look nice."

"You look nice."

She shook her head as she went to the front closet and removed a white fur jacket. "At least try to be civil there. I don't want anybody to know you're treating me like dirt."

"I'm not treating you like dirt, Cynthia. I gave you a chance to work on this relationship and you rejected it. So as far as I'm concerned, there's nothing else to say. Or do."

Shaking her head, she glared at him. "Don't start with

the divorce thing. Unless there's another woman, men like you don't leave their families."

Dad, please don't leave us with her.

He glanced at his watch. "Let's go." He'd had no choice but to take her to the Harvest Ball tonight. He had to attend, and she wouldn't think of missing it. Truthfully, he'd hope she'd go to the Hamptons to stay with her parents for a while and he could have gone to this fund-raiser alone. But instead, she was leaving tomorrow to spend the Thanksgiving holiday down there. She'd given no consideration to Trish or Bobby when making that decision, had said only it was his fault she had to get away.

What would Megan think when she saw him with Cynthia? He'd tried to call her several times, but Will had told him she'd taken a few days off; Will had thought the hiatus was to deal with her feelings about her father's birthday. Maybe she wouldn't even go to the ball tonight. No, she'd have to. This was a fund-raiser for her baby. And his.

He and Cynthia rode in silence to the Holloway House, a large Victorian mansion on East Avenue that had been turned into a commercial party house. The town held many social events there. They walked into the huge ballroom like strangers. It was only when she saw people she knew that she threaded her arm through his and began to play the happy wife. Man, he was sick of this.

The first half hour was torture, making nice with her friends, pretending things were just fine, and trying like hell not to look for Megan. When he spotted Zach and Grady at the bar set up in the dining room, he made his escape, leaving Cindy to talk about God-knew-what with the mayor.

As he reached the guys, he took note of their unhappy expressions. "Hey, this is a party, men. You look like it's a funeral."

Zach sipped his Manhattan. "Angie's here with Kellerman." He indicated Grady with an angling of his head. "I don't know what O'Connor's problem is."

Mitch gave Zach's shoulder a brief squeeze. "I'm sorry. Did you know Angie was coming with him?"

"Yep. She called to tell me." Zach eyed his brother carefully. "Where's Cynthia?"

"Talking to the higher-ups." Mitch sighed and leaned against the bar. He'd seen Zach again this week, but when his brother had asked about Megan, Mitch had told Zach it was something he couldn't discuss yet.

Mitch signaled the bartender. "Anybody want anything?"

Zach shook his head, but Grady didn't answer. He just stared into the crowd. After he ordered a beer, Mitch tracked his friend's gaze. Grady's eyes were glued to Jenn and her date—Councilman Steele. Jenn had outdone herself with the dress tonight. It was a little sage-green thing with a beaded top, long skirt with matching beads sprinkled at the bottom. Steele kept touching it—his arm around her waist, his hand resting on her hip. She'd move away; he'd move in. And she kept darting surreptitious glances toward the bar. At Grady?

Who was glowering now.

Mitch tried to joke. "Want us to go drag her away from him by the hair?"

Grady didn't answer.

Something about his demeanor. Mitch had a brief flash of the discussion they'd had when Mitch found out Grady and Jenn often spent the night together. "Hey, O'Connor. You look like a jealous lover. What's up?"

Still staring at Jenn, Grady said, "She shouldn't be out tonight."

Mitch and Zach exchanged glances. "Why?" Zach asked. "She's been fine since the elevator thing."

"No, she hasn't. She's taking tomorrow off. She doesn't feel well."

Zach straightened. "Jesus. Why'd you let her come here?"

Grady shot him a disgusted look.

"Did she see a doctor?" Mitch asked.

"She will next week."

Mitch caught something in Grady's tone. Not worry, really. Something else. Like possessiveness. He asked, "Anything going on here we should know about, Gray?"

Grady's head snapped around. "No, why?"

"Because you've been a bear for weeks, and you're acting stupid about Jenny all the time."

Averting his gaze, Grady sighed. "Sheila's accident."

"You were doing it before that."

"I—"

"Holy shit, look at that." Zach had turned and was distracted by something at the door.

Mitch looked to see what his brother meant—and froze. At the entrance to the room stood Megan on the arm of Will Rossettie.

At the first glimpse of her, Mitch's breath seized up She wore a shiny beige-and-brown dress, which hugged only one shoulder and was slit up the side showing leg to kingdom come.

Zach nudged him. "Close your mouth, bro."

Mitch tried to snap out of it. But, God, she looked good. In order not to gawk, he had to face the other way. Luckily, Grady had missed the exchange. He was still glaring at Jenn.

Geez, Mitch hoped there weren't any fireworks tonight. Angie with Kellerman. Jenn with Steele.

And Megan Hale looking sexier than a runway model.

WHEN THE DANCING started and Zach saw Angie and Kellerman head for the floor, he ducked out of the ball-room to find some place to have a cigarette. He ended up in the backyard, on a stone patio where a fire burned in a stone pit. Huge logs snapped and spit. As he approached it, he thought about Angie's call. . . .

Look, Zach, I know this is a fire department thing. But Ken's going to be our next principal; politically he needs to go. And I want to go with him.

Though it had cost him, Zach had tried to be gracious, had managed to be somewhat civil about it, but when she came in tonight in a blue dress that hugged every curve, clinging to another guy like he was her hero, Zach had felt ill.

Nothing you don't deserve.

It was cold outside, but the air felt good. A brisk slap in the face was what he needed. Besides, he could warm himself on the fire. He lit a cigarette and stared over the grounds wondering if he'd ever make sense of his life again.

You will, Zach, Harrison had promised. *It'll take time.*

He'd just butted out his smoke when he heard behind him, "Can I bum one of those?"

He turned to find a woman there. At first he couldn't make out who she was. Then she stepped into the light; it was Casey Brennan. Her hair was all fluffy and soft. And that dress—the pinkish color top was held up by minuscule straps and it looked like it was shot through with hundreds of multicolored ribbons. The skirt was really wide pants in a shimmery hot pink that slithered over her as she walked to him. Holy hell, he'd never known she was so buff. He tried not to drool. "Help yourself." He held out the pack. She took one and let him light it for her. After a long drag, she nodded. "Thanks. This ball thing's getting to me."

"Who'd you come with?"

"Ruscio."

"No wonder it's getting to you."

"He's okay. He's got issues."

"Don't we all."

She shivered. "What's yours, Malvaso?"

"My ex is here with her new beau."

"You care?"

"Now, I do." He peered out into the darkness as if he could find answers in the shadowy landscape. "I know the whole town wouldn't believe that, after what I've pulled. I've been such a jerk."

"Been there, done that." She waited. "Too bad it always comes back to haunt you."

"You married, Brennan?"

"I was." She shivered again.

Removing his tux jacket, he slipped it on her shoulders, without asking, since he knew he'd get the response she gave.

"I don't need this."

"Let me be a gentleman. My *ego* needs it."

She stared at him a while, then shrugged.

"Got any kids?" he asked.

Her shoulders stiffened. "I don't wanna go there."

He shrugged. "Fine."

She faced him, finally. "Can I ask you something? Would you be straight with me?"

"Sure."

"How do you think your group would feel about a woman taking Hunter's place when he retires at the beginning of the year?"

Zach thought about it. They'd accept Jenny in a minute. But Brennan? She was notorious for being a loner, and most groups wanted camaraderie. "I don't know. Word has it you don't get close to people."

"Jesus, I can't figure out why people like to talk about me. Just because I like to keep to myself?"

Again, he shrugged. He was staring directly into the fire when one of the huge logs shifted and settled with a loud whoosh. At the same time, fire sparked and the stink of charred wood assaulted him.

And suddenly Zach saw another fire, months ago. Heard another whoosh . . . a ceiling falling . . . and smelled everything burning . . .

The blaze burned brightly as he pulled up to it in his car. Mitch and Jenny were inside. He had to help. He bounded out of his car when he heard a whooshing sound. Jesus Christ, it came from inside Sinco's warehouse.

"Oh, God, Mitello, Genevieve," he breathed as he ran toward the blaze. When he reached the warehouse and headed inside, somebody grabbed him from behind.

"Let me go," he yelled to the person holding him back. "Malvaso . . ."

"I need to get to them. . . ."

Strong arms vised his chest. "You're not at the warehouse . . . you're at the Holloway House . . . Malvaso . . . come out of it. . . ."

The soothing voice calmed him. The fire receded and the world around him came into focus. He was outside the fancy house, on a covered portico and was pressed against a female body that, right now, imprisoned him in a steel grip.

"Easy," she whispered.

He sagged against her. She let him. Finally he was strong enough to stand on his own. Chagrin was setting in. Brennan. Shit. She'd seen him at his worst. Slowly he pivoted. "Oh, fuck."

Her pretty hairstyle was a wreck. The straps of her dress were off her shoulders. But it was the bruise on her cheek, already beginning to swell, that really got to him.

"Oh, Christ, Brennan. I'm sorry."

She straightened. Staring at him, she pulled up her dress and rubbed her cheek. "Ouch."

"I . . . what happened is . . ." He ran a hand through his hair.

"It's PTSD, isn't it?" she asked matter-of-factly. These attacks had scared the shit out of Angie.

He nodded. "I guess everybody knows."

"No, not that. I've seen it before. Someone . . ." She shook her head. "Never mind."

"You okay? Jesus, I don't know what I'm doing when these come."

"Yeah, that's the pattern. I'm fine." She rubbed her jaw. "You got a mean left hook, though."

He smiled.

She did, too, then as if she caught herself softening, she said, "I gotta go get cleaned up." Reaching down, she picked up his jacket. "Thanks." Handing it to him, she wandered off into the night.

Zach just stared after her.

"ARE YOU ALL right?"

The query came from Stan Steele as he whirled Jenn around the dance floor. Oh, yuck. Her stomach was doing flip-flops. It wasn't just because of the dancing and the few hors d'oeuvres she'd eaten, which she shouldn't have tried since she'd never had them before. There was ex-citement fluttering around inside her, too. She couldn't stop thinking about the baby she carried. Grady's baby.

She felt a kind of undiluted joy she'd never experienced before. And some measure of fear.

Though Grady couldn't have pulled through more for her today. Her emotions were on such a roller coaster, she didn't know how she would have handled it if he'd fallen apart. It was why she wouldn't do the test sooner, even when her period didn't come. But Grady had been great. . . .

As he drew a bath. "Not too hot, Jenn, ever when you're pregnant."

Smiling when she came downstairs. "You glow in that dress."

And just before Stan arrived. "No alcohol and no caffeine." Then his face darkened and he'd pulled her to him. "Don't let him put his hands on you, love."

She closed her eyes to savor the recollection as the dance ended.

"I think it's my turn, Steele."

Opening her eyes, she saw Grady had come up to them. It almost hurt to look at him. Rarely did he get dressed up, but tonight he made her mouth water. His tux was charcoal gray and he wore it with varying shades of gray underneath, shirt, vest, and tie. The monochromatic colors made his shoulders look a mile wide. Desire coursed through her. She'd read somewhere that pregnant women were horny as hell. Hell, she'd just found out today and already all she wanted to do was jump his bones. What would the next nine months be like?

After some banter, Stan handed her over to Grady. "You have her most of the time, O'Connor," he admonished. "Don't forget she's mine tonight."

"Yeah, don't bet on it," Grady whispered when Stan walked away. As he took Jenny in his arms, he added, "She is, after all, carrying *my* baby."

Jenn laid her head on his shoulder.

"You look a little peaked," he said rubbing his hand on her back.

"I don't feel so hot. It's like just confirming . . . you know, the baby . . . gave me permission to feel shitty."

He grinned against her cheek. "Go ahead, feel shitty."

He held her closer. "You shouldn't stay out too late."

"I won't."

"I told Mitch you didn't feel well and were taking to-morrow off."

"Oh." Pulling back, she gave him a half smile. "Self-fulfilling prophecy, I guess."

The dance floor was getting crowded. A couple bumped into them. They swayed gently to the music. All the while she relished the feel of Grady's body pressed up against hers.

"Geez, is it getting hot in here?" she asked.

He peered down at her. "Now your face is flushed." He kissed the top of her head. "Come on, we're getting you some air." Grasping her hand he led her to the French doors and out to the flagstone patio, where she started to see double.

"Grady!" She clapped her hand to her mouth.

He pivoted. "It's okay, honey." Quickly he dragged her out of sight off to the side.

Where she barfed like a kid sick on his first booze.

Dimly, she was aware of Grady holding her hair back, his arm braced around her. When she was done, he gave her his handkerchief to clean up. Then he took off his jacket and wrapped her in it. She sagged against him.

"That's it, I'm taking you home."

She was so weak she could barely stand. "Okay."

He led her around the outside of the club. By the time they reached the parking lot, she felt better. "What about Stan?"

"Fuck him."

"Grady . . ."

"All right, I'll get you in the car and go back and tell him you're ill."

"I should . . ."

"Shh. No arguments. I'm taking charge, now."

For some reason she liked the sound of that. Leaning heavily on his arm, she let Grady put her in his car.

*   *   *

MITCH DIDN'T WANT to dance with Cynthia but she insisted. Unfortunately, Megan was also on the floor with Steele; Mitch struggled to keep his eyes off of her.

It was almost eleven and he hadn't spoken with her all night.

"Your little detective friend seems pretty cozy with Jenny's date."

"I wonder where Jenn is. I haven't seen her in a while."

"Last I saw, she went outside with Grady."

They continued to dance, and Mitch continued to try not to watch Steele's hand flirt with Megan's hip. The floor got crowded, and he and Cynthia were inched toward the other couple. Shit. Mitch didn't want this.

As fate would have it, they ended up right next to Megan and Stan just as the dance ended. Immediately Cynthia went into socialite mode. "Well, hello, Councilman. Detective." She smiled sweetly up at Stan.

"Hello, Cynthia." Stan nodded to Mitch.

Megan said only, "Hi, you two."

"Where's Jenn?" Mitch asked.

For a minute, Steele's eyes darkened. "She felt ill. O'Connor spirited her away."

"Grady said she wasn't feeling well earlier."

"I'm sorry she's sick."

Cynthia fawned over him. "I've been wanting to talk to you all night, Stan. About a fund-raising idea I have." She peered coyly over at her husband. "You don't mind if I dance with the handsome councilman, do you dear?"

Mitch shrugged. She was trying to make him jealous. And hell, he was gonna end up dancing with Meggie. "No, of course not."

"Dance with the detective," Cynthia said and glided into Steele's arms.

Mitch looked fully at Megan. She couldn't refuse.

Her eyes told him she didn't want to, anyway. As Steele and Cynthia drifted away, he grasped her hand gently. It was warm, slender, feminine. She let him pull her close.

Megan felt like the fates were against her, or maybe working for her, depending on your viewpoint. After

Mitch's revelation last week, she'd gone to the cove to think about things. She'd stayed purposely away from temptation, and now she was in the arms of the man she'd been desperately trying to avoid, desperately trying not think about. This must be an example of the old joke about how God laughed whenever man said, "I have a plan."

"Don't scowl, Meg. What could we do?" His voice was soft, his tone teasing. Sometimes, a younger, less world-weary Mitch peeked out from the responsible captain and that part of him mesmerized her. It was as if she brought it out in him.

"This is crazy."

He stared at her. She loved his eyes. So brown. So warm. Tonight they had a sparkle in them that hadn't been there before. "You look stunning, Detective."

Her breath caught in her throat. She glanced down at his raven tux and pleated white shirt. It set off his dark coloring. "So do you. Do you own that tux?"

"Yeah, Cynthia thinks I'm a tuxedo kind of guy."

"Aren't you?"

"No, ma'am. I'm just a country boy at heart."

She smiled and he pulled her closer. She went, because the dance floor was crowded and semi-dark, and people wouldn't notice. And because she longed to be close to this man.

After a moment, he whispered, "You went away."

"Uh-huh."

"Where?"

"To Dad's cabin on the cove."

"Why?"

"To get away from you."

He stiffened.

Instinct, to protect him, to comfort him, made her squeeze his hand. "I had some thinking to do, Mitch."

"Did you think about me?" There was that boyish grin again.

"I thought about what you said."

"And?"

She shrugged. How did she tell him that although her

head told her not to get involved with a married man, her heart wouldn't listen. It kept insisting that Mitch was honest, was sincere. "I just thought about it."

"Do you believe me? What I said about my relationship with Cynthia?"

"Let's just say I'm not as upset as I was." For a moment, she lay her head on his shoulder, assimilating his warmth, seeking his strength. "Maybe this isn't the same thing. You know, as with Lance."

His hand tightened on her back. "I swear it isn't, Meg."

"I'm willing to wait it out. See what happens."

His heart thundered against hers. "You are?"

"Uh-huh."

Staring down at her, his jaw tightened. "Oh, God, I want to kiss you in the worst way."

She hid her face in the folds of his shirt.

"And touch you, Meg."

"Please stop. Don't do this. It's not time."

"All right."

Drawing her close, he just held her and danced. Blanking her mind, she basked in the feel of him.

EIGHTEEN

ON THANKSGIVING MORNING, Mitch put his arm around his mother and squeezed her tight as she stirred homemade applesauce at the stove. Sabina was a robust woman who wore her gray hair in a bun, house dresses, and sensible shoes. "So, Ma, who else did you invite *this* year?" Holidays at the Malvaso home always included legions; Sabina, who was a natural nurturer, loved taking in strays as well as coddling the entire family.

She pinched his cheek. "Noah Callahan's coming for dinner. And Will, of course."

Though the police chief had often kept them company on holidays, Mitch thought Will would spend Thanksgiving with Megan. God, he hoped she didn't go through today alone; her first Thanksgiving after her father's death was bound to be painful. He remembered vividly the first few holidays after his own father had died. He couldn't bear the thought of her being by herself. He could still feel her warm and supple in his arms on the dance floor Saturday night. Hmm. Maybe Will would bring her here. It never entered his mind he'd get to be with her today.

"You face is flushed, Mitello. Get away from the stove.

Go set up the buffet table while you talk to me." She smiled. "Like your father used to."

As he took the stacks of plates out of the cupboard, he thought about his dad. "Remember the story Pa told about that Thanksgiving at the station?" It was one of Mitch's favorites; he'd heard it several times, even after his father died.

"*Mamma mia.* He was stubborn, my Angelo."

"Yeah, the battalion chief he butted heads with all the time thought so, too."

Once, that particular BC got on his father's group about not scouring the kitchen. He said the table should be clean enough to eat off of. So that Thanksgiving, Angelo Malvaso was cooking, and the BC was eating with them; his father got the guys to help him "set the table." They put everything out—silverware, condiments, napkins—except plates.

"You really believe he did that, Ma? Served the meal right on the table?"

"Oh, my, I believe that." She smiled wistfully. "He could be a bad boy. He said he drew circles where the plates should have been and served turkey with all the trimmings right on the wood table."

"And the BC fumed."

They talked some more about his father, then Mitch crossed to the fridge for a beer. His mother glanced over her shoulder. "This early in the day, son?"

"It's eleven, Ma." He nodded into the living room where Zach sat sipping a Coors in front of the TV. "Zaccaria got a head start on me."

Sabina sighed. "It is a shame his boys can't come today." Nicky and Jason were spending today with their mother and her new boyfriend. "Divorce! See what it does?"

Mitch stilled.

His mother said, "And your wife. She should be here, too."

He wouldn't spoil his mother's Thanksgiving by telling her there would be another divorce in the family. But soon, he'd fill them all in. There was no harm in laying a little groundwork, though. "This is pretty typical of Cindy, don't you think, Ma?"

Sabina's dark eyes narrowed. "She is not a good wife, Mitello."

"Maybe I haven't been a good husband."

"Lord have mercy," she said, turning back to the stove. "You are the best."

"Not prejudiced, are you, Mama?"

She sniffed. "No."

There was commotion in the front of the house. "Somebody else is here."

"Hi, all." Paulie appeared in the doorway. He cocked his head at Mitch, then held out his hand. "Happy Thanksgiving, Mitello."

Mitch accepted the shake. "You too, Paolo."

His brother crossed to the stove and encircled his mother in a hug from behind. "Hello, beautiful."

"Oh, go on."

"Connie's here, too. We met in the driveway."

"I hear her girls."

"They're all over Zach." He glanced at Mitch. "Who isn't very happy right now."

Sabina harrumphed, and Mitch explained the situation.

Connie came to the kitchen and kissed Mitch, then Sabina. "What can I do, Mama?"

"Mitello peeled the onions. You can make the cream sauce."

Finding an apron, then donning it, Connie asked casually, "Where's Jenny?"

"She's not here yet." Mitch took a seat at the breakfast nook. "Grady called to say she's not feeling well and was going to rest a while before they came over."

Connie's actions stilled. "What's wrong with her?"

"I don't know. She got dizzy last week when we . . ." He trailed off, remembering his sister's and brother's feelings about the fire department. Lately, he suspected part of their animosity was rooted in fear.

"I read about it," Paulie told him. "You rappelled into an elevator shaft when the other car wasn't fully supported."

At the stove, Sabina crossed herself. Connie blanched

and turned away. Paulie started to leave. Mitch snagged his coat sleeve. "Wait a minute. Let's talk about this. It's been a wall between us for too long."

Paulie looked to Connie. She nodded.

And so Mitch frankly discussed the jeopardy in fire fighting. Yes, sometimes there were unusual dangers— like 9/11 of course, the Sinco fire, and on a smaller scale, the elevator shaft. But for the most part, firefighters were careful and didn't take unnecessary risks. They were also well trained. By the time Zach wandered into the kitchen, both Connie and Paulie had relaxed. Zach headed for the fridge, stopping to kiss his mother on the cheek. When he got another beer, Sabina looked to Mitch.

"Hey, buddy. It's a long day. Take it easy with the booze."

"Get off my back," Zach snarled.

Mitch waited a beat, then stood. "Let's go into the den and talk, Zach."

"No, I don't want to. Look, I'm sorry I snapped at you. I'm bummed about not having the boys. . . ."

"What did you expect?" Connie asked. "After what you did to Angie?"

Too late, Mitch saw the steam rise in his brother's face. "I know what I did to Angie. But what exactly did I do to you, Connie? Why do you hate me so much?"

"She does not hate you, Zaccaria." His mother had faced them fully. "Concetta, tell him."

Connie bristled. "I don't want to talk about this today."

"No, you just want to keep taking potshots at me on Thanksgiving."

Scowling, Connie bent over to get out a pan; Mitch started to intervene.

Zach said, "I'm going for a walk."

"I'll come," Mitch offered.

"No. I need some space." Zach stalked out of the room.

Connie's eyes clouded. They sought Paulie's. He said, "You gotta try, kid, like we talked about. It's not going to get any better if you don't."

Quietly, Mitch watched the byplay. When nobody said any more, he addressed them. "I want to say something.

How I appreciate what you're both doing with the camp. With me. I want us all to put the past behind us."

Connie stared after where Zach had gone. "I wish we could. But . . ." She shook her head. "I'm going to check on Al. See how he's doing with the baby."

Paulie went after her. Mitch sipped his beer and wondered why nothing was easy.

He went looking for Paulie a half hour later. His brother was in the den watching the small TV there. Since he had no kids of his own, sometimes the noise of family gatherings got to him. "Want some company?" Mitch asked.

"Sure."

"Connie okay?"

"As right as she'll ever be until she makes up with her siblings." He stared at the screen. "Nice pass."

Mitch grunted.

"Me, too," Paulie added. "You're right about letting go of things."

Sightlessly Mitch watch a punt. "Can I ask you something?"

Paulie nodded.

"If I needed some legal advice, could I come to you?"

His brother looked at him then. "What kind of legal advice?"

"Personal stuff. Maybe stuff you wouldn't want to get involved in."

"Are the kids in trouble again?"

Mitch shook his head.

Paulie raised his chin. "Are you finally fed up with Cynthia's shabby treatment of you?"

"Yeah, Paulie, I am. But I've got to protect Trish and Bobby in this. They can't live with her. Cynthia's a terrible mother."

"In a lot of ways, Cynthia's a terrible human being."

That surprised Mitch. Paulie never took much interest in his family. "Why do you say that?"

His brother stared at the TV, but Mitch had a feeling he was somewhere else. "Just how she's treated you."

"Yeah, well, my fault for letting it go on."

"It's never one person's fault." Paulie must be thinking of his own divorce five years ago. Of course, Mitch never knew what happened to break up him and his wife, only that his marriage ended abruptly. "But to answer your question, yes, I'd help you, especially if it's to get you out of Cynthia's clutches. Stop by and see me next week. We'll talk."

Just then Grady appeared in the doorway. "Hey, guys, Jenn and I are here. We'd like to talk to the family together. Could you come up to the kitchen?"

Mitch's heart did a somersault in his chest. He stood and felt his knees shake. "She's okay, isn't she? There's nothing seriously wrong with her, is there?"

Grady put a hand on his shoulder. "No, Mitch. She's fine. Honest. This is good news."

Despite Grady's assurances, Paulie and Mitch exchanged worried glances and followed Grady out.

JENN FELT HER stomach pitch as Mitch and Paulie came into the kitchen. Zach stood across the room scowling, and Connie was stirring something at the stove. Her mother's face was worried. Grady closed the door behind him and went to Jenn.

"You okay? You look a little green."

She put her hand on her stomach. "Jesus." She leaned into him. She'd been ill all morning, and nerves were making her tummy cramp. "Let's get it over with."

The room was ominously silent. Grady faced the Malvaso clan. "We have an announcement to make."

Questioning looks all around.

Jenn grabbed his hand, held it in a death grip. "I'm pregnant."

Connie dropped the spoon and it clattered to the stove top.

Sabina clapped her hands together, prayer fashion.

Paulie's mouth fell open.

And both Mitch and Zach stiffened like boxers ready to fight. Zach got particularly tense, then swore and chugged more beer.

"Jesus, Stan Steele isn't the father, is he?" Mitch asked.

"No!" Grady raised his chin and threw back his shoulders. "I'm the baby's father."

Mitch cocked his head. He looked at Jenny. "You said at the Sinco fire you wanted a baby. Did you like . . . do this . . . at a lab or something?"

"A lab, what does that mean?" Sabina asked.

"Artificial insemination, Mama." This from Connie who had stepped close and astounded Jenny by linking their arms. "Is that what you did, Jenny?"

Jenn sought her sister's gaze. "Well, we were going to do it that way, but . . ." She couldn't believe they were actually discussing this at one o'clock on Thanksgiving Day. "It, um, didn't turn out that way. Before we could . . . we . . ." She looked at Grady. "Help me out here."

Briefly he closed his eyes. A private man in many ways, this delving into his personal life had to be killing him. "All right. We conceived this baby the normal way. But that's our business, not yours. All you need to know is that it's a reality. And everything's going to be fine."

Mitch felt his temper rise. "Then you lied to us all these years? About the friendship? Christ, Grady, when I found out you slept together, you said it was just platonic."

"It was."

Paulie piped up with, "Platonic friends don't make babies."

Zach gulped the rest of his beer and wiped his mouth. "You guys dated a lot of other people. You were sleeping with each other at the same time? Jesus."

Grady's hands fisted. "Now hold on a minute."

Finally Connie stepped forward and faced Zach. "You have nerve criticizing *their* morals." Then she turned to Mitch and Paulie. "And you guys, this is none of your business. Jenny's thirty-six years old. She doesn't have to answer to you."

"No." Zach wavered a bit, then slapped his can on the table. "But he does."

Before Mitch could hold him back, before Jenn realized his intentions, Zach lunged at Grady. "You bastard, you been doin' my sister right under our noses."

It all happened so fast. Connie pulled Jenny out of the way. Zach tackled Grady; they fell to the floor, knocking over a kitchen chair. Jenn saw, almost in slow motion, her brother's arm come back, go forward, and land in Grady's jaw.

"Oh, God, stop this."

She lurched toward them, but Connie held her back. "Jenny, no, the baby."

Mitch and Paulie were on Zach, anyway. Each took an arm and yanked him off.

Grady, still on the floor, stared up at Zach. His mouth was bleeding. He said nothing.

Everybody was still until a voice came from the side of the room. They all turned to see the kitchen door was open and Will Rossettie was in the doorway. Megan Hale stood behind him.

Will said, "Well, looks like the cops arrived just in time."

BEFORE SHE INTRUDED on what was obviously a family thing, Megan ducked out of the kitchen and headed down the hall. This was private stuff, and she didn't want to be involved. She just hoped Mitch wasn't upset. What the hell could have made Grady and Zach scuffle like that?

Thinking about Mitch, she didn't see his son in the hall until she bumped right into him. He steadied her, much as Mitch would have. "Whoa!"

"Bobby."

He grinned. "Hi, Detective. Nobody told me you were coming."

"It was a last-minute thing." In truth, she'd fought Will tooth and nail about accompanying him here. She'd weakened when he said he wouldn't go without her; they'd cook for themselves at his place. She'd given in when he said it was too bad, too, because he was worried about the Malvaso *boys*. Sabina had told him Cynthia had gone to the Hamptons for the holidays. And Angie was taking Zach's kids with her to her boyfriend's house. Will had wanted to be there for moral support.

Bobby glanced over her shoulder. "What's going on out there?"

Geez, Bobby shouldn't see whatever it was that was happening. "Big family meeting, I think."

"Is it about Mom?"

Megan swallowed hard. "I don't think so." Why would Zach and Grady be fighting over Cynthia?

Bobby said, "I think I'll pass on my soda, then. People are really acting weird today." Again his grin. "Wanna come up to the attic with me and Trish? We got Ani DiFranco's album with 'School Night' on it."

Why not? She felt comfortable with these kids. "Sure."

They climbed the steps to the second floor. The Malvaso homestead was huge; she could see several bedrooms off the hallway. Bobby opened a door and music wafted down another set of stairs; they went up that flight.

As soon as she entered the attic space, she felt at home. Finished off in knotty pine on the high ceiling and walls, carpeted with a thick berber, it had beautiful angles from the dormer and roof lines. Across the room was a big bed. Trish sat on it, leafing through something. Her red hair was pulled back into braids today and she wore overalls and a navy shirt, making her seem very young and vulnerable. She glanced up when Megan entered. "Hey, Detective. Happy Thanksgiving."

"To you, too."

"No soda," Bobby said, dropping down on the floor at Trish's feet. "Big powwow in the kitchen."

"About Mom?" Trish asked.

Bobby looked to Megan. She reiterated her doubts. Trish held her gaze. "You know my mother didn't come, don't you?"

"Yes, honey, I know."

Trish's eyes teared. "Shit, I don't care."

Megan crossed to the bed. She sat down on the edge of the mattress. "It's okay to care, Trish, even when it hurts. I used to feel terrible I didn't have a mother like everybody else. My dad said that was all right to let the feelings come, to deal with them."

"Well, we don't really have a mother, either. We haven't for a long time."

Bobby said, "I don't wanna talk about her." His gaze narrowed on Megan. "Your dad? This is the first Thanksgiving he's dead, isn't it?"

A lump formed in her throat. Only a kid would be so starkly honest. "Yes."

"You feel bad?"

"Of course she does, dummy."

"Yep, I do." She looked around the room. And smiled despite the pain. "This was a bedroom, right?" She guessed whose it was.

"Yeah, Dad's." Bobby grinned. "We love to come up here. It reminds us what he used to be like."

Megan could see why. There were posters on the walls: Wilt Chamberlain, who would have been playing twenty-five years ago; Jane Fonda as *Barbarella* over the mirror. Photos that she wanted to examine up close were everywhere. A huge desk that looked handmade and a chair were by the large dormer window; a number was carved in the back of the chair. This was all evidence of the boy Mitch had once been. A boy she wished she'd known.

"He was a big basketball star, did you know that?" Trish said. "That's his number on the chair."

"No, I didn't know that." Hmm. Quick pictures of him dribbling, shooting, and stealing the ball from her came to mind.

"Yeah, come look." Trish indicated the book on her lap.

Feeling like she was getting sucked in by these kids, by this family, Megan scooted back against the wall.

Bobby asked, "Who do you want to hear?"

"Hmm. Ani, I think. Then Emm."

Bobby put Ani on the boom box and they listened to the soulful tunes while Trish showed her the book. "This is Dad's scrapbook. Grandma kept one on each of her kids, but Dad was the only sports star."

"Show me."

And so she got a glimpse of Mitch in his youth. He'd played varsity basketball in his freshman year as the sixth player. He was point guard for three seasons after that.

Megan devoured the pictures and articles Trish laughingly pointed out with a running commentary. "Look at that hair . . . I love this one where he's leaping off the floor. . . ."

Megan liked the one where he was poised at the foul-shot line. Trish said, "The score was tied with no time on the clock."

"And he made the basket, right?"

"Uh-huh. He was only a junior, too."

A broad smile breached her lips. "This is so cool."

Bobby who was still on the floor, scrambled up and onto the bed next to her. "Let me see. I haven't looked at these in ages."

It was how Mitch found her, a half hour later, on the bed sandwiched between his kids, taking a tour of his childhood and adolescence.

"Well, what's the draw in here?"

All three looked up. Something flashed across Mitch's face—something very profound.

Trish broke the moment. "We're checking out your scrapbooks, Daddycakes."

"Oh, Lord, you'll bore Detective Hale to death."

"Never." Megan felt mischievous. "I didn't know you were such a star. No wonder I had trouble beating you on the basketball court."

"You beat *Dad*?" Bobby said incredulously.

"Well," Mitch said, coming into the room and dragging out the chair to the desk. "That's a matter of opinion." He straddled it, his arms braced on the back. Megan was hard-pressed to take her eyes off of him. He wore navy slacks and a sweater of greens and blues, and his eyes danced. "Her team beat my team."

"Did you play ball in school?" Trish asked.

"Yep. High school and college." She glanced down at the books. "My dad kept these for me, too."

"Can we see them sometime?" Bobby asked.

Bobby's question threw her off balance, but warmed her. "Sure."

Mitch watched them, then seemed to shake himself out of a mood. "I need to talk to you guys." He glanced at Megan. "About what just happened downstairs."

"I should leave." Megan made to get off the bed.

"I'd rather you didn't. You'll need an explanation for what you saw. I don't wanna have to tell this twice."

She settled back in. Trish leaned close to her. "Is it bad news, Daddy?"

"No, princess. Well, at least I don't think it is."

Bobby's gaze was hard. "You tell them you're leaving Mom?"

"No." He drew in a breath. "Aunt Jenn's pregnant."

Both kids stared at him.

"Holy shit," Trish finally said.

"Trish . . ."

"Sorry, Dad. Um, who's the father?"

Megan hoped it wasn't Stan Steele.

"Uncle Grady."

"Hell." This from Bobby. "I don't get it. All these years they said they were just friends."

"They are."

"Da-ad." Trish's tone was very adult. "Friends don't . . ."

"I know, honey. But remember when I told you Aunt Jenn, Uncle Zach, and I all decided to change our lives after the Sinco fire? To live better?"

"Yeah. You decided to do the camp. Me and Bobby wanna help with it."

He smiled. "Good. But we also decided personal things. Aunt Jenn said she wanted to have a baby."

"So she just did it with Grady?" Trish blurted out.

"I don't think it's necessary for us to have all the details." He shook his head. "It's what got the fight going downstairs."

"Fight?" Bobby said. "There was, like, a *physical* fight?"

" 'Fraid so. Between Uncle Zach and Grady."

Trish's tone was wise. "Uncle Zach's pissed at Grady, isn't he?"

"Yeah."

"Are you?"

"Truthfully, I don't know what I feel about all this. I know Aunt Jenn really wanted a baby."

"Then it's mad-cool," Trish pronounced, surprising

Megan with her mature attitude. "Can we go see her?"

"Yes. She's lying down in Grandma's room now, but she said you guys could come in after I told you."

Trish and Bobby bolted off the bed and headed for the door. But before he left, Bobby turned around. "Dad?"

"Yeah, son?"

"What did you want to change about your life? Personally, after Sinco?"

"Well, for one thing, I wanted to get you guys on the straight and narrow. And spend more time with you."

"Anything else?"

"Yeah, but I don't want to go into it now."

"It's okay, I can guess." Bobby followed Trish out.

Megan felt like she'd peeked into somebody's bedroom window. She was further disconcerted when Mitch sat up straighter and stared meaningfully at her. "I vowed to do something about my marriage, Meg. When things were so bad at the Sinco warehouse."

She sighed, thinking how her relationship with him kept picking up speed, taking twists and turns like some emotional roller coaster. "As I said at the ball, I believe you. It . . . this thing between us . . . it's not like Lance."

"Do you want to talk about that?"

"No." She angled her head to the door. "Do you want to talk about *that*?"

He gripped the back of the chair. "Not much to say. I believed Grady when he said they were just friends."

"Maybe they were. Friendship can spark into something else," she added. "Without either person meaning to ignite it."

His eyes burned. "I know." Then he added, "But they've been buddies since they were five and Grady's parents moved to Hidden Cove."

She couldn't help but smile. "Well, something's changed. Is it so bad?"

"Hell, no. Not if it's working for them."

"You don't think it is?"

"I don't know. There's a lot of tension between them that was never there before. They don't seem as happy about the pregnancy as they should." His gaze dropped to the scrapbook Trish had dumped in her lap. "Sorry about the bragging my kids did." He stood and crossed to the bed. Reaching out, he said, "Here, I'll take it."

Hugging the book to her chest, she said, "Not a chance. I haven't finished looking at it."

"Meg."

Suddenly she felt lighter, like she was sixteen again and in a boy's room, upstairs, while his parents were off somewhere in the house. It made her pat the mattress next to her and say, "Come on, sit. Show the rest to me."

For a moment, he stared at her. As he knelt on the mattress, then eased back against the wall, he shook his head. "All right. But I warn you. I had some pretty intense fantasies when I used to sleep in this bed. Sittin' on it with you might not be the smartest thing we ever did."

"What's the harm? The door's open. Your family— your kids, for Christ's sake—are within hearing distance."

He cocked his head. "I'm not exactly rational where you're concerned, Meggie."

"Hush." Looking down, she turned the page.

Mitch said, "Oh, yeah, that game . . ."

Megan was mesmerized by his husky baritone as he recounted his high school athletic career. "This one time, I'd sprained my hand but didn't tell anybody so I could finish the game. . . ." A deep, rumbling laugh came forth when he read how he was quoted his junior year wanting to be the next Larry Byrd. . . . "Man, that last game. I was sayin' Hail Marys. . . ."

She was disappointed when they turned to the last page. Could anything be more precious than this experience with him? Than this stolen glimpse into Mitch as a young boy?

At the end of the book was an official-looking typed letter. Mitch stilled when he saw it. She looked down. The letterhead read Indiana University. The text congratulated Mitch for his acceptance. The school was awarding a full scholarship for basketball to play under Bobby Knight.

"I didn't know you went to IU."

His smile was sad. "I didn't."

She glanced down again. "But you got a full scholarship. Did you get hurt or something?"

He shook his head.

"Mitch?"

"My dad died, Megan. I couldn't leave my family."

"Couldn't leave them emotionally?"

"No. Physically. I had to work to help support them. Paulie was still in high school. The girls were only ten. Zach was seven. My mother couldn't swing it, even with Pa's fire department pension."

"Oh, Mitch, you gave *this* up for them."

"Of course."

Megan was overwhelmed by his unselfishness. "You are such a good man."

He shrugged off the compliment. "Anyone would have done it."

"No, that's not true."

"It's not . . ." He stopped. "All right, it was tough. Really tough." He leaned back against the wall and stared at the ceiling. "I wanted to go there so bad . . . play for Knight." He drew in a deep breath. "But other people had it tougher. Look at you. You've lost a lot more than me."

She smiled sadly.

"Today's hard, huh?"

His honesty called forth her own. "Yeah, it is."

"I'm glad you came. I'm surprised, though."

She told him about Will's blackmail.

"Ah, well, I'll have to thank him. I wanted you here today, Meg. With me. And my family."

"Mitch . . ."

"I know. We promised no words. I won't say anymore." They sat shoulder-to-shoulder nestled, on the bed. Just his nearness made her happy. So when he held out his hand, palm up, she not-so-reluctantly put her hand in it.

He linked their fingers. The contact was intimate. And tender. "Happy Thanksgiving, Meg," he said squeezing gently.

"Happy Thanksgiving, Mitch."

NINETEEN

"WELL, CONGRATULATIONS." FROM behind his desk, Chief Noah Callahan looked over at Jenn and watched her with cool green eyes. She wished she knew what he was really thinking. Grady had wanted to come with her today, Monday, to talk to the chief, but he had an appointment with Jack Harrison.

Shifting, Jenn smiled. "Thanks. I'm sorry if this throws things off at Quint Seven."

"As a matter of fact, it plays right into our hands."

She gave him a quizzical look.

"You're valuable on the line, Jenn, but Will and I have been lookin' for somebody to work full time on Project KidsCamp. Orchestrate the whole thing, keep track of what's been done, what needs to be done. Mitch and Megan have been released from duty one day a week to do it, but it's not enough."

A spurt of pleasure shot through Jenn. "Really? I'd much rather work on the camp than take an office job."

"You could always go to the academy."

"Am I being punished for something?" she joked. It was common knowledge that line workers dreaded their stint at the academy. Most smoke eaters didn't like it because they sought the adrenaline rush of being on the line. Jenn also believed it took a special kind of person to be a teacher.

Callahan smiled. One thing everybody liked about the man was that he had a sense of humor and didn't take himself too seriously. "Cute. So, if Will agrees, you interested?"

"I'd like to talk to Grady about it."

"O'Connor?"

"You might as well know, Chief, he's the father of my baby. It's no secret." Especially after Thanksgiving Day. Noah hadn't shown up until dinnertime so he'd missed the fireworks, but he'd been there for the tense aftermath.

"I see." He gave her a boyish look that belied his forty-seven years. "Does this have anything to do with the tension at Thanksgiving?"

"Yes. Zach's upset with Grady about the baby . . ." She broke off embarrassed by talking outside of the family.

Noah shook his head. "Zach has no right . . ." He trailed off, too, then refocused. "How is Grady, Jenn? There's been talk."

She stiffened. "About Grady?"

"Yes. He had trouble with that car accident two weeks ago. Took some personal leave."

How to protect Grady yet help garner the understanding he might need from the chief?

Noah added quickly, "I'm not lookin' for problems. He's the best medic I've ever had on staff. I'm asking as a concerned boss. And friend."

"He's had some rough spots in the past, Chief. Life dealt him some bad hands. But he's sorting it out."

Noah grinned and nodded to her stomach. "Well, looks like he hit the jackpot this time."

God, Jenn hoped Grady could come around to that thinking, too. And she hoped he was making headway with Harrison. Though she put up a good front, she was worried sick about him. How would digging into the past affect him? Moreso, would he make progress so that they could be together? Really together. She was grateful for his friendship and support. If necessary, she'd settle for it. But she wanted him in her bed. As her soul mate and her lover.

Would this baby make that happen? Or would it drive them further apart?

As Noah got out some schedules and stood to take her down to the space at headquarters that housed Project KidsCamp, Jenn said a silent prayer that Harrison would help Grady come to terms with his past.

She placed a hand over her stomach. And his future.

GRADY TRIED TO relax, but he found himself gripping the arms of the chair where he sat across from Jack Harrison. Though he'd never had much contact with the guy, he'd heard the department psychologist was good at his job. Not that he seemed to be helping Zach much. Grady rubbed his jaw. What a circus that had been Thanksgiving Day.

"So, Grady, tell me what brings you here."

Christ, it was hard to talk about this. "Where do I start, the past or present?"

"How about the present. Usually, the past comes up in the explanation."

Stretching his legs out to relieve some of the tension in his back, Grady nodded. "Well, I'm going to be a father."

Dark brows arched. "Congratulations." Harrison narrowed his eyes. "Or isn't it a happy occasion?"

"It is. I think. Though I didn't want this. Or I did at first."

The psychologist glanced down at Grady's hand. "You aren't married, are you?"

"No."

"That's a problem, then?"

"No." He raked restless fingers through his hair. "Jenny Malvaso's the mother. She's my best friend in world."

"Ah." Harrison waited a beat. "But it turned into more than friendship?"

"It turned into a volcano."

"What do you mean?"

Grady told him about Sinco, and Jenny's vow. Harrison said, "That damn fire has shifted everybody's life. It's been a zoo in here the past several months."

"I can imagine." Grady told him about Jenny's request and his counteroffer.

Harrison smiled. "It all sounds good to me, Grady."

"It was until I started seeing her differently. Things changed for her, too. We became sexually attracted."

"What's wrong with that?"

His heart started to beat like a patient going into cardiac arrest. "I . . ." He leaped out of the chair and began to pace. Could he talk about this? Could he get the words out? He conjured Jenny's image last night as he tucked her into bed. She'd vomited again, and he'd fed her tea and crackers. She'd looked up at him and her eyes shone with such love. . . .

"I was engaged once. Sheila couldn't handle the breakup. She's been on the skids since." He circled around and faced Harrison. "And I was married, too. Linda . . . she said I was bad at intimacy. That I couldn't handle a relationship with any woman."

"You seem to handle one with Jenn pretty well."

His laugh was raw. "You wouldn't say that if you saw her crying the last weeks over me."

"Why was she crying?"

"Because I hurt the women I love, Jack. I destroy them."

"People are responsible for their own actions, Grady."

"No, I killed Linda. And the baby she'd carried for seven months."

He saw a flicker of surprise in Harrison's eyes. "I knew about the suicide. Remember, I asked if you wanted to see me for a while. . . . You said no. But explain exactly how you think *you* killed her."

Suddenly the images came back. The sight and smell and sounds of Linda screaming at him not to leave her, of her accusations that he destroyed everything he loved. And the sickening smell of carbon monoxide and death when he came back hours later and found her in the front seat of the Mustang he'd just bought, slumped over the wheel, dead. With his baby inside her.

The horror of the vision made him whirl around. "She killed herself and the baby she was carrying because I . . . I . . . I'm so bad at relationships. . . ."

He didn't realize he was shaking, and sweating, until Harrison stood before him. He was as big as Grady, and as muscular. Very strong hands gripped his biceps. "O'Connor, listen to me. You got reason to be confused. And it isn't just the attraction to Jenn. You were bound to have some reaction to this whole baby thing with her after losing your child. Look, I'm sorry your wife killed herself and the baby. But *she* did it, not you."

Grady just stared at him.

"Do you hear me?"

Again, nothing.

"Grady?"

He came out of the past. Thought about Jenny and all he had at stake here. And straightened. "I hear you, Jack, but that's hard for me to internalize."

Harrison didn't let go.

"But I want to. Help me, would you? To believe that."

"That's why you're here, buddy. Now, let's sit and talk some more."

ZACH WAS IN the waiting room of Harrison's office, feeling like shit, when the door opened.

And out walked O'Connor. His friend stopped in the doorway, and just stared at Zach. They hadn't seen each other since Thanksgiving, when Zach lost it and attacked Grady. In deference to his mother, Zach had stayed for dinner, when he'd wanted to go home and bury himself in a bottle. But he'd been licking his wounds all weekend and hadn't faced up to what he'd done.

Just like the old Zach.

"Grady," Zach said.

Grady nodded.

Zach saw Harrison behind him. He guessed Grady was here to deal with what was going on with his sister, and had suspected for a long time there was a shitload of baggage the guy was dealing with because of his wife's death. Zach hadn't thought about that when he'd attacked Grady. He wondered if he'd made things worse.

In case he had, Zach asked, "Would you go back inside for a sec?"

"Why?"

"I wanna say some things, and maybe Harrison can help." Zach shrugged, feeling like the time he and Grady fought over a girl on the playground.

"That sounds like a great idea," Harrison put in.

Shoulders slumped, Grady headed back into the office and took a chair. Zach remained standing and glanced at Harrison.

"Go ahead, Zach. The ball's in your court."

He addressed his friend. "I'm sorry about Thanksgiving." Zach told the psychologist what had happened. Then he looked back to Grady. "I was half drunk and wallowing in self-pity because I didn't have my kids. I took it out on you."

Grady nodded. "The news about the baby . . . it was a shock, I know."

"But none of my business. Like you said." He took in a breath. "Since Sinco, I worry about Jenny and Mitch more." He shrugged. "And you, too. You're like a brother to me, Gray."

Grady's shoulders relaxed. "I feel the same."

Zach said, "You and Jenny. It was just a surprise."

"To me, too," Grady mumbled.

"She okay?"

"Yeah. She's sick, though. She's meeting with Noah right now about her position in the fire department."

"Can I do anything?"

"No, I'll take care of her. She'll be fine." Grady shot Harrison a worried look. "I promise, Zach, I'm going to handle all this right. I love Jenny." Standing, he crossed to Zach and socked him on the arm. "And you. And Mitch. I won't let you down."

"Yeah, well, I've let a lot of people down, Gray. So if you aren't perfect, I understand. I'll be better, too."

Then, like those little boys on the playground, they gave each other an embarrassed hug, and Grady left.

Zach faced Harrison. "I keep fucking up," he said simply.

From behind the desk, Harrison arched his brows. "Oh, I don't know, Malvaso, what I just saw seemed like progress to me. Now sit and let's talk about it."

JENN MALVASO WAS staring down at some papers when Megan came to the doorway of the office for Project KidsCamp, located just down the hall from Noah Callahan. "Hey, girlfriend, what's this I hear?"

Glancing up, Jenn smiled. Her eyes were the exact color of Mitch's. "They put me in charge." Those eyes filled with concern, like Mitch's often did. "That okay with you?"

"Are you kidding? We need all the help we can get. Your brother's running ragged, trying to do his job and work on the camp, too. Mitch is under too much pressure. You can ease it."

For a moment, Jenn assessed her. "You like Mitch, don't you?"

Megan's stomach clutched. "Yeah, doesn't everybody?"

Not looking fooled, Jenn said, "Sure, everybody does."

"So, how are you feeling? You were pretty green the last time I saw you."

"Hmm. Brawls do that to a girl."

Megan took a seat across the desk. "Wanna talk about it?" Everybody had put the scene in the kitchen behind them to enjoy the holiday. But it had lingered in the air, along with the smell of turkey and creamed onions.

Jenn stared at her. "Maybe. It'd be good to have a woman's view."

"I don't know much about pregnancy."

"No, I mean about men."

Rolling her eyes, she stretched out her legs. "You got me there, too."

"You were married once. You told me that day in the bathroom, and Mitch mentioned it again."

She fiddled with the hem of the cocoa-colored sweater she wore with matching corduroy jeans. "Yeah. Did Mitch bring it up?"

"Uh-huh. We were talking about you."

Don't ask. "When?"

"Thanksgiving night, after you and Will left. Mitch's kids couldn't say enough about how *mad-cool* you were. They grilled him on why you weren't married with kids of your own."

"Lance died before we could have them." Of course, his infidelity had slowed the process.

Like other pregnant women Megan had encountered, Jenn put her hand on her stomach. "You want kids?"

Megan's breath hitched. For a minute, she was hit by a wave of longing so bad—longing to have Mitch Malvaso's child—that she was silenced by it. Oh, my God, had it gone this far?

"Megan? I asked if you wanted a baby someday."

Megan nodded. "Yeah. I want a baby someday. I envy you."

"Am I interrupting?"

Megan turned to find Mitch in the doorway.

Jenn said, "No, Megan and I were doin' some old-fashioned girl talk."

"I heard."

Shit. Had he heard the longing in her voice, too?

He came into the room. "Hi, Meg." His words were all but a caress.

"Mitch." Hers was practically a croak.

Then he crossed to his sister. Squeezing her shoulder, he kissed her on the forehead. "You okay, kiddo?"

"Yep." She indicated the room. "You know about this?"

"Yeah, Noah called. So," he said, folding his arms over his chest and glanced toward Megan with a twinkle in his eyes. His face lit with that mischievousness she loved. "Should I leave so you two can talk baby talk?"

"Um, no, of course not." Great, Megan was stuttering.

She shook herself. "What . . . what do you think of our new director?"

Mitch held Megan's gaze briefly, then he smiled at his sister. "I think she'll be great."

Jenn stood. "I hope so. Right now, I need to visit the ladies' room."

Mitch frowned. "You sick again? Grady says you've had a tough time of it."

"No, I just have to pee. Be right back."

Jenn left them alone and Megan wondered if it was intentional. Mitch smiled after his sister. Then he went to the door, closed it, and leaned against it. He looked big and beautiful in his jeans and white sweater, as he was off duty today. She saw a muscle pulse just above the crew neck. "You want to have a baby, huh, Meggie?"

She averted her gaze. "Yeah, sure, someday."

He crossed to her, then, and towered over her. Lifting a strand of her hair, he rubbed it between his fingers. "A little girl. With hair as blond as this."

Mesmerized, she looked up at him and swallowed hard. He brushed his fingertips over her skin. "And high cheekbones like these."

Again she said nothing.

He stepped back. "Sorry . . ." He shrugged boyishly. "I just . . . when I heard . . . I thought about . . ." Sighing heavily, he shook himself. "Never mind . . ." He strode to the desk and stared down at the papers Jenn was reading. "Oh, wow, the figures for the Harvest Ball are in. We—"

"And brown velvety eyes," Megan interrupted.

His head snapped up. Brown velvety eyes stared over at her. "What?"

"I'd like her to have brown velvety eyes." She smiled. "I'm pretty partial to them."

"Are you, now?"

"Mmm."

His grin was broad. Then he sobered. Glanced at his watch. "I've got two appointments today."

"You do?"

"One with Harrison in an hour."

"The other?"

"With my brother Paulie. He's a lawyer."

"I know."

"Do you, Meg? Do you know?"

"I know," she said, her gaze never leaving his. "And I believe, Mitch."

"I'm glad."

"JESUS, HARRISON, YOU got us all today, didn't you?" After connecting with Megan, Mitch felt particularly lighthearted and didn't mind busting Jack Harrison's psychological balls a bit. "You giving group rates?"

"Don't know what you mean, Malvaso."

"Yeah, yeah, professional ethics. Well, I met Zach on the way in here today, and O'Connor told me he was seeing you earlier."

Harrison just looked at him.

"It's okay, we're not here about each other." Mitch frowned. "At least I think we aren't. Zach was pretty pissed at Grady about the baby. And I feel bad I didn't know about it . . . I could have done something. . . ."

"Do you always take responsibility for everything, Mitch?"

Mitch stared at the counselor. "Yeah, sure."

"Well, let's talk about that. Maybe it's the root of—"

Harrison's phone buzzed and he frowned. "Nobody's supposed to interrupt unless it's an emergency. I've got to take it."

"Go ahead . . ."

Harrison picked up his phone. "Yes, Mary?"

The doc listened, then frowned. "His brother? Yeah, send him in."

Before Mitch could question Harrison, Zach burst through the door. "Come quick, Mitch. Cynthia's on the warpath."

"Cynthia?" She'd breezed in late last night from the Hamptons for some kind of breakfast thing today. Mitch had only seen her briefly. She'd sniffled and pretended to be hurt, then stormed off to the bedroom. As far as Mitch knew, she'd never even said hello to the kids. "Where is she?"

"Looking for Megan Hale."

"What?" Mitch rose.

Zach headed for the door. "Come on, I'll fill you in on the way."

They flew out of the office and down the hall to the elevator. After punching the button, Zach faced him gravely. "She came to the camp office. I was there with Jenn and Grady. Cynthia's looking for Megan."

Please, God, no, don't let this be happening.

"Why Megan?"

As they got on the elevator, Zach threw him a sympathetic look. "I think you know why. Anyway, Jenn tried to calm her down; Grady tried, too. They couldn't. She stalked out, saying she was going up to Noah Callahan's office." Zach squeezed Mitch's arm. "About your whore."

Mitch felt his stomach heave. "No."

"It gets worse."

How could it?

"Megan's with Callahan and Will right now."

Lance cheated on me, Mitch . . . It hurt so much . . . I won't do that to another woman. I won't be the other woman.

They got to the chief's floor and hurried down the hall; as they approached the receptionist, Mitch saw Cynthia at the desk, her back to them. There were several people at desks in the area, watching her. "I don't care who he's with. I want to see him now."

Noah's office door opened and he stepped into the hall. "What's going on here?"

Cynthia crossed to him; Zach and Mitch caught up with her. "Oh, Noah, you won't believe what's happened." Her voice trembled.

She swept past him into the office just as Mitch said, "Cynthia, don't—"

The chief gave him a questioning look and stepped aside so Mitch could follow his wife in. Too late, because she halted in the middle of the room, staring at Megan, who sat at a round table with Will.

Cynthia pounced. "Well, if it isn't the little detective." She strode up to the table just as Megan stood.

"What can I do for you, Cynthia?"

"Cynthia, what are you *doing*?" Mitch asked on the heels of Megan's comment.

Cynthia whirled around. Her eyes were wild, her face flaming. "Here to defend your whore, Mitch?"

Mitch froze, Megan gasped, Will said, "Now, see here," and Noah closed the door. Zach came up to Mitch to stand by him.

The chief spoke. "Whatever's going on here—"

Cynthia faced Noah. "I'll tell you what's going on here. She stole my husband. She's a home wrecker."

Megan stood stock-still. Mitch wanted to go to her so badly he had to forcefully keep himself back.

Then Megan straightened. "I'm not your husband's whore, Cynthia."

Pure rage lit Cynthia's face. "I had breakfast with the mother of the department's financial secretary. She told me what really happened when you and he went to Keuka Lake." Cynthia edged in close to Megan, came nose-to-nose with her. "Try to talk your way out of this, Detective. There was only one motel bill submitted. Unless Mitch slept in the truck, you shared a room."

Megan stared at Cynthia, but said nothing. Her silence was as good as a signed confession.

Cynthia's voice rose a notch when she said, "I can see by your silence it's true." She whirled around to Mitch, her features taut. "And yours."

Mitch had seen her like this before. A rage was building inside her and, like wildfire, would burn everything in its path.

Cynthia circled back around. "How dare you do this?" Her voice peaked. "How *dare* you?" When Megan still said nothing, Cynthia faced Mitch again. "You son of a bitch."

"It's not what you think."

"No? Are you denying you slept with her?"

"Look, we slept in the same room. But we . . ." He

trailed off, knowing how trite this sounded. He gave Megan a look full of feeling and apology.

Cynthia caught it. "Jesus Christ. You think you're in love with her, don't you?"

Mitch looked away. He couldn't deny that, either.

Megan said, "Nothing's happened between us, Cynthia."

Cynthia addressed Megan again. "Oh, you deny you're screwing him?"

"Yes, I'm denying that."

"Do you deny you're in love with him?"

Megan looked at Mitch. She held his gaze. Finally, she said, "No, I'm not denying that. But nothing unethical has happened between us, Cynthia. Now, if you'll excuse me, I'm leaving."

Noah, Zach, and Will followed her out. Mitch faced Cynthia. "Proud of yourself?"

She was still trembling with rage. "I'm the wronged wife, darling. I'm getting all the sympathy in this situation."

"Don't bet on it."

"Yes, well, *you* can bet on this. No court in the land is going to let you have your precious children when they find out what an immoral bastard you are." She eyed him viciously. "I won this one, Mitch. I told you what would happened if you tried to leave me."

With that, she swept out of the room, leaving Mitch in the ashes of her tirade.

TWENTY

MEGAN BOUNCED THE ball hard on the wooden floor, then poised on her toes and arced it through the air. Two points. Heading in toward the hoop, she snagged the basketball, did a quick layup and dribbled to the other end of the court. There, she made another basket. This time she ran around the perimeter, pounding the ball on the floor as she went. It didn't help. Though she'd been relieved that no one was using the academy gym when she'd arrived at noon and changed into shorts and a T-shirt, now she felt suffocated. Voices and accusations filled the gym . . . *you're my husband's whore* . . . *do you deny you're screwing him* . . . *do you deny you're in love with him?* And the look on Mitch's face . . .

What had brought them to this point?

"Meg?"

She glanced to the side of the gym to see Mitch there. He stood stiffly in the doorway. Jamming his hands in his jeans pockets, he watched her trying to outrun the ghosts. She kept running. After a few laps, praying he'd just leave, she stopped at the far basket. From the foul line, she took two shots and sunk both. Mitch appeared under the backboard and said, "Go ahead, hotshot, I'll rebound." His voice was strained, but sure, somehow confident.

She held the ball, focused on the basket, and sent it flying through the air. Swish.

He threw it back to her.

Another basket.

Two more. Four. After ten, when he tossed the ball to her she cradled it in her arm, and sank cross-legged to the floor. He jogged over to her and dropped down next to her. He was too big to be comfortable sitting like her, so he stretched out his legs and braced his arms behind him.

"I'm sorry," was all he said.

She looked at him. "It's not your fault. It's just so sordid."

"It's exactly what you wanted to avoid."

She stared off over his shoulder. For a minute she saw Lila Jenkins's face, when Megan had run into her after Megan had reconciled with Lance. The woman had flushed, stuttered, and beat a hasty retreat. Now Megan wondered if she'd felt as . . . guilty as Megan did right now.

"I have to know something, Meg."

She nodded.

"Did you mean what you said?" he asked gently.

Do you deny you're in love with my husband?

No, I don't deny that.

She faced Mitch squarely. "I meant it." Though she didn't want to, she asked, "Did you mean it?"

"I meant it. I'm sorry, I hadn't planned for any of this. I wanted to wait until I was free. But when Cynthia asked, I couldn't deny it."

"Me, either. I just feel so bad."

"Me, too." He glanced at his watch. "I've got a meeting with Paulie in a half hour. I want to keep it more than ever, now. Then I'm going home. I'll do as much damage control as I can, for the kids mostly, but . . ." He shrugged. ". . . This whole thing just reached another level, and we have to deal with it."

"A very public level."

"Which you hate, I know. I reassured Rossettie and

Callahan that you've behaved ethically." She just stared at him. "But you're right, people will know. And gossip."

She looked up at the gym ceiling.

"I love you, Meg."

She sucked in a breath at hearing him say the words directly to her and let herself look at him. His face was ragged and strained. But in his eyes she saw something that made her know, wholeheartedly, that whatever happened now, they were in it together.

He rolled up to a squatting position in front of her. Briefly he grasped her jaw and brushed his thumb over her bottom lip. As he started to stand, she grabbed his hand, kept him poised in front of her. Staring up at him, she said, "I love you, too, Mitch."

His velvety brown eyes moistened. Cradling her neck, he brought her face to his chest. "That's all I need to hear, sweetheart." Then he kissed the top of her head, stood, and left her in the gym.

THINGS TOOK LONGER than he thought with Paulie, and by the time he swerved into the driveway at home, Trish's car was there. The kids were back from school.

I want a divorce, he'd told his brother. *I don't care about the money, we'll start over . . . I just want my kids . . . and legal freedom from her. . . .*

As he pulled into the garage, he remembered the look on Paulie's face when Mitch recounted what Cynthia had said about his immorality and a judge ruling against custody for him because of his relationship with Meg.

Paulie had said, *That's not exactly true . . . the kids will have a big say, given their ages . . . and Cynthia hasn't been an angel. . . .*

Mitch was thinking about the odd tone in Paulie's voice as he opened the garage door leading to the kitchen. All thought fled when he heard the crashing and banging upstairs.

Not again.

He followed the noise.

At the bottom of the stairs he heard, "Mom, please . . .

don't . . . Geez . . ." It was Trish's voice. Another crash.

"You bitch, get out of here. . . ." Bobby.

His heart catapulting in his chest, Mitch took the stairs two at a time, reached his son's bedroom, and scanned the scene. Bobby's computer lay on the floor. Posters hung half off the wall. Cynthia had Bobby's guitar raised over her head; Mitch dove toward her.

He didn't reach her in time. Bobby's treasured Gibson, which he'd saved for two years to buy, came crashing down on the chair. Mitch grabbed her then as she yelled almost incoherently.

He focused on his kids. "Go downstairs," he said quietly. "Call Aunt Jenn or Uncle Zach to come over right now. Stay down there until I can get this under control."

The kids gaped at them as they watched their mother struggle with their father. The look in Bobby's eyes was venomous. Trish was crying.

"Go, now, please. Do as I say."

Finally Trish dragged Bobby out. Once the door was closed, Mitch threw Cynthia on the bed and forcibly held her down. She looked up at him and he was hit by the fact that this was a woman he didn't even know anymore. "Calm down, Cindy."

She bucked against his restraint.

Vising her arms, he bent over her. Very clearly, he said, "This is the last straw. Do whatever you want. But I'm taking the kids out of here now."

"You can't have them."

"Oh, I'll have them, if I have to take them to Siberia to keep them away from you." He shook his head. "Now, I'm going to get up. I've never hit you, Cindy, but don't press your luck. After what you just did to my children, I won't be held responsible for what I do you if you start something else."

He made it to the door before she screamed at him, "They're my children, too."

"No," he said looking around the room at the shambles she'd made of everything Bobby loved. "Not anymore."

Feeling physically sick, he hurried downstairs.

"Bobby? Trish?"

His daughter came from the kitchen, her face tear-stained and her eyes hollow. She threw herself at Mitch. "Oh, Daddy."

"I'm so sorry, princess."

"Is it true? Have you been cheating on Mom?"

"No, honey, it's not true. But I need to talk to you and Bobby about Megan." He glanced toward the kitchen. "Is he out there?"

His daughter stiffened in his arms. "No." She buried her face in his chest. "He took my car. He's gone."

"Took your car? Trish, he doesn't have his license."

IN HER OFFICE, Megan tried to read some reports and keep her mind off what Mitch must be going through, but her gaze drifted out the window and she stared at the snow that had just begun to fall. It was dark and the wind was picking up, causing the big, fat flakes to flutter onto the glass.

I love you, Meg. . . .

You're his whore. . . .

Her door burst open. She looked up to see Mitch, hair windblown, jacket open, cheeks flushed. Something was wrong.

"It didn't go so well?" she asked.

"It was a nightmare." He ran a hand through his hair. "But there's more. Bobby's missing."

"Missing?"

"I got home later than I expected from seeing Paulie. The kids were back from school. Cynthia was throwing one of her tantrums." He began to pace, raking a hand through his hair. "She was upstairs with them. I went up . . . she'd destroyed Bobby's room . . . his guitar . . . I sent the kids downstairs. . . ." He stopped and stared at her, his eyes brimming with anguish. "Just for a bit . . . I told them to call Zach or Jenny . . . I had to calm Cynthia. . . ."

He didn't finish. Just stood there in the middle of the room, his hands fisted. "Jesus, Meggie, Bobby took Trish's car and was gone by the time I got down there."

She stood, her mind racing. "Did Trish know anything?"

"No. We spent the last few hours covering the city, looking for him. I checked his friends' houses. His haunts. Zach and Grady are still driving around. Trish is with Jenny."

Megan grabbed her pen from her desk. "All right. Tell me what he was wearing and give me a description of the car. We'll send out some black-and-whites. Then we'll look some more."

Whirling around, Mitch said, "Meg, he doesn't have his driver's license. He failed the test twice. We teased him about never being able to drive." His voice cracking, Mitch glanced out the window. "It's snowing. It's slippery . . . what if . . . I'll never forgive myself if something happens to him."

She stood and circled the desk. Without hesitation she wrapped her arms around his neck and pulled him to her. His arms vised around her, and he hung on as if to a lifeline. After a strong and meaningful hug, she pulled back and held up the pad. "The sooner we get this done, the sooner we find him."

After putting out the information on Bobby and getting Will involved, they all split up. By nine, there was still no sign of the boy. She'd talked to Mitch on the cell phone, and the last time he was frantic. On a hunch, Megan stopped at Jenny's to talk to Trish. Used to ferreting out information, she helped Trish think of a couple more places that Bobby might go.

Just as she was leaving, Trish grabbed her arm. "Megan?"

"Yeah, honey?"

"Bobby and I liked your the camp idea. We both wanted to work there. We drove out to look at the property one day." Her pretty blue eyes filled and Megan tugged her close. "Please find him, so we can do that. Work on the camp together."

Megan's police instincts kicked in. "I will, Trish."

It was dark on the road leading to her dad's property. She'd called Mitch and told him to check out Trish's other two ideas while she headed to the cove. They were in constant touch now. As she wended her way down the gravelly pavement, she prayed Bobby was here and that he was all right. She thought about her father and Lance and how she'd lost people she loved. She didn't want Mitch to suffer like that. *Oh, please, God, don't let him suffer that.* When she skidded off the road on a patch of ice, she forced herself to concentrate.

The cabin was about fifty feet back from the water. This far from the road, the area was pitch black except for the sliver of moon guiding her way. But there was enough light to see Trish's car parked at an angle in front of the cabin. She wanted to weep in relief.

Swerving up next to it, she bolted out of the car. The other vehicle was empty. She glanced at the cabin. It was dark, but she went inside, anyway. It, too, was unoccupied.

Outside, she zipped up her jacket, wishing she'd brought gloves and a hat to face the nighttime early December weather. She raced toward the beach.

Waves crashed viciously on the shore. A gust of wind stole her breath. She scanned the shoreline. Please, God, please, don't let him . . .

And then she saw him. A solitary figure perched on the end of the small dock, hunched over, staring down into the lake. The dark and *deadly* lake. Her heart pumping, she jogged down the slope and out over the dock. She didn't call out, afraid of Bobby's state of mind. Instead, she crept up behind him; just before she grasped onto him, she said, "Bobby, it's me, Megan Hale." Her hands gripped his biceps. Jesus, he wore only a bulky sweater and jeans. He was shivering badly.

He continued to face away from her but she felt him stiffen. He was slight but he had muscles. What if he shook her off? Was she strong enough to restrain him?

Instead, he put his head down and his body quaked— not from the cold.

"Oh, Bobby." Kneeling on the wet dock, she sidled up to him from behind and circled him in a motherly embrace; she pulled him as close to her chest as she could.

The young boy cried harder. "She . . . she trashed my guitar. She did it on purpose."

"I'm so sorry, honey."

He shook his head. "I'm never going back to that house. To her. I'll run away if . . ." His young voice choked with sobs.

"Your dad won't let that happen."

As if reminded, he stiffened again. Then he grasped one of her arms that was around him and held on tight. "She said . . . she said . . . it isn't true, is it? I told Trish she was lying . . . that you and Dad wouldn't . . ."

Megan sighed. How had such beautiful, honest feelings between her and Mitch had such far-reaching effects?

"What your mother said isn't true, Bobby." She kissed the boy's shaved head. "But let's go inside my cottage, get you warmed up, and call your dad. Then we'll talk about it."

Bobby sagged into her, like a child needing an adult to make the decisions. "Okay," he said grittily.

JENN SAT ON the edge of her bed and brushed back Trish's hair. "You okay, kid?"

"Yeah." Her niece hugged Bucky, who growled gently and nestled into her. "Can he stay here tonight?"

"Of course. You want me to stay with you?"

"No. You need your rest." She smiled tremulously. "But you can tell me a story before you go. One about Dad. And you."

"Okay." Jenn decided to tell her favorite story. "One time, when your dad had just become captain of the Rescue Squad, there was a big fire at an ordinary house in the city. People were trapped on the third floor. Quint Seven was first-in, and the Rescue Squad arrived simultaneously. Your dad volunteered to go up the fire escape, past fire shooting out the second-floor windows. Conditions were terrible and getting worse. Smoke was thick. He located an old man in an apartment and carried him down. He went back in and found four women and an infant. He'd gotten two of the women and the baby to the window and handed them out to me and Grady." Jenn could still remember Mitch's soot-covered face and slumped shoulders. "Then he went back for the others." She smiled at Trish. "Five people would have died in that fire alone without your dad, honey."

"It makes what happened with Mom today seem small."

"It wasn't small. But your father is a wonderful man who's just trying to do what's best."

"At least Bobby's okay."

"Your dad's gonna bunk in with him tonight."

"I want him to."

"It's all right if you want someone with you, sweetie." She shook her head. Her eyelids drooped. "No, I'm tired."

"All right." Jenn kissed Trish's cheek and made her way out of the bedroom. She bumped into her brother coming up the steps. "Megan leave?" Jenn asked when he reached her.

"Yeah." He looked as if he'd been hit by a train.

Thinking about all the rescues he'd made and all the good that he'd done, Jenn wrapped her arms around his waist and hugged him. His chest, always so big and safe, was tense and rock hard.

"You're a good man, Mitello."

"Harrmph." But he tugged her close. "Thanks for letting us stay here tonight."

"I want you to move in, Mitch, like I said. I can stay with Grady until you all get your bearings."

"Maybe we will." He kissed her forehead. "I can't make any decisions now." Drawing back, he swiped a thumb under her eye. "I need to explain some things to you. But you look exhausted."

"You don't need to explain anything to me. Go be with your son."

"Mom needs her rest."

Jenn smiled. "I'll get it." She kissed Mitch good night and made her way down the steps, over to Grady's side of the duplex, and up the stairs. At the top, she saw the

light on in Grady's bedroom. She went to the doorway.
"They're all settled in."

Dressed only in flannel pajama bottoms, he glanced up
from the book he was reading. "Good." He patted the bed.
"Come sit. You're about to fall down."

She crossed to the bed, climbed over him, and sat.
Adjusting pillows behind his head, he pulled her close.
She stretched out and went into his arms as naturally as
the sun set every night. She said against his bare chest,
"I'm so mad at Cynthia, Gray."

"She's a shrew."

"First all that stuff with Megan Hale. I had no idea
anything was going on between her and Mitch."

"I don't think there is." He brushed her arm absently.

"Zach said she admitted she loved him in front of
everybody."

"Him, too." He sighed. "Still, I wouldn't bet on Mitch
actually having an affair."

"I *hope* they're having an affair. My brother deserves
some happiness."

He kissed her head. "You, too." His hand crept to her
stomach. "How's he doing in there? With all this stress,
I worry."

"He or *she*'s just fine. I am exhausted, though."

"You want to sleep?"

"Yeah, I got ready for bed and brushed my teeth in my
bathroom before I tucked Trish in." His nearness felt so
good. So right. She wanted to stay with him so badly, she
ached with it. But he was just starting to see Harrison,
and the session had gone well, so she didn't want to rock
the boat. She made to get up. "I'll go into the spare room."

His hand locked around her waist. "I don't want you
in the spare room."

"We said Mitch and his kids could have my place as
long as they needed it."

"They can." Dragging her back to his chest, he reached
out and turned off the light. "I want you here, Jenny. Next
to me."

"Gray, I—"

"Shh. Just go to sleep. Life can get so fucked up. We gotta straighten ours out. We gotta stay close while we're doing it."

Her eyes were closing. "I know." Again, she nestled into him. "I love you."

"I love you, too, babe. Now sleep."

GRADY AWOKE, VIOLENTLY aroused. It was still dark out, and the clock said 4 A.M. They'd been asleep about five hours.

They. Jenn and he. They were nestled spoon fashion, his arms banded around her, her fanny bumping up against his groin.

Which right about now was throbbing.

His hand was closed over one of her breasts, the other rested on her stomach. Where his baby lay. Did he dare hope for this to work out? Did he dare plan a future with this woman? Could he keep her safe? From himself?

Harrison's words came back to him. *You know that's crazy thinking, Grady. You don't destroy people. You've had some bad breaks, but that's all they were. . . .*

He was so tired of all this. So worn out by the guilt. He'd told Harrison as much

Then get rid of it, the psychologist had said.

Sighing, Grady buried his face in Jenny's neck and inhaled her. She smelled like bath splash. He swelled harder against her and his hand flexed on her breast.

"Mmm."

She shimmied back, causing him great pain. He groaned aloud.

"Gray." Her arm came around his neck. Angling her head, she kissed his cheek.

"Go back to sleep, love."

She covered the hand that was on her breast, pressing his fingers into her. "I wanna make love." Her words were slurred, and he wondered if she was even awake.

"You need your sleep."

Taking his hand, she trailed it over her rib cage, past her waist, to settle over her intimately. Without consciously thinking about it, he cupped her hard.

"Oh, God, Grady."

For once, he didn't analyze what he was doing. Instead, he slipped his hand inside her boxers and slid his fingers through her curls.

Gently, he rubbed her there.

Not so gently, she ground against him.

His fingers parted her. His erection hardened impossibly when he found her wet and swollen. "Ah, Jenny."

She moved against him.

He let her.

Encouraged her.

Then he drove her over the edge, gently, slowly. Her cries were a sweet sexual chorus that made his entire body go rigid. He'd read pregnant women were erotic, but this was Jenny at her best. His heart galloped in his chest and he surged against her bottom. Still, he whispered, "Go back to sleep, love." He'd wait till she did, then get up and take care of this.

She circled around in his arms. Her eyes were wide open and shining like stars in the sky. Without a word, she slid her hand down his front, inside his pajamas, and grasped him. "Gray."

"Oh, God . . ."

She stroked him. "Please, come inside me. I don't care that nothing's solved. . . ."

He closed his eyes, savoring her touch. Then he put his hand to her lips. "Shh." He smiled. "I want this, too, Jenny." Carefully, as if he were unwrapping a priceless package, he slid off her bottoms and made quick work of his.

Lying on her side, she opened her legs. He pulled one over his hip and slipped into her. Cognizant of the baby, wanting to treat her like the precious thing she was, he thrust gently. She gripped his buttocks and pulled him closer, urging him to go harder, stronger. But it was tenderness Grady craved. And love. So he kept his own benevolent pace until she peaked again, crying out his name. He followed her then, in one long groundswell of feeling, consumed by the sound and smell and feel of the woman he loved.

The next thing Grady knew, there was a buzzing in his ear. It took him a minute to realize the sound came from the clock. Groping for it, he finally silenced it. Then he remembered. Jenny. Early this morning. They'd made love. Instead of the panic he might have expected, he felt . . . good. He turned over to reach for her, only to find she was gone. He sighed and looked around. The bathroom door was ajar.

"Jenn?"

No answer.

"Jenny?"

He heard a rustle.

Climbing out of bed, he headed for the john. Slowly he opened the door.

Jenny was on the floor, her back against the wall, as if she'd leaned on it and just slid down. Her eyes were wide and hollow.

"Aw, baby, are you sick again?"

She shook her head, then gripped her stomach, calling attention to her lower body. He glanced down. On her white Mickey Mouse boxers, he saw the bloodstains.

JENN SAT ON the examining table in a faded blue gown and gripped Grady's hand. The nurse had asked him to leave, but he'd refused. Jenn couldn't tell from his face what he was thinking. Was he glad that this pregnancy might end? The thought killed her. So she didn't ask. She simply took comfort in his physical presence.

Finally, the doctor she'd seen just last week swept into the room.

"Hi, Jenn." She nodded. "Grady." Small towns. They'd gone to school with Carolyn Jacobs. "What's this I hear about some bleeding?"

Jenn bit her lip. "Last night. Well, this morning really. I woke up and had to pee. When I went to the bathroom, I found the blood."

Carolyn crossed her hands over her chest. "Any cramps?"

"No."

"Did you pass any tissue?"

"No."

"Was the blood brown or bright red?"

"Brown."

"Well, all that's very good news." She angled her head. "As medics, surely you know that."

Grady shook his head. "Tell us anyway. It's different when it's you."

"All right. Your symptoms suggest this is fairly routine." She looked at Jenn's chart. "You're just six weeks along."

Jenn nodded.

"Did you do anything unusual last night?"

She couldn't speak.

"Lots of emotional stuff went down yesterday," Grady finally said. "And we made love early this morning." He cleared his throat. "We haven't since the baby was conceived."

Carolyn smiled. "Don't say it like you're confessing to a crime, Grady. Making love does *not* bring on miscarriage."

"What else could cause the bleeding, Carolyn?" Jenn asked.

"A myriad of things. Implantation of the fertilized egg in the uterus. The uterine walls beginning to thin because of the pregnancy. But let's not get ahead of ourselves. I want to examine you. If the cervix is closed, there's a good chance it's not miscarriage. Twenty-five percent of all pregnant women have vaginal bleeding in the first trimester. Approximately one-half of those women go on to have successful pregnancies. So this is not uncommon." She faced Jenn squarely. "The final determination will be getting the heartbeat at about ten to twelve weeks. But we can do a sonogram after the exam, which will give us more information." She looked at Grady. "You can wait over in X-ray, until I finish here."

He gripped Jenn's hand. "I'm not leaving Jenny."

Carolyn studied him. "Fine, I'll get the nurse." She left, and Jenn willed herself not to cry. Only *half* had successful pregnancies?

Moving in close, Grady put his hand on her neck and kissed her hair. "I'm here, honey, and I'm going to be here no matter what."

She looked at him, wondering again if he'd be glad if this pregnancy ended.

His eyes darkened. "Oh, Jenny, don't even think it. I wouldn't be glad about this."

Tears coursed down her cheeks. "If . . . if it's bad news, what then, Gray? Is this our last chance?"

He pressed her face to his chest. "We don't have to talk about that now."

When Carolyn Jacobs returned with the nurse and examined Jenny and when she pronounced that the cervix was indeed closed, not once did Grady let go of her hand or take his eyes from her face.

That was why she got to see the silent relief in his baby blues and the quick smile that tilted his mouth when he heard their child was most likely okay.

It was the first time Jenn realized Grady *did* want this baby.

ZACH'S MIND WAS reeling as he climbed the steps to the porch of his old house. He had to see his kids tonight.

Christ, yesterday and today should go down in the *Guinness World Records* book for worst days a family could experience. First, the scene at headquarters with Cynthia and Megan. Then Bobby running away and the long and unnerving search for him. To top it off, Jenn had a close call with her pregnancy this morning. Zach felt like he'd rappelled off the side of a bridge and lost his bearings.

He rang the doorbell, hoping Angie didn't mind his just showing up. Maybe they hadn't eaten and he could take them out.

Jason yanked open the door. "Dad!" Then, in a surprising move, given how the boy was still wary of him, Jason threw himself into his father's arms.

"Jay-Jay, what's wrong?"

Nicky called out, "Is that Dad?" Running, then his other son hurled himself at Zach. He held them both. "Hey, what's going on?"

Angie appeared in his line of vision. Her face was taut, her pretty eyes clouded. "Guys, come on, let your dad in." She didn't seem too upset to see him.

He stepped inside, a kid clinging on each side of him. "What's going on?"

Angie closed the door and faced him. "I—"

"She's getting married," Jason said. "To that guy."

Zach felt his stomach plummet to his knees. He'd suspected for a long time things weren't going to work out with him and Angie, but to hear it so starkly confirmed . . .

Turning, he caught Angie looking at him like he was Jack the Ripper. And suddenly he saw himself as she still saw him, the selfish, self-absorbed bastard he'd been all his life. She expected him to handle this badly.

He thought of Harrison's words. *You've changed, Zach, I believe it. But you have to show people you have. Your actions, if they're consistent, will prove it to people.*

He looked down at Jason, his eleven-year-old boy, who was sure to take his cue from Zach. He felt Nicky gripping his leg. And he saw Angie practically cringe before him.

Taking a deep breath, he dragged both his kids to the couch. He sat them down and dropped onto the scarred coffee table in front of them. Grasping each of their hands, he faced his boys—and the reality of his future. "Listen, guys, Mom's entitled to a life. There isn't a chance for me and her because I was a rotten husband to her. She loves somebody else now, and I'm the one to blame for that."

Jason said, "You've changed, Dad, haven't you?"

"Yeah, son, I have." He glanced at the woman he'd hurt more than any man had any right to hurt any woman. "But it's too late for me and Mom." The words choked him, but he got them out. "You have to accept Ken into your family."

"He won't be our dad."

"No, he'll be your stepfather. I'll always be your dad. And we'll spend even more time together, I promise."

Both boys looked at him with hope in their eyes. It gave him the courage to say, "Be happy for Mom, guys, and don't make her sad over this. She's been sad enough in her life." He smiled and whispered, "Now how about if you and me go to Mickey D's and talk about some of the things we're going to do together. We'll make our own plans for the future."

He felt a slender hand on his shoulder. He looked up and he saw something in his ex-wife's eyes he'd never seen before. Respect.

And though his heart was breaking, he smiled at her.

⌒ TWENTY-ONE

THE UNVEILING OF the architectural plans for Project KidsCamp took place in early December in Chief Callahan's conference room. Off to the side, both he and Chief Rossettie beamed like proud papas at the drawings displayed for the whole steering committee. As the chiefs pointed out the highlights, the press looked on.

"We have even more good news," Callahan announced.

Mitch shifted in his seat and tried not to stare at Megan, who he'd seen exactly three times since the night Bobby ran away.

"Megan, you want to tell it?" Callahan asked.

She looked gorgeous in a dark green skirt and blazer to match, which she wore with heels. He tore his gaze away from the way the skirt swirled around her legs as she approached the chiefs. Eyes sparkling, she held up a folder. "We just got a preliminary report on children who are interested in attending the camp. We already have fifteen kids who'd come."

Stan Steele, up front with the chiefs, moved in close to Megan. "Then the camp's a reality." He touched her arm. "Because of you, Detective."

"Yeah, it's a reality, but not just because of me. A lot of the credit goes to Captain Mitch Malvaso—" She smiled sweetly at Mitch, driving up his blood pressure, then nodded to Jenn. "—and Firefighter Jenn Malvaso."

His sister sat next to Grady at the round table. They were mellow these days, after the miscarriage scare, biding their time till they could hear the baby's heartbeat, though the sonogram showed all systems go. Grady seemed happier and Mitch knew he was seeing Harrison regularly. Everybody was taking things one day at a time.

When Jenn stood to speak, Megan asked her to come up front so the press could see her. "The volunteer list is growing. We're sure now we're going to have more people than we need."

"Is there a way to use everybody?" Steele asked. Mitch noticed he hadn't moved away from Megan.

"We're hoping to. Certainly with the construction."

"How's that progressing?" a reporter asked.

Everybody looked at Zach. "Great. If it gets warm in February we can dig then. March, at the latest. We got everybody lined up, all the volunteers, the equipment and its handlers." He held out his own folder. "People came out of the woodwork, so to speak, to sign up."

Mitch smiled and caught Megan doing the same. Looked like their project was a success. Now if only . . .

Jenn said, "My sister Connie Lewis can tell us how we're doing on the money end."

Mitch watched as one of his twin sisters approached the other and squeezed her arm. A side effect of Jenn's pregnancy had been bringing the girls closer. Mitch knew that Connie shared her own childbirth experiences with Jenn and they'd already done some shopping together. Too bad Connie hadn't made any progress with Zach. Although Cindy's antics had seemed to bring the Malvaso clan closer, something had driven an even deeper wedge between Zach and Connie. For the life of him, Mitch couldn't figure out what. It was too bad, too, because Zach was suffering over the Christmas wedding that was going to take place for Angie and Kellerman.

Paulie sat off to the side. Mitch tried not to panic thinking about the last news Paulie had given him. . . .

"Cynthia's filed suit from the Hamptons for full custody of both kids, Mitch. She's claiming adultery on your part."

Mitch had gripped the chair. "There's been no adultery."

"Well, admitting you and Megan loved each other in front of witnesses wasn't a good idea." He frowned. "But I still think the kids' preferences will count. And of course, with the tantrum she threw a few weeks ago, we have new information to prove her unfit. And unstable. Let's wait and see."

When the meeting wound down, Mitch told himself to leave right away. But Megan broke away from the small group who'd surrounded her and approached him before he could get out of there.

Her amber eyes were cautious. "Hi," she said simply. "I, um—" She glanced around the room and saw no one noticing them. "—I just needed some contact for a second."

"I know the feeling." He glanced at his brother. "I wish like hell Paulie hadn't told us to stay away from each other."

"It's for the best." She sighed. "I had a good time with Bobby and Trish at dinner last night."

"How did the driving lesson go beforehand?"

After his escapade with the car as an unlicensed driver, Bobby was ordered by the court to do community service and to take some driver's training. Megan had talked the judge into letting her give him lessons. "A little rocky at first." She smiled. "But okay." She smiled at him. "The kids are really excited about this camp."

"It's given us all something good to concentrate on." Since he was partly shielding her from everybody's gaze, he reached out and snagged the end of her sleeve and rubbed it between his fingers. "I have to think about them, sweetheart, but I'm not giving up on us."

"I know. We all need to regroup a bit."

He jammed his hands in his pockets. "What are you doing for Christmas?"

"I don't know."

"I wish—"

"Mitello?"

They turned to find Grady had come up to them. "You going back to our place now?"

Even though Cynthia had left town two weeks ago and not returned, he and the kids hadn't gone back home. They'd moved lock, stock, and barrel into Jenn's place. She and Grady seemed to like the company. And the kids loved the feel of family around.

"Yeah, I'm going back, why?"

"Give Jenny a ride, will you?"

"Where are you going?" Mitch asked.

"I've got to do something." With a few more words, he left.

Jenn came up to them. "I'm ready to go." She smiled at Megan. "What were you talking to Stan Steele about?"

Megan blanked. "Um, nothing."

Mitch thought of something. "Geez, now that Jenny ditched him, he's probably going to go after you, Meg."

When Megan looked away guiltily, he thought, *What the hell*? "Has he asked you out already?"

"Um, yeah. I said no," she hastily added.

"Excuse us for a second, will you, Jenn? Wait here." He nodded to Megan. "Come with me."

She scanned the room. "That's not a good idea."

"Fuck good ideas." He strode out and she followed. When he spotted one of the offices open—and empty— he dragged her inside.

"Mitch, what are you doing?"

"Just this." Closing the door, backing her up against the wall, he braced his arms on either side of her and took her mouth. For the very first time. The kiss was not gentle. Months of waiting made him ravenous, and so he devoured her. She tasted as he knew she would, sexy, hot, and hungry. He couldn't get enough of her mouth, of her. But he didn't put his hands on her; some remnant of sanity remained, and told him if he touched her now, he'd never let her go. But the kiss was long, and carnal, and very satisfying. When he drew back, she actually whimpered.

Damn, that made him feel like a kid in the backseat of his car with his best girl. He wanted more.

"What was that for?" she whispered.

"To let you know what's in store for you, woman." He pointed to the chief's office. "Stay away from Steele and any other man who wants you. You're mine, and as soon as I have a legal separation, I'm taking you."

With that he opened the door and walked out.

MEGAN WAS THINKING about Mitch's kiss on the trip home, Mitch was driving Jenn back to her place, Grady was on his way to see Sheila Madigan, Zach was heading over to tuck his kids into bed, Paulie and Connie were just getting into his car, and the chiefs were headed for Badges, when there was an explosion in one of the buildings in downtown Hidden Cove that rocked the whole city.

Everybody's thought was the same. Today was the nine-month anniversary of the Sinco fire.

BECAUSE OF ANOTHER fire and a bad car accident that had summoned a number of the town's on-duty firefighters and police officers, all available off-duty fire and police personnel were called to the scene through radio, television, and private scanners. By the time Grady, Mitch, and Zach raced to the firehouse, grabbed their gear, and sped to the fire, which was five minutes from Quint 7, Incident Command had been set up in the parking lot, hoses had been laid, and smoke eaters were attacking the building. The police were cordoning off the area and would assist with rescued victims. Chief Callahan himself was overseeing this one.

As Mitch bounded out of his truck, leaving Jenn inside, he was hit by a blast of cold air. Amidst the lightly falling snowflakes and freezing temperature, Creighton Manor, the pre-1940, four-story apartment house, showed fire from all four floors. Frantic occupants were attempting to flee by way of fire escapes. Some who were trapped called out from the windows. The building was bordered by a two-story retail structure on the west and an unoccupied strip mall to the north. The strip mall had had a fire during construction, and Mitch had fought the blaze himself. The Creighton had been damaged then. Mitch knew a major worry would be the fire spreading to the other buildings.

"What can I do, Chief?" Mitch asked when he reached Callahan.

Dressed in a turnout coat and thick gloves, the chief's face was already reddened by the cold. "It's startin' to roll," he said nodding to the structure. "The penthouse is fully involved and each floor has fire. We don't know about the basement. There was the explosion, and we don't know *why* the hell *that* happened. I hate sending men in without that information, but people are dyin'."

"We got no choice, Chief. Where do you want us?"

Callahan glanced at Zach and Grady, who'd joined them. "Our approach is three-pronged. We're attacking the fire on all four floors in an effort to control hallways and stairwells." He nodded to Engine 6's rig. "They're around back with Battalion Chief Jackson. Mitch, you go with them, but wait till I fill you in on the rest."

Mitch nodded and rubbed his hands together. He saw Zach and Grady put on their gloves. He yanked his out of his pocket as the chief continued.

"Engine Seventeen's providing top ventilation to remove the toxic gases." He glanced to the side. "Zach, you go there." He added gruffly, "Be careful. The roof's slippery."

Last, he indicated Grady. "O'Connor, help with occupant egress. Ladder Truck Five on the east side."

He faced them squarely. "This is a biggie, guys. We expect more firefighters on the scene, but you gotta hold the fort now."

Mitch was heading for the back of the building when he saw Megan's police vehicle pull in. Shit. He was already worried about his sister being here, as she'd insisted on driving over with him. Blanking his mind, he found the officer in charge at the rear of the structure.

Within twelve minutes, three of the four floors had two lines working and the aerial was laying a master stream with the stick on the top floor. Another company was hosing the nearest building in the strip mall to keep it safe. Mitch was teamed up with LoTurco and a rookie named Jamison.

"Take axes and ropes inside," he said to the two of them as he accepted a hose from one of 6's crew. "We don't know what we're gonna face in there."

Manning a two-inch hand line, he led the way into the building; their mission was to bring water to the back left corner of the first floor, which they suspected was the seat of the fire.

A shadowy curtain of smoke obscured their vision as they entered through the back door; the heat was suffocating in comparison to the cold outside. Five feet down the hallway, they came face-to-face with inferno-like flames surging from a back stairwell. Mitch spoke calmly into his radio, "I need water." In seconds, the hose charged. He felt LoTurco brace him at his back as water bucked through the latex. From the corner of his eye, he saw the rookie freeze. Blasting the flames, he yelled, "You okay, Jamison?"

Jamison backed up. "It's . . . it's coming at us. . . ."

"Get out of here," Mitch shouted as he continued to slap water on the fire. The smoke was thickening and he could just make out the guy. "Follow the hose out." The kid still didn't move. Mitch yelled, *"Now."*

The probie started out. Holding the hose steady, Mitch checked his progress over his shoulder. Jamison was a few feet away from the door when the floor went out from under him; the kid disappeared like thin white smoke.

"Fuck," Mitch said, passing off the hose to LoTurco. "Finish this."

Circling around, he raced to the hole in the first floor. It was about five feet in diameter. Though smoke clouded his vision, he could see well enough that the kid was splayed on his back, not moving.

"I need help," Mitch called out. "I gotta go down."

LoTurco came to his side and surveyed the situation. "Son of a bitch."

While LoTurco unfurled his rope and secured it to a sturdy-looking post, Mitch whipped off his airpack, shrugged out of his turnout coat, and put his SCBA back on. LoTurco tossed the rope into the hole. Gingerly Mitch got on his belly, feet extended toward the opening; gripping the rope, he edged toward the hole. He'd done this before over thin ice on the lake to save a skater who'd fallen through. When he reached the hole, he shimmied his way down the rope. His fingers and arms ached with the strain of carrying his weight and he shivered in the cold and dank atmosphere.

The basement was relatively free of smoke, making Mitch wonder what had caused the floor to collapse. The kid was still unconscious, but he had a pulse. Mitch said into the radio, "I need a backboard in the cellar. Jamison's breathing, but I don't dare move him by myself. . . ."

It was then that he heard it. An explosion rent the air and he caught sight of flames behind him.

MEGAN WARNED HERSELF to be calm as she bounded out of her police truck and headed for Incident Command. She'd almost reached home when she heard the call over the scanner. All available police and firefighters. Mitch. He'd go. It was his job.

Still, she worried.

Not watching where she was going, she slipped on the grass made wet by the lightly falling snow. Righting herself, she was more careful to make her way over to the chief. It was cold and she zipped up the too-thin leather jacket she'd worn to the meeting. She'd taken time only to change into jeans and a sweater she kept in the car. Will was standing to the side, assigning the off-duty cops who'd just arrived. "Cordon off all the streets leading here. Station black-and-whites on the corners. It's only nine o'clock and people will detour to see what all the fuss is about."

When he turned around, he saw Megan. "I'm glad you're here. This is a big one."

Another big one? Sinco had happened only nine months ago. "What can I do?" she asked, glancing at the building where Mitch was most likely inside. Flames shot out like angry fingertips from every floor and in places on the rooftop.

"Handle the press," he said, nodding to the street. "They're just starting to nose around. And send over all our guys who come in from now on."

Megan hesitated. "Will? Is it . . . what do you know about this fire?"

"Not much, except that it's suspicious. An explosion went off; we don't know what caused it."

"So it's dangerous to be inside?" She heard her voice quake.

"Yeah." She started to walk away and he snagged her sleeve. "He's a seasoned firefighter, Meggie. He can take care of himself."

She gave Will a brave smile that she didn't feel.

After dealing with the press and directing arriving officers to Will, Megan headed for Jenn, who was leaning against Mitch's Cherokee. Her light fleece coat was open and she wore no hat or gloves. Her face and hands were red.

Megan crossed to her friend. "Jenn? It's freezing out here. You should be home, or at least get inside the car."

"I sat in there for a while," she said, staring at the building. "I was going crazy."

Just then a firefighter jogged up to her. "Here, Malvaso, put this on." He slid a turnout coat around her shoulders. "You're gonna freeze to death."

She grabbed the guy's arm. "Hector, what's going on?"

"They think it's arson. The fire's really rolling like something's keeping it going in there."

"Where's everybody?"

For a minute, he stared at her. "Mitch is on the first floor with Engine Six. Zach's on the roof."

"Where's Grady?"

"He went in the second floor through a ladder with Judy Camp over on the east side."

When Hector left, Jenn just stared at the building.

Megan didn't want to mouth platitudes, and she was sick inside herself. She said only, "You okay?"

Jenn nodded and shivered.

"Come on, put your arms in this." She helped Jenny slide into the turnout gear. "Stuff your hands in the pockets at least," Megan told her friend as she buttoned up the coat.

Like a child, Jenn did as she was told.

"I'll be back." Megan squeezed Jenn's shoulder and hurried over to Incident Command. She came up behind Callahan, who was with Will, but talking into a radio. "Where is he, LoTurco?" A pause. "Holy hell. Get him out of there. We have reason to think incendiary devices are set to go . . ." The chief stopped talking when an explosion blew out the front cellar windows. "Jesus Christ."

"What happened?" Will asked.

"Something in the basement blew."

"Any of our guys down there?"

"A probie fell through the first floor. Mitch Malvaso went after him."

Megan froze. She thought—ludicrously—of that kiss he'd given her like a caveman claiming his mate.

Oh, God, was that all she'd ever have of him?

ZACH SLIPPED AROUND the guys heeling the ladder at ground level and ascended the rungs to the roof as quickly as he could, given the forty pounds of gear he wore, along with a pickax he carried. They'd ventilate the roof with a K-12 saw, but axes might be needed for shingle removal. The rungs were cold, even through his gloves, and the wind got worse the higher he rose.

Once he reached the top of the building, he saw the ranking officer from Engine 17 perched on the not-too-steep slope, holding a portable radio to keep in constant contact with Incident Command. *When* to ventilate was crucial to the firefighters in the building, two of whom were Zach's brother and best friend. The officer also had to ensure that only required openings were made, and the smoke eaters on the roof were safe.

The ladder had been placed with five rungs above the roof line and tied off to an existing support to keep it in place. From below, somebody was laying another ladder off to the right in case the crews needed an alternate escape route.

Two other firefighters were on the roof itself, Casey Brennan from 17 and Ed Snyder from the Rescue Squad. He held the K-12 saw while Brennan worked. Zach stayed on the ladder until he could see where he might be useful.

At the direction of the officer, Brennan marked off the two-by-four-foot rectangular opening. With the wind at her back, she took the saw from Snyder, braced her legs, and stood. Zach knew they would have already sounded out the roof for solid supports and rafters before picking a section to cut.

Though cold surrounded them, the three crew members from 17 were all sweating. As Brennan pulled the cord to start the saw, she slipped. The roof wasn't icy, but it was wet, making this maneuver dangerous. Regaining her footing, she pulled the cord. Zach stepped off the ladder, crossed to her, and stayed behind her to act as a brace if she needed it. She pulled the cord a third time. When nothing happened, she said, "Hell! It won't start. Didn't you test it before you brought it up the ladder, Snyder?"

"No, there wasn't time."

"You moron," she said, handing the saw to Zach. She glanced at the officer.

"Go ahead," Zach heard the officer say.

Zach moved away to fiddle with the saw.

"Stay back." From his peripheral view, he could see Brennan and Snyder raise their axes to remove the shingles and sheathing. They could cut through with an ax if necessary. They had half the shingles off when Zach got the saw started. Ear-splitting noise rent the air. He looked at her to see if she was too tired to make the cut. Reaching for the saw, she shook her head.

He gave her the K-12 and she bent over. Quickly she made the cut on the short side, away from her body. Then she moved and cut the longer side of the rectangle. In minutes the roof hole was done. As debris fell downward, Brennan stepped back. Fire often burst from the vent hole as the superheated gases got the oxygen they needed to burn. From behind, Zach braced her, just as angry flames shot through the opening.

"All right," the lieutenant yelled. "The roof's getting spongy. I want everybody off." He listened to his radio. "There's an emergency in the basement. I'm going down first so I can help."

Snyder crawled down next, carrying the saw and seeming pissed. Brennan looked at Zach, then headed for the ladder; he followed her down. He was just passing a window that had been blown out by fire when he heard something. He stopped. It sounded like crying. Leaning out and around the ladder, he poked his head inside the opening, careful to avoid the jagged glass. The wind was picking up again, and he held tight to the ladder rails. He saw a little girl and boy huddled in the corner. "Hey, you okay?"

They were across the room, sobbing.

"Look, I'm going to get you out. Come over to the window."

Frozen by fear, he guessed, they stayed where they were. Damn it to hell.

He felt weight on the ladder below him. "Why'd you stop, Malvaso?" It was Brennan. She'd come back up.

"Two kids, inside. They're scared shitless. I'm going in."

She came up flush. "Go on, I'll take them from out here."

Gingerly Zach braced his foot on the windowsill. He managed to slide it inside, but his other foot slipped on the rung of the ladder. He felt Brennan grab him and push him all the way in. Righting himself, he rushed toward the kids. They were about three and five. He grabbed the girl and hugged her to him. "Come with me, too," he said to the boy. After a hesitation, the kid followed him. At the window, he handed the girl out to Brennan. Because she was so little, Brennan cradled her to her chest. The child had her in a death grip and they descended the ladder.

He slid an arm around the boy. "She'll be right back and it'll be your turn."

"Can't you get me out of here?"

"No, I can't carry you out the window. Somebody has to be there to get you." He ruffled the kid's grimy hair. "You doin' okay, partner?"

The kid gulped back tears and nodded. Zach thought of his own boys.

In seconds, Brennan came back up the ladder. She took the boy from him. Since he was small, too, she brought him down the same way, descending quickly.

Zach was about to climb back out when he saw from his peripheral view fire licking through the closed door. Then the door exploded off its hinges, pitching him forward.

TEAMED WITH A female firefighter named Judy Camp from Engine 1, Grady entered the second floor through a window to do search and rescue. Lines had already been laid and another company was knocking down the part of the fire that had spread here, the north side of the building. Inside the apartment, they found an older man, thin and trembling, slumped by his front door. He was coughing and mumbled something in another language to them.

Grady bent over him. "Can you walk?"

The man sagged against the door. Grady pulled him up; Judy took one of the guy's arms and Grady took another. Grady yelled into the radio to have someone at the window ladder as they dragged him across the floor. In seconds, another firefighter appeared at the window. They handed off the man, just as he spoke again. "What's he saying?" Grady asked.

"Don't speak Italian," the firefighter told him. "These old guys always fall back on their native language when they're scared."

Judy and Grady turned and headed back in, hoping to

check other apartments. When they reached the door, Callahan's voice came over the radio. "O'Connor, the guy you just rescued said there's a woman in the apartment next to you in a wheelchair. She can't walk. We haven't gotten her out."

Grady said, "Let's go."

As soon as they opened the door, they saw flames coming down the second floor hallway. A line had been laid and firefighters slapped water on it, attempting to douse it, but the fire was winning this round.

Camp said, "Jesus, let's get out of here."

Grady made a split-second decision. His back against the wall, he slid down the hall to the next apartment; luckily he found the door ajar and hurled himself inside; the door slammed shut behind him. There was smoke here—gray and curling like fog—but the fire hadn't spread inside yet. He radioed his position as he got his bearings and made his way through the foyer. It wasn't hot enough yet to have to crawl, thank God. A quick scan of the small space and someone calling out sent him to the bathroom. He found the woman in her wheelchair inside. The frame of the john had been widened for accessibility, and its door swung outward. As he started to speak, the smoke darkened and he heard a blast outside the door, then felt the heat. Which meant the fire had come down the hallway. He'd have to get her out a window.

The woman was slumped in the chair, but she was awake, and lucid. "I was—"

"Not now, ma'am. No time to waste." Stepping inside, he maneuvered the chair, leaned over, and scooped her up in his arms. Just as he stepped toward the door, it slammed shut and he heard crashing in the living room. Setting her back down, Grady tried the door. It was huge, and heavy, and he couldn't budge it. Stepping back as far as he could, he rammed his shoulder against it. Still, it wouldn't open. He tried kicking it, twice, until his back ached. Nothing.

Thank God his radio was working. He spoke into it. "Chief, we got a problem." He explained the situation.

"Over, O'Connor. We'll be right in for you."

Callahan's reassuring tone calmed Grady. He soaked some towels with water and put them under the opening at the bottom of the door. Then he squatted down and faced the woman. "We're stuck in here. My guess is the door blew shut when somebody ventilated. And something fell in front of it. But I radioed the chief and we'll be rescued." He touched her parchment-like hand. "I promise."

She sputtered a bit and coughed. "I was in here when I heard the sirens and smelled the smoke. I didn't know where to go and there was water here."

Not a good idea, to trap yourself. "You did just fine, ma'am. There's a team coming with water to put this baby out," he said, lifting off his mask. "While we wait, I'm going to share this air with you. I've only been inside about ten minutes, and so we have at least twenty minutes of air left. As he put the mask to her face, he checked her pulse and other vitals. "What's your name?"

"Marlene. What's yours?"

"Grady. You're doing okay, Marlene. We just have to wait."

"All right." Then her eyes narrowed and after she'd had enough air, she asked, "Did Cosmo get out?"

"Who's Cosmo?"

More coughs. "The man next door. He was supposed to come over at seven. I fixed dinner. Left the door open while I came in here to get ready."

"Yes, he's out, Marlene. He's the one who told us where to find you."

The woman smiled. "He's my beau."

Grady smiled back. Took some more air.

"You got a girl?"

He thought about Jenny as he let the old woman breathe his air again. "Yeah, I do."

"You married?"

"No."

"How come?"

"Lots of reasons."

Marlene gripped his hand. "Silly boy." She closed her

eyes. "Me and Cosmo, we're getting married next week. Didn't tell nobody. His kids didn't want him to." She slapped the arm of the wheelchair with her palm. " 'Cause of this thing . . . Social Security . . . something about combined assets." She choked and he gave her more air.

Kneeling in front of her, he said, "You're going to get to marry your beau, Marlene. I promise."

She drew in the oxygen, then gave it back to him. "Well, that's all that's important."

Breathing in more air, Grady waited.

JENN PUSHED OFF from the Cherokee and raced to Incident Command when she heard another explosion. She bumped into Megan who was backing away from Rossettie. White as a ghost, Megan looked like she might be ill. "What happened?" Jenn asked.

"Mitch is in the basement." She stared past Callahan's shoulder. "The explosion before this one came from the cellar."

"Oh, God."

Hector approached them. "Megan, get Jenny out of here. It's not good for the baby."

"I'm staying. I . . ."

Suddenly, a horn blasted, three times, over the cacophony of sirens and shouts.

Jenn froze.

"What does that mean?" Megan asked, gripping her arm.

Callahan said gravely, "Evacuation. The building's fully involved."

Jenn felt her stomach roil. "Oh, God." She sank to the ground. Megan dropped down and gripped her arm. They just held each other, watching as firefighters left the building, praying hard.

Then it was a like the ending scene of a very tense movie. Somebody yelled, "Jenny, Megan, look."

They looked up. Several things were happening at once. From the left side of the building, firefighters carried out a stretcher.

"It's Malvaso," Callahan called out, after listening on his radio. "He's okay. He's got burns and something about his shoulder . . . but he's safe."

"Go," Jenny whispered to Megan.

Stumbling to her feet, Megan raced to Mitch.

Will pointed off to the front of the building. "Look, over there."

A smoke eater—Brennan—was descending a ladder. Hands braced on the rungs, she had somebody flush against her, her knee wedged between his legs. The descent was slow. She got to the bottom rung, where other smoke eaters took the victim, and she collapsed to her knees. Hector raced over to them. Jenn got to her feet and followed. When she reached them, she saw the blackened face and humped over body of her brother, Zach.

Who immediately started to cough and sputter, turned over on his side, and moaned.

Jenn thanked God both her brothers were all right.

But where was Grady?

Callahan touched her shoulder. "Look up there, Jenny."

From the east side of the building, the bucket was being lowered from the second floor.

When it hit the ground and the gate swung open, Grady stumbled out carrying a very frail-looking woman. His SCBA was gone, and he was grimy, but God, he was alive.

Jenn fell to her knees and wept.

TWENTY-TWO

HIDDEN COVE HOSPITAL had recently been remodeled and expanded. One of the additions was a huge emergency room, with state-of-the-art facilities. Right now, though, in the small treatment room, three disgruntled firefighters were unimpressed by their surroundings.

Jenn sat on Grady's bed, holding his hand in her lap. Mitch noticed they hadn't stopped touching each other since she climbed into the ambulance with him. Grady had wrenched his back trying to open the heavy bathroom door, and had some second-degree burns on his neck from wading through flames once they were freed from the bathroom.

Zach lay in the middle bed. He'd bumped his head bad enough to knock him out and had cuts on his wrists from the jagged window glass. When he'd fallen over the sill, another firefighter had burst into the room, and handed him off to Brennan, who'd dragged him out and down the ladder. Now, he was flanked by his boys, who climbed in bed with him as soon as Angie brought them over.

Both Zach and Grady suffered from smoke inhalation. Mitch himself held Trish's hand, while Bobby stood at the foot of his bed. Megan was back against the door, with Angie, Rossettie, and Callahan.

"How come you can't come home, Daddy, when Uncle Zach and Grady do?" Trish sounded like a little girl.

He shrugged, which made him wince. He'd dislocated his shoulder. Even after they popped it in place—that had been fun—it had been wrenched so badly he could hardly move. It was now in a sling. "They just want to keep an eye on me."

Bobby's eyes narrowed on the bandage at Mitch's temple—he had a concussion. He'd been thrown headfirst into a concrete beam during the explosion. "You were hurt worse than them, Dad."

"Yeah, son, I was."

Mitch discussed his injuries with his kids, then smiled and glanced down at what he wore. "Sure wish I had some pajamas. This thing's too tight." The faded blue hospital gown strained against his chest and barely closed at his back.

"Yeah, but you all look so cute in them," Callahan joked.

In deference to the kids, the injured smoke eaters didn't swear back at the chief or tell him to do something anatomically impossible.

Zach said to no one in particular, "How long before we can get out of here?"

"The doctor's coming to check you guys out in a few minutes." Callahan again. "Mitch'll be admitted to a room soon."

Grady, still gripping Jenny's hand, said in a voice made hoarse by smoke, "We'll wait around and get you settled, Mitello."

"No, you won't." Mitch used his best big-brother voice. "The staff can take care of me. Jenny needs to go home, and Zach, you go with your kids."

"Can we stay with Daddy tonight, Mom?" This from Nicky.

"It's a school night," Angie said.

Jason jumped in. "Please."

Zach gave her an ingratiating smile. "I'll bring them

home bright and early so they can change for school." He held onto their hands. "I think they need to be with me, Angel."

"All right. I'll drive you all to your place when you're ready."

Zach looked to Callahan. "Is Brennan okay? She cut the roof, rescued the kids with me, and then carried me down the ladder." He closed his eyes. "How embarrassing."

"Why'd you have to be carried down, Dad?"

"An explosion sent me forward into the windowsill and knocked me out, Jay. But I'm okay."

"That woman's tough as nails," Callahan said, "I know she had cuts on her wrists, but she refused to come here and get checked out."

"We had a choice?" Zach asked.

Mitch was trying to pay attention to the byplay, and not look at Megan, but he couldn't help it; his gaze kept straying to her. Wearing a thin leather coat, sweater, and jeans, she looked somehow fragile tonight. He caught her gaze and she smiled intimately at him. When they'd gotten him out of the basement—LoTurco, assisted by an ambulance crew, had managed to get both him and the rookie to safety—she'd raced over to him. Once he was on the stretcher he'd asked the EMTs to wait a second.

Tears in her eyes, she'd held his hand and brushed back his hair. Words had not been necessary.

But he whispered anyway, "I love you, Meg."

She'd returned the sentiment, adding, "I'm just glad you're all right."

When the doctor came to check them, Meg and Angie took the kids to get something to drink and the chiefs left. The doc declared Zach and Grady fit to leave and signed admitting papers for Mitch. As she left, two people appeared at the doorway.

Connie and Paulie.

Both their faces were ravaged, and it was obvious they'd gone through hell. Mitch felt bad that they worried so much about their siblings being firefighters; tonight must have been hard to handle for both of them.

"Hi," Paulie said, his voice sandpapery.

Connie stood stoically next to him as there were greetings all around.

"Can we talk to you a minute?" Paulie asked.

"All of us?" Jenn wanted to know.

"Yes." He nodded to the bed where she sat. "And Grady should stay. He should hear what I have to say."

Mitch sighed. "Look, if it's about the danger we were in—"

"No, Mitello, it's not."

Connie grasped Paulie's hand. "We watched the rescue on TV. It was awful, but you guys are so brave. . . ."

Kissing Connie's forehead, Paulie came fully into the room. He took a seat on the edge of Mitch's bed. In an uncharacteristic show of anxiety, he raked a hand through his hair. "It's when we watched the rescue I decided something."

"Paolo, that's not a good time to de—"

"Will you stop trying to make things all right for everybody, Mitch? I've got something to say. It's important."

Mitch exchanged glances with Jenn and Zach. "All right, go ahead."

Paulie drew himself up as if confessing a crime. "I . . . when I watched that tonight, and realized you might die, I decided I had to do something to help you get custody of your kids." He glanced at Connie, who nodded encouragement to him. "And to help you get free from Cynthia."

Mitch frowned. "You mean by being my lawyer?"

He shook his head. Up close, Mitch could see his brother's eyes were stricken. "Another way."

A chill ran down Mitch's spine. It was a reaction he occasionally got when fire was hiding in the wall or he was about to discover charred bodies. "How?"

"Cynthia's charging adultery and saying you're unfit as a parent."

"I know."

"Well, she's been unfaithful to you, and she's an unfit parent in the worst way."

Mitch's heart skipped a beat. "She was unfaithful? How do you know that?"

Connie glanced over at Zach.

Oh, God, no, please don't let that have happened. *Please.* Zach was his best friend as well as his brother.

"Because I slept with her, Mitch."

Mitch's head snapped back to Paulie. *"You?"*

"More than once. We had an affair. Five years ago during one of the rough patches in your marriage. You were talking divorce again. You, um, weren't sleeping together."

Speechless, Mitch stared at his younger brother.

"It's why my marriage broke up."

Still, Mitch could say nothing. He could hear a phone ring at the nurse's desk, and the wind bleating outside. Finally, he asked, "Why'd you do that, Paolo?"

"I thought I was in love with her. I was bewitched." He stared at Mitch. "But now I think, subconsciously, it had something to do with your cutting me out of your life all those years." He looked over to Jenn and Zach. "You don't know how much I hated that." He angled his head. "Connie, too. All we really wanted was to be close to you guys. But you were so tight . . . there wasn't room for us."

Jenn said, "Oh, Paolo. Concetta. I'm so sorry."

Connie stared at Zach. "I thought it was you."

Zach's eyebrows shot up. *"What?"*

"I thought, until tonight when Paulie told me, it was you that had an affair with Cynthia. It's why I haven't been able to . . . forgive anything."

"You knew about this?" Mitch asked. "How?"

Again Paulie looked to Mitch. "Connie's husband, Al, found out Cynthia had had an affair. He told Connie." When Mitch didn't say anything, Paulie grabbed his arm. "It gets worse, Mitello."

"How can it get worse?"

"Cynthia got pregnant."

Mitch gasped. *"What?"*

"It's when I told my wife about the affair. I thought Cindy was going to leave you. Instead, she had an abortion. Al found out when she went to a private clinic outside of town. You were away at a conference. She chose the place not knowing one of Al's patients was there. He found out accidentally that she was admitted and why; he tried to talk her out of the abortion because he thought the child was yours and you'd never want her to get rid of it. Cynthia told him she couldn't go through with the pregnancy because it wasn't your baby. And he'd better keep quiet about it because it would kill you to know she'd slept with your brother."

"And you automatically assumed it was me?" Zach said to Connie.

Connie began to cry. "Yes, I did. I'm so sorry, Zaccaria."

Standing, Jenn circled the bed and took Connie in her arms. "Shh, Connie, it's all right."

Zach just stared ahead. Finally he got out of bed, crossed to his sisters and enveloped them both in a bear hug. "It's okay, Con. I was such a shit, I can see why you thought it was me."

Mitch watched the trio, then looked at his brother Paulie.

Forgiveness would not come so easily from him.

ZACH CAUGHT SIGHT of Casey Brennan when he was leaving the hospital a half hour after Paulie dropped the emotional bomb on his family. Mitch was morose, and Zach was still reeling from the revelation. He met up with Brennan in the ER foyer, where she was just reaching the door to leave.

"Hey, Brennan, wait a sec."

Brennan turned. Her face was still smudged and there were circles under her eyes. Her wrist was bandaged.

Holding onto Nicky's hand and grasping Jason by the shoulder he nodded to her arm. "You get hurt?"

"Yeah." She glanced at the boys and her expression softened. "I got home and my wrist started to throb. I thought it was just the cuts from the window that the EMTs fixed up. But it kept hurting, so I came in here. Seems I sprained it when I yanked you through that win-

dow." She rolled her eyes. "You're no lightweight, Malvaso."

Nicky asked, "You the lady who carried my dad out?"

"Yep." She squatted down so she was eye level.
"What's your name?"

"Nicky. This is Jason, my brother." He grinned.
"Thanks for saving my dad."

Surprising the hell out of Zach—Brennan sure as hell
wasn't the motherly type—she shook hands with Nicky.
"You're welcome." Then she stood and shook hands with
Jason. "Nice to meet you." Navy-blue eyes studied Zach.
"You okay, Malvaso?"

"Yeah, mostly smoke inhalation." He held up his own
bandaged wrists. "And this."

"Oh, good." She turned to leave.

"Hey, Brennan?" She pivoted around. "Thanks for saving my life," he said, parroting Nicky.

No smile for him. Nothing. She just nodded.

"Remember what you asked about the vacancy on my
group?"

"Oh, that. Forget I—"

He grasped her sleeve. "I think you'd do great at our
firehouse, if you're still interested."

She shrugged. "Maybe," she said and walked out into
the night all alone.

Zach just stared after her, thinking how much she was
like the person he used to be.

He felt sorry for her.

AFTER SAYING GOOD night to Trish and Bobby—they
were cuddled up on Jenn's big bed together talking—Jenn
made her way to Grady's side of the house. He'd gone
straight to his bedroom to shower and when she looked
in on him, he was stretched out on the bed asleep. Tip-
toeing to his dresser, she snitched one of his pajama tops
and left his room. She'd made some life-changing decisions in the past hours because she'd never forget the gut-
wrenching fear she'd experienced when he was trapped in
a building that was fully involved. Determined, she went

to the guest room, got ready for bed there, and, wearing his clothes, she climbed under the covers.

She said a prayer of thanksgiving that he and her brothers were all right. Then, gently, she placed a hand over her stomach. "We'll be all right, too, baby," she whispered into the darkness. "Your daddy and I are gonna be better. This whole thing is so dumb. We can just be friends, like before, and take care of you that way. I promise, no more sex, no more—"

"Like hell!"

She looked up and could just make out Grady's silhouette in the doorway.

"Gray, I thought you were asleep."

"I was. I dozed off waiting for you." He scanned the guest room. "What are you doing in here?"

"I didn't want to disturb you."

"Oh, you disturb me, all right." There was something about his tone. . . .

"What did you mean, *like hell*?"

He came fully into the room and stood by her a minute. Then he bent over, turned on the small light next to the bed, and sat down. The room was cast in a mellow glow, and Jenn could hear the heat humming softly through the vents. Without saying anything, Grady drew back the covers, and lifted his hands to the top of the pj's she wore.

"You didn't ask if you could borrow this," he said, releasing the first button.

"Uh, no, I didn't."

"I want it back." Another button undone. "And you'll have to pay for taking it."

God, she hadn't seen this side of him in weeks. This was the old Grady, fun-loving, teasing, sexy. "I will?"

A third button. "Oh yeah, baby, you will." In seconds, all of the buttons were released. When he started to spread the material, she stayed his hands with hers. "Gray, we don't have to do this. We can do what you said before, just be friends."

His grin was cocky, and his eyes, his wonderful blue eyes, shone like polished sapphire. "Too late."

Jenn felt a clutch in her chest. "When you were in that fire, I realized it didn't matter how we were together, just that we were. And that I'd do anything to make you happy, even give up a sexual relationship."

A vee formed on his brow. "How can giving up sex make me happy?" he asked, batting her hands back and sliding one of his inside the open top. He closed it over her breast and smiled when she spontaneously arched into him. She'd never responded to anybody's touch like his. No surprise there.

"Hmm. I love watching you."

She struggled for sanity. "Gray, I don't understand."

"Well, I do. Now." He began to knead her. "I understand it's important to marry the woman I love, the woman I've loved since I was five."

Caught up in what his hand was doing, it took her a minute to understand. "Did you say marry?"

Leaning over, he brushed aside the flannel and kissed her breastbone. "Uh-huh. It's all falling into place, Jenny."

He drew back, but stayed over her. His hand moved to her stomach and rested there, just above the white cotton panties she wore. "I've been making progress with Harrison. I didn't want to say much, because I was afraid to disappoint you if I wasn't getting better. But after we made love again, and thinking hard about things, I was on the verge of something. I was going over to Sheila's tonight to see her."

"Why?"

"Because I'm sick of letting self-indulgent women, and ghosts, run my life. I finally was able to articulate that with Harrison. I'd decided before the fire to confront all this head-on."

"Oh, Gray."

"Then, being trapped with that old woman—she's marrying the old guy we rescued despite all the problems it will bring. She said that was all that mattered and it clicked for me. *We're* all that matters, Jenny, you, me, and the baby." His hand caressed her stomach. "I'll need more therapy, but I've crossed a hump, and this time I'm not backtracking. I promise."

Her heart swelled. "I love you so much, Gray."

"I know that. I've always known that." Finally he peeled back her shirt. And began to tug down her panties. "Now, I want you. Long. And slow. I want it to last. . . ."

She stayed his hand. "What about your back?"

"Hmm." He thought for a minute. "Got any ideas?"

Gently drawing him down to the mattress, she waited until he stretched out. "Oh, I got ideas all right. Lots and lots of them."

"Show me, Jenny."

She reached for his bottoms. "I will."

"Love me."

"I will. Forever."

THE MOON WAS slivering through the slats of the blinds shading the window of Mitch's room when Megan opened the door and slipped inside. Thank God he'd been given a private room. She had to see him. It was so hard watching his family fawn over him and not be able to touch him, hold him, make sure he was really all right. She waited until she was sure they were all gone to come back. If he was sleeping, she'd just sit by his side for a while.

She crept to the bed. He was still, his head averted to the opposite side. His shoulder was in a sling; she'd had a bad dislocation once herself and knew it hurt like hell. They'd probably given him painkillers and a sleeping pill.

But when she sat down, he turned his head to her. "Meggie?" he uttered hoarsely.

Megan was stunned by what she saw. She raised one hand to his cheek and found it wet, had seen the tears sparkling in the moonlight. "Mitch, why are you crying?"

He shook his head.

"What's happened?"

"I . . ." He drew in a heavy breath. "I found something out tonight."

"Something bad?"

His laugh was bitter. "Yeah, something bad that will let me keep my kids. Let me have you, probably."

Placing her hand on his arm, she frowned. "Isn't that good?"

She saw more tears stream down his cheeks. He lifted his hand and rubbed his thumb and forefinger over his eyes. "I don't know what it is."

"Please, tell me what happened."

"I'm not sure I can."

"Try. I'll help you with whatever it is."

Finally, he looked at her. "My . . . brother . . . Paulie . . . he had an affair with Cynthia, five years ago."

"Oh, my God." The woman was a monster. Megan had disliked her before. Now she hated her.

"They conceived a child."

"What?"

"She had an abortion."

"Oh, no, Mitch." She gripped his hand again. "I'm so sorry."

He held on tight to her. "It's partly my fault."

"Why do you say that?"

"Paulie did it because of our estrangement. He'd wanted to be a part of our lives and we wouldn't let him, or Connie." He shook his head. "Connie found out accidentally. She thought it was Zach's kid. I never could figure out why she resented him the most."

"Oh, Mitch." The effects of Cynthia's selfishness were so far reaching.

"I'm mad, Meg. Really mad."

"Well, that's good."

"I hate her for doing this. To Paulie. To Zach and Connie."

"And to you."

"Yeah, to me. I really tried to make the marriage work. I stayed in it for the two of us for a long time. Then for the kids. Part of that time, she was fucking my brother."

Raising his hand to her mouth, she kissed his knuckles.

"I never once cheated on her," he continued, emotion threading his voice, "no matter how bad things got. Until you, I never even looked at another woman." He tore his hand free, fisted it, and pounded it on the steel bed rail. "Son of a bitch."

Megan didn't know what to do, what to say. So she just sat there.

"It's going to take me awhile to work this through. Get past all this anger."

She said softly, "That's okay. You're entitled."

"I don't want you subjected to it."

"I want to be."

"I'm thinking about going away for a while." He indicated his shoulder. "The doctor said I can't work for two weeks. The kids are busy at school and could stay with Jenn and Grady. I need some time to myself."

Though it was hard for her to get the words out—she didn't want him to go away especially after the fear she'd felt all night—she said, "I think you should do it. You never take time for yourself. You deserve it."

He sighed.

"I'd help keep an eye on the kids. Spend time with them."

"That would be nice. They'd like that."

"You can go to the cabin."

"Project KidsCamp cabin?"

"Well, it's mine for a little while longer."

"Maybe I will."

"I'll get it ready for you."

"You'd do that for me? And let me go there for as long as I needed without a fuss?"

He was used to so little. The thought angered her, but also strengthened her resolve. She would make this man happy. She would take care of him, as he'd taken care of her. She cocked her head and brushed back a stray lock of his hair. "Yeah, I would, Mitello." Leaning over, she kissed his forehead. "I'd do *that*, I'd do *anything* for you."

~ TWENTY-THREE

TWO WEEKS LATER

The lake wind stung Mitch's cheeks and made his eyes water. Here, on Hidden Cove, a week before Christmas, winter unfurled around him in full force. But he'd taken this walk every morning since he'd gotten here and didn't want to break his record. There was something comforting in the routine of it all.

The lake hadn't frozen yet, and he stood for a minute watching the waves crash onto the shoreline. When he'd first come, the angry sea had reflected his mood. He'd been seething and, like the water, released his fury only in human ways—kicking wastebaskets, throwing stones in the lake until his good arm hurt as much as his other one, and when his shoulder healed enough, running till he could hardly breathe. The physical outlet had done him good. He'd been battered and needed to heal.

As he turned away from the water and headed up to the cabin, he thought about how his wintry mood had given way to the first buds of spring. As he'd fished, watched TV, slept, and did some reading and some journal writing, which Harrison had suggested but he wasn't very good at, he'd started to let go of the bubbling-over anger he felt for his wife, his brother, and at himself for handling his life as he had. He'd been unhappy, and so had Cynthia, and they'd let it go on too long till it built up to flashover.

His changing mood and acceptance of what had happened had also been furthered by his kids. Though he'd had no contact with anyone else, not even Megan, he'd talked to Trish and Bobby every night.

They'd accepted his sojourn here by the water, his need to be alone, with astonishing maturity. But they missed him. Harrison had said they'd be all right for a while, though, that Mitch should take time for himself. He did it, but still he needed to stay in touch.

In their nightly conversations, the kids chatted on about school, Bobby's gig at a local coffee shop and, surprisingly, Trish was trying out for the high school play. She also told him she'd gotten rid of her eyebrow ring—thank the good Lord!

They filled him in on the time they spent with Megan, and Mitch listened to how much they liked her, how much fun she was, and kept the knowledge close to his heart. He had to laugh at the stories Bobby told about her teaching him to drive.

He'd known before he left that the fire at the Creighton had been declared arson and an investigation was under way; the kids kept him apprised of those details, too. Apparently Chief Callahan was taking a lot of heat about inspections and safety. Mitch was sorry he couldn't be there for his friend, but he had his own demons to fight.

They also had family news.

Trish got to deliver the first tidbit.

Daddy, Aunt Jenn and Grady are getting married . . . a Valentine's Day wedding . . . this is so *cool.* Mitch didn't know exactly what had happened between his sister and his friend. Something hadn't been right through this whole pregnancy thing, but they hadn't shared it with anybody; and he knew Grady had been seeing Harrison, too. In any case, he was glad they were working it out.

Bobby told him about Zach.

Uncle Zach's buying a house. You should see it, Dad, it's big and beautiful, and he said we could live with him. . . . I don't want to go back to the other house. . . .

No, Mitch thought as he reached the cabin and swung open the door. They would never go back to the house they shared with Cynthia. He'd find them something else, smaller, warm and cozy. Something that felt like this cabin. He scanned the main room. He'd left a fire smoldering and crossed immediately to the big fireplace and stoked it. Soon it was burning brightly, crackling and snapping and filling the whole room with its smoky warmth.

The cabin was perfect for him, with a big living room, a bedroom off of it, and a kitchen in the back. As she'd promised, Megan had come here before him and cleaned up the place, stocked the fridge, and put linen on the bed. Getting coffee he'd fixed earlier, he made his way to the fire and sank down to the floor in front of it, his back against the sofa. She'd readied the cabin for him and let him go, *encouraged* him to go, willingly. But when he said good-bye, he could see the sadness in her eyes, the anxiety.

We'll be together, Meggie, I promise, he'd said when he picked up the key. *Please, tell me you believe me.*

He knew, after losing her husband and father, Megan didn't trust the fates much, didn't put stock in happily-ever-after like she used to. But she'd given him the key, kissed his cheek, and stepped back. He could still see her, standing in the little rented studio, arms wrapped around her waist and the phoniest smile on her face, telling him she believed him. She didn't, but he hadn't been in any position to convince her.

He dreamed about her frequently. Long, delicious dreams where she was in that big bed with him, doing things to him that had awakened him hot and hard and greedy for her.

Maybe it was time to go home. Maybe it was time to let summer into his life. He laid his head back against the sofa and closed his eyes. Was he ready? One thing he knew for sure. He wanted to see Megan. Even if things weren't settled—he doubted she'd make love with him until he had a legal separation—at least he could look at her, touch her hand, see her eyes light up when she talked about the camp . . . and when he walked into a room.

The door to the cabin, which he'd locked, opened. He heard keys jingle, then a vision swept inside. She was dressed in a big furry coat with the hood up; it obscured her face. But he'd recognize those long legs, now encased in black jeans, anywhere. She shut the door against the wind, shook off her hood, and scanned the interior until her gaze lighted on him.

And then she smiled. A full, luscious smile that held nothing back. In her eyes, he could see so much love and anticipation it humbled him. Maybe she did believe after all. "Hi, Captain."

"Detective. Fancy seeing you here."

Shrugging out of her coat, she hung it up on a hook on the wall and took something out of the pocket. When she circled around, he swallowed hard. She wore a simple maroon sweater with a cowl neck, but it hugged her curves so . . . obviously . . . he felt his whole body harden. Blond hair skimmed her shoulders—it looked curled, and fluffy—and her face glowed like a flame. In her hand she held an envelope. It was tied up with a red bow. Trying to control his visceral response to her, he let his gaze drop to it. "Did you bring me an early Christmas present?"

"Uh-huh. Two actually."

He held out his hand. "Come here, love."

Her smile was Eve's, Delilah's, Salome's. "Um, not yet. Here," she said, holding up the package, "catch." She tossed it to him. Grabbing it, he looked down. No clue from the outside.

"Open it," she said.

He struggled with the ribbon, then yanked up the flap. Inside were papers. He dragged them out. Quickly he scanned the first page. His pulse sped up. He read through them all. Then he peered up at her. "How . . . I thought . . . doesn't it take longer . . . explain this, Meg."

"Your brother Paulie came to see me," she said, perching her cute butt on the end of the small table by the wall.

"He brought these over to me; he thought I might want to take them to you."

Mitch grasped the papers tightly. "How'd he do it? Cynthia wouldn't have signed a separation agreement willingly and her lawyer told us she was going for full custody—" He stopped mid-sentence. "Oh, I get it. Paulie went to the Hamptons and talked to her."

Megan nodded, sending waves of blond hair into her eyes. "I gather it was quite a conversation. Something along the lines of, if she didn't sign the papers, agreeing to a legal separation and agreeing not to sue for custody, he'd make a stink about their affair to prove her unfit, and embarrass her and her parents."

Mitch glanced down at the legal terms of the agreement to separate: adultery and the respondent spouse's habitual intemperance or ill treatment of the other spouse to such a nature as to render their living together insupportable. "That works for me."

"Well enough for the court, too, I guess."

"Paulie did this to make up for what he did."

"I think so. He's really contrite."

"Yeah, I'm coming around to forgiving him." He glanced down at the papers. "I still can't believe she'd do this. There must be more to it."

"I agree. So does Paulie; he thinks she's enjoying her life in the Hamptons, and her father's running for some kind of local political office so she's helping with the campaign. But she also knew, deep in her heart, if she got the kids they'd make her life miserable. This was the nudge she needed."

Mitch felt as if one-hundred-pound weights were lifted off his shoulders. Somewhere inside him, he bemoaned the loss of twenty years of his life, but it diminished when he realized he was done with the fights and with trying to protect his kids from their mother. It vanished when he heard from across the room, "Don't you want to know what your second present is?"

His grin was all male. He tossed the papers to the floor and leaned back against the sofa, his arms spread on the cushions on either side of him. "Yeah, I wanna know."

Throwing back her head, straightening her shoulders, she gave him a sultry look. "I went shopping."

Shopping? Hell, he thought . . .

Slowly she placed her hands on the hem of the sweater. With excruciating slowness, she tugged the garment up. Her flat tummy . . . her gorgeous rib cage . . . and, oh, my God . . . black lace came into view. Black lace filled to capacity . . . overflowing . . .

Mitch was having trouble breathing by the time she pulled the sweater over her head. The why-bother bra hugged her breasts and, holy cow, she let one strap fall off one shoulder. "I don't usually wear things like this," she said, her voice husky. "I bought it for you. Like it?"

"Um, yeah. If I liked it anymore, I'd embarrass myself."

"Why, whatever do you mean, Captain?"

"Come here, Detective, and I'll show you."

"I'm not finished yet."

"Jesus. I don't think my heart can stand this."

Her hand went to her hips. She'd polished her fingernails. She'd never done that before. Her fingers slid sensuously to the fly button. It popped and Mitch felt his blood pressure skyrocket. Down came the zipper. Up went his temperature. Out peeked more black lace. Then, slowly she inched her jeans over her hips, exposing just enough creamy belly and sinful lace to make his mouth go dry. She stopped and let him look his fill, then braced a hand—hmm, it was shaking—on the table, bent over, and yanked off her boots and socks.

Then she shed the jeans.

Never, in his whole life, would he forget the vision of Megan, standing before him, dressed only in scraps of black lace. She was a private person, in some ways a shy one, who was offering herself to him this way. He loved her more than he could say.

But he sure as hell was gonna try to *show* her. He said, simply, "Come here, sweetheart."

Megan's knees were weak as she approached Mitch. She was out of her depth here, and she was going on pure instinct.

And love. She wanted to please this man so badly. . . .

When she reached him, she smiled innocently. "I'm, um, a little nervous. You gotta help me out here."

He chuckled. "Oh, I will." Tugging on her hand, he pulled her down so she straddled him. His groin thrust forward and she felt him hot and heavy against the thin barrier of her panties. He ran hands down her arms, back up, and closed one over her throat. Every single inch of skin he touched sizzled. Then it began to burn. "Do you have any idea how hard it's been, waiting to do this? To touch you like this?"

Locking her gaze with his, she nodded. "Yes."

He ran his knuckles down her breastbone, traced a finger along the scalloped lace. "I love my present."

"I love *you*."

"I love you, too, Meg. And I'm going to show you, right now, just how much." Gently, he eased her off his lap to lay beside the fire on the plush rug there.

Leaning over, he took her mouth. His was warm, insistent. Masterfully, his tongue explored her, possessed her. With the sureness of a man who knew what he was doing, he popped the front closure of her bra; his hands cupped her breasts and she startled. "You are so lovely."

Against his lips, she whispered, "Touch me, everywhere."

His fingers went to her waist, flexed there, then tugged off her panties. "Meg." He learned her body slowly—her belly, her knees, the inside of her ankle.

She responded with a moan or a sigh when he hit just the right nerve endings. "Mitch."

"Say it again," he breathed against her ear, still exploring her. "My name. Just like that."

"Mitch . . . Mitch . . . Mitch . . ."

Her hands went to his chest and felt the denim. "Too many clothes," she said, yanking on the first button. The second. All of them. His chest was covered with springy black hair, over a road map of muscles that leaped and pulsed at her touch. When she arched up and kissed his breastbone, he jerked toward her. When she went lower and cupped him boldly, he swore. "Damn . . . Meg . . . I'm never gonna last. . . ."

She grinned against his chest. Leaning over her, a shock of dark hair falling onto his forehead, his eyes sparkled with mischief and something else. . . .

Mitch gazed down at her, his heart so full it felt like bursting. He kissed her quick, then shrugged out of his shirt. Her hands were everywhere, bathing him in her touch. He wanted to drown in her. He couldn't stop kissing her, couldn't tear his mouth away. She was tugging on his jeans, and he felt the button release, the zipper come down. She couldn't get her hand inside, though, and swore. "Mitch, get . . . these . . . off."

Her impatience pleased him. "Yes, ma'am," he said, pulling back, stretching out awkwardly on the floor, and sliding off the rest of his clothes. And then he covered her, naked skin meeting naked skin. Every single inch possible. His penis nestled in the cradle of her thighs. His chest melded with her breasts. "I want to say something."

She was breathing hard, and the look of raw desire on her face made him throb. "Later. Now . . ." She thrust forward. ". . . now I want this." He opened his mouth to speak again, and she dug her nails into his palms. "Damn it, Mitch, we've talked enough. Let's just do this."

He laughed then, aloud. "Well, since you're being so romantic."

She laughed, too. It felt good.

Soon they sobered . . . when his mouth claimed hers . . . went lower and suckled her until she was writhing. When it skimmed her belly, nuzzled her curls, and covered that spot that made her arc off the floor.

Suddenly he found himself on his back then, and she returned the favors . . . tonguing his nipples until they were pebble hard, licking his abs, and then her mouth closed over him. His erection bucked in her mouth. "Meg!" He saw stars as she loved him. . . . "Oh. Shit. God. Fuck. Meg!"

He drew her up. She was grinning hugely.

So was he.

He stretched her out next to him then. Lying on his

side, his arms banded around her, and their legs entwined. Her hands went to his back and her head lay on his. The tenderness of the embrace, the fact that they just held each other, was in stark contrast to the dark sensuality of just moments before. He reveled in it.

Then, drawing back, he looked in her eyes, and slid inside her. "I love you, Meg. And I promise, I'll always be faithful, and do my best never to let you down."

She smiled back. "I know. And I trust you Mitch. I do."

"That means more than anything else to me." Then he grinned. "Well, and this," he whispered as he began to move inside her.

THEY STAYED IN front of the fireplace all day. They talked about Trish and Bobby—whom Mitch called at seven while Megan sat watching him, wearing just her socks and his shirt. They told his kids they'd be home tomorrow.

After he hung up, they talked about how to help Trish and Bobby through the upcoming divorce and accepting Megan into their lives, though they already had a good start on that part.

They also discussed Jenn and Grady and where those two would go from here. Mitch voiced concern about Zach and what they could do for him. Megan had some suggestions.

And late that night, after they'd made love again, Mitch wrapped Megan up in a quilt, sat her on the floor, and leaned her back against the couch. Then he dropped down across from her, tugged her leg out of the covers and positioned her foot in his lap.

"What are you doing?" she asked sleepily.

"Giving you a foot massage."

She grinned. "I don't have a headache."

"Ah, Meggie, foot massage has other . . . functions."

He began to knead her instep and she moaned. "Oh, God, that feels good."

"Close your eyes. Relax. Go to sleep if you want."

"Hmm." Her lids drifted shut. "Tell me a story."

His throat clogged at the meaningful request. She was, truly, his. "All right." He glanced around the cabin, which would soon be a part of the camp that had brought them together.

"One time, this firefighter I know—well—was floundering. His life was on the skids. His children were coming around but he needed something more to make him happy." Mitch remembered Sinco. "Then there was this big fire, and it devastated his town. After his family got out safely, the firefighter vowed he'd change his life."

"Did he?"

"Hmm." Mitch slid his hands over each toe, rubbing them individually. "Yeah, and somebody helped him."

Eyes closed, she smiled. "Who?"

"This incredibly sexy cop."

"Oh, I like that."

"I did . . . I mean *he* did, too. She was kind and loving and had a great ass."

She chuckled.

"Anyway, she had this idea for a camp. . . ." Mitch could hear the water outside lapping against the shore, and on it he pictured new docks, and a boathouse. In it, he heard kids laughing and playing water games. "So the cop, she sweet-talked the smoke eater into helping her build this camp."

"And being the kind, giving, and unselfish man he was—"

"Don't forget sexy."

"Oh, yeah, sexy," she purred as he dug his fingers into her heel. "He helped her make it a reality."

"He did." Mitch smiled, then switched feet and began the ministrations all over again. "And the camp opened that summer. . . ." He could see the cabins, the pavilion, the go-carts, and the basketball court. . . . "It was a miracle."

"A lot of things were." Her voice was husky and she opened her eyes to stare over at him lovingly.

"I know," Mitch told her, lifting her foot and kissing her ankle. "Not the least of which was Hale's Haven."

It took her a minute to get it. She bit her lip, he knew, so she wouldn't cry.

"You see the camp needed a name, and the firefighter met with the chiefs and he contacted his steering committee and they decided to name it after the man who brought this wonderful woman to the firefighter."

"Oh, Mitch," she whispered finally.

"The firefighter was going to save the news until Christmas, to tell the cop then." Mitch swallowed hard. "But I guess he couldn't wait."

Megan stared at him for a minute, then she drew back her leg and threw herself into his arms. "Oh, Mitello, I can't wait, either. For the camp. For us. For everything."

Then the firefighter smiled, sat back, and just held the cop close to his heart.

~ AUTHOR'S NOTE

Picture this: a hot, sweaty August afternoon. In the dead center of a large city, firefighters go about their daily chores: They do some in-house training, check out the rigs, make sure their equipment is in working order and mop the bays. A tone sounds over the static-filled PA system and everyone freezes. It's a run, and they're off—shoes flying, turnout gear donned; within minutes the truck is on its way. With me in it!

I began my research on fire fighting more than five years ago when I decided I wanted to write about this truly noble profession. I spent many hours with the Rochester Fire Department, in upstate New York, a five-hundred-plus organization of men and women dedicated to saving lives. I visited the station houses first, met with firefighters, paramedics, battalion chiefs and arson investigators; even the top guy, our fire chief, spent an afternoon with me. I talked at length with many of them and ate meals with them—firefighters love their food and go to great pains in fixing it. Some invited me to their homes to talk to them and their families. A truck was actually taken out of service for an hour to show me how to use the Hurst tools. From here I went on the ride-alongs, where you ride the trucks to actual calls with the firefighters. Imagine my shock when the first run I went to was a stabbing!

I also visited the Rochester Fire Academy. I met with instructors and recruits and sat in on numerous classes and drills. I can open an oxygen container now and know the basics of cutting through a roof with a K-12 saw. I dressed in their gear, posed for them as a patient in EMS drills, crawled through their maze with them and participated in night training evolutions.

As I did this primary research, I read about fire fighting: famous books like *Thirty Years on the Line*, by Leo Stapleton, *Report From Engine Company 82*, by Dennis Smith, *The Fire Inside*, by Steve Delsohn, and *Fighting Fire, A Personal Story* by Caroline Paul. I also read books on firehouse jokes, firefighting lore, fire museums, arson and firehouse cooking. I even subscribed to *Firehouse* magazine, though I confess my husband thought that this was going to an extreme. The most strenuous tome I read was the entire recruit manual on fire suppression (700 pages) and parts of the recruit texts on EMS—Emergency Medical Systems.

When I was looking for a focus for this Berkley series about firefighters, I remembered reading about a camp for the children of slain firefighters and police officers put on by the renowned Camp Good Days and Special Times on Keuka Lake. I interviewed the chairman (he, too, gave me hours of his valuable time) and asked to volunteer. Though that particular camp wasn't offered that year, I did spend almost a week at a similar one, a camp for kids affected by homicide, at the same residential facility. Much of the setup of my fictional camp in this book is based on this selfless, heart-warming endeavor. I plan to go back every summer to help Camp Good Days and Special Times provide a respite for kids dealing with life-altering problems.

My heartfelt thanks to everyone who helped me learn about their areas. Particular gratitude goes to Joe Giorgione, Rochester firefighter and paramedic, who steadfastly spent hours with me explaining techniques, developing plotlines, and figuring out answers to the unending questions I had. You can see a picture of Joe in the back of this book.

I think I've given an accurate portrayal of a fire department in upstate New York. Along the way, I took a requisite amount of poetic licenses—the books are fiction, after all, and they are clearly love stories—but I hope I stayed true to the character of these special men and women. They are among the most courageous, generous, interesting and exciting people I know. It is my sincerest hope that this book pays tribute to America's Bravest.

Return to Hidden Cove with

ON THE LINE,

Coming July 2004!
Turn the page for a preview . . .

BLACK SMOKE CURLED like an angry fist around Hidden Cove's newest restaurant while furious fingers of flame choked the air out of the building. It was a beautiful sight.

"You set this fire, mister?"

Startled, he stepped farther into the shadows then looked at the speaker. "What the hell are you doing here?"

"Just admiring my handiwork."

"Goddamn it, are you fucking nuts?"

"Nah, I'm a happy man." He nodded to Noah Callahan, chief of the town fire department, who barked orders into the radio. "How come he's at Incident Command? The cap's supposed to direct the maneuver."

"He's a control freak."

An ugly chuckle escaped his companion's lips. "The chief can't afford any more screw-ups."

Unable to resist, he allowed himself to take pleasure in what he'd already accomplished. "Yeah, like the Sinco fire."

"And the apartment complex on Jay Street."

And all those pesky problems with equipment and inspections, but he didn't say that out loud. No need for everybody to know everything. All told, several firefighters had been injured. Ten had died.

"Well, lookee there—another eruption of the Red Devil."

His head swung around. "Where?"

"On the west side of the structure."

He saw fire lick at what he knew was the small dining room off the larger one. He'd eaten there many times. "Perfect."

"Hey, I do good work."

Cloaked in inky blackness, he savored the moment. "Soon, very soon, Callahan's going down."

"Amen!"

THREE MONTHS LATER

"Chief Callahan?"

Feeling more like his beleaguered namesake from the Bible than a fire chief, Noah turned and, wiping the sweat from his brow on the sleeve of his navy T-shirt, came face-to-face with a woman he'd never seen before. She was dressed in a severe blue power suit, clasping a leather folder at her side. "I'm Noah Callahan."

"Eve Woodward." She held out her hand.

He shook it. Her grip was firm. "Nice to meet you." He gave her a quizzical look.

She squared her shoulders. "I'm the investigator from the Office of Fire Prevention and Control."

His gut clenched as he remembered the State Fire Commissioner's voice on the phone last week. . . .

We've got to come down there, Callahan. There have been an unusual number of fires, building inspection problems and shoddy equipment maintenance in your department. Mayor Johnson wants an unbiased investigator.

Noah had known then that he was in for weeks, maybe months, of some hotshot official from the state breathing down his neck. He just didn't realize it would start so soon.

"I thought you weren't comin' until next week."

"No. My memo read today." She frowned, marring the

smooth lines of her brow. Up close, he noticed her eyes were gray, reminding him of a cloudy sky just before it rained. "There must be some mix-up in your office. They told me you were out here working on the children's camp, and I wondered why." Her look clearly said, *Can't you guys get anything right?*

Damn it!

"Well," he said, covering glibly. "No harm done." He glanced down at the sweat-soaked shirt and jeans he wore. He'd come out here to work today because he needed a physical task to tax his body and numb his brain. Good hard labor had always been an antidote to what ailed him. "I'd be glad to meet with you after I clean up." He smelled like the fire academy's locker room after recruit fitness classes.

"No need to clean up. I work at fire scenes all the time and it gets plenty dirty." Shading her eyes, she surveyed the camp. "Nice place." A half smile. "Great idea."

It was. Hale's Haven, the summer residential camp for children of slain firefighters and police officers, to open in July, had been conceived and implemented by Hidden Cove's bravest and finest after a tragic loss of ten men in a fire the previous year. The incident still haunted Noah's midnights. "Thanks. Credit goes to my staff, though. It was their idea."

She nodded to the pavilion that had been completed last week. "Can we get out of the sun?" He noticed she was light-skinned and she'd covered her face with makeup, but still a few freckles peeked out.

"Sure. Let me tell Mitch I'm off hard labor." Mitch, a captain on his staff and a good friend, was crew boss this afternoon; at least today Noah didn't have to deal directly with Mitch's brother Zach, who sometimes filled that position.

"Fine, I'll wait over there." She headed toward the pavilion.

He noticed several men eye her. She wasn't all that attractive—pretty hair though, if she let it out of the knot at her neck. Its reddish highlights reminded him of the color of warm cedar. He supposed his people took note of the way she was dressed since the department had buzzed with rumors that he was on the line for a whole truckload of problems; they probably pieced her identity together.

As he headed for the hole where the foundation for the second cabin was being laid, to tell Mitch he'd be tied up for a while, he thought of the investigator's biblical namesake. And wondered if *Eve* Woodward would bring about his fall from grace just as hard and fast as the other Eve brought about Adam's.

EVE STARED OUT at the lake from under the pavilion and cursed her fair skin. It was only April, but the weather had warmed up and the sun bounced off the water sending dangerous noontime rays arcing down toward her. She stared out at the lake and enjoyed the soft *whoosh* of the waves on the shore; as she waited for Chief Callahan, she mentally calculated what she knew about him. Forty-seven. Widowed. A hometown boy. Fire chief in Hidden Cove, this sleepy town about a hundred miles outside of New York City, with a two-hundred-person fire department. He had numerous accolades, including a daring rescue when he went to help out in Oklahoma City after the 1995 bombing. He'd been HCFD chief for five years.

And had a bad track record. Craig was concerned.

Too many incendiary fires. Suspicion of kickbacks, fixing permits and ignoring code violations for profit. . . . The commissioner says it's hard to believe of Noah Callahan. But something's going on. What do you think, Evie?

Eve had looked at the man who'd been her mentor for years. *Sounds like the good-ole-boys network to me.*

Wanna check it out?

You bet.

Eve was good at her job, which was working for the Office of Fire Prevention and Control as a special investigator, sent to cities and towns to help out with, or expose, problems concerning fire safety. She liked nothing better than to catch people who were endangering the lives of others.

So far, if Noah Callahan was dirty, he'd been responsible for the deaths of ten, and the injuries of several more.

"Ms. Woodward?"

She turned.

Callahan stood before her. "So, when did you get in?"

"This morning. Albany's only an hour away."

"Yeah, I know. I went to college there."

"At the university?" When he nodded, Eve edged up against the picnic table which still smelled like fresh wood. "That's right, you have a bachelor's degree in Public Administration." And an associate's degree in fire science. And countless hours of training at the National Fire Academy. By all rights, he should be a top-notch chief. Too bad he succumbed to criminal activities.

"So, how do we start?" he asked.

She dug her notes out of her bag. "First, I'd like to see the reports on all the major incidents here in the last five years."

"Since I became chief."

"Yes." She glanced up. And was stunned by the naked pain on his chiseled features. She didn't know what to say.

Literally, he drew back and blanked his face. "Will you need somebody to interpret them?"

"Interpret them?"

"Explain the technical terminology."

"No."

"Oh. You're bringing them back to Albany?"

"No, I'm not."

He cocked his head.

"I can understand the reports, Chief. I'm a fire marshal." The premier investigator in the fire department hierarchy. Then she added, just so he'd know what he was dealing with, "And I have police certification." Which meant she could carry a gun and arrest people, though she no longer did either, preferring to turn criminals over to the state or local authorities.

"I see. What's your rank?"

"Captain."

His lips thinned. "Can you tell me how this is gonna shake out? Time lines and stuff."

"I'll need space at your headquarters. Access to reports and to the buildings themselves, for anything recent. I'll also need lists of personnel involved in those fires—arson investigators who handled the cases where that's applicable, firefighters who fought them, and inspectors who certified the buildings safe after construction or on routine inspections." She paused. "I'll want all the files on equipment problems in the past, oh, two years."

"Jesus."

Her eyes narrowed. "What, Chief? Didn't you think we'd be this thorough?"

He ran a hand through his full head of blond hair. It was sprinkled with gray and when he messed it up, he looked younger. "I didn't know this investigation was gonna include so much of my staff."

He glanced out over the grounds—a beautiful setting. Eve let herself admire it—and what he was doing here on the lake. Word of the children's camp had filtered over to OFPC and everyone in her office lauded him for it. Most had even sent money. He seemed to be doing so much good here, so the pieces didn't fit.

"Chief?"

He focused on her. "Will you be commuting between here and Albany?"

"No. I'm moving to Hidden Cove temporarily. I always reside in town when I'm on cases like these."

"Must be hard on your personal life."

Actually, it worked out perfectly for her and Ian. It gave them the needed time apart so they didn't get on each other's nerves. "So, when can I—"

"Pa-pa . . ."

Callahan turned as a tiny pink tornado raced toward them. His expression changed from one of grim displeasure to pure joy, like he'd been searching for victims in a burning building—and found one alive. The little girl reached him just as he bent down and scooped her up.

"Pa-pa . . ." she squealed again, burying her face in his chest. She resembled him so much—wheat-colored hair in pigtails, same angular features—it was eerie.

"How's my favorite girl?" he asked, hugging her close.

"Mommy, too. She's your favorite."

"That she is, pumpkin." They both glanced up at the sloping grass that spread from the parking lot to the shore. Its verdant color was a fitting backdrop to the stunning brunette who traversed it. Tall. Willowy. The kind of woman who always made Eve feel unfeminine.

And at least half Noah Callahan's age.

Hell. Did this guy fit every stereotype in the book?

ZACH MALVASO TURNED away from the sight of Noah Callahan, caught between his two worlds. The suit he was with must be from OFPC. Rumor had it the department was being investigated and Callahan's ass was on the line big time. To top it off, Mitch had told Zach that the chief's daughter and her kid had come to live with him after her marriage had broken up. Damn, the guy had a shitload to deal with. Not the least of which was Zach himself. As he lifted the bag to stack it on the others, he remembered the pure venom on Callahan's face. . . .

I gotta work with you, Malvaso, Callahan had said when Zach had repented his ways after the Sinco fire and gone to the chief to apologize for his past sins against the man. *But I'll never like you, or forget what happened between you and my wife.*

Well, that was okay. Zach would never forget—or forgive—himself for a lot of things, either, despite the fact that he was paying the piper big time for his mistakes. The post-traumatic stress he suffered since the Sinco fire, when he was buried under hot plaster and he thought for sure he was going to buy it, along with the chief's contempt, were just two of the things he had to live with.

"You gonna help me with this concrete or you gonna stay there daydreaming all day, Malvaso?" The harsh voice of Casey Brennan broke up his pity party.

Here was yet another stone in his shoe. *What* had he

been thinking when he recommended she join their fire station group after another crew member retired in January and she wanted to move from her former house? She'd done nothing but shoot sparks off all the guys in the two months she'd been at Quint/Midi 7, Group Two, where they worked.

"Quit complaining, Hulk." He'd given her the nickname when he discovered what kind of muscles she had. Hell, he bet she could outlift everybody at the station. Which was part of the reason some of the guys disliked her.

"Yeah, well get the lead out of your ass. We got a lot to do before dusk." Her sunny disposition was another.

"Take a break, Brennan. Live a little."

She glanced across the lake and for a minute, her face shadowed. If she wasn't so *hard* she'd be pretty—thick hair, pulled up like she wore it at work, nice cheekbones, eyes the deep blue of the sky at midnight. And that body. "No. I gotta be out of here a little early, so I wanna keep working."

"Got a hot date?" he asked.

Still staring out at the water, she watched a boat make waves as it cut through the lake. "Yeah, sure. Don't you know I'm working my way through the department. By recent tallies, I'll bet I've slept with at least half the guys."

Though she said it gruffly, he'd been around her enough now to hear the hurt beneath her saucy tone. "I don't believe that, Casey."

She glanced over her shoulder. "Don't go soft on me, Malvaso. I'm not big on warm fuzzies."

He shrugged. God, she was so much like he used to be. "Okay, fine. Then, do I get a turn?"

Pivoting, she hooked her fingers in the belt loops of her jeans. "No turn for the *new* you, buddy. Now, if you were the old Zach, I'd hop right into the sack with you. Word has it you were a legend between the sheets." She shook her head. "But now—you're milquetoast. I like my men tougher than me."

He socked her playfully in the shoulder. "You don't

fool me, Brennan. I've been where you are. Underneath that veneer, is a sweet and tender heart."

"Nah, I don't even have a heart."

" 'Course you do, darlin'." He gave her a bad-boy wink. "You just need the right guy to help you find it."

Again she glanced at the lake. "I already had—" She stopped abruptly. "Never mind." She donned a sassy look. "I only need a guy for one thing. Now, I'm getting back to work." Crossing to the pile, she hefted a fifty-pound bag of concrete like it was filled with feathers and strode toward the foundation.

Zach watched her go.

CASEY BRENNAN SWORE under her breath as she hefted another concrete bag and brought it to the mixer. Malvaso was getting to her. She found herself slipping up around him, and she didn't know why. Maybe because he'd been where she was.

Only he'd had a fucking epiphany, and those kind of men were the most dangerous. They thought everybody was salvageable. Which she definitely wasn't. She glanced out at the lake as she deposited the bag, and pictured the white clapboard house nestled on the opposite side, with its pretty bedrooms and swing set in the backyard.

Damn, she didn't need this. Turning, she let the concrete fall—grazing somebody's foot.

"Shit, Brennan, watch what you're doing."

"Whatsamatter, Snyder, I hurt your toesies?"

The wiry, nasty firefighter with an ego the size of Texas kicked the bag with his boot. "You bitch."

Her face flushed. "I—"

Mitch Malvaso, Snyder's captain on the Rescue Squad, came up to them. "What's going on here?" Mitch asked.

"Nothing." Casey shrugged. "Me and Snyder were just having one of our cozy chats."

"Look you two, you gotta find a way to get along. I'm sick of your sniping at each other."

Snyder regarded Mitch coldly. "She's the one that

transferred to our house. Which was about the dumbest move . . ."

"Oh, can it, Snyder. You don't like me because you're stupid and incompetent and I call you on it."

He took a step forward toward her. "I don't like you because you're a cu—"

Mitch stepped in between them. "*Enough.*"

"You're right." Casey yanked off her gloves and slapped them on her jeans. "I didn't come here on my day off to put up with this shit. I'm bookin'." She gave Snyder a disgusted look and strode away.

She'd just reached her Camaro when somebody grabbed her arm. "Hey, wait a sec," Malvaso said.

Since he was close, and since his concern dented her emotional armor, Casey whirled on him and attacked. "Back off, Malvaso. Jesus Christ, why are you always nagging at me?"

His eyes, the color of rich earth, narrowed. "Because I know you."

"What does that mean?"

"Casey, I've been where you are. I know the place your head's at."

For a brief minute, she stared at the man before her and wished that was true. Then she came to her senses. "You don't know me. What's more, I don't want you to."

"Why?"

"Shit, Malvaso, just leave it alone!"

Whipping open the door, she slid inside. She tore out of the lot faster than a rig on its way to a call.

That was *all* she needed. For Malvaso to find out her secrets. Too many people already knew about her drunken father. Some probably guessed she herself drank and smoked too much. And though her sexual exploits were exaggerated, she did like to sleep with men. It kept away the loneliness.

Which was caused, primarily, by her greatest secret of all, something nobody in the department knew about.

At that thought—and far enough away so she couldn't be seen by camp workers—Casey pulled off the road and opened the glove compartment. From inside, she drew out her wallet, and from the leather folds, a battered picture, crinkled with wear and tear, its edges ragged. Her throat tight, she stared down at the photo and lovingly traced the lines and swirls of the two images there. Her eight-year-old twin daughters, Shannon and Lindsay.

Who lived across the lake from the camp in a story-book home, with a storybook father, a not-so-wicked step-mother, and a life that Casey was incapable of giving them.

Jesus, all she needed was for anybody in the department to find out about that.